A Long-Ago Affair

TALES FROM CARAVAN

GW00507678

A LONG-AGO AFFAIR

TALES FROM CARAVAN

Volume Two

John Galsworthy

NONSUCH

First published 1926
Copyright © in this edition 2006
Nonsuch Publishing Ltd

Nonsuch Publishing Limited
The Mill, Brimscombe Port, Stroud, Gloucestershire, GL5 2QG
www.nonsuch-publishing.com

Nonsuch Publishing Ltd is an imprint of Tempus Publishing Group

For any comments or suggestions, please email the editor of this series at:
classics@tempus-publishing.com

All rights reserved. No part of this book may be reprinted or reproduced or
utilised in any form or by any electronic, mechanical or other means, now
known or hereafter invented, including photocopying and recording, or in any
information storage or retrieval system, without the permission in writing from
the Publishers.

British Library Cataloguing in Publication Data.
A catalogue record for this book is available from the British Library.

ISBN 1-84588-105-2

Typesetting and origination by Nonsuch Publishing Limited

Contents

INTRODUCTION TO THE MODERN EDITION

> Like some long caravan bearing merchandise of sorts, the tales of a
> writer wind through the desert of indifference towards the oasis of
> public favour. Whether they ever arrive, or drift to death among the
> shifting sands of popular taste, lies on the knees of the gods—the
> author has no say.

So wrote John Galsworthy in the foreword to the original
1926 edition of his collected tales. In saying this he summed up
both the essential unease of every writer, even a Nobel Prize-
winner such as Galsworthy, and the *raison d'être* of the Nonsuch
Classics series as a whole. To be condemned to 'the desert of
indifference', however, was never really to be Galsworthy's fate;
The Forsyte Saga, his best-known work, has been filmed several
times, including as recently as 2002, while 1931 saw *The Skin
Game* adapted and directed by Alfred Hitchcock. Galsworthy is
remembered today as a prolific writer, commercially successful
and politically influential, and as one of English literature's best-
loved sons.

John Galsworthy (1867–1933) was born at Kingston Hill in
Surrey, into a wealthy, middle-class family. At the age of fourteen
he began at Harrow, where he became head of his house and,
fashionably, was lauded more for his sporting than his academic
ability. From there he moved on to New College, Oxford, where
the heady life of an affluent, monocled undergraduate did not
prevent him from successfully reading law, and in 1890 he was
called to the Bar. His lack of interest in this august profession

soon became obvious, however, and he took to the seas. While Galsworthy's father hoped this might spark in his son an interest in maritime law, what actually resulted was a meeting with a young writer by the name of Joseph Conrad, who lit in Galsworthy a fire of an altogether different kind.

His first published work, *To the Four Winds*, appeared in 1897 under the nom de plume John Sinjohn. It was not until *The Island Pharisees* (1904) that Galsworthy published under his own name, as he considered this to be his best work to date. It was, however, two years later that he completed possibly the most important work of his career, *The Man of Property*. This book introduced the character of Soames Forsyte, and laid the foundation for *The Forsyte Saga*, which was to eventually bring Galsworthy the Nobel Prize.

A Long-Ago Affair is a collection of thirty-two tales making up the second volume of *Caravan*, which is in itself the definitive collection of the author's shorter tales. These tales, all written between 1900 and 1923, are grouped together in pairs, with an 'early' story being followed by a 'late' one. Each pair has also been grouped together to reflect similarities in theme, mood or technique.

Taken as a whole, Galsworthy's work constitutes a vast and wide-ranging examination of the deep divisions of social hierarchy, the vagaries and machinations of love, and the constant struggle between desire and honour. Together with the first volume, *The Apple Tree*, this collection represents Galsworthy as a master of his craft.

SPINDLEBERRIES

THE celebrated painter, Scudamore—whose studies of Nature had been hung on the line for so many years that he had forgotten the days when, not yet in the Scudamore manner, they depended from the sky—stood where his cousin had left him so abruptly. His lips, between comely grey moustache and comely pointed beard, wore a mortified smile, and he gazed rather dazedly at the spindleberries fallen on to the flagged courtyard from the branch she had brought to show him. Why had she thrown up her head as if he had struck her, and whisked round so that those dull-pink berries quivered and lost their rain-drops, and four had fallen? He had but said: "Charming! I'd like to use them!" And she had answered: "God!" and rushed away. Alicia really was crazed; who would have thought that once she had been so adorable? He stooped and picked up the four berries—a beautiful colour, that dull pink! And from below the coatings of success and the Scudamore manner a little thrill came up; the stir of emotional vision. Paint! What good? How express? He went across to the low wall which divided the courtyard of his expensively restored and beautiful old house from the first flood of the River Arun wandering silvery in pale winter sunlight. Yes, indeed! How express Nature, its translucence and mysterious unities, its mood never the same from hour to hour? Those brown-tufted rushes over there against the gold grey of light and water—those restless, hovering, white gulls. A kind of disgust at his own celebrated manner welled up within him—the disgust expressed in Alicia's "God!" Beauty! What use—how express it? Had she been thinking the same thing?

He looked at the four pink berries glistening on the grey stone of the wall and memory stirred. What a lovely girl she had been, with her grey-green eyes shining under long lashes, the rose-petal colour

in her cheeks and the too-fine dark hair—now so very grey—
always blowing a little wild. An enchanting, enthusiastic creature!
He remembered, as if it had been but last week, that day when they
started from Arundel Station by the road to Burpham, when he was
twenty-nine and she twenty-five, both of them painters and neither
of them famed—a day of showers and sunlight in the middle of
March and Nature preparing for full spring! How they had chattered
at first; and when their arms touched, how he had thrilled, and the
colour had deepened in her rain-wet cheeks; and then, gradually,
they had grown silent; a wonderful walk, which seemed leading so
surely to a more wonderful end. They had wandered round through
the village and down past the chalk-pit and Jacob's ladder, into the
field path and so to the river bank. And he had taken her ever so
gently round the waist, still silent, waiting for that moment when
his heart would leap out of him in words and hers—he was sure—
would leap to meet it. The path entered a thicket of blackthorn with
a few primroses close to the little river running full and gentle. The
last drops of a shower were falling, but the sun had burst through,
and the sky above the thicket was cleared to the blue of speedwell
flowers. Suddenly she had stopped and cried: "Look, Dick! Oh,
look! It's heaven!" A high bush of blackthorn was lifted there, starry
white against the blue and that bright cloud. It seemed to sing, it was
so lovely; the whole of spring was in it. But the sight of her ecstatic
face had broken down all his restraint, and tightening his arm round
her he had kissed her lips. He remembered still the expression of her
face, like a child's startled out of sleep. She had gone rigid, gasped,
started away from him, quivered and gulped, and broken suddenly
into sobs. Then, slipping from his arm, she had fled. He had stood at
first, amazed and hurt, utterly bewildered; then, recovering a little,
had hunted for her full half an hour before at last he found her
sitting on wet grass, with a stony look on her face. He had said
nothing, and she nothing, except to murmur: "Let's go on; we shall
miss our train!" And all the rest of that day and the day after, until
they parted, he had suffered from the feeling of having tumbled
down off some high perch in her estimation. He had not liked it
at all; it had made him very angry. Never from that day to this had

he thought of it as anything but a piece of wanton prudery. Had
it—had it been something else?

He looked at the four pink berries, and, as if they had uncanny power
to turn the wheel of memory, he saw another vision of his cousin five
years later. He was married by then, and already hung on the line. With
his wife he had gone down to Alicia's country cottage. A summer night,
just dark and very warm. After many exhortations she had brought into
the little drawing-room her last finished picture. He could see her now
placing it where the light fell, her tall, slight form already rather sharp
and meagre, as the figures of some women grow at thirty, if they are not
married; the nervous, fluttering look on her charming face, as though
she could hardly bear this inspection; the way she raised her shoulder
just a little as if to ward off an expected blow of condemnation. No
need! It had been a beautiful thing, a quite surprisingly beautiful study
of night. He remembered with what a really jealous ache he had gazed
at it—a better thing than he had ever done himself. And, frankly, he had
said so. Her eyes had shone with pleasure.

"Do you really like it? I tried so hard!"

"The day you show that, my dear," he had said, "your name's
made!" She had clasped her hands and simply sighed: "Oh, Dick!"
He had felt quite happy in her happiness, and presently the three
of them had taken their chairs out, beyond the curtains, on to the
dark verandah, had talked a little, then somehow fallen silent. A
wonderful warm, black, grape-bloom night, exquisitely gracious
and inviting; the stars very high and white, the flowers glimmering
in the garden-beds, and against the deep, dark blue, roses hanging,
unearthly, stained with beauty. There was a scent of honeysuckle, he
remembered, and many moths came fluttering by toward the tall,
narrow chink of light between the curtains. Alicia had sat leaning
forward, elbows on knees, ears buried in her hands. Probably they
were silent because she sat like that. Once he heard her whisper to
herself: "Lovely, lovely! Oh, God! How lovely!" His wife, feeling
the dew, had gone in, and he had followed; Alicia had not seemed
to notice. But when she too came in, her eyes were glistening with
tears. She said something about bed in a queer voice; they had taken
candles and gone up. Next morning, going to her little studio to

give her advice about that picture, he had been literally horrified to see it streaked with lines of white—Alicia, standing before it, was dashing her brush in broad smears across and across. She heard him and turned round. There was a hard red spot in either cheek, and she said in a quivering voice: "It was blasphemy. That's all!" And turning her back on him she had gone on smearing it with white. Without a word, he had turned tail in simple disgust. Indeed, so deep had been his vexation at that wanton destruction of the best thing she had ever done or was ever likely to do, that he had avoided her for years. He had always had a horror of eccentricity. To have planted her foot firmly on the ladder of fame and then deliberately kicked it away; to have wantonly foregone this chance of making money—for she had but a mere pittance! It had seemed to him really too exasperating, a thing only to be explained by tapping one's forehead. Every now and then he still heard of her, living down there, spending her days out in the woods and fields, and sometimes even her nights, they said, and steadily growing poorer and thinner and more eccentric; becoming, in short, impossibly difficult, as only Englishwomen can. People would speak of her as "such a dear," and talk of her charm, but always with that shrug which is hard to bear when applied to one's relations. What she did with the productions of her brush he never inquired, too disillusioned by that experience. Poor Alicia!

The pink berries glowed on the grey stone, and he had yet another memory. A family occasion when Uncle Martin Scudamore departed this life, and they all went up to bury him and hear his will. The old chap, whom they had looked on as a bit of a disgrace, money-grubbing up in the little grey Yorkshire town which owed its rise to his factory, was expected to make amends by his death, for he had never married—too sunk in industry, apparently, to have the time. By tacit agreement, his nephews and nieces had selected the Inn at Bolton Abbey, nearest beauty spot, for their stay. They had driven six miles to the funeral, in three carriages. Alicia had gone with him and his brother, the solicitor. In her plain black clothes she looked quite charming, in spite of the silver threads already thick in her fine dark hair, loosened by the moor wind. She had talked of painting to him with all her old enthusiasm, and her eyes had seemed to linger on his face as if she still had a little weakness for him. He had quite enjoyed that drive. They had come rather abruptly on the small grimy town clinging to the river banks, with old Martin's long, yellow-brick house dominating it, about two hundred yards above the mills. Suddenly, under the rug, he felt Alicia's hand seize his with a sort of desperation, for all the world as if she were clinging to something to support her. Indeed, he was sure she did not know it was his hand she squeezed. The cobbled streets, the muddy-looking water, the dingy, staring factories, the yellow, staring house, the little dark-clothed, dreadfully plain work-people, all turned out to do a last honour to their creator; the hideous new grey church, the dismal service, the brand-new tombstones—and all of a glorious autumn day! It was inexpressibly sordid—too ugly for words! Afterwards the will was read to them seated decorously on bright mahogany chairs in the yellow mansion, a very satisfactory will, distributing in perfectly adjusted portions, to his own kinsfolk and nobody else, a very considerable wealth. Scudamore had listened to it dreamily, with his eyes fixed on an oily picture, thinking, 'My God! What a thing!' and longing to be back in the carriage smoking a cigar to take the reek of black clothes and sherry—sherry!—out of his nostrils. He happened to look at Alicia. Her eyes were closed; her lips, always sweet-looking, quivered amusedly. And at that very moment the will came to her name. He saw those eyes open wide, and marked a beautiful pink flush, quite like that of old days, come into her thin cheeks. 'Splendid!' he had thought; 'it's really jolly for her. I *am* glad! Now she won't have to pinch. Splendid!' He shared with her to the full the surprised relief showing in her still beautiful face.

All the way home in the carriage he felt at least as happy over her good fortune as over his own, which had been substantial. He took her hand under the rug and squeezed it, and she answered with a long, gentle pressure, quite unlike the clutch when they were driving in. That same evening he strolled out to where the river curved below the Abbey. The sun had not quite set, and its last smoky radiance slanted into the burnished autumn woods. Some white-faced Herefords were grazing in lush grass, the river rippled and gleamed all over golden scales. About that scene was the magic which had so often startled the hearts of painters, the wistful gold—the enchantment of a dream.

For some minutes he had gazed with delight which had in it a sort of despair. A little crisp rustle ran along the bushes; the leaves fluttered, then hung quite still. And he heard a voice—Alicia's—speaking. 'The lovely, lovely world!" And moving forward a step, he saw her standing on the river bank, braced against the trunk of a birch tree, her head thrown back, and her arms stretched wide apart as though to clasp the lovely world she had apostrophised. To have gone up to her would have been like breaking up a lovers' interview, and he turned round instead and went away.

A week later he heard from his brother that Alicia had refused her legacy. "I don't want it," her letter had said simply; "I couldn't bear to take it. Give it to those poor people who live in that awful place." Really eccentricity could go no further! They decided to go down and see her. Such mad neglect of her own good must not be permitted without some effort to prevent it. They found her very thin and charming, humble, but quite obstinate in her refusal. "Oh! I couldn't really! I should be so unhappy. Those poor little stunted people who made it all for him! That little, awful town! I simply couldn't be reminded. Don't talk about it, please. I'm quite all right as I am." They had threatened her with lurid pictures of the workhouse and a destitute old age. To no purpose; she would not take the money. She had been forty when she refused that aid from heaven—forty, and already past any hope of marriage. For though Scudamore had never known for certain that she had ever wished or hoped for marriage, he had his theory—that all her eccentricity came from wasted sexual instinct. This last folly had seemed to him monstrous enough to be pathetic, and he no longer avoided her. Indeed, he would often walk over to tea in her little hermitage. With Uncle Martin's money he had bought and restored the beautiful old house over the River Arun, and was now only five miles from Alicia's, across country. She, too, would come tramping over at all hours, floating in with wild flowers or ferns, which she would put into water the moment she arrived. She had ceased to wear hats, and had by now a very doubtful reputation for sanity about the countryside. This was the period when Watts was on every painter's tongue, and he seldom saw Alicia without a disputation concerning that famous symbolist. Personally, he had no use for Watts, resenting his

faulty drawing and crude allegories, but Alicia always maintained with
her extravagant fervour that he was great because he tried to paint the
soul of things. She especially loved a painting called "Iris"—a female
symbol of the rainbow, which indeed, in its floating eccentricity, had a
certain resemblance to herself. "Of course he failed," she would say; "he
tried for the impossible and went on trying all his life. Oh! I can't bear
your tales and catchwords, Dick; what's the good of them! Beauty's too
big, too deep!" Poor Alicia! She was something very wearing.

He never knew quite how it came about that she went abroad
with them to Dauphiné in the autumn of 1904—a rather disastrous
business. Never again would he take anyone travelling who did not
know how to come in out of the cold. It was a painter's country, and
he had hired a little *château* in front of Glandaz mountain—himself,
his wife, their eldest girl, and Alicia. The adaptation of his famous
manner to that strange scenery, its browns and French greys and
filmy blues, so preoccupied him that he had scant time for becoming
intimate with these hills and valleys. From the little gravelled terrace
in front of the annexe, out of which he had made a studio, there was
an absorbing view over the pantiled old town of Die. It glistened
below in the early or late sunlight, flat-roofed and of pinkish
yellow, with the dim, blue River Drôme circling one side, and cut,
dark cypress trees dotting the vineyarded slopes. And he painted it
continually. What Alicia did with herself they none of them very
much knew, except that she would come in and talk ecstatically of
things and beasts and people she had seen. One favourite haunt of
hers they did visit—a ruined monastery high up in the amphitheatre
of the Glandaz mountain. They had their lunch up there, a very
charming and remote spot, where the watercourses and ponds and
chapel of the old monks were still visible, though converted by the
farmer to his use. Alicia left them abruptly in the middle of their
praises, and they had not seen her again till they found her at home
when they got back. It was almost as if she had resented laudation
of her favourite haunt. She had brought in with her a great bunch
of golden berries, of which none of them knew the name; berries
almost as beautiful as these spindleberries glowing on the stone of
the wall. And a fourth memory of Alicia came.

Christmas Eve, a sparkling frost, and every tree round the little *chateau* rimed so that they shone in the starlight as though dowered with cherry blossom. Never were more stars in clear black sky above the whitened earth. Down in the little town a few faint points of yellow light twinkled in the mountain wind keen as a razor's edge. A fantastically lovely night—quite "Japanese," but cruelly cold. Five minutes on the terrace had been enough for all of them except Alicia. She—unaccountable, crazy creature—would not come in. Twice he had gone out to her, with commands, entreaties, and extra wraps; the third time he could not find her. She had deliberately avoided his onslaught and slid off somewhere to keep this mad vigil by frozen starlight. When at last she did come in she reeled as if drunk. They tried to make her really drunk, to put warmth back into her. No good! In two days she was down with double pneumonia; it was two months before she was up again—a very shadow of herself. There had never been much health in her since then. She floated like a ghost through life, a crazy ghost, who would steal away, goodness knew where, and come in with a flush in her withered cheeks, and her grey hair wild blown, carrying her spoil—some flower, some leaf, some tiny bird or little soft rabbit. She never painted now, never even talked of it. They had made her give up her cottage and come to live with them, literally afraid that she would starve herself to death in her forgetfulness of everything. These spindleberries even! Why probably, she had been right up this morning to that sunny chalk-pit in the lew of the Downs to get them, seven miles there and back, when you wouldn't think she could walk seven hundred yards, and as likely as not had lain there on the dewy grass looking up at the sky, as he had come on her sometimes. Poor Alicia! And once he had been within an ace of marrying her! A life spoiled! By what, if not by love of beauty? But who would have ever thought that the intangible could wreck a woman, deprive her of love, marriage, motherhood, of fame, of wealth, of health? And yet—by George!—it had!

Scudamore flipped the four pink berries off the wall. The radiance and the meandering milky waters; that swan against the brown tufted rushes; those far, filmy Downs—there was beauty! *Beauty*! But, damn it all—moderation! Moderation! And, turning his back on that prospect, which he had painted so many times, in his celebrated manner, he went in, and up the expensively restored staircase to his studio. It had great windows on three sides, and perfect means for regulating light. Unfinished studies melted into walls so subdued that they looked like atmosphere. There were no completed pictures—they sold too fast. As he walked over to his easel his eye was caught by a spray of colour—the branch of spindleberries set in water, ready for him to use, just where the pale sunlight fell so that their delicate colour might glow and the few tiny drops of moisture still clinging to them shine. For a second he saw Alicia herself as she must have looked, setting them there, her transparent hands hovering, her eyes shining, that grey hair of hers all fine and loose. The vision vanished! But what had made her bring them after that horrified "God!" when he spoke of using them? Was it her way of saying: "Forgive me for being rude?" Really she was pathetic, that poor devotee! The spindleberries glowed in their silver-lustre jug, sprayed up against the sunlight. They looked triumphant—as well they might, who stood for that which had ruined—or was it saved?—a life! Alicia! She had made a pretty mess of it, and yet who knew what secret raptures she had felt with her subtle lover, Beauty, by starlight and sunlight and moonlight, in the fields and woods, on the hilltops, and by riverside? Flowers, and the flight of birds, and the ripple of the wind, and all the shifting play of light and colour which made a man despair when he wanted to use them; she had taken them, hugged them to her with no afterthought, and been happy! Who could say that she had missed the prize of life? Who could say it? . . . Spindleberries! A bunch of spindleberries to set such doubts astir in him! Why, what was beauty but just the extra value which certain forms and colours, blended, gave to things—just the extra value in the human market! Nothing else on earth, nothing! And the spindleberries glowed against the sunlight, delicate, remote!

Taking his palette, he mixed crimson lake, white, and ultra marine. What was that? Who sighed, away out there behind him? Nothing!

'Damn it all!' he thought; 'this is childish. This is as bad as Alicia!' And he set to work to paint in his celebrated manner—spindleberries.
[1918]

SALTA PRO NOBIS

(A Variation)

"THE dancer, my Mother, is very sad. She sits with her head on her hands. She looks into the emptiness. It is frightful to watch. I have tried to make her pray, my Mother, but the poor girl—she does not know how; she has no belief. She refuses even to confess herself. She is pagan—but quite pagan. What could one do for her, my Mother—to cheer her a little during these hours? I have tried to make her tell me of her life. She does not answer. She sits and looks always into the emptiness. It does me harm in the heart to see her. Is there nothing one can do to comfort her a little before she dies? To die so young—so full of life; for her who has no faith! To be shot—so young, so beautiful; but it is frightful, my Mother!"

When she had finished speaking thus, the little elderly Sister raised her hands, and crossed them quietly on her grey-clothed breast. Her eyes, brown and mild, looked up, questioning the face before her, wax pale under its coif and smooth grey hair. Straight, thin, as it were bodiless, beneath the grey and white of her garb, the Mother Superior stood pondering. The spy-woman in her charge, a dancer with gypsy blood they said—or was it Moorish?—who had wormed secrets from her French naval lover, and sold them to the Germans in Spain. At the trial they said there was no doubt. And they had brought her to the Convent saying, "Keep her for us till the fifteenth. She will be better with you than in prison." To be shot—a woman! It made one shiver! And yet—it was war! It was for France!

Looking down at the little Sister with the soft brown eyes, the Mother Superior answered:

"One must see, my daughter. Take me to her cell."

Along the corridor they passed, and went in gently. The dancer was sitting on her bed, with legs crossed under her. There was no colour in her skin, save the saffron sprinkled into it by Eastern blood. The face was oval, the eyebrows slanted a little up; black hair formed on her forehead a V reversed; her lips, sensuous but fine, showed a gleam of teeth. Her arms were crossed, as though compressing the fire within her supple body. Her eyes, colour of Malaga wine, looked through and beyond the whitened walls, through and beyond her visitors, like the eyes of a caged leopard.

The Mother Superior spoke:

"What can we do for you, my daughter?"

The daughter shrugged her body from the waist; one could see its supple shivering beneath her silk garment.

"You suffer, my daughter. They tell me you do not pray. It is a pity."

The dancer smiled—that quickly passing smile had sweetness, as of something tasted, of a rich tune, of a long kiss; she shook her head.

"One would not say anything to trouble you, my daughter; one feels pity for your suffering. One comprehends. Is there a book you would read; some wine you would like; in a word, anything which could distract you a little?"

The dancer untwined her arms, and clasped them behind her neck. The movement was beautiful, sinuous—all her body beautiful; and into the Mother Superior's waxen cheeks a faint colour came.

"Will you dance for us, my daughter?"

Again the smile, like the taste of a sweet wine, came on the dancer's face, and this time did not pass.

"Yes," she said, "I will dance for you—willingly. It will give me pleasure, Madame!"

"That is good. Your dresses shall be brought. This evening in the refectory, after the meal. If you wish music—one can place a piano. Sister Mathilde is a good musician."

"Yes, music—some simple dances. Madame, could I smoke?"

"Certainly, my daughter. I will have cigarettes brought to you."

The dancer stretched out her hand. Between her own, fragile with thin blue veins, the Mother Superior felt its supple warmth, and shivered. To-morrow it would be cold and stiff!

"*Au revoir*! then, my daughter . . ."

"The dancer will dance for us!" This was the word. One waited; expectant, as for a marvel. One placed the piano; procured music; sat eating the evening meal—whispering. The strangeness of it! The intrusion! The little gay ghosts of memories! Ah! the dramatic, the strange event! Soon the meal was finished; the tables cleared, removed; against the wall, on the long benches sixty grey figures with white coifs waited—in the centre the Mother Superior, at the piano Sister Mathilde.

The little elderly Sister came first; then, down the long whitened refectory, the dancer walking slowly over the dark oak floor. Every head was turned—alone the Mother Superior sat motionless, thinking: 'If only it does not put notions into some light heads!'

The dancer wore a full skirt of black silk, she had silvery shoes and stockings, round her waist was a broad tight network of gold, over her bust tight silvery tissue, with black lace draped; her arms were bare; a red flower was set to one side of her black hair; she held a black and ivory fan. Her lips were just touched with red, her eyes just touched with black; her face was like a mask. She stood in the very centre, with eyes cast down. Sister Mathilde began to play. The dancer lifted her fan. In that dance of Spain she hardly moved from where she stood, swaying, shivering, spinning, poised; only the eyes of her face seemed alive, resting on this face and on that of the long row of faces, where so many feelings were expressed—curiosity and doubt, pleasure, timidity, horror, curiosity. Sister Mathilde ceased playing, the dancer stood still; a little murmur broke along the line of nuns, and the dancer smiled. Then Sister Mathilde began again to play, a Polish dance; for a moment the dancer listened as if to catch the rhythm of music strange to her; then her feet moved, her lips parted, she was sweet and gay, like a butterfly, without a care; and on the lips of the watching faces smiles came, and little murmurs of pleasure escaped.

The Mother Superior sat without moving, her thin lips pressed together, her thin fingers interlaced. Images from the past kept starting out, and falling back, like figures from some curious old musical box. That long-ago time—she was remembering—when her lover was killed in the Franco-Prussian war, and she entered religion. This supple figure from the heathen world, the red flower in the black hair, the whitened face, the sweetened eyes, stirred up remembrance, sweet and yearning, of her own gay pulses, before they had seemed to die, and she brought them to the Church to bury them.

The music ceased; began again a Habañera, reviving memories of the pulses after they were buried—secret, throbbing, dark. The Mother Superior turned her face to left and right. Had she been wise? So many light heads, so many young hearts! And yet, why not soothe the last dark hours of this poor heathen girl? She was happy, dancing. Yes, she was happy! What power! And what abandonment! It was frightening. She was holding every eye—the eyes even of Sister Louise—holding them as a snake holds a rabbit's eyes. The Mother Superior nearly smiled. That poor Sister Louise! And then, just beyond that face of fascinated horror, the Mother Superior saw young Sister Marie. How the child was staring—what eyes, what lips! Sister Marie—so young—just twenty—her lover dead in the war—but one year dead! Sister Marie
—prettiest in all the Convent! Her hands—how tightly they seemed pressed together on her lap! And—but yes—it was at Sister Marie that the dancer looked; at Sister Marie she twirled and writhed those supple fiery limbs! For Sister Marie the strange sweet smile came and went on those enticing reddened lips. In dance after dance—like a bee on a favourite flower—to Sister Marie the dancer seemed to cling. And the Mother Superior thought: 'Is this the Blessed Virgin's work I have done, or—the Devil's?'

Close along the line of nuns the dancer was sweeping now; her eyes glowed, her face was proud, her body supreme. Sister Marie! What was it? A look, a touch with the fan! The music ceased! The dancer blew a kiss. It lighted—where? "*Gracias, Señoras! Adios!*"

Slowly, swaying, as she had come, she walked away over the dark floor; and the little old Sister followed.

A sighing sound from the long row of nuns; and—yes—one sob!

"Go to your rooms, my daughters! Sister Marie!"

The young nun came forward; tears were in her eyes.

"Sister Marie, pray that the sins of that poor soul be forgiven. But yes, my child, it is sad. Go to your room. Pray!"

With what grace the child walked! She, too, had the limbs of beauty. The Mother Superior sighed. . . .

Morning, cold, grey, a sprinkle of snow on the ground; they came for the dancer during Mass. A sound of firing! With trembling lips, the Mother Superior prayed for the soul dancing before her God. . . .

That evening they searched for Sister Marie, but could not find her. After two days a letter came:

> "Forgive me, my Mother. I have gone back to
> life.
> "MARIE."

The Mother Superior sat quite still. Life in death! Figures starting out from that old musical box of memory; the dancer's face, red flower in the hair, dark sweetened eyes, lips, touched with flying finger, parted in a kiss!

[*1922*]

THE PACK

"It's only," said H., "when men run in packs that they lose their sense of decency. At least that's my experience. Individual man—I'm not speaking of savages—is more given to generosity than meanness, rarely brutal, inclines in fact to be a gentleman. It's when you add three or four more to him that his sense of decency, his sense of personal responsibility, his private standards, go by the board. I am not at all sure that he does not become the victim of a certain infectious fever. Something physical takes place, I fancy . . . I happen to be a trustee, with three others, and we do a deal of cheeseparing in the year, which as private individuals we should never dream of."

"That's hardly a fair example," said D., "but on the whole, I quite agree. Single man is not an angel; collective man is a. bit of a brute."

The discussion was carried on for several minutes, and then P., who had not yet spoken, said: "They say a pinch of illustration is worth a pound of argument. When I was at the 'Varsity there was a man at the same college with me called Chalkcroft, the son of a high ecclesiastic, a perfectly harmless, well-mannered individual, who had the misfortune to be a Radical, or, as some even thought, a Socialist—anyway, he wore a turn-down collar, a green tie, took part in Union debates on the shady side, and no part in college festivities. He was, in fact, a 'smug'—a man, as you know, who, through some accident of his early environment, incomprehensibly fails to adopt the proper view of life. He was never drunk, not even pleasantly, played no games connected with a ball, was believed to be afraid of a horse or a woman, took his exercise in long walks with a man from another college, or solitarily in a skiff upon the river; he also read books, and was prepared to discuss abstract propositions. Thus,

in one way or another he disgusted almost every self-respecting
undergraduate. Don't imagine, of course, that his case was unusual;
we had many such at M—— in my time; but about this Chalkcroft
there was an unjustifiable composure, a quiet sarcasm, which made
him conspicuously intolerable. He was thought to be a 'bit above
himself,' or, rather, he did not seem conscious, as any proper 'smug'
should, that he was a bit below his fellows; on the contrary, his figure,
which was slim, and slightly stooping, passed in and about college
with serene assurance; his pale face with its traces of reprehensible
whisker, wore a faint smile above his detested green tie; besides, he
showed no signs of that poverty which is, of course, some justification
to 'smugs' for their lack of conformity. And as a matter of fact, he was
not poor, but had some of the best rooms in college, which was ever
a remembered grievance against him. For these reasons, then," went
on P., "it was decided one evening to bring him to trial. This salutary
custom had originated in the mind of a third-year man named
Jefferies, a dark person with a kind of elephant-like unwieldiness
in his nose and walk, a biting, witty tongue, and very small eyes
with a lecherous expression. He is now a baronet. This gentleman
in his cups had quite a pretty malice, and a sense of the dignity of
the law. Wandering of a night in the quadrangles, he never had any
difficulty in gathering a troop of fellows in search of distraction, or
animated by public and other spirits; and, with them whooping and
crowing at his heels, it was his beneficial practice to enter the rooms
of any person, who for good and sufficient reasons merited trial,
and thereupon to conduct the same with all the ceremony due to
the dispensation of British justice. I had attended one of these trials
before, on a chuckle-headed youth whose buffoonery was really
offensive. The ceremony was funny enough, nor did the youth seem
to mind, grinning from ear to ear, and ejaculating continually, 'Oh!
I say, Jefferies!'

"The occasion of which I am going to speak now was a different
sort of affair altogether. We found the man Chalkcroft at home,
reading before his fire by the light of three candles. The room was
panelled in black oak, and the yellow candle flames barely lit up the
darkness as we came whooping in.

"'Chalkcroft,' said Jefferies, 'we are going to try you.' Chalkcroft stood up and looked at us. He was in a Norfolk jacket, with his customary green tie, and his face was pale.

"He answered: 'Yes, Jefferies? You forgot to knock.'

"Jefferies put out his finger and thumb and delicately plucked Chalkcroft's tie from out of his waistcoat.

"'You wear a green tie, sir,' he said.

"'Chalkcroft went the colour of the ashes in the grate; then, slowly, a white-hot glow came into his cheeks.

"'Don't look at me, sir,' said Jefferies; 'look at the jury!' and he waved his hand at us. 'We are going to try you for ——' He specified an incident of a scabrous character which served as the charge on all such humorous occasions, and was likely to be peculiarly offensive to 'smugs,' who are usually, as you know, what is called 'pi.'

"We yelped, guffawed, and settled ourselves in chairs; Jefferies perched himself on a table and slowly swung his thin legs; he always wore very tight trousers. His little black eyes gleamed greedily above his unwieldy nose. Chalkcroft remained standing.

"It was then," pursued P., "that I had my first qualm. The fellow was so still and pale and unmoved; he looked at me, and, when I tried to stare back, his eyes passed me over, quiet and contemptuous. And I remember thinking: 'Why are we all here—we are not a bit the kind of men to do this sort of thing?' And really we were not. With the exception of Jefferies, who was, no doubt, at times inhabited by a devil, and one Anderson, a little man in a long coat, with a red nose and very long arms, always half-drunk—a sort of desperate character, and long since a schoolmaster—there wasn't one of us who, left to himself, would have entered another man's rooms unbidden (however unpopular he might be, however much of a 'smug'), and insulted him to his face. There was Beal, a very fair, rather good-looking man, with bowed legs and no expression to speak of, known as Boshy Beal; Dunsdale, a heavy, long-faced, freckled person, prominent in every college disturbance, but with a reputation for respectability; Horden (called Jos), a big, clean-cut Kentish man with nice eyes, and fists like hammers; Stickland, fussy, with mild habits; Sevenoax, now in the House of Lords; little Holingbroke, the cox;

and my old school-fellow, Fosdyke, whose dignity even then would certainly have forbidden his presence had he not previously dined. Thus, as you see, we were all or nearly all from the 'best' schools in the country, in the 'best' set at M——, and naturally, as individuals, quite—oh! quite—incapable of an ungentlemanlike act.

"Jefferies appointed Anderson gaoler, Dunsdale Public Prosecutor, no one counsel for the defence, the rest of us jury, himself judge, and opened the trial. He was, as I have said, a witty young man, and, dangling his legs, fastening his malevolent black eyes on Chalkcroft, he usurped the functions of us all. The nature of the charge precludes me from recounting to you the details of the trial, and, in fact, I have forgotten them, but as if he were standing here before us, I remember, in the dim glow of those three candles, Chalkcroft's pale, unmoved, ironic face; his unvarying, 'Yes, Jefferies'; his one remonstrance: 'Are you a gentleman, Jefferies?' and our insane laughter at the answer: 'No, sir, a by-our-Lady judge.' As if he were standing here before us I remember the expression on his face at the question: 'Prisoner, are you guilty—yes or no?' the long pause, the slow, sarcastic: 'As you like, Jefferies.' As if he were standing here before us I remember his calm and his contempt. He was sentenced to drink a tumbler of his own port without stopping; whether the sentence was carried out I cannot tell you; for with one or two more I slipped away.

"The next morning I had such a sense of discomfort that I could not rest till I had sent Chalkcroft a letter of apology. I caught sight of him in the afternoon walking across the quad with his usual pale assurance, and in the evening I received his answer. It contained, at the end, this sentence: 'I feel sure you would not have come if it hadn't been for the others.' It has occurred to me since that he may have said the same thing to us all—for anything I know, we may all of us have written."

There was a silence. Then H. said: "The Pack! Ah! What second-hand devil is it that gets into us when we run in packs?"
[*1905*]

"THE DOG IT WAS THAT DIED"

UNTIL the Great War was over I had no idea that some of us who stayed at home made the great sacrifice.

My friend Harburn is, or rather was, a Northumbrian or some kind of northerner, a stocky man of perhaps fifty with close-clipped grizzled hair and moustache and a deep-coloured face. He was a neighbour of mine in the country, and we had the same kind of dogs—Airedales, never less than three at a time, so that for breeding purposes we were useful to each other. We often, too, went up to town by the same train. His occupation was one which gave him opportunity of prominence in public life, but until the war he took little advantage of this, sunk in a kind of bluff indifferentism which was almost cynical. I used to look on him as a typically good-natured, blunt Englishman, rather enjoying his cynicism, and appreciating his open-air tendencies—for he was a devotee of golf and fond of shooting when he had the chance; a good companion, too, with an open hand to people in distress. He was unmarried, and dwelled in a bungalow-like house not far from mine and next door to a German family called Holsteig, who had lived in England nearly twenty years. I knew them pretty well also—a very united trio— father, mother, and one son. The father, who came from Hanover, was something in the city, the mother was Scotch, and the son—the one I knew best and liked most—had just left his public school. This youth had a frank, open, blue-eyed face, and thick light hair brushed back without a parting—an attractive, rather Norwegian-looking type. His mother was devoted to him—she was a real West Highlander; slight, with dark hair going grey, high cheek bones, a sweet but ironical smile, and those grey eyes which have second sight in them. I several times met Harburn at their house, for he would go in to play billiards with Holsteig in the evenings, and the whole family were on friendly terms with him. The third morning after we had declared war on Germany, Harburn, Holsteig, and I went up to town in the same carriage. Harburn and I talked freely. But Holsteig, a fair, well-set-up man of about fifty, with a pointed beard and blue eyes like his son, sat immersed in his paper, till Harburn said rather suddenly:

"I say, Holsteig, is it true that your boy was going off to join the German Army?"

Holsteig looked up.

"Yes," he said. "He was born in Germany, so he's liable to military service. Thank heaven—it isn't possible for him to go!"

"But his mother?" said Harburn. "She surely wouldn't have let him."

"She was very miserable, of course, but she thought duty came first."

"Duty! Good God—my dear man! Half British, and living in this country all his life! I never heard of such a thing!" Holsteig shrugged his shoulders.

"In a crisis like this what can you do except follow the law strictly? He is of military age and a German subject. We were thinking of his honour; but, of course, we're most thankful he can't get over to Germany."

"Well, I'm damned!" said Harburn. "You Germans are too bally conscientious altogether."

Holsteig did not answer.

I travelled back with Harburn the same evening, and he said to me:

"Once a German, always a German. Didn't that chap Holsteig astonish you this morning? In spite of living here so long and marrying a British wife, his sympathies are dead German, you see."

"Well," I replied, "put yourself in his place."

"I can't; I could never have lived in Germany. I say, Cumbermere," he added, "I wonder if the chap's all right?"

"Of course he's all right." Which was the wrong thing to say to Harburn if one wanted to re-establish his confidence in the

Holsteigs, as I certainly did, for I liked them and was sure of their good faith. If I had said: "Of course he's a spy," I should have rallied all Harburn's confidence in Holsteig, for he was naturally contradictious.

I only mention this little passage to show how early Harburn's thoughts began to turn to the subject which afterwards completely absorbed and inspired him till he—er—died for his country.

I am not sure what paper first took up the question of interning all the Huns; but I fancy the point was raised originally rather from the instinct, deeply implanted in so many journals, to do what would please the public than out of any deep animus. At all events, I remember meeting a sub-editor who told me he had been opening letters of approval all the morning. "Never," said he, "have we had a stunt catch on so quickly. 'Why should that bally German round the corner get my custom?' and so forth. Britain for the British!"

"Rather bad luck," I said, "on people who've paid us the compliment of finding this the best country to live in?"

"Bad luck, no doubt," he replied, "but war's war. You know Harburn, don't you? Did you see that article he wrote? By Jove! he pitched it strong."

When next I met Harburn himself he began talking on this subject at once.

"Mark my words," he said, "I'll have every German out of this country." His grey eyes seemed to glint with the snap and spark as of steel and flint and tinder; and I felt I was in the presence of a man who had brooded so over the German atrocities in Belgium that he was possessed by a sort of abstract hate.

"Of course," I said, "there have been many spies, but——"

"Spies and ruffians," he cried, "the whole lot of them."

"How many Germans do you know personally?" I asked him.

"Thank God! not a dozen."

"And are they spies and ruffians?"

He looked at me and laughed, but that laugh was uncommonly like a snarl.

"You go in for fairness," he said, "and all that slop; take 'em by the throat—it's the only way."

It trembled on the tip of my tongue to ask him whether he meant to take the Holsteigs by the throat, but I swallowed it for fear of doing them an injury. I was feeling much the same general abhorrence myself, and had to hold myself in for fear it should gallop over my common sense of justice. But Harburn, I could see, was giving it full rein. His whole manner and personality somehow had changed. He had lost geniality and the cynicism which had made him an attractive companion; he was as if gnawed at inwardly—in a word, he already had a fixed idea.

Now, a cartoonist, like myself, has to be interested in the psychology of men, and I brooded over Harburn, for it seemed to me quite remarkable that one whom I had always associated with good humour and bluff indifference should be thus obsessed. And I found this theory about him: "Here"—I said to myself—"is one of Cromwell's Ironsides, born out of his age. In the slack times of peace he discovered no outlet for the grim within him—his fire could never be lighted by love, therefore he drifted in the waters of indifferentism. Now, suddenly, in this grizzly time he has found himself, a new man, girt and armed by this new passion of hate, stung and uplifted, as it were, by the sight of that which he can smite with a whole heart. It really is most deeply interesting. Who could have dreamed of such a reincarnation; for what on the surface could possibly be less like an 'Ironside' than Harburn as I've known him up to now?" I used his face for the basis of a cartoon which represented a human weather-vane continually pointing to the East, no matter from what quarter the wind blew. He recognised himself, and laughed when he saw me—rather pleased, in fact; but in that laugh there was a sort of truculence as if the man had the salt taste of blood at the back of his mouth.

"Ah!" said he, "you may joke about it, Cumbermere, but I've got my teeth into the swine!"

And there was no doubt he had—the man had become a force; unhappy Germans—a few of them spies, no doubt, but the great majority as certainly innocent—were being wrenched from their trades and families and piled into internment camps all day and every day—and the faster they were piled in, the higher grew his "stock" as a servant of his country. I'm sure he did not do it to gain credit; the thing was a crusade to him, something sacred—"his bit"; but I believe he also felt for the first time in his life that he was really living, getting out of life the full of its juice. Was he not smiting hip and thigh? He longed, I am sure, to be in the thick of the actual fighting, but age debarred him, and he was not of that more sensitive type which shrinks from smiting the defenceless if it cannot smite anything stronger. I remember saying to him once:

"Harburn, do you ever think of the women and children of your victims?"

He drew his lips back, and I saw how excellent his teeth were.

"The women are worse than the men, I believe," he said. "I'd put them in, too, if I could. As for the children, they're all the better for being without fathers of that kidney."

He really was a little mad on the subject; no more so, of course, than any other man with a fixed idea, but certainly no less.

In those days I was here, there, and everywhere, and had let my country cottage, so I saw nothing of the Holsteigs, and, indeed, had pretty well forgotten their existence. But coming back at the end of 1917 from a long spell with the Red Cross, I found among my letters one from Mrs. Holsteig.

> "Dear Mr. Cumbermere,
> "You were always so friendly to us that I have summoned up courage to write this letter. You know, perhaps, that my husband was interned over a year ago, and repatriated last September; he has lost everything, of course, but so far he is well and able to get along in Germany. Harold and I have been jogging on here as best we can on my own little income—'Huns in our midst' as we are, we see practically nobody. What a pity we cannot all look into each other's hearts, isn't it? I used to think we were a 'fair-play' people, but I have learned the bitter truth, that there is no such thing when pressure comes. It's much worse for Harold than

for me; he feels his paralysed position intensely, and would, I'm sure, really rather be 'doing his bit' as an interned than be at large, subject to everyone's suspicion and scorn. But I am terrified all the time that they will intern him. You used to be intimate with Mr. Harburn. We have not seen him since the first autumn of the war, but we know that he has been very active in the agitation and is very powerful in this matter. I have wondered whether he can possibly realise what this indiscriminate internment of the innocent means to the families of the interned. Could you not find a chance to try and make him understand? If he and a few others were to stop hounding on the Government, it would cease, for the authorities must know perfectly well that all the dangerous have been disposed of long ago. You have no notion how lonely one feels in one's native land nowadays; if I should lose Harold, too, I think I might go under, though that has never been my habit.

"Believe me, dear Mr. Cumbermere,

"Most truly yours,

"Helen Holsteig."

On receiving this letter I was moved by compassion, for it required no stretch of imagination to picture the life of that lonely British mother and her son; and I thought very carefully over the advisability of speaking to Harburn, and consulted the proverbs: "Speech is silver, but silence is gold—When in doubt, play trumps." "Second thoughts are best—He who hesitates is lost." "Look before you leap—Delays are dangerous." They balanced so perfectly that I had recourse to commonsense, which told me to abstain. But meeting Harburn at the club a few days later and finding him in a genial mood, I let impulse prevail.

"By the way," I said, "you remember the Holsteigs? I had a letter from poor Mrs. Holsteig the other, day; she seems terrified that they'll intern her son, that particularly nice boy. Don't you think it's time you let up on these unhappy people?" The moment I reached the word Holsteig I saw I had made a mistake, and only went on because to have stopped at that would have been worse still. The hair had bristled up on his back, as it were, and he said:

"Holsteig! That young pup who was off to join the German Army if he could? By George, is he at large still? This Government will never learn. I'll remember him."

"Harburn," I stammered, "I spoke of this in confidence. The boy is half British and a friend of mine. I thought he was a friend of yours, too."

"Of mine?" he said. "No, thank you. No mongrels for me. As to confidence, Cumbermere, there's no such thing in war time over what concerns the country's safety."

"Good God!" I exclaimed. "You really are crazy on this subject. That boy—with his bringing-up!"

He grinned. "We're taking no risks," he said, "and making no exceptions. The British Army or an internment camp. I'll see that he gets the alternative."

"If you do," I said, rising, "we cease to be friends. I won't have my confidence abused!"

"Oh! Hang it all," he grumbled, "sit down! We must all do our duty."

"You once complained to Holsteig himself of that German peculiarity."

He laughed. "I did," he said; "I remember—in the train. I've changed since then. That pup ought to be in with all the other swine-hounds. But let it go."

There the matter rested, for he had said: "Let it go," and he was a man of his word. It was, however, a lesson to me not to meddle with men of temperament so different from my own. I wrote to young Holsteig and asked him to come and lunch with me. He thanked me, but could not, of course, being confined to a five-mile radius. Really anxious to see him, I motorbiked down to their house. I found a very changed youth; moody and introspective, thoroughly forced in upon himself, and growing bitter. He had been destined for his father's business, and, marooned as he was by his nationality, had nothing to do but raise vegetables in their garden and read poetry and philosophy, not occupations to take a young man out of himself. Mrs. Holsteig, whose nerves were evidently at cracking point, had become extremely bitter and lost all power of seeing the war as a whole. All the ugly human qualities and hard people which the drive and pressure of a great struggle inevitably bring to the fore seemed viewed by her now as if they were the normal character of her fellow-countrymen, and she made no allowance for the fact that those fellow-countrymen had not commenced this struggle, nor for the certainty that the same ugly qualities and hard people were just as surely to the fore in every other of the fighting countries. The certainty she felt about her husband's honour had made her regard his internment and subsequent repatriation as a personal affront as well as a wicked injustice. Her tall, thin figure and high cheekboned face seemed to have been scorched and withered by some inner flame; she could not have been a wholesome companion for her boy in that house, empty even of servants. I spent a difficult afternoon in muzzling my sense of proportion, and journeyed back to town sore, but very sorry.

I was off again with the Red Cross shortly after, and did not return to England till August of 1918. I was unwell, and went down to my cottage, now free to me again.

The influenza epidemic was raging, and there I developed a mild attack; when I was convalescent my first visitor was Harburn, who had come down to his bungalow for a summer holiday. He had not been in the room five minutes before he was off on his favourite topic. My nerves must have been on edge from illness, for I cannot express the disgust with which I listened to him on that occasion. He seemed to me just like a dog who mumbles and chews a mouldy old bone with a sort of fury. There was a kind of triumph about him, too, which was unpleasant, though not surprising, for he was more of a force than ever.

'God save me from the fixed idea!' I thought, when he had gone. That evening I asked my old housekeeper if she had seen young Mr. Holsteig lately.

"Oh! no," she said, "he's been put away this five month. Mrs. Holsteig goes up once a week to see 'im. She's nigh out of her mind, poor lady, the baker says—that fierce she is about the Government for takin' 'im off."

I confess I could not bring myself to go and see her.

About a month after the armistice had been signed I came down to my cottage again. Harburn was in the same train, and he gave me a lift from the station. He was more like his old good-humoured self, and asked me to dinner the next day. It was the first time I had met him since the victory. We had a most excellent repast, and drank the health of the Future in some of his oldest port. Only when we had drawn up to the blazing wood fire in that softly lighted room, with our glasses beside us and two Airedales asleep at our feet, did he come round to his hobby.

"What do you think?" he said, suddenly leaning toward the flames. "Some of these blazing sentimentalists want to release our Huns. But I've put my foot on it; they won't get free till they're out of this country and back in their precious Germany." And I saw the familiar spark and smoulder in his eyes.

"Harburn," I said, moved by an impulse which I couldn't resist, "I think you ought to take a pill."

He stared at me.

"This way madness lies," I went on: "Hate is a damned insidious disease, men's souls can't stand very much of it, you know. You want purging."

He laughed.

"Hate! I thrive on it. The more I hate the brutes the better I feel. Here's to the death of every cursed Hun!"

I looked at him steadily. "I often think," I said, "that there could have been no more unhappy men on earth than Cromwell's Ironsides or the red revolutionaries in France when their work was over and done with."

"What's that to do with me?" he asked, amazed.

"They too smote out of hate and came to an end of their smiting. When a man's occupation is gone——"

"You're drivelling," he said sharply.

"Far from it," I answered, nettled. "Yours is a curious case, Harburn. Most of our professional Hun-haters have found it a good stunt or are merely weak sentimentalists; they can drop it easily enough when it ceases to be a good stunt or a parrot's war cry. You can't. With you it's mania, religion. When the tide ebbs and leaves you high and dry——"

He struck his fist on the arm of his chair, upsetting his glass and awakening the Airedale at his feet.

"I won't let it ebb," he said. "I'm going on with this—mark me!"

"Remember Canute!" I muttered. "May I have some more port?" I had got up to fill my glass when I saw to my astonishment that a woman was standing in the long window which opened on to the verandah. She had evidently only just come in, for she was still holding the curtain in her hand. It was Mrs. Holsteig, with her fine grey hair blown about her face, looking strange and almost ghostly in a grey gown. Harburn had not seen her, so I went quickly towards her, hoping to get her to go out again as silently and speak to me on the verandah; but she held up her hand with a gesture as if she would push me back, and said:

"Forgive my interrupting; I came to speak to that man."

Startled by the sound of her voice, Harburn jumped up and spun round towards it.

"Yes," she repeated quite quietly, "I came to speak to you; I came to put my curse on you. Many have put their curses on you silently; I do so to your face. My son lies between life and death in your prison—*your* prison. Whether he lives or dies I curse you for what you have done to poor wives and mothers—to British wives and mothers. Be for ever accursed! Good-night!"

She let the curtain fall and had vanished before Harburn had time to reach the window. She vanished so swiftly and silently, she had spoken so quietly, that both he and I stood rubbing our eyes and ears.

"Pretty theatrical!" he said at last.

"But quite real," I answered slowly; "you have been cursed by a live Scotswoman. Look at those dogs!"

The two Airedales were standing stock-still with the hair bristling on their backs.

Harburn suddenly laughed, and it jarred the whole room.

"By George!" he said, "I believe that's actionable."

But I was not in that mood and answered tartly:

"If it is, we are all food for judges."

He laughed again, this time uneasily, slammed the window to, and bolted it, and sat down again in his chair.

"He's got the 'flu, I suppose," he said. "She must think me a prize sort of idiot to have come here with such tomfoolery." But our evening was spoiled, and I took my leave almost at once. I went out into the roupy raw December night pondering deeply. Harburn had made light of it, and though I suppose no man likes being cursed to his face in the presence of a friend, I felt his skin was quite tough enough to stand it. Besides, it was too cheap and crude a way of carrying on. Any body can go into his neighbour's house and curse him—and no bones broken. And yet—what she had said was no doubt true—hundreds of women—of his fellow-countrywomen—must silently have put their curse on one who had been the chief compeller of their misery. Still, he had put *his* curse on the Huns and their belongings, and I felt he was man enough to take what he had given. 'No,' I thought, 'she has only fanned the flame of his hate. But, by Jove! that's just it! Her curse has fortified my prophecy.' It was *of his own state of mind* that he would perish, and she had whipped and deepened that state of mind. And, odd as it may seem, I felt sorry for him, as one is for a dog that goes mad, does what harm he can, and dies. I lay awake that night a long time thinking of him, and of that unhappy half-crazed mother, whose son lay between life and death.

Next day I went to see her, but she was up in London hovering round the cage of her son, no doubt. I heard from her, however, some days later, thanking me for coming and saying he was out of danger. But she made no allusion to that evening visit. Perhaps she was ashamed of it. Perhaps she was demented when she came and had no remembrance thereof.

Soon after this I went to Belgium to illustrate a book on Reconstruction, and found such subjects that I was not back in town till the late summer of 1918. Going into my club one day I came on

Harburn in the smoking-room. The curse had not done him much harm, it seemed, for he looked the picture of health.

"Well, how are you?" I said. "You look at the top of your form."

"Never better," he replied.

"Do you remember our last evening together?"

He uttered a sort of gusty grunt and did not answer.

"That boy recovered," I said. "What's happened to him and his mother since?"

"Ironical young brute! I've just had this from him." And he handed me a letter with a Hanover post-mark.

> "Dear Mr. Harburn,
> "It was only on meeting my mother here yesterday that I learned of her visit to you one evening last December. I wish to apologise for it, since it was my illness which caused her to so forget herself. I owe you a deep debt of gratitude for having been at least partly the means of giving me the most wonderful experience of my life. In that camp of sorrow—where there was sickness of mind such as I am sure you have never seen or realised, such endless, hopeless mental anguish of poor huddled creatures turning and turning on themselves year after year—I learned to forget myself and to do my little best for them. And I learned, and I hope I shall never forget it, that good will towards his fellow-creatures is all that stands between man and death in life; I was going fast the other way before I was sent there. I thank you from my heart, and beg to remain,
> "Very faithfully yours,
> "Harold Holsteig."

I put it down and said:

"That's not ironical. He means it."

"Bosh!" said Harburn, with the old spark and smoulder in his eyes. "He's pulling my leg—the swinelet Hun-prig."

"He is not, Harburn; I assure you."

Harburn got up.

"He *is*; I tell you he *is*. Ah! those brutes! Well! I haven't done with them yet."

And I heard the snap of his jaw and saw his eyes fixed fiercely on some imagined object. I changed the subject hurriedly and soon took my departure. But going down the steps an old jingle came into my head and has hardly left it since:

> "The man recovered of the bite,
> The dog it was that died."

[*1919*]

A KNIGHT

At Monte Carlo, in the spring of the year 189—, I used to notice an old fellow in a grey suit and sunburnt straw hat with a black ribbon. Every morning at eleven o'clock, he would come down to the *Place*, followed by a brindled German boar- hound, walk once or twice round it, and seat himself on a bench facing the casino. There he would remain in the sun, with his straw hat tilted forward, his thin legs apart, his brown hands crossed between them, and the dog's nose resting on his knee. After an hour or more he would get up, and, stooping a little from the waist, walk slowly round the *Place* and return up hill. Just before three, he would come down again in the same clothes and go into the casino, leaving the dog outside.

One afternoon, moved by curiosity, I followed him. He passed through the hall without looking at the gambling-rooms, and went into the concert. It became my habit after that to watch for him. When he sat in the *Place* I could see him from the window of my room. The chief puzzle to me was the matter of his nationality.

His lean, short face had a skin so burnt that it looked like leather; his jaw was long and prominent, his chin pointed, and he had hollows in his cheeks. There were wrinkles across his forehead; his eyes were brown; and little white moustaches were brushed up from the corners of his lips. The back of his head bulged out above the lines of his lean neck and high, sharp shoulders; his grey hair was cropped quite close. In the Marseilles buffet, on the journey out, I had met an Englishman, almost his counterpart in features—but somehow very different! This old fellow had nothing of the other's alert, autocratic self-sufficiency. He was quiet and undemonstrative, without looking, as it were, insulated against shocks and foreign substances. He was certainly no Frenchman. His eyes, indeed, were brown, but hazel-brown, and gentle—not the red brown sensual eye of the Frenchman. An American? But was ever an American so passive? A German? His moustache was certainly brushed up, but in a modest, almost pathetic way, not in the least Teutonic. Nothing seemed to fit him. I gave him up, and nicknamed him "the Cosmopolitan."

Leaving at the end of April, I forgot him altogether. In the same month, however, of the following year I was again at Monte Carlo, and going one day to the concert found myself seated next this same old fellow. The orchestra was playing Meyerbeer's "Prophète," and my neighbour was asleep, snoring softly. He was dressed in the same grey suit, with the same straw hat (or one exactly like it) on his knees, and his hands crossed above it. Sleep had not disfigured him—his little white moustache was still brushed up, his lips closed; a very good and gentle expression hovered on his face. A curved mark showed on his right temple, the scar of a cut on the side of his neck, and his left hand was covered by an old glove, the little finger of which was empty. He woke up when the march was over and brisked up his moustache.

The next thing on the programme was a little thing by Poise from *Le joli Gilles*, played by Mons. Corsanego on the violin. Happening to glance at my old neighbour, I saw a tear caught in the hollow of his cheek, and another just leaving the corner of his eye; there was a faint smile on his lips. Then came an interval; and while orchestra and audience were resting, I asked him if he were fond of music. He looked up without distrust, bowed, and answered in a thin, gentle voice: "Certainly. I know nothing about it, play no instrument, could never sing a note; but—fond of it! Who would not be?" His English was correct enough, but with an emphasis not quite American nor quite foreign. I ventured to remark that he did not care for Meyerbeer. He smiled.

"Ah!" he said, "I was asleep? Too bad of me. He *is* a little noisy—I know so little about music. There is Bach, for instance. Would you believe it, he gives me no pleasure? A great misfortune to be no musician!" He shook his head.

I murmured, "Bach is too elevating for you perhaps."

"To me," he answered, "any music I *like* is elevating. People say some music has a bad effect on them. I never found any music that gave me a bad thought—no—no—quite the opposite; only sometimes, as you see, I go to sleep. But what a lovely instrument the violin!" A faint flush came on his parched cheeks. "The human soul that has left the body. A curious thing, distant bugles at night have given me the same feeling." The orchestra was now coming back, and, folding his hands, my neighbour turned his eyes towards them. When the concert was over we came out together. Waiting at the entrance was his dog.

"You have a beautiful dog!"

"Ah! yes. Freda, *mia cara, da su mano!*" The dog squatted on her haunches, and lifted her paw in the vague, bored way of big dogs when requested to perform civilities. She was a lovely creature— the purest brindle, without a speck of white, and free from the unbalanced look of most dogs of her breed.

"*Basta! basta!* He turned to me apologetically. "We have agreed to speak Italian; in that way I keep up the language; astonishing the number of things that dog will understand!" I was about to take my leave, when he asked if I would walk a little way with him—"If you are free, that is." We went up the street with Freda on the far side of her master.

"Do you never 'play' here?" I asked him.

"Play? No. It must be very interesting; most exciting, but as a matter of fact, I can't afford it. If one has very little, one is too nervous."

He had stopped in front of a small hairdresser's shop. "I live here," he said, raising his hat again. "*Au revoir!*—unless I can offer you a glass of tea. It's all ready. Come! I've brought you out of your way; give me the pleasure!"

I have never met a man so free from all self-consciousness, and yet so delicate and diffident—the combination is a rare one. We went up a steep staircase to a room on the second floor. My companion threw the shutters open, setting all the flies buzzing. The top of a plane-tree was on a level with the window, and all its little brown balls were dancing, quite close, in the wind., As he had promised, an urn was hissing on a table; there was also a small brown teapot, some sugar, slices of lemon, and glasses. A bed, washstand, cupboard, tin trunk, two chairs, and a small rug were all the furniture. Above the bed a sword in a leather sheath was suspended from two nails. The photograph of a girl stood on the closed stove. My host went to the cupboard and produced a bottle, a glass, and a second spoon. When the cork was drawn, the scent of rum escaped into the air, He sniffed at it and dropped a teaspoonful into both glasses.

"This is a trick I learned from the Russians after Plevna; they had my little finger, so I deserved something in exchange." He looked round; his eyes, his whole face, seemed to twinkle. "I assure you it was worth it—makes all the difference. Try!" He poured off the tea.

"Had you a sympathy with the Turks?"

"The weaker side———" He paused abruptly, then added: "But it was not that." Over his face innumerable crow's feet had suddenly appeared, his eyes twitched; he went on hurriedly, "I had to find something to do just then—it was necessary." He stared into his glass; and it was some time before I ventured to ask if he had seen much fighting.

"Yes," he replied gravely, "nearly twenty years altogether; I was one of Garibaldi's *Mille* in '60."

"Surely you are not Italian?"

He leaned forward with his hands on his knees. "I was in Genoa at that time learning banking; Garibaldi was a wonderful man! One could not help it." He spoke quite simply. "You might say it was like seeing a little man stand up to a ring of great hulking fellows; I went, just as you would have gone, if you'd been there. I was not long with them—*our* war began; I had to go back home." He said this as if there had been but one war since the world began. "In '61," he mused, "till '65. Just think of it! The poor country. Why, in my State, South Carolina—I was through it all—nobody could be spared there—we were one to three."

"I suppose you have a love of fighting?"

"H'm!" he said, as if considering the idea for the first time. "Sometimes I fought for a living, and sometimes—because I was obliged; one must try to be a gentleman. But won't you have some more?"

I refused more tea and took my leave, carrying away with me a picture of the old fellow looking down from the top of the steep staircase, one hand pressed to his back, the other twisting up those little white moustaches, and murmuring, "Take care, my dear sir, there's a step there at the corner."

"To be a gentleman!" I repeated in the street, causing an old French lady to drop her parasol, so that for about two minutes we stood bowing and smiling to each other, then separated full of the best feeling.

II

A week later I found myself again seated next him at a concert. In the meantime I had seen him now and then, but only in passing. He seemed depressed. The corners of his lips were tightened, his tanned cheeks had a greyish tinge, his eyes were restless; and, between two numbers of the programme, he murmured, tapping his fingers on his hat, "Do you ever have bad days? Yes? Not pleasant, are they?"

Then something occurred from which all that I have to tell you followed. There came into the concert-hall the heroine of one of those romances, crimes, follies, or irregularities, call it what you will, which had just attracted the "world's" stare. She passed us with her partner, and sat down in a chair a few rows to our right. She kept turning her head round, and at every turn I caught the gleam of her uneasy eyes. Some one behind us said: "The brazen baggage!"

My companion turned full round, and glared at whoever it was who had spoken. The change in him was quite remarkable. His lips were drawn back from his teeth; he frowned; the scar on his temple had reddened.

"Ah!" he said to me. "The hue and cry! Contemptible! How I hate it! But you wouldn't understand—I——" he broke off, and slowly regained his usual air of self-obliteration; he even seemed ashamed, and began trying to brush his moustaches higher than ever, as if aware that his heat had robbed them of neatness.

"I'm not myself, when I speak of such matters," he said suddenly; and began reading his programme, holding it upside down. A minute later, however, he said in a peculiar voice: "There are people to be found who object to vivisecting animals; but the vivisection of a woman, who minds that? Will you tell me it's right, that because of some tragedy like this—believe me, it is always a tragedy—we should hunt down a woman? That her fellow-women should make an outcast of her? That we, who are *men*, should make a prey of her? If I thought that—" Again he broke off, staring very hard in front of him. "It is we who make them what the are; and even if that is not so—why, if I thought there was a woman in the world I could not take my hat off to—I—I—couldn't sleep at night." He got up from his seat, put on his old straw hat with trembling fingers, and, without a glance back, went out, stumbling over the chair-legs.

I sat there, horribly disturbed; the words, "One must try to be a gentleman!" haunting me. When I came out, he was standing by the entrance with one hand on his hip and the other on his dog. In that attitude of waiting he was such a patient figure; the sun glared down and showed the threadbare nature of his clothes and the thinness of his brown hands, with their long fingers and nails yellow from tobacco. Seeing me he came up the steps again, and raised his hat.

"I am glad to have caught you; please forget all that."

I asked him if he would do me the honour of dining at my hotel.

"Dine?" he repeated with the sort of smile a child gives if you offer him a box of soldiers; "with the greatest pleasure. I seldom dine out, but I think I can muster up a coat. Yes—yes—and at what time shall I come? At half-past seven, and your hotel is——! Good! I shall be there. Freda, *mia cara*, you will be alone this evening. You do not smoke *caporal*, I fear. I find it fairly good; though it has too much bite." He walked off with Freda, puffing at his thin roll of *caporal*.

Once or twice he stopped, as if bewildered or beset by some sudden doubt or memory; and every time he stopped, Freda licked his hand. They disappeared round the corner of the street, and I went to my hotel to see about dinner. On the way I met Jules le Ferrier, and asked him to come too.

"My faith, yes!" he said, with the rosy pessimism characteristic of the French editor. "Man must dine!"

At half-past six we assembled. My "Cosmopolitan" was in an old frock-coat braided round the edges, buttoned high and tight, defining more than ever the sharp lines of his shoulders and the slight kink of his back; he had brought with him, too, a dark-peaked cap of military shape, which he had evidently selected as more fitting to the coat than a straw hat. He smelled slightly of some herb.

We sat down to dinner, and did not rise for two hours. He was a charming guest, praised everything he ate—not with commonplaces, but in words that made you feel it had given him real pleasure. At first, whenever Jules made one of his caustic remarks, he looked quite pained, but suddenly seemed to make up his mind that it was bark, not bite; and then at each of them he would turn to me and say, "Aha! that's good—isn't it?" With every glass of wine he became more gentle and more genial, sitting very upright, and tightly buttoned-in; while the little white wings of his moustache seemed about to leave him for a better world.

In spite of the most leading questions, however, we could not get him to talk about himself, for even Jules, most cynical of men, had recognised that he was a hero of romance. He would answer gently and precisely, and then sit twisting his moustaches, perfectly unconscious that we wanted more. Presently, as the wine went a little to his head, his thin, high voice grew thinner, his cheeks became flushed, his eyes brighter; at the end of dinner he said: "I hope I have not been noisy."

We assured him that he had not been noisy enough. "You're laughing at me," he answered. "Surely I've been talking all the time!"

"*Mon Dieu!*" said Jules, "we have been looking for some fables of your wars; but nothing—nothing, not enough to feed a frog!"

The old fellow looked troubled.

"To be sure!" he mused. "Let me think! there is that about Colhoun at Gettysburg; and there's the story of Garibaldi and the Miller." He plunged into a tale, not at all about himself, which would have been extremely dull, but for the conviction in his eyes, and the way he stopped and commented. "So you see," he ended, "that's the sort of man Garibaldi was! I could tell you another tale of him." Catching an introspective look in Jules's eye, however, I proposed taking our cigars over to the *café* opposite.

"Delightful!" the old fellow said: "We shall have a band and the fresh air, and clear consciences for our cigars. I can not like this smoking in a room where there are ladies dining."

He walked out in front of us, smoking with an air of great enjoyment. Jules, glowing above his candid shirt and waistcoat, whispered to me, "Mon cher Georges, how he is good!" then sighed, and added darkly: "The poor man!"

We sat down at a little table. Close by, the branches of a plane-tree rustled faintly; their leaves hung lifeless, speckled like the breasts of birds, or black against the sky; then, caught by the breeze, fluttered suddenly.

The old fellow sat, with head thrown back, a smile on his face, coming now and then out of his enchanted dreams to drink coffee, answer our questions, or hum the tune that the band was playing. The ash of his cigar grew very long. One of those bizarre figures in Oriental garb, who, night after night, offer their doubtful wares at a great price, appeared in the white glare of a lamp, looked with a furtive smile at his face, and glided back, discomfited by its unconsciousness. It was a night for dreams! A faint, half-Eastern scent in the air, of black tobacco and spice; few people as yet at the little tables, the waiters leisurely, the band soft! What was he dreaming of, that old fellow, whose, cigar-ash grew so long? Of youth, of his battles, of those things that must be done by those who try to be gentlemen; perhaps only of his dinner; anyway of something gilded in vague fashion as the light was gilding the branches of the plane-tree.

Jules pulled my sleeve: "He sleeps." He had smilingly dropped off; the cigar-ash—that feathery tower of his dreams—had broken and fallen on his sleeve. He awoke, and fell to dusting it.

The little tables round us began to fill. One of the bandsmen played a czardas on the czymbal. Two young Frenchmen, talking loudly, sat down at the adjoining table. They were discussing the lady who had been at the concert that afternoon.

"It's a bet," said one of them, "but there's the present man. I take three weeks, that's enough—*elle est déclassée; ce n'est que le premier pas*—"

My old friend's cigar fell on the table. "Monsieur," he stammered, "you speak of a lady so, in a public place?"

The young man stared at him. "Who is this person?" he said to his companion.

My guest took up Jules's glove that lay on the table; before either of us could raise a finger, he had swung it in the speaker's face. "Enough!" he said, and, dropping the glove, walked away.

We all jumped to our feet. I left Jules and hurried after him. His face was grim, his eyes those of a creature who has been struck on a raw place. He made a movement of his fingers which said plainly, "Leave me, if you please!"

I went back to the *café*. The two young men had disappeared, so had Jules, but everything else was going on just as before; the bandsman still twanging out his czardas; the waiters serving drinks; the Orientals trying to sell their carpets. I paid the bill, sought out the manager, and apologised. He shrugged his shoulders, smiled and said: "An eccentric, your friend, *nicht wahr*?" Could he tell me where Mr. le Ferrier was? He could not. I left to look for Jules; could not find him, and returned to my hotel disgusted. I was sorry for my old guest, but vexed with him too; what business had he to carry his Quixotism to such an unpleasant length? I tried to read. Eleven o'clock struck; the casino disgorged a stream of people; the *Place* seemed fuller of life than ever; then slowly it grew empty and quite dark. The whim seized me to go out. It was a still night, very warm, very black. On one of the seats a man and woman sat embraced, on another a girl was sobbing, on a third—strange sight—a priest dozed. I became aware of some one at my side; it was my old guest.

"If you are not too tired," he said, "can you give me ten minutes?"

"Certainly; will you come in?"

"No, no; let us go down to the Terrace. I shan't keep you long."

He did not speak again till we reached a seat above the pigeon-shooting grounds; there in a darkness denser for the string of lights still burning in the town, we sat down.

"I owe you an apology," he said; "first in the afternoon, then again this evening—your guest—your friend's glove. I have behaved as no gentleman should." He was leaning forward with his hands on the handle of a stick. His voice sounded broken and disturbed.

"Oh!" I muttered. "It's nothing!"

"You are \very good," he sighed; "but I feel that I must explain. I consider I owe this to you, but I must tell you I should not have the courage if it were not for another reason. You see I have no friend." He looked at me with an uncertain smile. I bowed, and a minute or two later he began.

III

"You will excuse me if I go back rather far. It was in '74, when I had been ill with Cuban fever. To keep me alive they had put me on board a ship at Santiago, and at the end of the voyage I found myself in London. I had very little money; I knew nobody. I tell you, sir, there are times when it's hard for a fighting man to get anything to do. People would say to me: 'Afraid we've nothing for a man like you in our business.' I tried people of all sorts; but it was true—I had been fighting here and there since '60, I wasn't fit for anything——" He shook his head. "In the South, before the war, they had a saying, I remember, about a dog and a soldier having the same value. But all this has nothing to do with what I have to tell you." He sighed again and went on, moistening his lips: "I was walking along the Strand one day, very disheartened, when I heard my name called. It's a queer thing, that, in a strange street. By the way," he put in with dry ceremony, "you don't know my name, I think; it is Brune— Roger Brune. At first I did not recognise the person who called me. He had just got off an omnibus—a square-shouldered man with heavy moustaches, and round spectacles. But when he shook my hand I knew him at once. He was a man called Dalton, who was taken prisoner at Gettysburg; one of you Englishmen who came to fight with us—a major in the regiment where I was captain. We were comrades during two campaigns. If I had been his brother he couldn't have seemed more pleased to see me. He took me into a bar for the sake of old times. The drink went to my head, and by the time we reached Trafalgar Square I was quite unable to walk. He made me sit down on a bench. I was in fact—drunk. It's disgraceful to be drunk, but there was some excuse. Now I tell you, sir" (all through his story he was always making use of that expression, it seemed to infuse fresh spirit into him, to help his memory in obscure places, to give him the mastery of his emotions; it was like the piece of paper a nervous man holds in his hand to help him through a speech), "there never was a man with a finer soul than my friend Dalton. He was not clever, though he had read much; and sometimes perhaps he was too fond of talking. But he was a gentleman; he listened to me as if I had been a child; he was not ashamed of me—and it takes a gentleman not to be ashamed of a drunken man in the streets of London; God knows what things I said to him while we were sitting there! He took me to his home and put me to bed himself; for I was down again with fever." He stopped, turned slightly from me, and put his hand up to his brow. "Well, then it was, sir, that I first saw her. I am not a poet and I can not tell you what she seemed to me. I was delirious, but I always knew when she was there. I had dreams of sunshine and cornfields, of dancing waves at sea, young trees—never the same dreams, never anything for long together; and when I had my senses I was afraid to say so for fear she would go away. She'd be in the corner of the room, with her hair hanging about her neck, a bright gold colour; she never worked and never read, but sat and talked to herself in a whisper, or looked at me for a long time together out of her blue eyes, a little frown between them, and her upper lip closed firm on her lower lip, where she had an uneven tooth. When her father came, she'd jump up and hang on to his neck until he groaned, then run away, but presently come stealing back on tiptoe. I used to listen for her footsteps on the stairs, then the knock, the door flung back or opened quietly—you never could tell which; and her voice, with a little lisp, 'Are you better to-day, Mr. Brune? What funny things you say when you're delirious! Father says you've been in heaps of battles?'"

He got up, paced restlessly to and fro, and sat down again. "I remember every word as if it were yesterday, all the things she said, and did; I've had a long time to think them over, you see. Well, I must tell you, the first morning that I was able to get up, I missed her. Dalton came in her place, and I asked him where she was. 'My dear fellow,' he answered, 'I've sent Eilie away to her old nurse's inn down on the river; she's better there at this time of year.' We looked at each other, and I saw that he had sent her away because he didn't trust me. I was hurt by this. Illness spoils one. He was right, he was quite right, for all he knew about me was that I could fight and had got drunk; but I am very quick-tempered. I made up my mind at once to leave him. But I was too weak—he had to put me to bed again. The very next morning he came and proposed that I should go into partnership with him. He kept a fencing-school and pistol-gallery. It seemed like the finger of God; and perhaps it was—who knows?" He fell into a reverie, and taking out his *caporal*, rolled himself a cigarette; having lighted it, he went on suddenly: "There, in the room above the school, we used to sit in the evenings, one on each side of the grate. The room was on the second floor, I remember, with two windows, and a view of nothing but the houses opposite. The furniture was covered up with chintz. The things on the bookshelf were never disturbed, they were Eilie's—half-broken cases with butterflies, a dead frog in a bottle, a horse-shoe covered with tinfoil, some shells too, and a cardboard box with three speckled eggs in it, and these words written on the lid: 'Missel thrush from Lucy's tree—second family, only one blown.'" He smoked fiercely, with puffs that were like sharp sighs.

"Dalton was wrapped up in her. He was never tired of talking to me about her, and I was never tired of hearing. We had a number of pupils; but in the evening when we sat there, smoking—our talk would sooner or later come round to her. Her bedroom opened out of that sitting-room; he took me in once and showed me a narrow little room the width of a passage, fresh and white, with a photograph of her mother above the bed, and an empty basket for a dog or cat." He broke off with a vexed air, and resumed sternly, as if trying to bind himself to the narration of his more important facts: "She was then fifteen—her mother had been dead twelve years—a beautiful face, her mother's; it had been her death that sent Dalton to fight with us. Well, sir, one day in August, very hot weather, he proposed a run into the country, and who should meet us on the platform when we arrived but Eilie, in a blue sunbonnet and frock—flax blue, her favourite colour. I was angry with Dalton for not telling me that we should see her; my clothes were not quite—my hair wanted cutting. It was black then, sir," he added, tracing a pattern in the darkness with his stick. "She had a little donkey-cart; she drove, and, while we walked one on each side, she kept looking at me from under her sunbonnet. I must tell you that she never laughed—her eyes danced, her cheeks would go pink, and her hair shake about on her neck, but she never laughed. Her old nurse, Lucy, a very broad, good woman, had married the proprietor of the inn in the village there. I have never seen anything like that inn; sweetbriar up to the roof! And the scent—I am very susceptible to scents!" His head drooped, and the cigarette fell from his hand. A train passing beneath sent up a shower of sparks. He started, and went on: "We had our lunch in the parlour—I remember that room very well, for I spent the happiest days of my life afterwards in that inn . . . We went into a meadow after lunch, and my friend Dalton fell asleep. A wonderful thing happened then. Eilie whispered to me, 'Let's have a jolly time.' She took me for the most glorious walk. The river was close by. A lovely stream, your river Thames, so calm and broad; it is like the spirit of your people. I was bewitched; I forgot my friend, I thought of nothing but how to keep her to myself. It was such a day! There are days that are the devil's, but that was truly one of God's. She took me to a little pond under an elm-tree, and we dragged it, we two, an hour, for a kind of tiny red worm to feed some creature that she had. We found them in the mud, and while she was bending over, the curls got in her eyes. If you could have seen her then, I think, sir, you would have said she was like the first sight of spring . . . We had tea afterwards, all together, in the long grass under some fruit-trees. If I had the knack of words, there are things that I could say—" He bent, as though in deference to those unspoken memories. "Twilight came on while we were sitting there. A wonderful thing is twilight

in the country! It became time for us to go. There was an avenue
of trees close by—like a church with a window at the end, where
golden light came through. I walked up and down it with her. 'Will
you come again?' she whispered, and suddenly she lifted up her
face to be kissed. I kissed her as if she were a little child. And when
we said good-bye, her eyes were looking at me across her father's
shoulder, with surprise and sorrow in them. 'Why do you go away?'
they seemed to say . . . But I must tell you," he went on hurriedly,
"of a thing that happened before we had gone a hundred yards.
We were smoking our pipes, and I, thinking of her—when out she
sprang from the hedge and stood in front of us. Dalton cried out,
'What are you here for again, you mad girl!' She rushed up to him
and hugged him; but when she looked at me, her face was quite
different—careless, defiant, as one might say—it hurt me. I couldn't
understand it, and what one doesn't understand frightens one.

IV

"Time went on. There was no swordsman, or pistolshot like me in
London, they said. We had as many pupils as we liked—it was the
only part of my life when I have been able to save money. I had no
chance to spend it. We gave lessons all day, and in the evening were
too tired to go out. That year I had the misfortune to lose my dear
mother. I became a rich man—yes, sir, at that time I must have had
not less than six hundred a year.

"It was a long time before I saw Eilie again. She went abroad to
Dresden with her father's sister to learn French and German. It was
in the autumn of 1875 when she came back to us. She was seventeen
then—a beautiful young creature." He paused, as if to gather his
forces for description, and went on.

"Tall, as a young tree, with eyes like the sky. I would not say she
was perfect, but her imperfections were beautiful to me. What is it
makes you love—ah! sir, that is very hidden and mysterious. She had
never lost the trick of closing her lips tightly when she remembered

her uneven tooth. You may say that was vanity, but in a young girl—
and which of us is not vain, eh? 'Old men and maidens, young men
and children!'

"As I said, she came back to London to her little room, and in
the evenings was always ready with our tea. You mustn't suppose
she was housewifely; there is something in me that never admired
housewifeliness—a fine quality, no doubt, still
——" He sighed.

"No," he resumed, "Eilie was not like that, for she was never quite
the same two days together. I told you her eyes were like the sky—
that was true of all of her. In one thing, however, at that time, she
always seemed the same—in love for her father. For me! I don't
know what I should have expected; but my presence seemed to have
the effect of making her dumb: I would catch her looking at me
with a frown, and then, as if to make up to her own nature—and a
more loving nature never came into this world, that I shall maintain
to my dying day—she would go to her father and kiss him. When I
talked with him she pretended not to notice, but I could see her face
grow cold and stubborn. I am not quick, and it was a long time be
fore I understood that she was jealous, she wanted him all to herself.
I've often wondered how she could be his daughter, for he was the
very soul of justice and a slow man too—and she was as quick as a
bird. For a long time after I saw her dislike of me, I refused to believe
it—if one does not want to believe a thing there are always reasons
why it should not seem true, at least so it is with me, and I suppose
with all selfish men.

"I spent evening after evening there, when, if I had not thought
only of myself, I should have kept away. But one day I could no
longer be blind.

"It was a Sunday in February. I always had an invitation on Sundays
to dine with them in the middle of the day. There was no one in
the sitting-room; but the door of Eilie's bed room was open. I heard
her voice: 'That man, always that man!' It was enough for me, I went
down again without coming in, and walked about all day.

"For three weeks I kept away. To the school of course I came as
usual, but not upstairs. I don't know what I told Dalton—it did not

signify what you told him, he always had a theory of his own, and was persuaded of its truth—a very single-minded man, sir.

"But now I come to the most wonderful days of my life. It was an early spring that year. I had fallen away already from my resolution, and used to slink up—seldom, it's true—and spend the evening with them as before. One afternoon I came up to the sitting-room; the light was failing—it was warm, and the windows were open. In the air was that feeling which comes to you once a year, in the spring, no matter where you may be, in a crowded street, or alone in a forest; only once—a feeling like—but I cannot describe it.

"Eilie was sitting there. If you don't know, sir, I can't tell you what it means to be near the woman one loves. She was leaning on the window-sill, staring down into the street. It was as though she might be looking out for some one. I stood, hardly breathing. She turned her head, and saw me. Her eyes were strange. They seemed to ask me a question. But I couldn't have spoken for the world. I can't tell you what I felt—I dared not speak, or think, or hope. I have been in nineteen battles—several times in positions of some danger, when the lifting of a finger perhaps meant death; but I have never felt what I was feeling at that moment. I knew something was coming; and I was paralysed with terror lest it should not come!" He drew a long breath.

"The servant came in with a light and broke the spell. All that night I lay awake and thought of how she had looked at me, with the colour coming slowly up in her cheeks.

"It was three days before I plucked up courage to go again; and then I felt her eyes on me at once—she was making a 'cat's cradle' with a bit of string, but I could see them stealing up from her hands to my face. And she went wandering about the room, fingering at everything. When her father called out: 'What's the matter with you, Eilie?' she stared at him like a child caught doing wrong. I looked straight at her then, she tried to look at me, but she couldn't; and a minute later she went out of the room. God knows what sort of nonsense I talked—I was too happy.

"Then began our love. I can't tell you of that time. Often and often Dalton said to me: 'What's come to the child?' Nothing I can do pleases her.' All the love she had given him was now for me; but he was too simple and straight to see what was going on. How many times haven't I felt criminal towards him! But when you're happy, with the tide in your favour, you become a coward at once . . .

"Well, sir," he went on, "we were married on her eighteenth birthday. It was a long time before Dalton became aware of our love. But one day he said to me with a very grave look:

"'Eilie has told me, Brune; I forbid it. She's too young, and you're—too old!' I was then forty-five, my hair as black and thick as a rook's feathers, and I was strong and active. I answered him: 'We shall be married within a month!' We parted in anger. It was a May night, and I walked out far into the country. There's no remedy for anger, or, indeed, for anything, so fine as walking. Once I stopped— it was on a common, without a house or light, and the stars shining like jewels. I was hot from walking, I could feel the blood boiling in my veins—I said to myself: 'Old, are you?' And I laughed like a fool. It was the thought of losing her—I wished to believe myself angry, but really I was afraid; fear and anger in me are very much the same. A friend of mine, a bit of a poet, sir, once called them 'the two black wings of self.' And so they are, so they are! . . . The next morning I went to Dalton again, and somehow I made him yield. I'm not a philosopher, but it has often seemed to me that no benefit can come to us in this life without an equal loss somewhere, but does that stop us? No, sir, not often . . .

"We were married on the 30th of June, 1876, in the parish church. The only people present were Dalton, Lucy, and Lucy's husband—a big, red-faced fellow, with blue eyes and a golden beard parted in two. It had been arranged that we should spend the honeymoon down at their inn on the river. My wife, Dalton and I, went to a restaurant for lunch. She was dressed in grey, the colour of a pigeon's feathers." He paused, leaning forward over the crutch handle of his stick; trying to conjure up, no doubt, that long-ago image of his young bride in her dress "the colour of a pigeon's feathers," with her blue eyes and yellow hair, the little frown between her brows, the firmly shut red lips, opening to speak the words, "For better, for worse, for richer, for poorer, in sickness and in health."

"At that time, sir," he went on suddenly, "I was a bit of a dandy. I wore, I remember, a blue frock-coat with white trousers, and a grey top hat. Even now I should always prefer to be well dressed . . .

"We had an excellent lunch, and drank Veuve Clicquot, a wine that you cannot get in these days! Dalton came with us to the railway station. I can't bear partings; and yet, they must come.

"That evening we walked out in the cool under the aspen trees. What should I remember in all my life if not that night—the young bullocks snuffling in the gateways—the campion flowers all lighted up along the hedges—the moon with a halo too, in and out among the stems, and the shadows of the cottages as black and soft as that sea down there. For a long time we stood on the river-bank beneath a lime-tree. The scent of the lime flowers! A man can only endure about half his joy; about half his sorrow. Lucy and her husband," he went on, presently, "his name was Frank Tor—a man like an old Viking, who ate nothing but milk, bread, and fruit—were very good to us! It was like Paradise in that inn—though the commissariat I am bound to say, was limited. The sweetbriar grew round our bedroom windows; when the breeze blew the leaves across the opening—it was like a bath of perfume. Eilie grew as brown as a gipsy while we were there. I don't think any man could have loved her more than I did. But there were times when my heart stood still; it didn't seem as if she understood how much I loved her. One day, I remember, she coaxed me to take her camping. We drifted down stream all the afternoon, and in the evening pulled into the reeds under the willow-boughs and lit a fire for her to cook by—though as a matter of fact, our provisions were cooked already—but you know how it is; all the romance was in having a real fire. 'We won't pretend,' she kept saying. While we were eating our supper a hare came to our clearing—a big fellow—how surprised he looked! 'The tall hare,' Eilie called him. After that we sat by the ashes and watched the shadows, till at last she roamed away from me. The time went very slowly; I got up to look for her. It was past sundown. I called and called. It was a long time before I found her—and she was like a wild thing, hot and flushed, her pretty frock torn, her hands and face scratched, her hair down, like some beautiful creature of the woods. If one loves, a little thing will scare one. I didn't think she had noticed my fright; but when we got back to the boat she threw her arms round my neck, and said, 'I won't ever leave you again.'

"Once in the night I woke—a water-hen was crying, and in the moonlight a kingfisher flew across. The wonder on the river—the wonder of the moon and trees, the soft bright mist, the stillness! It was like another world, peaceful, enchanted, far holier than ours. It seemed like a vision of the thoughts that come to one—how seldom! and go if one tries to grasp them. Magic—poetry—sacred!" He was silent a minute, then went on in a wistful voice: "I looked at her, sleeping like a child, with her hair loose, and her lips apart, and I thought: 'God do so to me, if ever I bring her pain!' How was I to understand her? the mystery and innocence of her soul?—The river has had all my light and all my darkness, the happiest days, and the hours when I've despaired; and I like to think of it, for, you know, in time bitter memories fade, only the good remain . . . Yet the good have their own pain, a different kind of aching, for we shall never get them back. Sir," he said, turning to me with a faint smile, "it's no use crying over spilt milk. In the neighbourhood of Lucy's inn, the Rose and Maybush—Can you imagine a prettier name? I have been all over the world, and nowhere found names so pretty as in the English country. There, too, every blade of grass, and flower, has a kind of pride about it; knows it will be cared for; and all the roads, trees, and cottages, seem to be certain that they will live for ever . . . But I was going to tell you: Half a mile from the inn was a quiet old house which we used to call the 'Convent'—though I believe it was a farm. We spent many afternoons there, trespassing in the orchard—Eilie was fond of trespassing; if there were a long way round across somebody else's property, she would always take it. We spent our last afternoon in that orchard, lying in the long grass. I was reading *Childe Harold* for the first time—a wonderful, a memorable poem! I was at that passage—the bull-fight—you remember:

> "'Thrice sounds the clarion; lo! the signal falls,
> The din expands, and expectation mute'—

when suddenly Eilie said: 'Suppose I were to leave off loving you?' It
was as if some one had struck me in the face. I jumped up, and tried
to take her in my arms, but she slipped away; then she turned, and
began laughing softly. I laughed too. I don't know why.

VI

"We went back to London the next day; we lived quite close to the
school, and about five days a week Dalton came to dine with us. He
would have come every day, if he had not been the sort of man who
refuses to consult his own pleasure. We had more pupils than ever.
In my leisure I taught my wife to fence. I have never seen any one
so lithe and quick; or so beautiful as she looked in her fencing dress,
with embroidered shoes.

"I was completely happy. When a man has obtained his desire he
becomes careless and self-satisfied; I was watchful, however, for I
knew that I was naturally a selfish man. I studied to arrange my time
and save my money, to give her as much pleasure as I could. What
she loved best in the world just then was riding. I bought a horse for
her, and in the evenings of the spring and summer we rode together;
but when it was too dark to go out late, she would ride alone, great
distances, sometimes spend the whole day in the saddle, and come
back so tired she could hardly walk upstairs—I can't say that I liked
that. It made me nervous, she was so headlong—but I didn't think it
right to interfere with her. I had a good deal of anxiety about money,
for though I worked hard and made more than ever, there never
seemed enough. I was anxious to save—I hoped, of course—but we
had no child, and this was a trouble to me. She grew more beautiful
than ever, and I think was happy. Has it ever struck you that each one
of us lives on the edge of a volcano? There is, I imagine, no one who
has not some affection or interest so strong that he counts the rest for
nothing, beside it. No doubt a man may live his life through without
discovering that. But some of us——! I am not complaining; what
is—is." He pulled the cap lower over his eyes, and clutched his hands

firmly on the top of his stick. He was like a man who rushes his horse at some hopeless fence, unwilling to give himself time, for fear of craning at the last moment. "In the spring of '78, a new pupil came to me, a young man of twenty-one who was destined for the army. I took a fancy to him, and did my best to turn him into a good swordsman; but there was a kind of perverse recklessness in him; for a few minutes one would make great impression, then he would grow utterly careless. 'Francis,' I would say, 'if I were you I would be ashamed.' 'Mr Brune,' he would answer, 'why should I be ashamed? I didn't make myself.' God knows, I wish to do him justice, he had a heart—one day who had shut himself a child; he drove up in a cab, and brought in his poor dog, who had been run over, and was dying. For half an hour he shut himself up with its body, we could hear him sobbing like a child; he came out with his eyes all red, and cried: 'I know where to find the brute who drove over him,' and off he rushed. He had beautiful Italian eyes; a slight figure, not very tall; dark hair, a little dark moustache; and his lips were always a trifle parted—it was that, and his walk, and the way he dropped his eyelids, which gave him a peculiar, soft, proud look. I used to tell him that he'd never make a soldier! 'Oh!' he'd answer, 'that'll be all right when the time comes!' He believed in a kind of luck that was to do everything for him, when the time came. One day he came in as I was giving Eilie her lesson. This was the first time they saw each other. After that he came more often, and sometimes stayed to dinner with us. I won't deny, sir, that I was glad to welcome him; I thought it good for Eilie. Can there be anything more odious," he burst out, "than such a self-complacent blindness? There are people who say, 'Poor man, he had such faith!' Faith, sir! Conceit! I was a fool—in this world one pays for folly . . .

"The summer came; and one Saturday in early June Eilie, I and Francis—I won't tell you his other name—went riding. The night had been wet; there was no dust, and presently the sun came out—a glorious day! We rode a long way. About seven o'clock we started back—slowly, for it was still hot, and all the cool of night before us. It was nine o'clock came to Richmond Park. A grand place, Richmond Park; and in that half-light wonderful, the deer moving so softly, you might have thought they were spirits. We were silent too—great trees have that effect on me . . . say when changes come? Like a shift of the wind, the old passes, the new is on you. I am telling you now of a change like that. Without a sign of warning, Eilie put her horse into a gallop. 'What are you doing?' I shouted. She looked back with a smile, then he dashed past me too. A hornet might have stung them both: they galloped over fallen trees, under low-hanging branches, up hill and down. I had to watch that madness! My horse was not so fast. I rode like a demon; but fell far behind. I am not a man who takes things quietly When I came up with them at last, I could not speak for rage. They were riding side by side, the reins on the horses' necks, looking in each other's faces. 'You should take care.' I said. 'Care!' she cried; 'life is not all taking care!' My anger left me. I dropped behind, as grooms ride behind their mistresses . . . Jealousy! No torture is so ceaseless or so black . . . In those minutes a hundred things came up in me—a hundred memories, true, untrue, what do I know? My soul was poisoned. I tried to reason with myself, it was absurd to think such things! It was unmanly . . . Even if it were true, one should try to be a gentleman! But I found myself laughing; yes, sir, laughing at that word." He spoke faster, as if pouring his heart out not to a live listener, but to the night. "I could not sleep that night. To lie near her with those thoughts in my brain was impossible! I made an excuse, and sat up with some papers. The hardest thing in life is to see a thing coming and be able to do nothing to prevent it. What could I do? Have you noticed how people may become utter strangers without a word? It only needs a thought . . . The very next day she said: 'I want to go to Lucy's.' 'Alone?' 'Yes.' I had made up my mind by then that she must do just

as she wished. Perhaps I acted wrongly; I do not know what one ought to do in such a case; but before she went I said to her: 'Ellie, what is it?' 'I don't know,' she answered; and I kissed her—that was all . . . A month passed; I wrote to her nearly

every day, and I had short letters from her, telling me very little of herself. Dalton was a torture to me, for I could not tell him; he had a conviction that she was going to become a mother. 'Ah, Brune!' he said, 'my poor wife was just like that.' Life, Sir, is a somewhat ironical affair! . . . *He*—I find it hard to speak his name—came to the school two or three times a week. I used to think I saw a change, a purpose growing up through his recklessness; there seemed a violence in him as if he chafed against my blade. I had a kind of joy feeling I had the mastery, and could toss the iron out of his hand any minute like a straw. I was ashamed, and yet I gloried in it. Jealousy is a low thing, sir—a low, base thing! When he asked me where my wife was, I told him; I was too proud to hide it. So after that he came no more to the school.

"One morning, when I could bear it no longer, I wrote and said I was coming down. I would not force myself on her, but asked her to meet me in the orchard of the old house we called, the convent. I asked her to be there at four o'clock. It has always been my belief that a man must neither beg anything of a woman, nor force anything from her. Women are generous—they will give you what they can. I sealed my letter, and posted it myself. All the way down I kept on saying to myself, 'She must come—surely she will come!'

VII

"I was in high spirits, but the next moment trembled like a man with ague. I reached the orchard before my time. She was not there. You know what it is like to wait? I stood still and listened; I went to the point whence I could see farthest; I said to myself, 'a watched pot never boils; if I don't look for her she will come.' I walked up and down with my eyes on the ground. The sickness of it! A hundred times I took out my watch. Perhaps it was fast, perhaps hers was slow—I can't tell you a thousandth part of my hopes and fears. There was a spring of water in one corner. I sat beside it, and thought of the last time I had been there—and something seemed to burst in me. It was five o'clock before I lost all hope; there comes a time when you're glad that hope is dead, it means rest. 'That's over,' you say, 'now I can act.' But what was I to do? I lay down with my face to the ground; when one's in trouble, it's the only thing that helps—something to press against and cling to what can't give way. I lay there for two hours, knowing all the time that I should play the coward. At seven o'clock I left the orchard and went towards the inn; I had broken my word, but I felt happy. I should see her—and, sir, nothing—nothing seemed to matter beside that. Tor was in the garden snipping at his roses. He came up, and I could see that he couldn't look me in the face. 'Where's my wife?' I said. He answered, 'Let's get Lucy.' I ran indoors. Lucy met me with two letters; the first—my own—unopened; and the second, this:—

> "'I have left you. You were good to me, but now—it is no use.
> EILIE.'

"She told me that a boy had brought a letter for my wife the day before, from a young gentleman in a boat. When Lucy delivered it she asked, 'Who is he, Miss Eilie? What will Mr. Brune say?' My wife looked at her angrily, but gave her no answer—and all that day she never spoke. In the evening she was gone, leaving this note on the bed . . . Lucy cried as if her heart would break. I took her by the shoulders and put her from the room; I couldn't bear the noise. I sat down and tried to think. While I was sitting there Tor came in with a letter. It was written on the notepaper of an inn twelve miles up the river: these were the words:—

> "'Eilie is mine. I am ready to meet you where you like.'

He went on with a painful evenness of speech. "When I read those words, I had only one thought—to reach them; I ran down to the river, and chose out the lightest boat. Just as I was starting, Tor came running. 'You dropped this letter, sir,' he said. 'Two pairs of arms are better than one.' He came into the boat. I took the sculls and I pulled out into the stream. I pulled like a madman; and that great man, with his bare arms crossed, was like a huge, tawny bull sitting there opposite me. Presently he took my place, and I took the rudder lines. I could see his chest, covered with hair, heaving

up and down, it gave me a sort of comfort—it meant that we were
getting nearer. Then it grew dark, there was no moon, I could barely
see the bank: there's something in the dark which drives one into
oneself. People tell you there comes a moment when your nature
is decided—'saved' or 'lost' as they call it—for good or evil. That is
not true, your self is always with you, and cannot be altered; but, sir,
I believe that in a time of agony one finds out what are the things
one can do, and what are those one cannot. You get to *know* yourself,
that's all. And so it was with me. Every thought and memory and
passion was so clear and strong! I wanted to kill him. I wanted to kill
myself. But her—no! We are taught that we possess our wives, body
and soul, we are brought up in that faith, we are commanded to
believe it—but when I was face to face with it, those words had no
meaning; that belief, those commands, they were without meaning
to me, they were—vile. Oh yes, I *wanted* to find comfort in them, I
wanted to hold on to them—but I couldn't. You may force a body;
how can you force a soul? No, no—cowardly! But I wanted to—I
wanted to kill him and force her to come back to me! And then,
suddenly, I felt as if I were pressing right on the most secret nerve
of my heart. I seemed to see her face, white and quivering, as if I'd
stamped my heel on it. They say this world is ruled by force; it may
be true—I know I have a weak spot in me . . . I couldn't bear it. At
last I jumped to my feet and shouted out, 'Turn the boat round!' Tor
looked up at me as if I had gone mad. And I *had* gone mad. I seized
the boat-hook and threatened him; I called him fearful names. 'Sir,'
he said, 'I don't take such names from any one!' 'You'll take them
from me,' I shouted; 'turn the boat round, you idiot, you hound, you
fish!' . . . I have a terrible temper, a perfect curse to me. He seemed
amazed, even frightened; he sat down again suddenly and pulled the
boat round. I fell on the seat, and hid my face. I believe the moon
came up; there must have been a mist too, for I was cold as death.
In this life, sir, we cannot hide our faces—but by degrees the pain of
wounds grows less. Some will have it that such blows are mortal; it
is not so. Time is merciful.

"In the early morning I went back to London. I had fever on
me—and was delirious. I dare say I should have killed myself if I

had not been so used to weapons—they and I were too old friends, I suppose—I can't explain. It was a long while before I was up and about. Dalton nursed me through it; his great heavy moustache had grown quite white. We never mentioned her; what was the good? There were things to settle of course, the lawyer—this was unspeakably distasteful to me. I told him it was to be as she wished, but the fellow would come to me, with his—there, I don't want to be unkind. I wished him to say it was my fault, but he said—I remember his smile now—he said, that was impossible, would be seen through, talked of collusion—I don't understand these things, and what's more, I can't bear them, they are—dirty.

"Two years later, when I had come back to London, after the Russo-Turkish war, I received a letter from her. I have it here." He took an old, yellow sheet of paper out of a leathern pocket-book, spread it in his fingers, and sat staring at it. For some minutes he did not speak.

"In the autumn of that same year she died in childbirth. He had deserted her. Fortunately for him, he was killed on the Indian frontier, that very year. If she had lived she would have been thirty-two next June; not a great age . . . I know I am what you call a crank; doctors will tell you that you can't be cured of a bad illness, and be the same man again. If you are bent, to force yourself straight must leave you weak in another place. I *must* and will think well of women—everything done, and everything said against them is a stone on her dead body. Could *you* sit, and listen to it?" As though driven by his own question, he rose, and paced up and down. He came back to the seat at last.

"That, sir, is the reason of my behaviour this afternoon, and again this evening. You have been so kind, I wanted—I wanted to tell you. She had a little daughter—Lucy has her now. My friend Dalton is dead; there would have been no difficulty about money, but I am sorry to say that he was swindled—disgracefully. It fell to me to administer his affairs—he never knew it, but he died penniless; he had trusted some wretched fellows—had an idea they would make his fortune. As I very soon found, they had ruined him. It was impossible to let Lucy—such a dear woman—bear that burden.

I have tried to make provision; but, you see," he took hold of my sleeve, "I, too, have not been fortunate; in fact, it's difficult to save a great deal out of £190 a year; but the capital is perfectly safe—and I get £47 10s. a quarter, paid on the nail. I have often been tempted to reinvest at a greater rate of interest, but I've never dared. Anyway, there are no debts—I've been obliged to make a rule not to buy what I couldn't pay for on the spot. Now I am really plaguing you—but I wanted to tell you—in case—anything should happen to me." He seemed to take a sudden scare, stiffened, twisted his moustache, and muttering, "Your great kindness! Shall never forget!" turned hurriedly away.

He vanished; his footsteps and the tap of his stick grew fainter and fainter. They died out. He was gone. Suddenly I got up and hastened after him. I soon stopped—what was there to say?

VIII

The following day I was obliged to go to Nice, and did not return till midnight. The porter told me that Jules le Ferrier had been to see me. The next morning, while I was still in bed, the door was opened, and Jules appeared. His face was very pale; and the moment he stood still drops of perspiration began coursing down his cheeks.

"Georges!" he said, "he is dead. There, there! How stupid you look! My man is packing. I have half an hour before the train; my evidence shall come from Italy. I have done my part, the rest is for you. Why did you have that dinner? The Don Quixote! The idiot! The *poor* man! Don't move! Have you a cigar? Listen! When you followed him, I followed the other two. My infernal curiosity! Can you conceive a greater folly? How fast they walked, those two! feeling their cheeks, as if he had struck them both, you know; it was funny. They soon saw me, for their eyes were all round about their heads; they had the mark of a glove on their cheeks." The colour began to come back into Jules's face; he gesticulated with his cigar and became more and more dramatic. "They waited for me.

'*Tiens!*' said one, 'this gentleman was with him. My friend's name is
M. le Baron de ——. The man who struck him was an odd-looking
person; kindly inform me whether it is possible for my friend to
meet him?' Eh!" commented Jules, "he was offensive! Was it for me
to give our dignity away? 'Perfectly, monsieur!' I answered. 'In that
case,' he said, 'please give me his name and address.' . . . I could
not remember his name, and as for the address, I never knew it! .
. . I reflected. 'That,' I said, 'I am unable to do, for special reasons.'
'Aha!' he said, 'reasons that will prevent our fighting him, I suppose?'
'On the contrary,' I said, 'I will convey your request to him; I may
mention that I have heard he is the best swordsman and pistol-shot
in Europe. Good-night!' I wished to give them something to dream
of, you understand . . . Patience, my dear! Patience! I was coming to
you, but I thought I would let them sleep on it—there was plenty
of time! But yesterday morning I came into the *Place*, and there he
was on the bench, with a big dog. I declare to you he blushed like
a young girl. 'Sir,' he said, 'I was hoping to meet you; last evening
I made a great disturbance. I took an unpardonable liberty'—and
he put in my hand an envelope. My friend, what do you suppose it
contained—a pair of gloves! Señor Don Punctilioso, *hein*? He was
the devil, this friend of yours; he fascinated me with his gentle eyes
and his white moustachettes, his humility, his flames—poor man! .
. . I told him I had been asked to take him a challenge. 'If any thing
comes of it,' I said, 'make use of me!' 'Is that so?' he said. 'I am most
grateful for your kind offer. Let me see—it is so long since I fought a
duel. The sooner it's over the better. Could you arrange to-morrow
morning? Weapons? Yes; let them choose.' . . . You see, my friend,
there was no hanging back here; *nous voilà en train.*"

Jules took out his watch. "I have sixteen minutes. It is lucky for
you that you were away yesterday, or you would be in my shoes
now. I fixed the place, right hand of the road to Roquebrune, just
by the railway cutting, and the time—five-thirty of the morning.
It was arranged that I should call for him. Disgusting hour; I
have not been up so early since I fought Jacques Tirbaut in '85.
At five o'clock I found him ready and drinking tea with rum
in it—singular man! he made me have some too, brrr! He was

shaved, and dressed in that old frock-coat. His great dog jumped
into the carriage, but he bade her get out, took her paws on his
shoulders, and whispered in her ear some Italian words; a charm,
hein! and back she went, the tail between the legs. We drove slowly,
so as not to shake his arm. He was more gay than I. All the way
he talked to me of you: how kind you were! how good you had
been to him! 'You do not speak of yourself!' I said. 'Have you no
friends, nothing to say? Sometimes an accident will happen!' 'Oh!'
he answered, 'there is no danger; but if by any chance—well there
is a letter in my pocket.' 'And if you should kill *him*?' I said. 'But I
shall not,' he answered slyly: 'do you think I am going to fire on
him? No, no, he is too young.' 'But,' I said, 'I am not going to stand
that!' 'Yes,' he replied, 'I owe him a shot; but there is no danger—
not the least danger.' We had arrived; already they were there. Ah!
bah! You know the preliminaries, the politeness—this duelling, you
know, it is absurd, after all. We placed them at twenty paces. It is
not a bad place. There are pine-trees round, and rocks; at that hour
it was cool and grey as a church. I handed him the pistol. How can
I describe him to you, standing there, smoothing the barrel with
his fingers! 'What a beautiful thing a good pistol!' he said. 'Only a
fool or a madman throws away his life,' I said. 'Certainly,' he replied,
'certainly; but there is no danger,' and he regarded me, raising his
moustachette.

"There they stood then, back to back, with the mouths of their
pistols to the sky. '*Un*!' I cried, '*deux*! *tirez*!' They turned, I saw the
smoke of his shot go straight up like a prayer; his pistol dropped. I
ran to him. He looked surprised, put out his hand, and fell into my
arms. He was dead. Those fools came running up. 'What is it?' cried
one. I made him a bow. 'As you see,' I said; 'you have made a pretty
shot. My friend fired in the air. Messieurs, you had better breakfast
in Italy.' We carried him to the carriage, and covered him with a rug;
the others drove for the frontier. I brought him to his room. Here
is his letter." Jules stopped; tears were running down his face. "He is
dead; I have closed his eyes. Look here, you know, we are all of us
cads—it is the rule; but this—this, perhaps, was the exception." And
without another word he rushed away.

Outside the old fellow's lodging a dismounted *cocher* was standing disconsolate in the sun. "How was I to know they were going to fight a duel?" he burst out on seeing me. "He had white hair—I call you to witness he had white hair. This is bad for me: they will ravish my licence. Aha! you will see—this is bad for me!" I gave him the slip and found my way upstairs. The old fellow was alone, lying on the bed, his feet covered with a rug as if he might feel cold; his eyes were closed, but in this sleep of death, he still had that air of faint surprise. At full length, watching the bed intently, Freda lay, as she lay nightly when he was really asleep. The shutters were half open: the room still smelt slightly of rum. I stood for a long time looking at the face: the little white fans of moustache brushed upwards even in death, the hollows in his cheeks, the quiet of his figure; he was like some old knight . . . The dog broke the spell. She sat up, and resting her paws on the bed, licked his face. I went downstairs—I couldn't bear to hear her howl. This was his letter to me, written in a pointed handwriting:

"My dear Sir,—Should you read this, I shall be gone. I am ashamed to trouble you—a man should surely manage so as not to give trouble; and yet I believe you will not consider me importunate. If, then, you will pick up the pieces of an old fellow, I ask you to have my sword, the letter enclosed in this, and the photograph that stands on the stove buried with me. My will and the acknowledgments of my property are between the leaves of the Byron in my tin chest; they should go to Lucy Tor—address thereon. Perhaps you will do me the honour to retain for yourself any of my books that may give you pleasure. In the *Pilgrim's Progress* you will find some excellent recipes for Turkish coffee, Italian and Spanish dishes, and washing wounds. The landlady's daughter speaks Italian, and she would, I know, like to have Freda; the poor dog will miss me. I have read of old Indian warriors taking their horses and dogs with them to the happy hunting-grounds. Freda would come—noble animals are dogs! She eats once a day—a good large meal—and requires much salt. If you have animals of your own, sir, don't forget—all animals require salt. I have no debts, thank God! The money

in my pockets would bury me decently—not that there is any danger. And I am ashamed to weary you with details—the least a man can do is not to make a fuss—and yet he must be found ready.—Sir, with profound gratitude, your servant,
"Roger Brune."

Everything was as he had said. The photograph on the stove was that of a young girl of nineteen or twenty, dressed in an old-fashioned style, with hair gathered backward in a knot. The eyes gazed at you with a little frown, the lips were tightly closed; the expression of the face was eager, quick, wilful, and, above all, young.

The tin trunk was scented with dry fragments of some herb, the history of which in that trunk man knoweth not . . . There were a few clothes, but very few, all older than those he usually wore. Besides the Byron and *Pilgrim's Progress* were Scott's *Quentin Durward*, Captain Marryat's *Midshipman Easy*, a pocket Testament, and a long and frightfully stiff book on the art of fortifying towns, much thumbed, and bearing date 1863. By far the most interesting thing I found, however, was a diary, kept down to the preceding Christmas. It was a pathetic document, full of calculations of the price of meals; resolutions to be careful over this or that; doubts whether he must not give up smoking; sentences of fear that Freda had not enough to eat. It appeared that he had tried to live on ninety pounds a year, and send the other hundred pounds home to Lucy for the child; in this struggle he was always failing, having to send less than the amount—the entries showed that this was a nightmare to him. The last words, written on Christmas Day, were these: "What is the use of writing this, since it records nothing but failure!"

The landlady's daughter and myself were at the funeral. The same afternoon I went into the concert-room, where I had spoken to him first. When I came out Freda was lying at the entrance, looking into the faces of every one that passed, and sniffling idly at their heels. Close by the landlady's daughter hovered, a biscuit in her hand, and a puzzled, sorry look on her face.

[*September, 1900*]

THE JURYMAN

"Don't you see, brother, I was reading yesterday
the Gospel about Christ, the little Father; how He
suffered, how He walked on the earth. I suppose
you have heard about it?"

"Indeed, I have," replied Stepanuitch; "but we
are people in darkness; we can't read."—Tolstoy.

MR. Henry Bosengate, of the London Stock Exchange, seated himself
in his car that morning during the Great War with a sense of injury.
Major in a Volunteer Corps; member of all the local committees;
lending this very car to the neighbouring hospital, at times even
driving it himself for their benefit; subscribing to funds, so far as
his diminished income permitted—he was conscious of being an
asset to the country, and one whose time could not be wasted with
impunity. To be summoned to sit on a jury at the local assizes, and
not even the grand jury at that! It was in the nature of an outrage.

Strong and upright, with hazel eyes and dark eyebrows, pinkish-
brown cheeks, a forehead white, well-shaped, and getting high, with
greyish hair glossy and well-brushed, and a trim moustache, he
might have been taken for that colonel of Volunteers which indeed
he was in a fair way of becoming.

His wife had followed him out under the porch, and stood bracing
her supple body clothed in lilac linen. Red rambler roses formed a
sort of crown to her dark head; her ivory-coloured face had in it just
a suggestion of the Japanese.

Mr. Bosengate spoke through the whirr of the engine:

"I don't expect to be late, dear. This business is ridiculous. There
oughtn't to *be* any crime in these days."

His wife—her name was Kathleen—smiled. She looked very pretty and cool, Mr. Bosengate thought. To one bound on this dull and stuffy business everything he owned seemed pleasant—the geranium beds beside the gravel drive, his long, red-brick house mellowing decorously in its creepers and ivy, the little clock-tower over stables now converted to a garage, the dovecote, masking at the other end the conservatory which adjoined the billiard-room. Close to the red-brick lodge his two children, Kate and Harry, ran out from under the acacia trees, and waved to him, scrambling bare-legged on to the low, red, ivy-covered wall which guarded his domain of eleven acres. Mr. Bosengate waved back, thinking: 'Jolly couple—by Jove, they are!' Above their heads, through the trees, he could see right away to some Downs, faint in the July heat haze. And he thought: 'Pretty a spot as one could have got, so close to town!'

Despite the war he had enjoyed these last two years more than any of the ten since he built "Charmleigh" and settled down to semi-rural domesticity with his young wife. There had been a certain piquancy, a savour added to existence, by the country's peril, and all the public service and sacrifice it demanded. His chauffeur was gone, and one gardener did the work of three. He enjoyed—positively enjoyed—his committee work; even the serious decline of business and increase of taxation had not much worried one continually conscious of the national crisis and his own part therein. The country had wanted waking up, wanted a lesson in effort and economy; and the feeling that he had not spared himself in these strenuous times had given a zest to those quiet pleasures of bed and board which, at his age, even the most patriotic could retain with a good conscience. He had denied himself many things—new clothes, presents for Kathleen and the children, travel, and that pine-apple house which he had been on the point of building when the war broke out; new wine, too, and cigars, and membership of the two Clubs which he had never used in the old days. The hours had seemed fuller and longer, sleep better earned—wonderful, the things one could do without when put to it! He turned the car into the high road, driving dreamily, for he was in plenty of time. The war was going pretty well now; he was no fool optimist, but now that conscription was in force, one might reasonably hope for its end within a year. Then there would be a boom, and one might let oneself go a little. Visions of theatres and supper with his wife at the Savoy afterwards, and cosy night drives back into the sweet-smelling country behind your own chauffeur once more teased a fancy which even now did not soar beyond the confines of domestic pleasures. He pictured his wife in new dresses by Jay—she was fifteen years younger than himself, and "paid for dressing" as they said. He had always delighted—as men older than their wives will—in the admiration she excited from others not privileged to enjoy her charms. Her rather queer and ironical beauty, her cool irreproachable wifeliness, was a constant balm to him. They would give dinner parties again, have their friends down from town, and he would once more enjoy sitting at the foot of the dinner table while Kathleen sat at the head, with the light soft on her ivory shoulders, behind flowers she had arranged in that original way of hers, and fruit which he had grown in his hot-houses; once more he would take legitimate interest in the wine he offered to his guests—once more stock that Chinese cabinet wherein he kept cigars. Yes—there was a certain satisfaction in these days of privation, if only from the anticipation they created.

The sprinkling of villas had become continuous on either side of the high road; and women going to shop, tradesmen's boys delivering victuals, young men in khaki, began to abound. Now and then a limping or bandaged form would pass—some bit of human wreckage! and Mr. Bosengate would think mechanically: 'Another of those poor devils! Wonder if we've had his case before us!'

Running his car into the best hotel garage of the little town, he made his way leisurely over to the court. It stood back from the market-place, and was already lapped by a sea of persons having, as in the outer ring at race meetings, an air of business at which one must not be caught out, together with a soaked or flushed appearance. Mr. Bosengate could not resist putting his handkerchief to his nose. He had carefully drenched it with lavender water, and to this fact owed, perhaps, his immunity from the post of foreman on the jury—for, say what you will about the English, they have a deep instinct for affairs.

He found himself second in the front row of the jury box, and through the odour of "Sanitas" gazed at the judge's face expressionless up there, for all the world like a be-wigged bust. His fellows in the box had that appearance of falling between two classes characteristic of jurymen. Mr. Bosengate was not impressed. On one side of him the foreman sat, a prominent upholsterer, known in the town as "Gentleman Fox." His dark and beautifully brushed and oiled hair and moustache, his radiant linen, gold watch and chain, the white piping to his waistcoat, and a habit of never saying "Sir" had long marked him out from commoner men; he undertook to bury people too, to save them trouble; and was altogether superior. On the other side Mr. Bosengate had one of those men who, except when they sit on juries, are never seen without a little brown bag, and the appearance of having been interrupted in a drink. Pale and shiny, with large loose eyes shifting from side to side, he had an underdone voice and uneasy, flabby hands. Mr. Bosengate disliked sitting next to him. Beyond this commercial traveller sat a dark pale young man with spectacles; beyond him again, a short old man with grey moustache, mutton chops, and innumerable wrinkles; and the front row was completed by a chemist. The three immediately behind, Mr. Bosengate did not thoroughly master; but the three at the end of the second row he learned in their order of an oldish man in a grey suit, given to winking; an inanimate person with the mouth of a moustachioed codfish, over whose long bald crown three wisps of damp hair were carefully arranged; and a dried, dapperish, clean-shorn man, whose mouth seemed terrified lest it should be surprised without a smile. Their first and second verdicts were recorded without the necessity for withdrawal, and Mr. Bosengate was already sleepy when the third case was called. The sight of khaki revived his drooping attention. But what a weedy-looking specimen! This prisoner had a truly nerveless, pitiable, dejected air. If he had ever had a military bearing it had shrunk into him during his confinement. His ill-shaped brown tunic, whose little brass buttons seemed trying to keep smiling, struck Mr. Bosengate as ridiculously short, used though he was to such things. 'Absurd,' he thought—'Lumbago! Just where they ought to be covered!' Then the officer and gentleman stirred in him, and he added to himself: ' Still, there must be some distinction made!' The little soldier's visage had once perhaps been tanned, but was now the colour of dark dough; his large brown eyes with white showing below the iris, as so often in the eyes of very nervous people—wandered from face to face, of judge, counsel, jury, and public. There were hollows in his cheeks, his dark hair looked damp; around his neck he wore a bandage. The commercial traveller on Mr. Bosengate's left turned, and whispered: "*Felo de se*! My hat! what a guy!" Mr. Bosengate pretended not to hear—he could not bear that fellow!— and slowly wrote on a bit of paper: "Owen Lewis." Welsh! Well, he looked it—not at all an English face. Attempted suicide—not at all an English crime! Suicide implied surrender, a putting-up of hands to Fate—to say nothing of the religious aspect of the matter. And suicide in khaki seemed to Mr. Bosengate particularly abhorrent; like turning tail in face of the enemy; almost meriting the fate of a deserter. He looked at the prisoner, trying not to give way to this prejudice. And the prisoner seemed to look at him, though this, perhaps, was fancy.

The counsel for the prosecution a little, alert, grey, decided man, above military age, began detailing the circumstances of the crime. Mr. Bosengate, though not particularly sensitive to atmosphere could perceive sort of current running through the court. It was as if jury and public were thinking rhythmically in obedience to the same unexpressed prejudice of which he himself was conscious. Even the Cæsar-like pale face up there, presiding, seemed in its ironic serenity responding to that current.

"Gentlemen of the jury, before I call my evidence, I direct your attention to the bandage the accused is still wearing. He gave himself this wound with his Army razor, adding, if I may say so, insult to the injury he was inflicting on his country. He pleads not guilty; and before the magistrates he said that absence from his wife was preying on his mind" —the advocate's close lips widened—"Well, gentlemen if such an excuse is to weigh with us in these days, I'm sure I don't know what's to happen to the Empire."

'No, by George!' thought Mr. Bosengate.

The evidence of the first witness, a room-mate who had caught the prisoner's hand, and of the sergeant, who had at once been summoned, was conclusive, and he began to cherish a hope that they would get through without withdrawing, and he would be home before five. But then a hitch occurred. The regimental doctor failed to respond when his name was called; and the judge having for the first time that day showed himself capable of human emotion, intimated that he would adjourn until the morrow.

Mr. Bosengate received the announcement with equanimity. He would be home even earlier! And gathering up the sheets of paper he had scribbled on, he put them in his pocket and got up. The would-be suicide was being taken out of the court—a shambling drab figure with shoulders hunched. What good were men like that in these days! What good! The prisoner looked up. Mr. Bosengate encountered in full the gaze of those large brown eyes, with the white showing underneath. What a suffering, wretched, pitiful face! A man had no business to give you a look like that! The prisoner passed on down the stairs, and vanished. Mr. Bosengate went out and across the market place to the garage of the hotel where he had left his car. The sun shone fiercely and he thought: 'I must do some watering in the garden.' He brought the car out, and was about to start the engine, when some one passing said: "Good evenin'. Seedy-lookin' beggar that last prisoner, ain't he? We don't want men of that stamp." It was his neighbour on the jury, the commercial traveller, in a straw hat, with a little brown bag already in his hand and the froth of an interrupted drink on his moustache. Answering curtly: "Good evening!" and thinking: 'Nor of yours, my friend!' Mr. Bosengate started the car with unnecessary clamour. But as if brought back to life by the commercial traveller's remark, the prisoner's figure seemed to speed along too, turning up at Mr. Bosengate his pitifully unhappy eyes. Want of his wife!—queer excuse that for trying to put it out of his power ever to see her again. Why! Half a loaf, even a slice, was better than no bread. Not many of that neurotic type in the Army—thank Heaven! The lugubrious figure vanished, and Mr. Bosengate pictured instead the form of his own wife bending over her "Gloire de Dijon" roses in the rosery, where she generally worked a little before tea now that they were short of gardeners. He saw her, as often he had seen her raise herself and stand, head to one side, a gloved hand on her slender hip, gazing as it were ironically from under drooped lids at buds which did not come out fast enough. And the word 'Caline,' for he was something of a French scholar, shot through his mind: 'Kathleen—Caline!' If he found her there when he got in, he would steal up on the grass and—ah! but with great care not to crease her dress or disturb her hair! 'If only she weren't quite so self-contained,' he thought. 'It's like a cat you can't get near, not really near!'

The car, returning faster than it had come down that morning, had already passed the outskirt villas, and was breasting the hill to where, among fields and the old trees, Charmleigh lay apart from commoner life. Turning into his drive, Mr. Bosengate thought with a certain surprise: 'I wonder what she *does* think of! I wonder!' He put his gloves and hat down in the outer hall and went into the lavatory to dip his face in cool water and wash it with sweet-smelling soap— delicious revenge on the unclean atmosphere in which he had been stewing so many hours. He came out again into the hall dazed by soap and the mellowed light, and a voice from half-way up the stairs said: "Daddy! Look!" His little daughter was standing up there with one hand on the banisters. She scrambled on to them and came sliding down, her frock up to her eyes, and her holland knickers to her middle. Mr. Bosengate said mildly:

"Well, that's elegant!"

"Tea's in the summer-house. Mummy's waiting. Come on!"

With her hand in his, Mr. Bosengate went on, through the drawing-room, long and cool, with sunblinds down, through the billiard-room, high and cool, through the conservatory, green and sweet-smelling, out on to the terrace and the upper lawn. He had never felt such sheer exhilarated joy in his home surroundings, so cool, glistening and green under the July sun; and he said:

"Well, Kit, what have you all been doing?"

"I've fed my rabbits and Harry's; and we've been in the attic; Harry got his leg through the skylight."

Mr. Bosengate drew in his breath with a hiss.

"It's all right, Daddy; we got it out again, it's only grazed the skin. And we've been making swabs—I made seventeen—Mummy made thirty-three, and then she went to the hospital. Did you put many men in prison?"

Mr. Bosengate cleared his throat. The question seemed to him untimely.

"Only two."

"What's it like in prison, Daddy?"

Mr. Bosengate, who had no more knowledge than his little daughter, replied in an absent voice:

"Not very nice."

They were passing under a young oak tree, where the path wound round to the rosery and summer-house. Something shot down and clawed Mr. Bosengate's neck. His little daughter began to hop and suffocate with laughter.

"Oh, Daddy! Aren't you caught! I led you on purpose!" Looking up, Mr. Bosengate saw his small son lying along a low branch above him—like the leopard he was declaring himself to be (for fear of error), and thought blithely: 'What an active little chap it is!'

"Let me drop on your shoulders, Daddy—like they do on the deer."

"Oh, yes! Do be a deer, Daddy!"

Mr. Bosengate did not see being a deer; his hair had just been brushed. But he entered the rosery buoyantly between his offspring. His wife was standing precisely as he had imagined her, in a pale blue frock open at the neck, with a narrow black band round the waist, and little accordion pleats below. She looked her coolest. Her smile, when she turned her head, hardly seemed to take Mr. Bosengate seriously enough. He placed his lips below one of her half-drooped eyelids. She even smelled of roses. His children began to dance round their mother, and Mr. Bosengate, firmly held between them, was also compelled to do this, until she said:

"When you've quite done, let's have tea!"

It was not the greeting he had imagined coming along in the car. Earwigs were plentiful in the summer-house—used perhaps twice a year, but indispensable to every country residence—and Mr.

Bosengate was not sorry for the excuse to get out again. Though all was so pleasant, he felt oddly restless, rather suffocated; and lighting his pipe, began to move about among the roses, blowing tobacco at the greenfly; in war-time one was never quite idle! And suddenly he said:

"We're trying a wretched Tommy at the assizes."

His wife looked up from a rose. "What for?"

"Attempted suicide."

"Why did he?"

"Can't stand the separation from his wife."

She looked at him, gave a low laugh, and said:

"Oh dear!"

Mr. Bosengate was puzzled. Why did she laugh? He looked round, saw that the children were gone, took his pipe from his mouth, and approached her.

"You look very pretty," he said. "Give me a kiss!"

His wife bent her body forward from the waist, and pushed her lips out till they touched his moustache. Mr. Bosengate felt a sensation as if he had arisen from breakfast without having eaten marmalade. He mastered it and said:

"That jury are a rum lot."

His wife's eyelids flickered. "I wish women sat on juries."

"Why?"

"It would be an experience."

Not the first time she had used that curious expression! Yet her life was far from dull, so far as he could see; with the new interests created by the war, and the constant calls on her time made by the perfection of their home life, she had a useful and busy existence. Again the random thought passed through him: 'But she never tells me anything!' And suddenly that lugubrious khaki-clad figure started up among the rose bushes. "We've got a lot to be thankful for!" he said abruptly. "I must go to work!" His wife, raising one eyebrow, smiled. "And I to weep!" Mr. Bosengate laughed—she had a pretty wit! And stroking his comely moustache where it had been kissed, he moved out into the sunshine. All the evening, throughout his labours, not inconsiderable, for this jury business had put him behind time, he was afflicted by that restless pleasure in his surroundings; would break off in mowing the lower lawn to look at the house through the trees; would leave his study and committee papers to cross into the drawing-room and sniff its dainty fragrance; paid a special good-night visit to the children having supper in the schoolroom; pottered in and out from his dressing-room to admire his wife while she was changing for dinner; dined with his mind perpetually on the next course; talked volubly of the war; and in the billiard-room afterwards, smoking the pipe which had taken the place of his cigar, could not keep still, but roamed about, now in conservatory, now in the drawing-room, where his wife and the governess were still making swabs. It seemed to him that he could not have enough of anything. About eleven o'clock he strolled out—beautiful night, only just dark enough—under the new arrangement with Time—and went down to the little round fountain below the terrace. His wife was playing the piano. Mr. Bosengate looked at the water and the flat dark water-lily leaves which floated there; looked up at the house, where only narrow chinks of light showed, because of the Lighting Order. The dreamy music drifted out; there was a scent of heliotrope. He moved a few steps back, and sat in the children's swing under an old lime tree. Jolly—blissful—in the warm, bloomy dark! Of all hours of the day, this before going to bed was perhaps the pleasantest. He saw the light go up in his wife's bedroom, unscreened for a full minute, and thought: 'Aha! If I did my duty as a special, I should "strafe" her for that.' She came to the window, her figure lighted, hands up to the back of her head, so that her bare arms gleamed. Mr. Bosengate wafted her a kiss, knowing he could not be seen. 'Lucky chap!' he mused; 'she's a great joy!' Up went her arm, down came the blind—the house was dark again. He drew a long breath. 'Another ten minutes,' he thought, 'then I'll go in and shut up. By Jove! The limes are beginning to smell already!' And, the better to take in that acme of his well-being, he tilted the swing, lifted his feet from the ground, and swung himself toward the scented blossoms. He wanted to whelm his senses in their perfume, and closed his eyes. But instead of the domestic vision he expected, the face of the little Welsh soldier, hare-eyed, shadowy, pinched and dark and pitiful, started up with such disturbing vividness that he opened his eyes again at once. Curse! The fellow almost haunted one! Where would he be now—poor little devil! lying in his cell, thinking—thinking of his wife! Feeling suddenly morbid, Mr. Bosengate arrested the swing and stood up. Absurd!—all his well-being and mood of warm anticipation had deserted him! 'A d——d world!' he thought. 'Such a lot of misery! Why should I have to sit in judgment on that poor beggar, and condemn him?' He moved up on to the terrace and walked briskly, to rid himself of this disturbance before going in. 'That commercial traveller chap,' he thought, 'the rest of those fellows—they see nothing!' And, abruptly turning up the three stone steps, he entered the conservatory, locked it, passed into the billiard-room, and drank his barley water. One of the pictures was hanging crooked; he went up to put it straight. Still life. Grapes and apples, and lobsters! They struck him as odd for the first time. Why lobsters? The whole picture seemed dead and oily. He turned off the light, and went upstairs, passed his wife's door, into his own room, and undressed. Clothed in his pyjamas he opened the door between the rooms. By the light coming from his own he could see her dark head on the pillow. Was she asleep? No—not asleep, certainly. The moment of fruition had come; the crowning of his pride and pleasure in his home. But he continued to stand there. He had suddenly no pride, no pleasure, no desire; nothing but a sort of dull resentment against everything. He turned back, shut the door, and slipping between the heavy curtains and his open window, stood looking out at the night. 'Full of misery!' he thought. 'Full of d——d misery!'

II

Filing into the jury box next morning, Mr. Bosengate collided slightly with a short juryman, whose square figure and square head of stiff yellow-red hair he had only vaguely noticed the day before. The man looked angry, and Mr. Bosengate thought:

'An ill-bred dog, that!'

He sat down quickly, and, to avoid further recognition of his fellows, gazed in front of him. His appearance on Saturdays was always military, by reason of the route march of his Volunteer Corps in the afternoon. Gentleman Fox, who belonged to the corps too, was also looking square; but that commercial traveller on his other side seemed more *louche*, and as if surprised in immorality, than ever; only the proximity of Gentleman Fox on the other side kept Mr. Bosengate from shrinking. Then he saw the prisoner being brought in, shadowy and dark behind the brightness of his buttons, and he experienced a sort of shock, this figure was so exactly that which had several times started up in his mind. Somehow he had expected a fresh sight of the fellow to dispel and disprove what had been haunting him, had expected to find him just an outside phenomenon, not, as it were, a part of his own life. And he gazed at the carven immobility of the judge's face, trying to steady himself, as a drunken man will, by looking at a light. The regimental doctor, unabashed by the judge's comment on his absense the day before, gave his evidence like a man who had better things to do, and the case for the prosecution was forthwith rounded in by a little speech from counsel. The matter—he said—was clear as daylight. Those who wore His Majesty's uniform, charged with the responsibility and privilege of defending their country, were no more entitled to desert their regiments by taking their own lives than they were entitled to desert in any other way. He asked for a conviction. Mr. Bosengate felt a sympathetic shuffle passing through all feet; the judge was speaking:

"Prisoner, you can either go into the witness box and make your statement on oath, in which you may be cross-examined on it; or you can make your statement there from the dock, in which case you will not be cross-examined. Which do you elect to do?"

"From here, my lord."

Seeing him now full face, and, as it might be, come to life in the effort to convey his feelings, Mr. Bosengate had suddenly a quite different impression of the fellow. It was as if his khaki had fallen off, and he had stepped out of his own shadow, a live and quivering creature. His pinched clean-shaven face seemed to have an irregular, wilder, hairier look, his large nervous brown eyes darkened and glowed; he jerked his shoulders, his arms, his whole body, like a man suddenly freed from cramp or a suit of armour. He spoke, too, in a quick, crisp, rather high voice, pinching his consonants a little, sharpening his vowels, like a true Welshman.

"My lord and misters the jury," he said: "I was a hairdresser when the call came on me to join the army. I had a little home and a wife. I never thought what it would be like to be away from them, I surely never did; and I'm ashamed to be speaking it out like this—how it can squeeze and squeeze a man, how it can prey on your mind when you're nervous like I am. 'Tis not everyone that cares for his home—there's a lots o' them never wants to see their wives again. But for me 'tis like being shut up in a cage, it is!" Mr. Bosengate saw daylight between the skinny fingers of the man's hand thrown out with a jerk. "I cannot bear it shut up away from wife and home like what you are in the army. So when I took my razor that morning I was wild—an' I wouldn't be here now but for that man catching my hand. There was no reason in it, I'm willing to confess. It was foolish; but wait till you get feeling like what I was, and see how it draws you. Misters the jury, don't send me back to prison; it is worse still there. If you have wives you will know what it is like for lots of us; only some is more nervous than others. I swear to you, sirs, I could not help it——" Again the little man flung out his hand, his whole thin body shook and Mr. Bosengate felt the same sensation as when he drove his car over a dog—"Misters the jury, I hope you may never in your lives feel as I've been feeling."

The little man ceased, his eyes shrank back into their sockets, his figure back into its mask of shadowy brown and gleaming buttons, and Mr. Bosengate was conscious that the judge was making a series of remarks; and, very soon, of being seated at a mahogany table in the jury's withdrawing room, hearing the voice of the man with hair like an Irish terrier's saying: "Didn't he talk through his hat, that little blighter!" Conscious, too, of the commercial traveller, still on his left—always on his left!—rnopping his brow, and muttering: "Phew! It's hot in there to-day!" when an effluvium, as of an inside accustomed to whisky, came from him. Then the man with the underlip and the three plastered wisps of hair said:

"Don't know why we withdrew, Mr. Foreman!"

Mr. Bosengate looked round to where, at the head of the table, Gentleman Fox sat, in defensive gentility and the little white piping to his waistcoat. "I shall be happy to take the sense of the jury," he was saying blandly.

There was a short silence, then the chemist murmured:

"I should say he must have what they call claustrophobia."

"Clauster fiddlesticks! The feller's a shirker, that's all. Missed his wife—pretty excuse! Indecent, I call it!"

The speaker was the little wire-haired man; and emotion, deep and angry, stirred in Mr. Bosengate. That ill-bred little cur! He gripped the edge of the table with both hands.

"I think it's d——d natural!" he muttered. But almost before the words had left his lips he felt dismay. What had he said—he, nearly a colonel of volunteers—endorsing such a want of patriotism! And hearing the commercial traveller murmuring: "''Ear, 'ear!" he reddened violently.

The wire-headed man said roughly:

"There's too many of these blighted shirkers, and too much pampering of them."

The turmoil in Mr. Bosengate increased; he remarked in an icy voice:

"I agree to no verdict that'll send the man back to prison."

At this a real tremor seemed to go round the table, as if they all saw themselves sitting there through lunch time. Then the large grey-haired man given to winking, said:

"Oh! Come, sir—after what the judge said! Come, sir! What do you say, Mr. Foreman?"

Gentleman Fox—as who should say 'This is excellent value, but I don't wish to press it on you!'—answered:

"We are only concerned with the facts. Did he or did he not try to shorten his life?"

"Of course he did—said so himself," Mr. Bosengate heard the wire-haired man snap out, and from the following murmur of assent he alone abstained. Guilty! Well—yes! There was no way out of admitting that, but his feelings revolted against handing "that poor little beggar" over to the tender mercy of his country's law. His whole soul rose in arms against agreeing with that ill-bred little cur, and the rest of this job-lot. He had an impulse to get up and walk out, saying: "Settle it your own way. Good-morning."

"It seems, sir," Gentleman Fox was saying, "that we're all agreed to guilty, except yourself. If you will allow me, I don't see how you can go behind what the prisoner himself admitted."

Thus brought up to the very guns, Mr. Bosengate, red in the face, thrust his hands deep into the side pockets of his tunic, and, staring straight before him, said:

"Very well; on condition we recommend him to mercy."

"What do you say, gentlemen; shall we recommend him to mercy?"

"'Ear 'ear!" burst from the commercial traveller, and from the chemist came the murmur:

"No harm in that."

"Well, I think there is. They shoot deserters at the front, and we let this fellow off. I'd hang the cur."

Mr. Bosengate stared at that little wire-haired brute. "Haven't you *any* feeling for others?" he wanted to say. "Can't you see that this poor devil suffers tortures?" But the sheer impossibility of doing this before ten other men brought a slight sweat out on his face and hands; and in agitation he smote the table a blow with his fist. The effect was instantaneous. Everybody looked at the wire-haired man, as if saying:

"Yes, you've gone a bit too far there!" The "little brute" stood it for a moment, then muttered surlily:

"Well, commend 'im to mercy if you like; I don't care."

"That's right; they never pay any attention to it," said the grey-haired man, winking heartily. And Mr. Bosengate filed back with the others into court.

But when from the jury box his eyes fell once more on the hare-eyed figure in the dock, he had his worst moment yet. Why should this poor wretch suffer so—for no fault, no fault; while he, and these others, and that snapping counsel, and the Cæsar-like judge up there, went off to their women and their homes, blithe as bees, and probably never thought of him again? And suddenly he was conscious of the judge's voice:

"You will go back to your regiment, and endeavour to serve your country with better spirit. You may thank the jury that you are not sent to prison, and your good fortune that you were not at the front when you tried to commit this cowardly act. You are lucky to be alive."

A policeman pulled the little soldier by the arm; his drab figure, with eyes fixed and lustreless, passed down and away. From his very soul Mr. Bosengate wanted to lean out and say: "Cheer up, cheer up! *I* understand."

It was nearly ten o'clock that evening before he reached home, motoring back from the route march. His physical tiredness was abated, for he had partaken of a snack and a whisky and soda at the hotel but mentally he was in a curious mood. His body felt appeased, his spirit hungry. To-night he had a yearning, not for his wife's kisses, but for her understanding. He wanted to go to her and say: "I've learnt a lot to-day—found out things I never thought of. Life's a wonderful thing, Kate, a thing one can't live all to oneself; a thing one shares with everybody, so that when another suffers, one suffers too. It's come to me that what one *has* doesn't matter a bit—it's what one does, and how one sympathises with other people. It came to me in the most extraordinary vivid way, when I was on that jury watching that poor little rat of a soldier in his trap; it's the first time I've ever felt—the—the spirit of Christ, you know. It's a wonderful thing, Kate—wonderful! We haven't been close—really close, you and I, so that we each understand what the other is feeling. It's all in that, you know; understanding—sympathy—it's priceless. When I saw that poor little devil taken down and sent back to his regiment to begin his sorrows all over again—wanting his wife, thinking and thinking of her just as you know I would be thinking and wanting you, I felt what an awful outside sort of life we lead, never telling each other what we really think and feel, never being really close. I daresay that little chap and his wife keep nothing from each other—

live each other's lives. That's what we ought to do. Let's get to feeling
that what really matters is—understanding and loving, and not only
just saying it as we all do, those fellows on the jury, and even that
poor devil of a judge—what an awful life, judging one's fellow-
creatures! When I left that poor little Tommy this morning, and ever
since, I've longed to get back here quietly to you and tell you about
it, and make a beginning. There's something wonderful in this, and I
want you to feel it as I do, because you mean such a lot to me."

This was what he wanted to say to his wife, not touching, or
kissing her, just looking into her eyes, watching them soften and
glow as they surely must, catching the infection of his new ardour.
And he felt unsteady, fearfully unsteady with the desire to say it all
as it should be said: swiftly, quietly, with the truth and fervour of his
feeling.

The hall was not lit up, for daylight still lingered under the new
arrangement. He went towards the drawing-room, but from the very
door shied off to his study and stood irresolute under the picture of
a "Man catching a flea" (Dutch school), which had come down to
him from his father. The governess would be in there with his wife!
He must wait. Essential to go straight to Kathleen and pour it all
out, or he would never do it. He felt as nervous as an undergraduate
going up for his *viva voce*. This thing was so big, so astoundingly and
unexpectedly important. He was suddenly afraid of his wife, afraid
of her coolness and her grace, and that something Japanese about
her—of all those attributes he had been accustomed to admire; most
afraid, as it were, of her attraction. He felt young to-night, almost
boyish; would she see that he was not really fifteen years older than
herself, and she not really a part of his collection, of all the admirable
appointments of his home; but a companion spirit to one who
wanted a companion badly? In this agitation of his soul he could
keep still no more than he could last night in the agitation of his
senses; and he wandered into the dining-room. A dainty supper was
set out there, sandwiches, and cake, whisky and cigarettes—even an
early peach. Mr. Bosengate looked at this peach with sorrow rather
than disgust. The perfection of it was of a piece with all that had
gone before this new and sudden feeling. Its delicious bloom seemed

to heighten his perception of the hedge around him, that hedge of the things he so enjoyed, carefully planted and tended these many years. He passed it by uneaten, and went to the window. Out there all was darkening, the fountain, the lime tree, the flower-beds, and the fields below, with the Jersey cows who would come to your call; darkening slowly, losing form, blurring into soft blackness, vanishing, but there none the less—all there—the hedge of his possessions. He heard the door of the drawing-room open, the voices of his wife and the governess in the hall, going up to bed. If only they didn't look in here! If only——! The voices ceased. He was safe now—had but to follow in a few minutes, to make sure of Kathleen alone. He turned round and stared down the length of the dark dining-room, over the rosewood table, to where in the mirror above the sideboard at the far end, his figure bathed, a stain, a mere blurred shadow; he made his way down to it along the table edge, and stood before himself as close as he could get. His throat and the roof of his mouth felt dry with nervousness; he put out his finger and touched his face in the glass. 'You're an ass!' he thought.'Pull yourself together, and get it over. She will see; of course she will!'He swallowed, smoothed his moustache, and walked out. Going up the stairs, his heart beat painfully; but he was in for it now, and marched straight into her room.

Dressed only in a loose blue wrapper, she was brushing her dark hair before the glass. Mr. Bosengate went up to her and stood there silent, looking down. The words he had thought of were like a swarm of bees buzzing in his head yet not one would fly from between his lips. His wife went on brushing her hair under the light which shone on her polished elbows. She looked up at him from beneath one lifted eyebrow.

"Well, dear—tired?"

With a sort of vehemence the single word "No" passed out. A faint, a quizzical smile flitted over her face; she shrugged her shoulders ever so gently. That gesture—he had seen it before! And in desperate desire to make her understand, he put his hand on her lifted arm.

"Kathleen, stop—listen to me!" His fingers tightened in his agitation and eagerness to make his great discovery known. But before he could get out a word he became conscious of that cool round arm, conscious of her eyes half-closed, sliding round at him, of her half-smiling lips, of her neck under the wrapper. And he stammered:

"I want—I must—Kathleen, I—"

She lifted her shoulders again in that little shrug. "Yes—I know; all right!"

A wave of heat and shame, and of God knows what came over Mr. Bosengate; he fell on his knees and pressed his forehead to her arm; and he was silent, more silent than the grave. Nothing—nothing came from him but two long sighs. Suddenly he felt her hand stroke his cheek—compassionately it seemed to him. She made a little movement towards him; her lips met his, and he remembered nothing but that . . .

In his own room Mr. Bosengate sat at his wide-open window, smoking a cigarette; there was no light. Moths went past, the moon was creeping up. He sat very calm, puffing the smoke out into the night air. Curious thing—life! Curious world! Curious forces in it—making one do the opposite of what one wished; always—always making one do the opposite, it seemed! The furtive light from the creeping moon was getting hold of things down there, stealing in among the boughs of the trees. 'There's something ironical,' he thought, 'which walks about. Things don't come off as you think they will. I meant, I tried—but one doesn't change like that all of a sudden, it seems. Fact is, life's too big a thing for me! All the same, I'm not the man I was yesterday—not quite!' He closed his eyes, and in one of those flashes of vision which come when the senses are at rest, he saw himself as it were far down below—down on the floor of a street narrow as a grave, high as a mountain, a deep dark slit of a street—walking down there, a black midget of a fellow, among other black midgets—his wife, and the little soldier, the judge, and those jury chaps—*fantoches* straight up on their tiny feet, wandering down there in that dark, infinitely tall, and narrow street. 'Too much for one!' he thought. 'Too high for one—no getting on top of it. We've got to be kind, and help one another, and not expect too much, and not think too much. That's—all!' And, squeezing out his cigarette, he took six deep breaths of the night air, and got into bed.

[*1910*]

TIMBER

Sɪʀ Arthur Hirries Baronet, of Hirriehugh, in a northern county, came to the decision to sell his timber in that state of mind—during the War—which may be called patrio-profiteering. Like newspaper proprietors, writers on strategy, shipbuilders, owners of works, makers of arms and the rest of the working classes at large, his mood was "Let me serve my country, and if thereby my profits are increased, let me put up with it, and invest in National Bonds."

With an encumbered estate and some of the best coverts in that northern county, it had not become practical politics to sell his timber till the Government wanted it at all costs. To let his shooting had been more profitable, till now, when a patriotic action and a stroke of business had become synonymous. A man of sixty-five, but not yet grey, with a reddish tinge in his moustache, cheeks, lips, and eyelids, slightly knock-kneed, and with large, rather spreading feet, he moved in the best circles in a somewhat embarrassed manner. At the enhanced price, the timber at Hirriehugh would enfranchise him for the remainder of his days. He sold it therefore one day of April when the War news was bad, to a Government official on the spot. He sold it at half five in the afternoon, practically for cash down, and drank a stiff whisky and soda to wash away the taste of the transaction; for, though no sentimentalist his great-great-grandfather had planted most of it, and his grandfather had planted the rest. Royalty too had shot there in its time; and he himself (never much of a sportsman) had missed more birds in the rides and hollows of his fine coverts than he cared to remember. But the country was in need, and the price considerable. Bidding the Government official good-bye, he lighted a cigar, and went across the Park to take a farewell stroll among his timber.

He entered the home covert by a path leading through a group of pear trees just coming into bloom. Smoking cigars and drinking whisky in the afternoon in preference to tea, Sir Arthur Hirries had not much sense of natural beauty. But those pear trees impressed him, greenish white against blue sky and fleecy thick clouds which looked as if they had snow in them. They were deuced pretty, and promised a good year for fruit, if they escaped the late frosts, though it certainly looked like freezing to-night! He paused a moment at the wicket gate to glance back at them—like scantily-clothed maidens posing on the outskirts of his timber. Such, however, was not the vision of Sir Arthur Hirries, who was considering how he should invest the balance of the cash down after paying off his mortgages. National Bonds—the country was in need!

Passing through the gate he entered the ride of the home covert. Variety lay like colour on his woods. They stretched for miles, and his ancestors had planted almost every kind of tree—beech, oak, birch, sycamore, ash, elm, hazel, holly, pine; a lime tree and a hornbeam here and there, and further in among the winding coverts, spinneys and belts of larch. The evening air was sharp, and sleet showers came whirling from those bright clouds; he walked briskly, drawing at his richly fragrant cigar, the whisky still warm within him. He walked thinking, with a gentle melancholy slowly turning a little sulky, that he would never again be pointing out with his shooting stick to such or such a guest where he was to stand to get the best birds over him. The pheasants had been let down during the War, but he put up two or three old cocks who went clattering and whirring out to left and right; and rabbits crossed the rides quietly to and fro, within easy shot. He came to where Royalty had stood fifteen years ago during the last drive. He remembered Royalty saying: "Very pretty shooting at that last stand, Hirries; birds just about as high as I like them." The ground indeed rose rather steeply there, and the timber was oak and ash, with a few pines sprinkled into the bare greyish twiggery of the oaks, always costive in spring, and the just greening feather of the ashes.

'They'll be cutting those pines first,' he thought—strapping trees, straight as the lines of Euclid, and free of branches, save at their

tops. In the brisk wind those tops swayed a little and gave forth
soft complaint. 'Three times my age,' he thought; 'prime timber.'
The ride wound sharply and entered a belt of larch, whose steep
rise entirely barred off the rather sinister sunset—a dark and wistful
wood, delicate dun and grey, whose green shoots and crimson tips
would have perfumed the evening coolness, but for the cigar smoke
in his nostrils. 'They'll have this spinney for pit props.' he thought;
and, taking a cross ride through it, he emerged in a heathery glen of
birch trees. No forester, he wondered if they would make anything
of those whitened, glistening shapes. His cigar had gone out now,
and he leaned against one of the satin-smooth stems, under the
lacery of twig and bud, sheltering the flame of a relighting match.
A hare lopped away among the bilberry shoots; a jay, painted like a
fan, squawked and flustered past him up the glen. Interested in birds,
and wanting just one more jay to complete a fine stuffed group of
them, Sir Arthur, though devoid of a gun, followed, to see where
"The beggar's" nest was. The glen dipped rapidly, and the character
of the timber changed, assuming greater girth and solidity. There was
a lot of beech here—a bit he did not know, for though taken in by
the beaters, no guns could be stationed there because of the lack of
undergrowth. The jay had vanished, and light had begun to fail. 'I
must get back,' he thought, 'or I shall be late for dinner.' He debated
for a moment whether to retrace his steps or to cut across the
beeches and regain the home covert by a loop. The jay, reappearing
to the left, decided him to cross the beech grove. He did so, and took
a narrow ride up through a dark bit of mixed timber with heavy
undergrowth. The ride, after favouring the left for a little, bent away
to the right; Sir Arthur followed it hurriedly, conscious that twilight
was gathering fast. It must bend again to the left in a minute! It
did, and then to the right, and, the undergrowth remaining thick,
he could only follow on, or else retrace his steps. He followed on,
beginning to get hot in spite of a sleet shower falling through the
dusk. He was not framed by Nature for swift travelling—his knees
turning in and his toes turning out—but he went at a good bat,
uncomfortably aware that the ride was still taking him away from
home, and expecting it at any minute to turn left again. It did not,

and hot, out of breath, a little bewildered, he stood still in three-quarter darkness, to listen. Not a sound save that of wind in the tops of the trees, and a faint creaking of timber, where two stems had grown athwart and were touching.

The path was a regular will-o'-the-wisp. He must make a bee line of it through the undergrowth into another ride! He had never before been amongst his timber in the dusk, and he found the shapes of the confounded trees more weird, and as if menacing, than he had ever dreamed of. He stumbled quickly on in and out of them among the undergrowth, without coming to a ride.

'Here I am stuck in this damned wood!' he thought. To call these formidably encircling shapes "a wood" gave him relief. After all, it was *his* wood, and nothing very untoward could happen to a man in his own wood, however dark it might get; he could not be more than a mile and a half at the out side from his dining-room! He looked at his watch, whose hands he could just see—nearly half-past seven! The sleet had become snow, but it hardly fell on him, so thick was the timber just here. But he had no overcoat, and suddenly he felt that first sickening little drop in his chest, which presages alarm. Nobody knew he was in this damned wood! And in a quarter of an hour it would be black as your hat! He *must* get on and out! The trees amongst which he was stumbling produced quite a sick feeling now in one who hitherto had never taken trees seriously. What monstrous growths they were! The thought that seeds, tiny seeds or saplings, planted by his ancestors, could attain such huge impending and imprisoning bulk—ghostly great growths mounting up to heaven and shutting off this world, exasperated and unnerved him. He began to run, caught his foot in a root and fell flat on his face. The cursed trees seemed to have a down on him! Rubbing elbows and forehead with his snow-wetted hands, he leaned against a trunk to get his breath, and summon the sense of direction to his brain. Once as a young man he had been "bushed" at night in Vancouver Island; quite a scary business! But he had come out all right, though his camp had been the only civilised spot within a radius of twenty miles. And here he was, on his own estate, within a mile or two of home, getting into a funk. It was childish! And he laughed. The wind answered, sighing and threshing in the tree tops. There must be a regular blizzard blowing now, and, to judge by the cold, from the north—but whether north-east or north-west was the question. Besides, how keep definite direction without a compass, in the dark? The timber, too, with its thick trunks, diverted the wind into keen, directionless draughts. He looked up, but could make nothing of the two or three stars that he could see. It was a mess! And he lighted a second cigar with some difficulty, for he had begun to shiver. The wind in this blasted wood cut through his Norfolk jacket and crawled about his body, which had become hot from his exertion, and now felt clammy and half-frozen. This would mean pneumonia, if he didn't look out! And, half feeling his way from trunk to trunk, he started on again, but, for all he could tell he might be going round in a circle, might even be crossing rides without realising, and again that sickening drop occurred in his chest. He stood still and shouted. He had the feeling of shouting into walls of timber, dark and heavy, which threw the sound back at him.

'Curse you!' he thought; 'I wish I'd sold you six months ago!' The wind fleered and moved in the tree tops; and he started off again at a run in that dark wilderness; till, hitting his head against a low branch, he fell stunned. He lay several minutes unconscious, came to himself deadly cold, and struggled up on to his feet.

'By Jove!' he thought, with a sort of stammer in his brain; 'this is a bad business! I may be out here all night!' For an unimaginative man, it was extraordinary what vivid images he had just then. He saw the face of the Government official who had bought his timber, and the slight grimace with which he had agreed to the price. He saw his butler, after the gong had gone, standing like a stuck pig by the sideboard, waiting for him to come down. What would they do when he didn't come? Would they have the *nous* to imagine that he might have lost his way in the coverts, and take lanterns and search for him? Far more likely they would think he had walked over to "Greenlands" or "Berrymoor," and stayed there to dinner. And, suddenly, he saw himself slowly freezing out here, in the snowy night, among this cursed timber. With a vigorous shake, he butted again into the darkness among the tree trunks. He was angry now—with himself, with the night, with the trees; so angry that he actually let out with his fist at a trunk against which he had stumbled, and scored his knuckles. It was humiliating; and Sir Arthur Hirries was not accustomed to humiliation. In anybody else's wood—yes; but to be lost like this in one's own coverts! Well, if he had to walk all night, he would get out! And he plunged on doggedly in the darkness.

He was fighting with his timber now, as if the thing were alive and each tree an enemy. In the interminable stumbling exertion of that groping progress his angry mood gave place to half-comatose philosophy. Trees! His great-great-grandfather had planted them! His own was the fifth man's life, but the trees were almost as young as ever; they made nothing of a man's life! He sniggered: And a man made nothing of theirs! Did they know they were going to be cut down? All the better if they did, and were sweating in their shoes. He pinched himself—his thoughts were becoming so queer! He remembered that once, when his liver was out of order, trees had seemed to him like solid, tall diseases—bulbous, scarred, cavernous, witch-armed, fungoid emanations of the earth. Well, so they were! And he was among them, on a snowy pitch-black night, engaged in this death-struggle! The occurrence of the word death in his thoughts brought him up all standing. Why couldn't he concentrate his mind on getting out; why was he mooning about the life and nature of trees instead of trying to remember the conformation of his coverts, so as to re-kindle in himself some sense of general direction? He struck a number of matches to get a sight of his watch again. Great heaven! He had been walking nearly two hours since he last looked at it; and in what direction? They said a man in a fog went round and round because of some kink in his brain! He began now to feel the trees, searching for a hollow trunk. A hollow would be some protection from the cold—his first conscious confession of exhaustion. He was not in training, and he was sixty-five. The thought: 'I can't keep this up much longer,' caused a second explosion of sullen anger. Damnation! Here he was—for all he could tell—standing where he had sat perhaps a dozen times on his spread shooting stick; watching sunlight on bare twigs, or the nose of his spaniel twitching beside him, listening to the tap of the beaters' sticks, and the shrill, drawn-out: "Marrk! Cock over!" Would they let the dogs out, to pick up his tracks? No! ten to one they would assume he was staying the night at the Summertons', or at Lady Mary's, as he had done before now, after dining there. And suddenly his strained heart leaped. He had struck a ride again! His mind slipped back into place like an elastic let-go, relaxed, quivering gratefully. He had only to follow this ride, and somewhere, somehow, he would come out. And be hanged if he would let them know what a fool he had made of himself! Right or left—which way? He turned so that the flying snow came on his back, hurrying forward between the denser darkness on either hand, where the timber stood in walls, moving his arms, across and across his body, as if dragging a concertina to full stretch, to make sure that he was keeping in the path. He went what seemed an interminable way like this, till he was brought up all standing by trees, and could find no outlet, no continuation. Turning in his tracks, with the snow in his face now, he retraced his steps till once more he was brought up short by trees. He stood panting. It was ghastly—ghastly! And in a panic he dived this way and that to find the bend, the turning, the way on. The sleet stung his eyes, the wind fleered and whistled, the boughs sloughed and moaned. He struck matches, trying to shade them with his cold, wet hands but one by one they went out, and still he found no turning. The ride must have a blind alley at either end, the turning be down the side somewhere! Hope revived in him. Never say die! He began a second retracing of his steps, feeling the trunks along one side, to find a gap. His breath came with difficulty. What would old Brodley say if he could see him, soaked, frozen, tired to death, stumbling along in the darkness among this cursed timber—old Brodley who had told him his heart was in poor case! . . . A gap? Ah! No trunks—a ride at last! He turned, felt a sharp pain in his knee and pitched forward. He could not rise—the knee dislocated six years ago was out again. Sir Arthur Hirries clenched his teeth. Nothing more could happen to him! But after a minute—blank and bitter—he began to crawl along the new ride. Oddly he felt less discouraged and alarmed on hands and knee—for he could use but one. It was a relief to have his eyes fixed on the ground, not peering at the tree trunks; or perhaps there was less strain for the moment on his heart. He crawled, stopping every minute or so to renew his strength. He crawled mechanically waiting for his heart, his knee, his lungs to stop him. The earth was snowed over, and he could feel its cold wetness as he scraped along. Good tracks to follow, if anybody struck them! But in this dark forest——! In one of his halts, drying his hands as best he could, he struck a match, and sheltering it desperately fumbled out his watch. Past ten o'clock! He wound the watch, and put it back against his heart. If only he could wind his heart! And squatting there he counted his matches—four! 'Well,' he thought grimly, 'I won't light them to show me my blasted trees. I've got a cigar left; I'll keep them for that.' And he crawled on again. He must keep going while he could! He crawled till his heart and lungs and knee struck work; and, leaning his back against a tree, sat huddled together, so exhausted that he felt nothing save a sort of bitter heartache. He even dropped asleep, waking with a shudder, dragged from a dream armchair at the Club into this cold, wet darkness and the blizzard moaning in the trees. He tried to crawl again, but could not, and for some minutes stayed motionless, hugging his body with his arms. 'Well,' he thought vaguely, 'I *have* done it!' His mind was in such lethargy that he could not even pity himself. His matches: could he make a fire? But he was no woodsman, and, though he groped around, could find no fuel that was not soaking wet. He scraped a hole and with what papers he had in his pockets tried to kindle the wet wood. No good! He had only two matches left now, and he remembered his cigar. He took it out, bit the end off, and began with infinite precautions to prepare for lighting it. The first burned, and the cigar drew. He had one match left, in case he dozed and let the thing go out. Looking up through the blackness he could see a star. He fixed his eyes on it, and leaning against the trunk, drew the smoke down into his lungs. With his arms crossed tightly on his breast he smoked very slowly. When it was finished—what? Cold, and the wind in the tree until the morning! Halfway through the cigar, he dozed off, slept a long time, and woke up so cold that he could barely summon vitality enough to strike his last match. By some miracle it burned, and he got his cigar to draw again. This time he smoked it nearly to its end, without mentality, almost without feeling, except the physical sense of bitter cold. Once with a sudden clearing of the brain, he thought faintly: 'Thank God, I sold the trees, and they'll all come down!' The thought drifted away in frozen incoherence, drifted out like his cigar smoke into the sleet; and with a faint grin on his lips he dozed off again.

An under-keeper found him at ten o'clock next morning, blue from cold, under a tall elm tree, within a mile of his bed, one leg stretched out, the other hunched up toward his chest, with its foot dug into the undergrowth for warmth, his head huddled into the collar of his coat, his arms crossed on his breast. They said he must have been dead at least five hours. Along one side snow had drifted against him; but the trunk had saved his back and other side. Above him, the spindly top boughs of that tall tree were covered with green-gold clusters of tiny crinkled elm flowers, against a deep blue sky—gay as a song of perfect praise. The wind had dropped, and after the
cold of the night the birds were singing their clearest in the sunshine.

They did not cut down the elm tree under which they found his body, with the rest of the sold timber, but put a little iron fence round it, and a little tablet on its trunk.

[*1920*]

SANTA LUCIA

RETURNING from the English church at Monte Carlo towards his hotel, old Trevillian paused at a bend in the road to rest his thin calves. Through a mimosa tree the sea was visible, very blue, and Trevillian's eyes rested on it with the filmy brown stare of old age.

Monte Carlo was changed, but that blue, tideless, impassive sea was the same as on his first visit forty-five years ago, and this was pleasant to one conservative by nature. Since then he had married; made money, and inherited more; "raised," as Americans called it, a family—all, except his daughter Agatha, out in the world; had been widowed, and developed old man's cough. He and Agatha now left The Cedars, their country house in Hertfordshire, for the Riviera with the annual regularity of swallows. Usually they stayed at Nice or Cannes; but this year, because a friend of Agatha's was the wife of the English chaplain, they had chosen Monte Carlo.

It was near the end of their stay, and the April sun hot.

Trevillian passed a thin hand down his thin brown hairy face, where bushy eyebrows were still dark, but the pointed beard white; and the effect, under a rather wide-brimmed brown hat, almost too Spanish for an English Bank Director. He was fond of saying that some of the best Cornish families had Spanish blood in their veins, whether Iberian or Armadesque he did not specify. The theory in any case went well with his formalism, growing more formal every year.

Agatha having stayed in with a cold, he had been to service by himself. A poor gathering! The English out here were a rackety lot! Among the congregation to whom he had that morning read the Lessons he had noted, for instance, that old blackguard Telford, who had run off with two men's wives in his time, and was now living with a French woman, they said. What on earth was *he* doing in

church? And that ostracised couple, the Gaddenhams, who had the
villa near Roquebrune? She used his name, but they had never been
married—for Gaddenham's wife was still alive. And, more seriously,
had he observed Mrs. Rolfe, who before the war used to come with
her husband—now in India—to The Cedars, to shoot the coverts in
November. Young Lord Chesherford was hanging about her, they
said. That would end in a scandal to a certainty! Never without
uneasiness did he see that woman, with whom his daughter was on
terms of some intimacy. Grass widows were dangerous, especially in
a place like this. He must give Agatha a hint. Such doubtful people,
he felt, had no business to attend divine service; yet it was difficult to
disapprove of people coming to church, and after all—most of them
did not! A man of the world, however strong a Churchman, could,
of course, rub shoulders with anyone; but it was different when they
came near one's womenfolk, or into the halls of one's formal beliefs.
To encroach like that showed no sense of the fitness of things. He
must certainly speak to Agatha!

The road had lain uphill, and he took breaths of the mimosa-
scented air, carefully regulating them so as not to provoke his cough.
He was about to proceed on his way when a piano organ across
the road burst into tune. The man who turned the handle was the
usual moustachioed Italian, with restive eyes and a game leg; the
animal who drew it the customary little grey donkey; the singer, the
proverbial dark girl with an orange head-kerchief; the song she sang,
the immemorial "Santa Lucia." Her brassy voice blared out the full
metallic a's which seemed to hit the air, as hammers hit the wires
of a czymbal. Trevillian had some music in his soul; he often started
out for the Casino concert, though he generally arrived in the
playing-rooms, not indeed to adventure more than a five-franc piece
or two, for he disapproved of gambling, but because their motley
irregularity titillated his formalism, made him feel like a boy a little
out of school. He could distinguish, however, between several tunes,
and knew this to be neither "God save the King," "Rule, Britannia,"
"Tipperary," nor "Funiculi-Funicula!" Indeed, it had to him a kind
of separate ring, a resonance oddly intimate, as if in some other
life it had been the beating—the hammering rhythm of his heart.

Queer sensation—quite a queer sensation! And he stood, blinking.
Of course, he knew that tune now that he heard the words—Santa
Lucia; but in what previous existence had its miauling awakened
something deep, hot, almost savage within him, sweet and luring
like a strange fruit or the scent of a tropical flower? "San-ta Luci-
i-a! San-ta Luci-i-a!" Lost! And yet so close to the fingers of his
recollection that they itched! The girl stopped singing and came
across to him—a gaudy baggage, with her orange scarf, her beads,
the whites of her eyes, and all those teeth! These Latins, emotional,
vibrant, light-hearted and probably light-fingered—an inferior race!
He felt in his pocket, produced a franc, and moved on slowly.

But at the next bend in the road he halted again. The girl had
recommenced, in gratitude for his franc—"Santa Luci-ia!" What
was it buried in him, under the fallen leaves of years and years?

The pink clusters of a pepper tree drooped from behind a low
garden wall right over him, while he stood there. The air tingled
with its faint savorous perfume, true essence of the South. And again
that conviction of a previous existence, of something sweet, burning,
poignant, caught him in the Adam's apple veiled by his beard. Was it
something he had dreamed? Was that the matter with him now—
while the organ wailed, the girl's song vibrated? Trevillian's stare
lighted on the prickly pears and aloes above the low pink wall. The
savagery of those plants jerked his mind forward almost to the pitch
of—what? A youth passed, smoking a maize-coloured cigarette,
leaving a perfume of Latakia, that tobacco of his own youth, when
he too smoked cigarettes made of its black, strong fragrant threads.
He gazed blankly at the half-obliterated name on the dilapidated
garden gate, and spelled it aloud: "V lla Be u S te. Villa Beau Site!
Beau—— ! By God! I've got it!"

At the unbecoming vigour of his ejaculation, a smile of release,
wrinkling round his eyes, furrowed his thin brown cheeks. He went
up to the gate. What a coincidence! The very——! He stood staring
into a tangled garden, through the fog of forty-five years, resting his
large prayer-book with its big print on the top rail of the old green
gate; then, looking up and down the road like a boy about to steal
cherries, he lifted the latch and passed in.

Nobody lived here now, he should say. The old pink villa, glimpsed some sixty yards away at the end of that little wilderness, was shuttered, and its paint seemed peeling off. Beau Site! That *was* the name! And this the gate he had been wont to use into this lower garden, invisible from the house. And—yes—here was the little fountain, broken and discoloured now, with the same gargoyle face, and water still dripping from its mouth! And here—the old stone seat his cloak had so often covered. Grown over now—all of it; unpruned the lilacs, mimosas, palms making that dry rustling when the breeze crept into them. He opened his prayer-book, laid it on the seat, and carefully sat down—he never sat on unprotected stone. He had passed into another world, screened from any eye by the overgrown shrubs and tangled foliage. And, slowly, while he sat there the frost of nearly half a century thawed.

Yes! Little by little, avidly, yet as it were unwillingly, he remembered—sitting on his prayer-book, out of the sun, under the flowering tangled trees.

He had been twenty-six, just after he went into the family bank— he recollected—such a very sucking partner. A neglected cold had given him the first of those bronchial attacks of which he was now reaping the aftermath. Those were the days when, in the chill of a London winter, he would—dandy-like—wear thin underclothes and no overcoat. Still coughing at Easter, he had taken three weeks off and a ticket to Mentone. A cousin of his was engaged to a Russian girl whose family had a villa there, and he had pitched his tent in a little hotel almost next door. The Russians of *that* day were the Russians of the Turgenev novels, which Agatha had made him read. A simple, tri-lingual family of gentlefolk, the Rostakovs, father, mother, and two daughters—what was it they had called *him*— Philip Philipovitch? Monsieur Rostakov, with his beard, his witty French stories, imperfectly understood by young Trevillian, his zest for food and drink, his thick lips, and, as they said, his easy morals— quite a dog in his way! And Madame, née Princesse Nogárin (a Tartar strain in her, his cousin said); "spirituelle," somewhat worn out by Monsieur Rostakov and her belief in the transmigration of souls. And Varvara, the eldest daughter—the one engaged; only

seventeen, with deep-grey, truthful eyes, a broad grave face, dark
hair, and a candour—by George!—which had almost frightened
him. And the little one, Katrina, blue-eyed, snub-nosed, fair-haired,
with laughing lips, yet very serious too—charming little creature,
whose death from typhoid three years later had given him quite a
shock! Delightful family, seen through the mists of time. And now,
in all the world you couldn't find a Russian family like that—gone,
vanished from the face of the earth! Their estates had been—ah!—
somewhere in South Russia, and a house near Yalta. Cosmopolitan,
yet very Russian, with their samovar, and their "Zakouskas "—a
word he had never learned to spell—and Rostakov's little glasses of
white vodka, and those caviare sandwiches that the girls and he used
to take on their picnics to Gorbio, and Castellar, and Belle Enda,
riding donkeys, and chaperoned by that amiable young German
lady, their governess . . . Germans, in those days—how different they
were! How different the whole of life! The girls riding in their wide
skirts, under parasols, the air unspoiled by the fumes of petrol, the
carriages with their jangling-belled little horses and bright harness;
priests in black, soldiers in bright trousers and yellow shakoes; and
beggars—plenty. The girls would gather wild flowers, and press them
afterwards; and in the evening Varvara would look at him with her
grave eyes and ask him whether he believed in a future life. He had
no beliefs to speak of, then, if he remembered rightly; they had
come with increasing income, family, and business responsibilities.
It had always seemed to hurt her that he thought of sport and
dress, and not of his soul. The Russians, in those days, seemed so
tremendously concerned about the soul—an excellent thing, of
course, but not what one talked of. Still, that first fortnight had been
quite idyllic. He remembered one Sunday afternoon—queer how
such a little thing could stay in the mind—on the beach near Cap
Martin, flicking sand off his boots with his handkerchief, and Varvara
saying: "And then to your face again, Philip Philipovitch?" She was
always saying things which made him feel uncomfortable. And in the
little letter which Katrina wrote him a year later, with blue forget-
me-nots all about the paper, she had reminded him of how he had
blushed! Charming young girls—simple—no such, nowadays! The

dew was off. They had thought Monte Carlo a vulgar place—what would they think of it now, by Jove! Even Rostakov only went there on the quiet—a viveur, that fellow, who would always be living a double life. Trevillian recollected how, under the spell of that idyllic atmosphere, and afraid of Varvara's eyes, he himself had put off from day to day his visit to the celebrated haunt, until one evening when Madame Rostakov had *migraine* and the girls were at a party, he had sauntered to the station and embarked on a Monte Carlo train. How clearly it came back to him—the winding path up through the Gardens, a beautiful still evening, scented and warm, the Casino orchestra playing the Love music from "Faust"—the one opera that he knew well. The darkness, strange with exotic foliage, glimmering with golden lamps—none of this glaring white electric light—had deeply impressed him, who, for all his youthful dandyism, had Puritanism in his blood and training. It was like going up to—well, not precisely heaven! And in his white beard old Trevillian uttered a slight cackle. Anyway, he had entered "the rooms" with a beating heart. He had no money to throw away in those days; by Jove! no! His father had kept him strictly to an allowance of four hundred a year, and his partnership was still in the apprentice stage. He had only some ten or twenty pounds to spare. But to go back to England and have his fellows say: "What? Monte Carlo, and never played?" was not to be thought of.

His first sensation in the "rooms" was disappointing. The decorations were florid, the people foreign, queer, ugly! For some time he stood still listening to the chink of rake against coin, and the nasal twang of the croupiers' voices. Then he had gone up to a table to watch the game, which he had never played. That, at all events, was the same as now; that, and the expression on the gamblers' faces—the sharp, blind, crab-like absorption like no other human expression. And what a lot of old women! A nervous excitement had crept into his brain while he stood there, an itch into his fingers. But he was shy. All these people played with such deadly calm, seemed so utterly familiar with it all. At last he had reached over the shoulder of a dark-haired woman sitting in front of him, put down a five-franc piece and called out the word: "*Vingt.*" A rake shovelled it forward on to the number with an indifferent click. The ball rolled: "*Quatorze, Rouge pair et manque.*" His five-franc piece was raked away; but he—Philip Trevillian—had gambled at Monte Carlo, and at once he had seemed to see Varvara's eyes with something of amusement in their candour, and to hear her voice: "But to gamble! How silly, Philip Philipovitch!" Then the man sitting to his, left got up, and he had slipped down into the empty chair. Once seated he knew that he must play. So he pushed another five-franc piece on to black, and received its counterpart. Now he was quits; and continuing that simple stake with varying success he began taking in the faces of his neighbours. On his left he had an old Englishman in evening dress, ruddy, with chubby lips, who played in gold pieces and seemed winning rather heavily; opposite, in a fabulous shawl, a bird-like old woman, with a hook nose, and a man who looked like a Greek bandit in a frock coat. To his right was the dark-haired woman over whose shoulder he had leaned. An agreeable perfume, as of jasmine blossoms, floated from her. She had some tablets, and six or seven gold pieces before her, but seemed to have stopped playing. Out of the tail of his eye Trevillian scrutinised her profile. She was by far the most attractive woman he had seen in here. And he felt, suddenly, uninterested in the fate of his five-franc pieces. Under the thin dark brows a little drawn down, he could see that her eyes were dark and velvety. Her face was rather pointed, delicate, faintly powdered in the foreign fashion. She wore a low dress, but with a black lace scarf thrown over her gleaming shoulders, and something that glimmered in her dark hair. She was not English; but what he could not tell. He won twice running on black, left his stake untouched, and was conscious that she pushed one of her own gold pieces on to the black. Again black won; again he left his stake, and she hers. To be linked with her by that following of his luck was agreeable to young Trevillian. The devil might care—he would leave his winnings down! Again, and again, till he had won eight times on black, he left his stake, and his neighbour followed suit. A pile of gold was mounting in front of each of them. The eyes of the hawk-like old woman opposite, like those of a crustacean in some book of Natural History, seemed pushed out from her face; a little hard smile on her thin lips seemed saying: "Wait, it will all go back!" The jasmine perfume from his neighbour grew stronger, as though disengaged by increasing emotion; he could see her white neck heave under its black lace. She reached her hand out as though to gather in her winnings. In bravado Trevillian sat unmoving. Her eyes slid round to his, she withdrew her hand. The little ball rolled. Black! He heard her sigh of relief; she touched his arm. "*Retirez!*" she whispered, "*retirez*, Monsieur!" and, sweeping in her winnings, she got up. Trevillian hesitated just a moment, then with the thought: 'If I stay, I lose sight of her!' he too reached out, and, gathering in his pile, left the table. Starting with a five-franc piece, in nine successful coups he had won just over a hundred pounds. His neighbour, who had started with a louis, in seven coups—he calculated rapidly—must have won the same. "*Seize, Rouge pair et manque!*" Just in time! Elated, Trevillian turned away. There was the graceful figure of his dark neighbour, threading the throng; and without deliberate intention, yet longing not to lose sight of her, he followed. A check in her progress brought him so close, however, that he was at infinite pains to seem unconscious. She turned and saw him. "Ah! *Merci, Monsieur!* I tank you moch." "It's for me to thank you!" he stammered. The dark lady smiled. "I have the instinct," she said in her broken English, "for others—not for myself. I am unlucky. It is the first time you play, Sare? I tought so. Do not play again. Give me that promise; it will make me 'appy."

Her eyes were looking into his. Never in his life had he seen anything so fascinating as her face with its slightly teasing smile; her figure in the lacy black dress swinging out Spanish fashion from the hips, and the scarf flung about her shoulders. He had made the speech, then, which afterwards seemed to him so foreign.

"Charmed to promise anything that will make you happy, Madame."

She clasped her hands like a pleased child.

"That is a bargain; now I have repaid you."

"May I find your carriage?"

"I am walkin', Monsieur."

With desperate courage, he had murmured:

"Then may I escort you?"

"But certainly."

Sitting on his prayer-book, Trevillian burrowed into the past. What had he felt, thought, fancied, in those moments while she had gone to get her cloak? Who and what was she? Into what whirlpool drawing him? How nearly he had bolted—back to the idyllic, to Varvara's searching candour, and Katrina's laughing innocence, before she was there beside him, lace veiling her hair, face, eyes, like an Eastern woman, and her fingers had slipped under his sleeve . . . What a walk! What sense of stepping into the unknown; strange intimacy, and perfect ignorance! Perhaps every man had some such moment in his life—of pure romance; of adventuring at all and any cost! He had restrained the impulse to press that slender hand closely to his side, had struggled to preserve the perfect delicacy worthy of the touching confidence of so beautiful a lady. Italian, Spanish, Polish, Bohemian? Married, widowed? She told him nothing—he asked no questions. Instinct or shyness kept him dumb, but with a whirling brain. And the night above them had seemed the starriest ever seen, the sweetest scented, the most abandoned by all except himself and her. They had come to the gate of this very garden; and, opening it, she had said:

"Here is my home. You have been perfect for me, Monsieur."

Her lightly resting fingers were withdrawn. Trevillian remembered—with a sort of wonder—how he had kissed those fingers.

"I am always at your service, Madame."

Her lips had parted; her eyes, had an arch sweetness he had never seen before or since in woman.

"Every night I play. *Au revoir!*"

He had listened to her footsteps on the path—watched lights go up in the house which looked so empty now behind him, watched them put out again; and, retracing his steps, had learned by heart their walk from the Casino, till he was sure he could not miss his way to that garden gate by day or night . . . A fluster of breeze came into the jungle where he sat, and released the dry rustle of the palm tree leaves. "*On fait des folies!*" as the French put it. Loose lot—the

French! Queer, what young men would go through when they were
"making madnesses." And, plucking a bit of lilac, old Trevillian put
it to his nose, as though seeking explanation for the madnesses of
youth. What had he been like then? Thin as a lath, sunburnt—he
used to pride himself on being sunburnt—a little black moustache;
a dandy about clothes! The memory of his youthful looks warmed
him, sitting there, chilly from old age . . .

   "*On fait des folies!*" All next day he had been restless, uneasy at the
Villa Rostakov under the question in Varvara's eyes—and Lord knew
what excuse he had made for not going there that evening! Ah! And
what of his solemn resolutions to find out all about his dark lady,
not to run his head into some foreign noose, not to compromise
her or himself? They had all gone out of his head the moment he
set eyes on her again, and he had never learned anything but her
name, Iñez, in all those three weeks; nor told anything of himself—
as if both had felt the knowledge would destroy romance. When
had he known himself of interest to her—the second night—the
third? The look in her eyes; the pressure of her arm against his own!
On this very seat, with his cloak spread to guard her from the chill,
he had whispered his turbulent avowals! Not free! No such woman
could be free. What did it matter? Disinheritance—Ostracism—
Exile! All such considerations had burned like straws in the fire
he had felt, sitting by her in the darkness, his arm about her, her
shoulder pressed to his. With mournful mockery she had gazed at
him, kissed his forehead, slipped away up the dark garden. God!
What a night after that! Wandering, up and down, along by the
sea—devoured! Funny to look back on—deuced funny! A woman's
face to have such power! And with a little shock he remembered
that never in all the few weeks of that mad business had he seen
her face by daylight! Of course, he had left Mentone at once—no
offering his madness up to the candid eyes of those two girls, to
the cynical stare of that old *viveur* Rostakov! But no going home,
though his leave was up; he was his own master yet awhile, thanks
to his winnings. And then—the deluge! Literally—a night when
the rain came down in torrents, drenching him through cape and
clothes while he stood waiting for her. It was after that drenching

night which had kept them apart that she had returned his passion
. . . A wild young devil! the madness of those nights, beneath
these trees by the old fountain! How he used to sit waiting on
this bench in the darkness with heart fluttering, trembling, aching
with expectancy! . . . Gad! how he had ached and fluttered on that
seat! What fools young men could be! And yet, in all his life had
there been weeks so wildly sweet as those? Weeks the madness of
which could stir in him still this strange youthful warmth. Rubbing
his veined thin hands together, he held them out into a streak of
sunlight and closed his eyes . . . There, coming through the gate
into the deeper shadow, dark in her black dress—always black—
the gleam of her neck when she bent and pressed his head to it!
Through the rustling palm leaves the extinct murmuring of their
two voices, the beating of their two hearts . . . Madness indeed!
His back gave a little crick. He had been very free from lumbago
lately! Confound it—a premonitory twinge! Close to his feet, a
lizard rustled out into the patch of sunlight, motionless but for
tongue and eyes, looked at him with head to one side—queer quick
dried-looking little object! . . . And then, the end! What a Jezebel
of cruelty he had thought her! Now he could see its wisdom and
its mercy. By George! She had blown their wild weeks out like
a candle flame! Vanished! Vanished into the unknown as she had
come from the unknown; left him to go, haggard
and burnt-up, back to England and Bank routine, to the social and
moral solidity of a pillar of society . . .

Like that lizard whisking its tail and vanishing beneath the dead
dry leaves, so she had vanished—as if into the earth. Could she
ever have felt for him as he for her? Did women ever know such
consuming fires? Trevillian shrugged his thin shoulders. She had
seemed to; but—how tell? Queer cattle—women!

Two nights he had sat here—waiting—sick with anxiety and
longing. A third day he had watched outside the villa, closed,
shuttered, abandoned—not a sound from it, not a living thing, but
one white and yellow cat. He pitied himself even now, thinking of
that last vigil. For three days more he had hung around, haunting
Casino, garden, villa No sign—no sign!

Trevillian rose; his back had given him another twinge. He examined the seat and his open prayer-book. Had he overlapped it on to damp stone? He frowned, smoothing superstitiously the pages a little creased and over-flattened by his weight. Closing the book he went towards the gate. Had those passionate hours been the best or the worst of his life? He did not know.

He moved out into the hot sunshine and up the road. Round the corner he came suddenly abreast of the old villa. 'It was here I stood,' he thought: 'Just here.' What was that caterwauling? Ah! The girl and the organ—there they were again! What! Why, of course! That long-ago morning a barrel organ had come while he stood there in despair. He could see it still, grinding away, with a monkey on it, and a woman singing that same silly tune. With a dry dusty feeling he turned and walked on. What had he been thinking of before? Oh! Ah! The Rolfe woman, and that young fool Chesherford. Yes, he would certainly warn Agatha; certainly warn her! They were a loose lot out here!

[*1921*]

THE MOTHER STONE

IT was after dinner, and five elderly Englishmen were discussing the causes of the war.

"Well," said Travers, a big, fresh-coloured grey-beard, with little twinkling eyes and very slow speech, "you gentlemen know more about it than I do, but I bet you I can lay my finger on the cause of the war at any minute."

There was an instant clamour of jeering. But a man called Askew, who knew Travers well, laughed and said: "Come, let's have it!" Travers turned those twinkling little eyes of his slowly round the circle, and with heavy, hesitating modesty began:

"Well, Mr. Askew, in was in '67 or '68 that this happened to a great big fellow of my acquaintance named Ray—one of those fellers, you know, that are always on the lookout to make their fortunes and never do. This Ray was coming back south one day after a huntin' trip he'd been in what's now called Bechuanaland, and he was in a pretty bad way when he walked one evenin' into the camp of one of those wanderin' Boers. That class of Boer has disappeared now. They had no farms of their own, but just moved on with their stock and their boys; and when they came to good pasture they'd outspan and stay there till they'd cleared it out—and then trek on again. Well, this old Boer told Ray to come right in and take a meal; and Heaven knows what it was made of, for those old Boers they'd eat the devil himself without onion sauce, and relish him. After the meal the old Boer and Ray sat smokin' and yarnin' in the door of the tent, because in those days these wanderin' Boers used tents. Right close by in the front the children were playin' in the dust, a game like marbles with three or four round stones, and they'd pitch 'em up to another stone they called the Moer-Klip, or Mother Stone—one, two, and pick up;

two, three, and pick up—you know the game of marbles. Well, the sun was settin', and presently Ray noticed this Moer-Klip that they were pitchin' 'em up to shinin'; and he looked, at it, and he said to the old Boer: 'What's that stone the children are playin' with?' And the old Boer looked at him and looked at the stone, and said: 'It's just a stone,' and went on smokin'.

"Well, Ray went down on his knees and picked up the stone and weighed it in his hand. About the size of a hazel-nut it was and looked—well, it looked like a piece of alum; but the more he looked at it the more he thought: 'By Jove, I believe it's a diamond!'

"So he said to the old Boer: 'Where did the children get this stone?' And the old Boer said: 'Oh! the shepherd picked it up somewhere.' And Ray said: 'Where did he pick it up?' And the old Boer waved his hand, and said : 'Over the kopje, there, beyond the river. How should I know, brother?—a stone is a stone!' So Ray said: 'You let me take this stone away with me.' And the old Boer went on smokin', and he said: 'One stone's the same as another. Take it, brother.' And Ray said: 'If it's what I think, I'll give you half the price I get for it.'

"The old Boer smiled and said: 'That's all right, brother; take it,' take it!'

"The next morning Ray left this old Boer, and, when he was going, he said to him: 'Well,' he said, 'I believe this is a valuable stone!' And the old Boer smiled because he knew one stone was the same as another.

"The first place Ray came to was C——, and he went to the hotel; and in the evenin' he began talkin' about the stone, and they all laughed at him, because in those days nobody had heard of diamonds in South Africa. So presently he lost his temper and pulled out the stone and showed it round; but nobody thought it was a diamond, and they all laughed at him the more. Then one of the fellers said: 'If it's a diamond it ought to cut glass.'

"Ray took the stone, and, by Jove! he cut his name on the window, and there it is—I've seen it—on the bar window of that hotel. Well, next day, you bet, he travelled straight back to where the old Boer told him the shepherd had picked up the stone, and he went to a native chief called Jointje, and said to him: 'Jointje,' he said, 'I go a journey.

While I go, you go about and send all your "boys" about, and look for all the stones that shine like this one; and when I come back, if you find me plenty, I give you gun.' And Jointje said: 'That all right, boss.'

"And Ray went down to Cape Town and took the stone to a jeweller, and the jeweller told him it was a diamond of about 30 or 40 carats, and gave him five hundred pound for it. So he bought a waggon and a span of oxen to give to the old Boer, and went back to Jointje. The niggers had collected skinfuls of stones of all kinds, and out of all the skinfuls Ray found three or four diamonds. So he went to work and got another feller to back him, and between them they made the Government move. The rush began, and they found that place near Kimberley; and after that they found De Beers, and after that Kimberley itself."

Travers stopped and looked around him.

"Ray made his fortune, I suppose?"

"No, Mr. Askew; the unfortunate feller made next to nothin'. He was one of those fellers that never do any good for themselves."

"But what has all this to do with the war?"

Again Travers looked round, and more slowly than ever said:

"Without that game of marbles, would there have been a Moer-Klip—without the Moer-Klip, would there have been a Kimberley—without Kimberley, would there have been a Rhodes—without a Rhodes would there have been a Raid—without a Raid, would the Boers have started armin'—if the Boers hadn't armed, would there have been a Transvaal War? And if there hadn't been the Transvaal War, would there have been the incident of those two German ships we held up, and all the general feelin' in Germany that gave the Kaiser the chance to start his Navy programme in 1900? And if the Germans hadn't built their Navy, would their heads have swelled till they challenged the world, and should we have had this war?"

He slowly drew a hand from his pocket and put it on the table. On the little finger was blazing an enormous diamond.

"My father," he said, "bought it of the jeweller."

The Mother Stone glittered and glowed, and the five Englishmen fixed their eyes on it in silence. Some of them had been in the Boer War, and three of them had sons in this. At last one of them said:

"Well, that's seeing God in a dew-drop with a vengeance. What about the old Boer?"

"Well," he said, "Ray told me the old feller just looked at him as if he thought he'd done a damn silly thing to give him a waggon; and he nodded his old head and said, laughin' in his beard: 'Wish you good luck, brother, with your stone.' You couldn't humbug that old Boer; he, knew one stone was the same as another."

[1914]

PEACE MEETING

COLIN Wilderton, coming from the west on his way to the Peace Meeting, fell in with John Rudstock, coming from the north, and they walked on together. After they had commented on the news from Russia and the inflation of money, Rudstock said abruptly:

"We shall have a queer meeting, I expect."

"God knows!" answered Wilderton.

And both smiled, conscious that they were uneasy, but predetermined not to show it under any circumstances. Their smiles were different, for Rudstock was a black-browed man with dark beard and strong, thick figure, and Wilderton a very light-built, grey-haired man, with kindly eyes and no health. He had supported the war an immense time, and had only recently changed his attitude. In common with all men of warm feelings, he had at first been profoundly moved by the violation of Belgium. The horrors of the German advance through that little country and through France, to which he was temperamentally attached, had stirred in him a vigorous detestation, freely expressed in many ways. Extermination, he had felt all those early months, was hardly good enough for brutes who could commit such crimes against humanity and justice; and his sense of the need for signal defeat of a noxious force riding rough-shod over the hard-won decency of human life had survived well into the third year of the war. He hardly knew himself when his feeling had begun—not precisely to change, but to run, as it were, in a different channel. A man of generous instincts, artistic tastes and unsteady nerves too thinly coated with that God-given assurance which alone fits a man for knowing what is good for the world, he had become gradually haunted by the thought that he was not laying down his own life, but only the lives of his own and other people's sons. And the consideration that he was laying them down for the benefit of their own future had lost its grip on him. At moments he was still able to see that the war he had so long supported had not yet attained sufficient defeat of the Prussian military machine to guarantee that future; but his pity and distress for all these young lives cut down without a chance to flower had grown till he had become, as it were, a gambler. What good—he would think—to secure the future of the young in a Europe which would soon have no young? Every country was suffering hideously—the criminal country not least, thank God! Suppose the war were to go for another year, two, three years, and then stop from sheer exhaustion of both sides, while all the time these boys were being killed and maimed, for nothing more, perhaps, than could be obtained to-day. What then? True the Government promised victory, but they never promised it within a year. Governments did not die; what if they were to go on promising it a year hence, till everybody else was dead! Did history ever show that victory in the present could guarantee the future? Besides, even if not so openly defeated as was desirable, this damnable Prussianism had got such a knock that it could never again do what it had in the past. These last, however, were but side reflections, toning down for him the fact that his nerves could no longer stand this vicarious butchery of youth. And so he had gradually become that "traitor to his country, a weak-kneed, peace-by-negotiation man." Physically his knees really were weak, and he used to smile a wry smile when he read the expression.

John Rudstock, of vigorous physique, had opposed the war, on principle, from the start, not because, any more than Wilderton, he approved of Prussianism, but because, as an essentially combative personality, he opposed everything supported by a majority; the greater the majority, the more bitterly he opposed it; and no one would have been more astonished than he at hearing that this was his principle. He preferred to put it that he did not believe in opposing force by force. In peace-time he was a "stalwart," in war-time a "renegade."

The street leading to the chapel which had been engaged seemed quiet enough. Designed to make an impression on public opinion, every care had been taken that the meeting should not attract the public eye. God's protection had been enlisted, but two policemen also stood at the entrance, and half a dozen others were suspiciously near by. A thin trickle of persons, mostly women, were passing through the door. Colin Wilderton, making his way up the aisle to the platform, wrinkled his nose, thinking: 'Stuffy in here.' It had always been his misfortune to love his neighbours individually, but to dislike them in a bunch. On the platform some fifteen men and women were already gathered. He seated himself modestly in the back row, while John Rudstock, less retiring, took his place at the chairman's right hand. The speakers began with a precipitancy hardly usual at a public meeting. Wilderton listened, and thought: 'Dreadfully *cliché*; why can't someone say straight out that boys enough have been killed?' He had become conscious, too, of a muttering noise, as of the tide coming in on a heavy wind; it broke suddenly into component parts—human voices clamouring outside. He heard blows raining on the door, saw sticks smashing in the windows. The audience had risen to its feet, some rushing to defend the doors, others standing irresolute. John Rudstock was holding up the chair he had been sitting on. Wilderton had just time to think: 'I thought so,' when a knot of young men in khaki burst into the chapel, followed by a crowd. He knew he was not much good in a scrimmage, but he placed himself at once in front of the nearest woman. At that moment, however, some soldiers, pouring through a side-door, invaded the platform from behind, and threw him down the steps. He arrived at the bottom with a bump, and was unable to get up because of the crowd around him. Someone fell over him; it was Rudstock, swearing horribly. He still had the chair in his hand, for it hit Wilderton a nasty blow. The latter saw his friend recover his feet and swing the weapon, and with each swing down went some friend or foe, until he had cleared quite a space round him. Wilderton, still weak and dizzy from his fall, sat watching this Homeric battle. Chairs, books, stools, sticks were flying at Rudstock, who parried them, or diverted their course so that they carried on and hit Wilderton, or crashed against the platform. He heard Rudstock roar like a lion and saw him advance, swinging his chair;

down went two young men in khaki, down went a third in mufti; a very tall young soldier, also armed with a chair, dashed forward, and the two fought in single combat. Wilderton had got on his feet by now, and, adjusting his eyeglass, for he could see little without, he caught up a hymn-book, and, flinging it at the crowd with all his force, shouted: "Hoobloodyray!" and followed with his fists clenched. One of them encountered what must have been the jaw of an Australian, it was so hard against his hand; he received a vicious punch in the ribs and was again seated on the ground. He could still hear his friend roaring, and the crash of chairs meeting in mid-air. Something fell heavily on him. It was Rudstock—he was insensible. There was a momentary lull, and peering up as best he could from underneath the body, Wilderton saw that the platform had been cleared of all its original inhabitants, and was occupied mainly by youths in navy blue and khaki. A voice called out:

"Order! Silence!"

Rubbing Rudstock's temples with brandy from a flask which he had had the foresight to slip into his pocket, he listened as best he could, with the feet of the crowd jostling his anatomy.

"Here we are, boys," the voice was saying, "and here we'll always be when these treacherous blighters try their games on. No peace, no peace at any price! We've got to show them that we won't have it. Leave the women alone—though they ought to be ashamed of themselves; but for the men—the skunks—shooting's too good for them. Let them keep off the course or we'll make them. We've broken up this meeting, and we'll break up every meeting that tries to talk of peace. Three cheers for the old flag!"

During the cheers which followed Wilderton was discovering signs of returning consciousness in his friend; for Rudstock had begun to breathe heavily. Pouring some brandy into his mouth, he propped him up as best he could against a wooden structure, which he suddenly perceived to be the chapel's modest pulpit. A thought came to his dazed brain. If he could get up into that, as if he had dropped from Heaven, they might almost listen to him. He disengaged his legs from under Rudstock and began crawling up the steps on hands and knees. Once in the pulpit he sat on the floor below the level of visibility, getting his breath and listening to the cheers. Then, smoothing his hair, he rose, and waited for the cheers to stop. He had calculated rightly. His sudden appearance, his grey hair, eyeglass and smile deceived them for a moment. There was a hush.

"Boys!" he said, "listen to me a second. I want to ask you something. What on earth do you think we came here for? Simply and solely because we can't bear to go on seeing you killed day after day, month after month, year after year. That's all, and it's Christ's truth. Amen!"

A strange gasp and mutter greeted this little speech; then a dull voice called out:

"Pro-German!"

Wilderton flung up his hand.

"The Germans to hell!" he said simply.

The dull voice repeated:

"Pro-German!" And the speaker on the platform called out: "Come out of that! When we want you to beg us off we'll let you know."

Wilderton spun round to him.

"You're all wonderful!" he began, but a hymn-book hit him fearfully on the forehead, and he sank down into the bottom of the pulpit. This last blow, coming on the top of so many others, had deprived him of intelligent consciousness; he was but vaguely aware of more speeches, cheers and tramplings, then of a long hush, and presently found himself walking out of the chapel door between Rudstock and a policeman. It was not the door by which they had entered, and led to an empty courtyard.

"Can you walk?" said the policeman.

Wilderton nodded.

"Then walk off!" said the policeman, and withdrew again into the house of God.

The two walked, holding each other's arms, a little unsteadily at first. Rudstock had a black eye and a cut on his ear, the blood from which had stained his collar and matted his beard. Wilderton's coat was torn, his forehead bruised, his cheek swollen, and he had a pain in his back which prevented him from walking very upright. They did not speak, but in an archway did what they could, with pins and handkerchiefs and by turning up Rudstock's coat collar, to regain something of respectability. When they were once more under way Rudstock said coldly:

"I heard you. You should have spoken for yourself. I came, as you know, because I don't believe in opposing force by force. At the next meeting we hold I shall make that plainer."

Wilderton murmured:

"Yes, yes; I saw you—I'm sure you will. I apologise; I was carried away."

Rudstock went on in a deep voice:

"As for those young devils, they may die to a man if they like! Take my advice and let them alone."

Wilderton smiled on the side which was not swollen.

"Yes," he said. sadly, "it does seem difficult to persuade them to go' on living. Ah, well!"

"Ah, well" he said again, five minutes later, "they're wonderful— Poor young beggars! I'm very unhappy, Rudstock!"

"I'm not," said Rudstock, "I've enjoyed it in a way! Good-night!"

They shook hands, screwing up their mouths with pain, for their fists were badly bruised, and parted, Rudstock going to the north, Wilderton to the west.

[*1917*]

A STRANGE THING

NOT very long ago, during a sojourn in a part of the West Country never yet visited by me, I went out one fine but rather cold March morning for a long ramble. I was in one of those disillusioned moods which come to writers bankrupt of ideas, bankrupt of confidence, a prey to that recurrent despair, the struggle with which makes the profession of the pen—as a friend once said to me—"a manly one." 'Yes,' I was thinking, for all that the air was so brisk, and the sun so bright, 'nothing comes to me nowadays, no flashes of light, none of those suddenly shaped visions that bring cheer and warmth to a poor devil's heart, and set his brain and pen to driving on. A bad business!' And my eyes, wandering over the dip and rise, the woods, the moor, the rocks of that fine countryside, took in the loveliness thereof with the profound discontent of one who, seeing beauty, feels that he cannot render it. The high lane- banks had just been pollarded; one could see right down over the fields and gorse and bare woods tinged with that rosy brown of beech and birch twigs, and the dusty saffron of the larches. And suddenly my glance was arrested by something vivid, a sort of black and white excitement in the air. 'Aha!' I thought, 'a magpie. Two! Good! Is it an omen?' The birds had risen at the bottom of a field, their twining, fluttering voyage—most decorative of all bird flights—was soon lost in the wood beyond, but something it had left behind—in my heart; I felt more hopeful, less inclined to think about the failure of my spirit, better able to give myself up to this new country I was passing through. Over the next rise in the very winding lane I heard the sound of brisk church bells, and not three hundred yards beyond came to a village green, where knots of men dressed in the dark clothes, light ties and bowler hats of village festivity, and of women smartened up beyond belief, were gathered, chattering, round the yard of an old, grey, square-towered church.

'What's going on?' I thought. 'It's not Sunday, not the birthday of a potentate, and surely they don't keep saint days in this manner. It must be a wedding. Yes—there's a favour! Let's go in and see!' And, passing the expectant groups, I entered the church and made my way up the aisle. There was already a fair sprinkling of folk all turned round towards the door, and the usual licensed buzz and whisper of a wedding congregation. The church, as seems usual in remote parishes, had been built all those centuries ago to hold a population in accordance with the expectations of its tenet, "Be fruitful and multiply." But the whole population could have been seated in a quarter of its space. It was lofty and unwarmed save by excitement and the smell of bear's-grease. There was certainly more animation than I had ever seen or savoured in a truly rural district.

The bells, which had been ringing with a sort of languid joviality, fell now into the hurried crashing which marks the approach of a bride, and the people I had passed outside came thronging in. I perceived a young man—little more than a boy—who by his semi-detachment, the fumbling of his gloved hands, and the sheepishness of the smile on his good-looking, open face, was obviously the bridegroom. I liked the looks of him—a cut above the usual village bumpkin—something free and kind about his face. But no one was paying him the least attention. It was for the bride they were waiting; and I myself began to be excited. What would this young thing be like? Just the ordinary village maiden with tight cheeks and dress, coarse veil, high colour, and eyes like a rabbit's; or something—something like that little Welsh girl on the hills whom I once passed and whose peer I have never since seen? Bending forward, I accosted an apple-faced woman in the next pew. "Can you tell me who the bride is?"

Regarding me with the grey, round, defensive glance that one bestows on strangers, she replied:

"Aw, don't 'ee know? 'Tes Gwenny Mara—prettiest, brightest maid in these parts." And jerking her thumb towards the neglected bridegroom, she added: "He's a lucky young chap. She'm a sunny maid, for sure, and a gude maid, tu."

Somehow the description did not reassure me, and I prepared for the worst.

A bubble, a stir, a rustle!

Like everyone else, I turned frankly round. She was coming up the aisle on the arm of a hard-faced, rather gipsy-looking man dressed in a farmer's very best.

I can only tell you that to see her coming down the centre of that grey church amongst all those dark-clothed people was like watching the dance of a sunbeam. Never had I seen a face so happy, sweet, and radiant. Smiling, eager, just lost enough to her surroundings, her hair unconquerably golden through the coarse veil; her dancing eyes clear and dark as a great pool—she was the prettiest sight. One could only think of a young apple tree with the spring sun on its blossom. She had that kind of infectious brightness which comes from very simple goodness. It was quite a relief to have taken a fancy to the young man's face and to feel that she was passing into good hands.

The only flowers in the church were early daffodils, but those first children of the sun were somehow extraordinarily appropriate to the wedding of this girl. When she came out she was pelted with them, and with that miserable confetti, without which not even the simplest souls can pass to bliss, it seems. There are things in life which make one feel good—sunshine, most music, all flowers, many children, some animals, clouds, mountains, bird-songs, blue sky, dancing, and here and there a young girl's face. And I had the feeling that all of us there felt good for the mere seeing of her.

When she had driven away, I found myself beside a lame old man with whiskers and delightful eyes, who continued to smile after the carriage had quite vanished. Noticing, perhaps, that I, too, was smiling, he said : "'Tes a funny thing, tu, when a maid like that gets married—makes you go all of a tremble— so it du." And to my nod he added: "Brave bit o' sunshine—we'll miss her hereabout; not a doubt of it. We ain't got another one like that."

"Was that her father?" I asked, for the want of something to say. With a sharpish look at my face he shook his head.

"No, she ain't got no parents, Mr. Mara bein' her uncle, as you may say. No, she ain't got no parents," he repeated, and there was something ill at ease, yet juicy, about his voice, as though he knew things that he would not tell.

Since there was nothing more to wait for, I went up to the little inn and ordered bread and cheese. The male congregation was wetting its whistle noisily within, but, as a stranger, I had the verandah to myself, and, finishing my simple lunch in the March sunlight, I paid and started on. Taking at random one of the three lanes which debouched from the bottom of the green, I meandered on between high banks, happy in the consciousness of not knowing at all where it would lead me—that essential of a country ramble. Except one cottage in a bottom and one farm on a rise, I passed nothing, nobody. The spring was late in these parts, the buds had hardly formed as yet on any trees, and now and then between the bursts of sunlight a few fine specks of snow would come drifting past me on the wind. Close to a group of pines at a high corner the lane dipped sharply down to a long farmhouse standing back in its yard, where three carts were drawn up and an empty waggonette with its shafts in the air. And suddenly, by some broken daffodils on the seats and confetti on the ground, I perceived that I had stumbled on the bride's home, where the wedding feast was, no doubt, in progress.

Gratifying but by no means satisfying my curiosity by gazing at the lichened stone and thatch of the old house, at the pigeons, pigs, and hens at large between it and the barns, I passed on down the lane, which turned up steeply to the right beside a little stream. To my left was a long larch wood, to my right rough fields with many trees. The lane finished at a gate below the steep moorside crowned by a rocky tor. I stood there leaning on the top bar, debating whether I should ascend or no. The bracken had, most of it, been cut in the autumn, and not a hundred yards away the furze was being swaled; the little blood-red flames and the blue smoke, the yellow blossoms of the gorse, the sunlight, and some flecks of drifting snow were mingled in an amazing tangle of colour.

I had made up my mind to ascend the tor and was pushing through the gate when suddenly I saw a woman sitting on a stone under the wall bordering the larch wood. She was holding her head in her hands, rocking her body to and fro, and her eyes were evidently shut, for she had not noticed me. She wore a blue serge dress, her hat reposed beside her, and her dark hair was straggling about her face. That face, all blowsy and flushed, was at once wild and stupefied. A face which has been beautiful, coarsened and swollen by life and strong emotion, is a pitiful enough sight. Her dress, hat, and the way her hair had been done were redolent of the town, and of that unnameable something which clings to women whose business it is to attract men. And yet there was a gipsyish look about her, as though she had not always been of the town.

The sight of a woman's unrestrained distress in the very heart of untouched nature is so rare that one must be peculiar to remain unmoved. And there I stood, not knowing what on earth to do. She went on rocking herself to and fro, her stays creaking, and a faint moaning sound coming from her lips; and suddenly she drooped over her lap, her hands fallen to her sides, as though she had gone into a kind of coma. How go on and leave her thus? Yet how intrude on what did not seem to me mere physical suffering?

In that quandary I stood and watched. This corner was quite sheltered from the wind, the sun almost hot, and the breath of the swaling reached one in the momentary calms. For three full minutes she had not moved a finger, till, beginning to think she had really fainted, I went up to her. From her drooped body came a scent of heat and of stale violet powder, and I could see, though the east wind had outraddled them, traces of rouge on her cheeks; their surface had a sort of swollen defiance, but underneath, as it were, a wasted look. Her breathing sounded faint and broken.

Mustering courage, I touched her on the arm. She raised her head and looked up. Her eyes were the best things she had left; they must have once been very beautiful. Blood-shot now from the wind, their wild, stupefied look passed after a moment into the peculiar, half-bold, half-furtive stare of women of a certain sort. She did not speak, and in my embarrassment I drew out the flask of port I always take with me on my rambles, and stammered:

"I beg your pardon—are you feeling faint? Would you care——?" And, unscrewing the top, I held out the flask. She stared at it a moment blankly, then taking it, said:

"That's kind of you. I feel to want it, tu." And, putting it to her lips, she drank, tilting back her head. Perhaps it was the tell-tale softness of her u's, perhaps the naturally strong lines of her figure thus bent back, but somehow the plumage of the town bird seemed to drop off her suddenly.

She handed back the flask, as empty as it had ever been, and said, with a hard smile:

"I daresay you thought me funny sittin' 'ere like that."

"I thought you were ill."

She laughed without the faintest mirth, and muttered:

"I did go on, didn't I?" Then, almost fiercely, added: "I got some reason, too. Seein' the old place again after all these years." Her dark eyes, which the wine seemed to have cleared and boldened, swept me up and down, taking me in, making sure, perhaps, whether or no she had ever seen me, and what sort of a brute I might be. Then she said: "I was born here. Are you from these parts?" I shook my head. "No, from the other side of the county."

She laughed. Then, after a moment's silence, said abruptly:

"I been to a weddin'—first I've seen since I was a girl."

Some instinct kept me silent.

"My own daughter's weddin', but nobody didn't know me—not likely."

I had dropped down under the shelter of the wall on to a stone opposite, and at those words looked at her with interest indeed. She—this coarsened, wasted, suspiciously-scented woman of the town—the mother of that sweet, sunny child I had just seen married? And again instinctively silent about my own presence at the wedding, I murmured:

"I thought I saw some confetti in that farmyard as I came up the lane."

She laughed again.

"Confetti—that's the little pink and white and blue things—plenty o' that,"; and she added fiercely: "My own brother didn' know me—let alone my girl. How should she?—I haven't seen her since she was a baby—she was a laughin' little thing;" and she gazed past me with that look in the eyes as of people who are staring back into the bygone. "I guess we was laughin' when we got her. 'Twas just here—summer-time. I 'ad the moon in my blood that night, right enough." Then, turning her eyes on my face, she added: "That's what a girl *will* 'ave, you know, once in a while, and like as not it'll du for her. Only thirty-five now, I am, an' pretty nigh the end o' my tether. What can you expect?—I'm a gay woman. Did for me right enough. Her father's dead, tu."

"Do you mean," I said, "because of your child?"

She nodded. "I suppose you can say that. They made me bring an order against him. He wouldn't pay up, so he went and enlisted, an' in tu years 'e was dead in the Boer War—so it killed him right enough. But there she is, a sweet sprig if ever there was one. That's a strange thing, isn't it?" And she stared straight before her in a sudden silence. Nor could I find anything to say, slowly taking in the strangeness of this thing. That girl, so like a sunbeam, of whom the people talked as though she were a blessing in their lives—her coming into life to have been the ruin of the two who gave her being!

The woman went on dully: "Funny how I knew she was goin' to be married—'twas a farmer told me—comes to me regular when he goes to Exeter market. I always knew he came from near my old home. 'There's a weddin' on Tuesday,' 'e says, 'I'd like to be the bridegroom at. Prettiest, sunniest maid you ever saw;' an' he told me where she come from, so I knew. He found me a bit funny that afternoon. But he don't know who I am, though he used to go to school with me; I'd never tell, not for worlds." She shook her head vehemently. "I don't know why I told you; I'm not meself to-day, and that's a fact." At her half-suspicious, half-appealing look, I said quickly:

"I don't know a soul about here. It's all right."

She sighed. "It was kind of you; and I feel to want to talk sometimes. Well, after he was gone, I said to myself: 'I'll take a holiday and go an' see my daughter married.'" She laughed—"I never had no pink and white and blue little things myself. That was all done up for me that night I had the moon in me blood. Ah! my father was a proper hard man. 'Twas bad enough before I had my baby; but after, when I couldn't get the father to marry me, an' he cut an' run, proper life

they led me, him and stepmother. Cry! Didn' I cry—I was a soft
hearted thing—never went to sleep with me eyes dry—never. 'Tis a
cruel thing to make a young girl cry."

I said quietly: "Did you run away, then?"

She nodded. "Bravest thing I ever did. Nearly broke my 'eart to
leave my baby; but 'twas that or drownin' meself. I was soft then.
I went off with a young fellow—bookmaker that used to come
over to the sports meetin', wild about me—but he never married
me"—again she uttered her hard laugh—"knew a thing worth tu o'
that." Lifting her hand towards the burning furze, she added: "I used
to come up here an' help 'em light that when I was a little girl." And
suddenly she began to cry. It was not so painful and alarming as her
first distress, for it seemed natural now.

At the side of the cart-track by the gate was an old boot thrown
away, and it served me for something to keep my eyes engaged.
The dilapidated black object among the stones and wild plants
on that day of strange mixed beauty was as incongruous as this
unhappy woman herself revisiting her youth. And there shot into
my mind a vision of this spot as it might have been that summer
night when she had "the moon in her blood"—queer phrase—and
those two young creatures in the tall soft fern, in the warmth and
the darkened loneliness, had yielded to the impulse in their blood.
A brisk fluttering of snowflakes began falling from the sky still blue,
drifting away over our heads towards the blood-red flames and
smoke. They powdered the woman's hair and shoulders, and with
a sob and a laugh she held up her hand, and began catching them
as a child might.

"'Tis a funny day for my girl's weddin'," she said. Then with a
sort of fierceness added: "She'll never know her mother—she's in
luck there, tu!" And, grabbing her feathered hat from the ground,
she got up. "I must be gettin' back for my train, else I'll be late for
an appointment."

When she had put her hat on, rubbed her face, dusted and
smoothed her dress, she stood looking at the burning furze. Restored
to her town plumage, to her wonted bravado, she was more than
ever like that old discarded boot, incongruous.

"I'm a fool ever to have come," she said; "only upset me—and you don't want no more upsettin' than you get, that's certain. Good-bye, and thank you for the drink—it lusened my tongue praaper, didn't it?" She gave me a look—not as a professional—but a human, puzzled look. "I told you my baby was a laughin' little thing. I'm glad she's still like that. I'm glad I've seen her." Her lips quivered for a second; then, with a faked jauntiness, she nodded. "So long!" and passed through the gate down into the lane.

I sat there in the snow and sunlight some minutes after she was gone. Then, getting up, I went and stood by the burning furze. The blowing flames and the blue smoke were alive and beautiful; but behind them they were leaving blackened skeleton twigs.

'Yes,' I thought, 'but in a week or two the little green grass-shoots will be pushing up underneath into the sun. So the world goes! Out of destruction! It's a strange thing!'

[1916]

THE NIGHTMARE CHILD

I SET down here not precisely the words of my friend, the country doctor, but the spirit of them:

"You know there are certain creatures in this world whom one simply dare not take notice of, however sorry one may be for them. That has often been borne in on me. I realised it, I think, before I met that little girl. I used to attend her mother for varicose veins— one of those women who really ought not to have children, since they haven't the very least notion of how to bring them up. The wife of a Sussex agricultural labourer called Alliner, she was a stout person, with most peculiar prominent epileptic eyes, such eyes as one usually associates with men of letters or criminals. And yet there was nothing in her. She was just a lazy, slatternly, easy-going body, rather given to drink. Her husband was a thin, dirty, light-hearted fellow, who did his work and offended nobody. Her eldest daughter, a pretty and capable girl, was wild, got into various kinds of trouble, and had to migrate, leaving two illegitimate children behind her with their grandparents. The younger girl, the child of this story, who was called Emmeline, of all names—pronounced Em'leen, of course—was just fifteen at the time of my visits to her mother. She had eyes like a hare's, a mouth which readily fell open, and brown locks caught back from her scared and knobby forehead. She was thin, and walked with her head poked a little forward, and she so manœuvred her legs and long feet, of which one turned in rather and seemed trying to get in front of the other, that there was something clod-hopperish in her gait. Once in a way you would see her in curl-papers, and then indeed she was plain, poor child! She seemed to have grown up without ever having had the least attention paid to her. I don't think she was ill-treated—she was simply not treated at all. At school they had been kind enough, but had regarded her as almost deficient. Seeing that her father was paid about fifteen shillings a week, that her mother had no conception of housekeeping, and that there were two babies to be fed, they were, of course, villainously poor, and Em'leen was always draggle-tailed and badly shod. One side of her too-short dress seemed ever to hang lower than the other, her stockings always had one hole at least, and her hats—such queer hats—would seem about to fly away. I have known her type in the upper classes pass muster as 'eccentric' or 'full of character.' And even in Em'leen there was a sort of smothered natural comeliness, trying pathetically to push through, and never getting a chance. She always had a lost-dog air, and when her big hare's eyes clung on your face it seemed as if she only wanted a sign to make her come trailing at your heels, looking up for a pat or a bit of biscuit.

"She went to work, of course, the moment she left school. Her first place was in a small farm where they took lodgers, and her duties were to do everything, without, of course, knowing how to do anything. She had to leave because she used to take soap and hair-pins, and food that was left over, and was once seen licking a dish. It was just about then that I attended her mother for those veins in her unwieldy legs, and the child was at home, waiting to secure some other fate. It was impossible not to look at that little creature kindly and to speak to her now and then; she would not exactly light up, because her face was not made that way, but she would hang towards you as if you were a magnet, and you had at once the uncomfortable sensation that you might find her clinging, impossible to shake off. If one passed her in the village, too, or coming down from her blackberrying in the thickets on the Downs—their cottage lay just below the South Downs—one knew that she would be lingering along, looking back till you were out of sight. Somehow one hardly thought of her as a girl at all; she seemed so far from all human hearts, so wandering in a queer lost world of her own, and to imagine of what she could be thinking was as impossible as it is with animals. Once I passed her and her mother dawdling slowly in a lane, then heard the dot-and-go-one footsteps pattering after me, and the childish voice, rather soft and timid, say behind my shoulders: 'Would you please buy some blackberries, sir?' She was almost pretty at that moment, flushed and breathless at having actually spoken to me, but her eyes hanging on my face brought a sort of nightmare feeling at once of being unable to get rid of her.

"Isn't it a cruel thing, when you come to think of it, that there should be born into the world poor creatures—children, dogs, cats, horses—who want badly to love and be loved, and yet whom no one can quite put up with, much less feel affection for!

"Well, what happened to her is what will always happen to such as those, one way or another, in a world where the callous abound; for, however unlovable a woman or girl, she has her use to a man, just as a dog or a horse has to a master who cares nothing for it.

"Soon after I bought those blackberries I went out to France on military duty. I got my leave a year later and went home. It was late September, very lovely weather, and I took a real holiday walking or lying about up on the Downs, and only coming down at sunset. On one of those days when you really enter heaven, so pure are the lines of the hills, so cool the blue, the green, the chalk-white colouring under the smile of the afternoon sun—I was returning down that same lane, when I came on Em'leen sitting in a gap on the bank, with her dishevelled hat beside her, and her chin sunk on her hands. My appearance seemed to drag her out of a heavy dream—her eyes awoke, became startled, rolled furtively; she scrambled up, dropped her little old school curtsey, then all confused, faced the bank as if she were going to climb it. She was taller, her dress longer, her hair gathered up, and it was very clear what was soon going to happen to her. I walked on in a rage. At her age—bare sixteen even, yet! I am a doctor accustomed to most things, but this particular crime against children of that hopeless sort does make my blood boil. Nothing, not even passion to excuse it—who could feel passion for that poor child?—nothing but the cold, clumsy lust of some young ruffian. Yes, I walked on in a rage, and went straight to her mother's cottage. That wretched woman was incapable of moral indignation, or else the adventures of her elder daughter had exhausted her powers of expression 'Yes,' she admitted, 'Em'leen had got herself into trouble too; but she would not tell, she wouldn't say nothin' against nobody. It was a bad business, surely, an' now there would be three o' them, an' Alliner was properly upset, that he was!' That was all there was to be had out of *her*. One felt that she knew or suspected more, but her fingers had been so burned over the elder girl that anything to her was better than a fuss.

"I saw Alliner; he was a decent fellow, though dirty, distressed in his simple, shallow-pated way, and more obviously ignorant than his wife. I spoke to the school-mistress, a shrewd and kindly married woman.

"Poor Emmeline! Yes, she had noticed. It was very sad and wicked! She hinted, but would not do more than hint, at the son of the miller, but he was back again, fighting in France now, and, after all, her evidence amounted to no more than his reputation with girls. Besides, one is very careful what one says in a country village. I, however, was so angry that I should not have been careful if I could have got hold of anything at all definite.

"I did not see the child again before my leave was up. The very next news I heard of her was from a newspaper—Emmeline Alliner, sixteen, had been committed for trial for causing the death of her illegitimate child by exposure. I was on the sick list in January, and went home to rest. I had not been there two days before I received a visit from a solicitor of our assize town, who came to ask me if I would give evidence at the girl's trial as to the nature of her home surroundings. I learned from him the details of the lugubrious business. It seems that she had slipped out one bitter afternoon in December, barely a fortnight after her confinement, carrying her baby. There was snow on the ground and it was freezing hard, but the sun was bright, and it was that, perhaps, which tempted her. She must have gone up towards the Downs by the lane where I had twice met her; gone up, and stopped at the very gap in the bank where she had been sitting lost in that heavy dream when I saw her last. She appears to have subsided there in the snow, for there she was found by the postman just as it was getting dark; leaning over her knees as if stupefied, with her chin buried in her hands—and the baby stiff and dead in the snow beside her. When I told the lawyer how I had seen her there ten weeks before, and of the curious dazed state she had been in, he said at once: 'Ah! the exact spot! That's very important; it looks uncommonly as if it were there that she came by her misfortune. What do you think? It's almost evidence that she'd lost sense of her surroundings, baby and all. I shall ask you to tell us about that at the trial. She's a most peculiar child; I can't get anything out of her. I keep asking her for the name of the man, or some indication of how it came about, but all she says is: "Nobody—nobody!" Another case of immaculate conception! Poor little creature! She's very pathetic, and that's her best chance. Who could condemn a child like that?'

"And so, indeed, it turned out. I spared no feelings in my evidence. The mother and father were in court, and I hope Mrs. Alliner liked my diagnosis of her maternal qualities. My description of how Em'leen was sitting when I met her in September tallied so exactly with the postman's account of how he met her that I could see the jury were impressed. And then there was the figure of the child herself, lonely there in the dock. The French have a word, *hébétée*. surely there never was a human object to which it applied better. She stood like a little tired pony, whose head hangs down, half-sleeping after exertion; and those hare eyes of hers were glued to the judge's face, for all the world as if she were worshipping him. It must have made him extraordinarily uncomfortable. He summed up very humanely, dwelling on the necessity of finding intention in her conduct towards the baby; and he used some good strong language against the unknown man. The jury found her not guilty, and she was discharged. The school mistress and I, anticipating this, had found her a refuge with some sisters of mercy who ran a sort of home not far away, and to that we took her, without a 'by your leave' to the mother.

"When I came home the following summer I found an opportunity of going to look her up. She was amazingly improved in face and dress, but she had attached herself to one of the sisters—a broad, fine-looking woman—to such a pitch that she seemed hardly alive when out of her sight. The sister spoke of it to me with real concern.

"'I really don't know what to do with her,' she said; 'she seems incapable of anything unless I tell her; she only feels things through me. It's really quite trying, and sometimes very funny, poor little soul! but it's tragic for her. If I told her to jump out of her bedroom window, or lie down in that pond and drown, she'd do it without a moment's hesitation. She can't go through life like this; she must learn to stand on her own feet. We must try and get her a good place, where she can learn what responsibility means and get a will of her own.'

"I looked at the sister, so broad, so capable, so handsome, and so puzzled, and I thought, 'Yes, I know exactly. She's on your nerves; and where in the world will you find a place for her where she won't become a sort of nightmare to someone with her devotion, or else get it taken advantage of again?' And I urged them to keep her a little longer. They did; for when I went home for good, six months later, I found that she had only just gone into a place with an old lady patient of mine in a small villa on the outskirts of our village. She used to open the door to me when I called there on my rounds once a week. She retained vestiges of the neatness which had been grafted on her by the sister, but her frock was already beginning to sag down on one side and her hair to look ill-treated. The old lady spoke to her with a sort of indulgent impatience, and it was clear that the girl's devotion was not concentrated upon her. I caught myself wondering what would be its next object, never able to help the feeling that if I gave a sign it would be myself. You may be sure I gave no sign. What's the good? I hold the belief that people should not force themselves to human contacts or relationships which they cannot naturally and without irritation preserve. I've seen these heroic attempts come to grief so often; in fact, I don't think I've ever seen one succeed, not even between blood relations. In the long run they merely pervert and spoil the fibre of the attempter without really benefiting the attemptee. Behind healthy relationships between human beings, or even between human beings and animals, there must be at least some rudimentary affinity. That's the tragedy of poor little souls like Em'leen. Where on earth can they find the affinity which makes life good? The very fact that they must worship is their destruction. It was a soldier—or so they said—who had brought her to her first grief; I had seen her adoring the judge at the trial, then the handsome uniformed sister. And I, as the village doctor, was a sort of tin-pot deity in those parts, so I was very careful to keep my manner to her robust and almost brusque.

"And then one day I passed her coming from the post office; she was looking back, her cheeks were flushed, and she was almost pretty. There by the inn a butcher's cart was drawn up. The young butcher, new to our village (he had a stiff knee and had been discharged from the army), was taking out a leg of mutton. He had a dare-devil face and eyes that had seen much death. He had evidently been chatting with her, for he was still smiling, and even as I passed him he threw her a jerk of the head.

"Two Sundays after that I was coming down past Wiley's copse at dusk and heard a man's coarse laugh. There, through a tiny gap in the nut-bushes, I saw a couple seated. He had his leg stiffly stretched out and his arm round the girl, who was leaning towards him; her lips were parted, and those hare's eyes of hers were looking up into his face. Adoration!

"I don't know what it was my duty to have done; I only know that I did nothing, but slunk on with a lump in my throat.

"Adoration! There it was again! Hopeless! Incurable devotions to those who cared no more for her than for a slice of suet-pudding to be eaten hot, gulped down, forgotten, or loathed in the recollection. And there they are, these girls, one to almost every village of this country—a nightmare to us all. The look on her face was with me all that evening and in my dreams.

"I know no more, for two days later. I was summoned north to take up work in a military hospital."

[*1917*]

A REVERSION TO TYPE

WE sat smoking after dinner in a country house. Someone was saying: "They're either too conceited, too much in earnest, too much after advertisement, too effeminate, or too dirty—I never found literary men amusing."

There was a murmur of approval, till a sallow man who had not spoken all the evening, except to ask for matches, emerged from the shadow of his chair . . .

"You're wrong," he said. "The most diverting thing I ever came across was in connection with two literary men. It happened some years ago at an Italian inn, in a place where there were ruins. I was travelling with poor B——, and at that inn we came across a literary man, a regular Classicist, looking up items for an historical romance. He was very good company—a prosperous, clever, satirical creature, who wore a moustache, and thought it wicked not to *change* for dinner. In spite of this, he had his limitations—but we all have *them*, even we sitting here. This inn was a queer place—at a crossing of two roads in the midst of brown hills—with blistered eucalyptus trees throwing ragged shadows on it, and two old boar-spears fastened up over the door. We were the only people there, and it was very hot. We used to dine outside the entrance, in the shade of the eucalyptus trees. There was a wonderful tap of wine; and, after toiling over ruins in the sun all day, we used to punish it—the Classicist especially; it sharpened his wit and thickened his tongue. He was a man of culture, great believer in physical sports, and knew all about everybody's ancestors—was himself fifteen degrees removed from a murderer of Thomas A'Becket, and a friend of the champion tennis player. We got on very well; he was quite amusing and affable.

"It was about sunset on the fourth evening when the other literary person turned up. He came just as we were going to dinner—a long, weedy fellow, slouching in under a knapsack, covered with dust, in a battered 'larrikin' hat, unshaved, with eyes as keen as sword-points, a lot of hair, and an emotional mouth, like a girl's. He sprawled down on a bench close to our table, unslung his pack, and appeared to lose himself in the sunset. When our host came out with the soup, he asked for wine and a bed. B—— suggested that he should join us; he accepted, and sat down forthwith. I sat at one end, B—— opposite; this fellow and the Classicist, who wore a smoking jacket, and smelt tremendously of soap, faced each other. From the first moment it was a case of 'two of a trade.' The moment their eyes met, ironical smiles began wandering about their mouths. There was little enough talk till we had broached our third bottle. The Classicist was a noble drinker; this wild man of the ways a nobler, or perhaps more thirsty. I remember the first words they exchanged. The Classicist, in his superior, thick, satirical voice, was deploring 'the unmanly tricks' introduced nowadays into swordsmanship, to the detriment of its dignity and grace.

"' It would be interesting to know, sir,' said the other, 'when you're fighting for life, what is the good of those "tickle points of niceness"?' The Classicist looked at him: 'You would wish, I should imagine, to "play the game," sir?'

"'With my enemy's sword through the middle of me?'

"The Classicist answered: 'I should have thought it a matter of "good form"; however, if you don't feel that—of course—'

"'I have not the good fortune to be a swordsman; but if I were, I should be concerned to express my soul with the point of my sword, not with attitudes.'

"'Noble aspiration!'

"'Just as I drink off at a draught this most excellent wine.'

"'Evidently you are not concerned with flavours?'

"'Its flavour, sir, is the feeling it gives me—Burn Academy, and all its works!'

"The Classicist turned to me elaborately and asked:

"'Do you know young D——, the author of ——? You ought to; there's no d—d nonsense about *him*.' The man on the other side of the table laid his soiled hand on his soiled chest. 'A hit. I feel honoured.'

"The Classicist continued his remarks. 'No "expressions of soul" and that sort of thing about D——!'

"'Oh! happy D——!' murmured our visitor. 'And is the happy B—— an artist in his writings?'

"The Classicist turned and rent him. 'He's a public school man, sir, and a gentleman, which, in my humble opinion, is much better.'

"The newcomer drank. 'That is very interesting. I must read D———. Has he given us any information about the inner meaning of life in public schools?'

"'No, sir; he is not a prig.'

"'Indeed! He must have English blood in him, this gentleman!'

"'He knows the meaning of "good form," anyway.'

"Our visitor clutched his glass and shook it in the air. 'Sir,' he said, 'with all my heart, with all my blood, I revolt against those words "good form"; I revolt against the commercial snobbery that underlies them; I revolt against the meanness and the Pharisaism of them; I revolt—' and still he went on shaking his glass and saying 'I revolt.'

"The Classicist ironically murmured: *Sparge rosas! Inania verba!*

"'No, sir; "winged words," that I will drive home with my last breath.'

"The Classicist smiled: 'An Emotional,' he began, 'an Emotional . . .'

"Gentlemen, it was time to interfere, so I upset the bottle. The wine streamed across the table. We ordered more. Darkness had gathered; the moon was rising; over the door the reflections of those old boar-spears branched sharp and long on the pale wall; they had an uncanny look, like cross-bones. How those two fellows disliked each other! Whole centuries of antagonism glared out of their eyes. They seemed to sum up in some mysterious way all that's significant and opposed in the artist and the man of action. It was exceedingly funny. They were both learned pigs. But the ancestors of the one might from time immemorable have been burning and stamping on the other, and the ancestors of the other stabbing desperately up at the one. One represented a decent well-fed spirit of satisfaction with things as they are, and the other a ravening shade, whom centuries of starvation had engrained with strife. For all I know they may both have been the sons of chemists. But, anyway, some instinct made each recognise the other as typical of what he had most cause to hate. Very obscure the reasons of such things—very obscure everything to do with origins!

"We ordered another bottle. Any other two men, having discovered such hostility, would have held their tongues; these couldn't—I have noticed it with members of their profession. The Emotionalist proposed a toast: 'I give you,' he said, 'the country most immersed in the slough of commercialism, the country that suffocates truth in its cradle with the smell of money, the country of snobs and stockjobbers!' He drank his own toast with enthusiasm; needless to say, nobody else did. The Classicist showed the first signs of excitement. 'I give you,' he responded, 'the whipping of all high-falutin' upstarts!'

"'Good!' replied the other; 'I drink that too!' It again became necessary to upset something—a glass this time. Presently we tumbled somehow on the subject of the Sagas. Gentlemen, the Sagas were deep in the affections of both those fellows; and nothing could have better roused their hostility to boiling-point than this common affection. You could see it by their faces. To the one a Saga was the quintessence of sport, of manly valour, and aristocratic tyranny; to the other some thing lawless and beautiful, freedom in a mist of primitive emotions, a will-o'-the-wisp hovering over bogs, a draught of blood and wine.

"Have you ever noticed two men discussing a picture, a book, a person, which one loves and the other hates? What happens? Indifference or mutual contempt—nothing more. But let them chance on that which each loves; then you may cry 'havoc!'

"We left our chairs, and stood about, and in the moonlight those creatures talked. First one went to the table and drained his glass, then the other. Their words were as bitter as bitter; they kept closing and hastily recoiling. They were like two men defending the honour of some woman who belonged to both of them—a priceless possession, which neither would abandon to the other. So, in the age of Sagas, a forbear of the one, some wild heathman, may have hewn a lord in sunder; or, in a foray, the other's ancestor trodden into the earth a turbulent churl. It was being done over again that evening—with words—by two lights of our high civilisation. B—— went to sleep. I woke him, and we left them disputing in the moonlight.

"And now, gentlemen, I come to the diverting part of my story. It may have been a quarter, it may have been half an. hour after B—— and I had retired, when the landlord came to call us.

"There, in a pool of moonlight, shadows, blood, and wine, they lay—they had carved each other up with the boar-spears.

"The Classicist was quite dead, with a sneer on his face; the Emotionalist still lived, with a gash right through his chest. There was nothing to be learnt from him, however; before his death he fixed his eyes on me. I bent, thinking to hear words of remorse or terror. But all he said was:

"The snob!' and died.

"They took alarm at the inn and wanted to smother it up. They called it fever. Well, gentlemen, so it *was*: the ineradicable fever of type. A good many years ago. You must have seen it in the papers . . ."

The sallow man was silent.

[*1901*]

EXPECTATIONS

NOT many years ago a couple were living in the south of England whose name was Wotchett—Ralph and Eileen Wotchett; a curious name, derived, Ralph asserted, from a Saxon Thegn called Otchar, mentioned in Domesday, or at all events—when search of the book had proved vain—on the edge of that substantial record.

He—possibly the thirtieth descendant of the Thegn—was close on six feet in height and thin, with thirsty eyes, and a smile which had fixed itself in his cheeks, so on the verge of appearing was it. His hair waved and was of a dusty shade bordering on grey. His wife, of the same age and nearly the same height as himself, was of sanguine colouring and a Cornish family, which had held land in such a manner that it had nearly melted in their grasp. All that had come to Eileen was a reversion on the mortgageable value of which she and Ralph had been living for some time. Ralph Wotchett also had expectations. By profession he was an architect, but, perhaps because of his expectations, he had always had bad luck. The involutions of the reasons why his clients died, became insolvent, abandoned their projects, or otherwise failed to come up to the scratch, were followed by him alone in the full of their maze-like windings. The house they inhabited, indeed, was one of those he had designed for a client, but the "fat chough" had refused to go into it for some unaccountable reason; he and Eileen were only perching there, however, on the edge of settling down in some more permanent house when they came into their expectations.

Considering the vicissitudes and disappointments of their life together, it was remarkable how certain they remained that they would at last cross the bar and reach the harbour of comfortable circumstances. They had, one may suppose, expectations in their blood. The germ of getting "something for nothing" had infected their systems, so that, though they were not selfish or greedy people, and well knew how to rough it, they dreamed so of what they had not that they continually got rid of what they had in order to obtain more of it. If, for example, Ralph received an order, he felt so strongly that this was the chance of his life if properly grasped, that he would almost as a matter of course increase and complicate the project till it became unworkable, or in his zeal omit some vital calculation such as a rise in the price of bricks; nor would anyone be more surprised than he at this, or more certain that all connected with the matter had been "fat choughs" except—himself. On such occasions Eileen would get angry, but if anyone suggested that Ralph had over-reached himself, she would get still angrier. She was very loyal, and unfortunately rather fly-away both in mind and body; before long she always joined him in his feeling that the whole transaction had been just the usual "skin-game" on the part of Providence to keep them out of their expectations. It was the same in domestic life. If Ralph had to eat a breakfast, which would be almost every morning, he had so many and such imaginative ways of getting from it a better breakfast than was in it that he often remained on the edge of it, as it were. He had special methods of cooking, so as to extract from everything a more than ordinary flavour, and these took all the time that he would have to eat the results in. Coffee he would make with a whole egg, shell and all, stirred in; it had to be left on the hob for an incomparable time, and he would start to catch his train with his first cup in his hand; Eileen would have to run after him and take it away. They were, in fact, rather like a kitten which knows it has a tail, and will fly round and round all day with the expectation of catching that desirable appendage. Sometimes indeed, by sheer perseverance, of which he had a great deal in a roundabout way, Ralph would achieve something, but, when this happened, something else, not foreseen by him, had always happened first, which rendered that accomplishment nugatory and left it expensive on his hands. Nevertheless, they retained their faith that some day they would get ahead of Providence and come into their own.

In view of not yet having come into their expectations, they
had waited to have children; but two had rather unexpectedly been
born. The babes had succumbed, however, one to preparation for
betterment too ingenious to be fulfilled, the other
to fulfillment itself, a special kind of food having been treated so
ingeniously that it had undoubtedly engendered poison. And they
remained childless.

They were about fifty when Ralph received one morning a
solicitor's letter announcing the death of his godmother, Aunt
Lispeth. When he read out the news they looked at their plates a
full minute without speaking. Their expectations had matured. At
last they were to come into something in return for nothing. Aunt
Lispeth, who had latterly lived at Ipswich in a house which he had
just not built for her, was an old maid. They had often discussed
what she would leave them—though in no mean or grasping spirit,
for they did not grudge the "poor old girl" her few remaining years,
however they might feel that she was long past enjoying herself. The
chance would come to them some time, and when it did, of course,
must be made the best of. Then Eileen said:

"You must go down at once, Ralph!"

Donning black, Ralph set off hurriedly, and just missed his train;
he caught one, however, in the afternoon, and arrived that evening
in Ipswich. It was October, drizzling and dark; the last cab moved
out as he tried to enter it, for he had been detained by his ticket,
which he had put for extra readiness in his glove, and forgotten—as
if the ticket collector couldn't have seen it there, the "fat chough!"
He walked up to his aunt's house, and was admitted to a mansion
where a dinner-party was going on. It was impossible to persuade
the servant that this was his aunt's, so he was obliged to retire to an
hotel and wire to Eileen to send him the right address—the "fat
choughs" in the street did not seem to know it. He got her answer
the following midday, and, going to the proper number, found the
darkened house. The two servants who admitted him described the
manner of their mistress's death and showed him up into her room.
Aunt Lispeth had been laid out daintily. Ralph contemplated her
with the smile which never moved from his cheeks and with a sort

of awe in his thirsty eyes. The poor old girl! How thin, how white! It had been time she went! A little stiffened twist in her neck where her lean head had fallen to one side at the last had not been set quite straight, and there seemed the ghost of an expression on her face, almost cynical; by looking closer he saw that it came from a gap in the white lashes of one eye, giving it an air of not being quite closed, as though she were trying to wink at him. He went out rather hastily, and, ascertaining that the funeral was fixed for noon next day, paid a visit to the solicitor.

There he was told that the lawyer himself was sole executor, and he—Ralph—residuary legatee. He could not help a feeling of exultation, for he and Eileen were at that time particularly hard pressed. He restrained it, however, and went to his hotel to write to her. He received a telegram in answer next morning at ten o'clock: "For goodness' sake leave all details to lawyer.—Eileen," which he thought very peculiar. He lunched with the lawyer after the funeral, and they opened his aunt's will. It was quite short and simple, made certain specific bequests of lace and jewellery, left a hundred pounds to her executor, the lawyer, and the rest of her property to her nephew, Ralph Wotchett. The lawyer proposed to advertise for debts in the usual way, and Ralph, with considerable control, confined himself to urging all speed in the application for probate and disposal of the estate. He caught a late train back to Eileen. She received his account distrustfully; she was sure he had put his finger in the pie, and if he had it would all go wrong. Well, if he hadn't, he soon would! It was really as if loyalty had given way in her now that their expectations were on the point of being realised.

They had often discussed his aunt's income, but they went into it again that night, to see whether it could not by fresh investment be increased. It was derived from Norwich and Birmingham Corporation Stocks, and Ralph proved that by going into industrial concerns the four hundred a year could quite safely be made into six. Eileen agreed that this would be a good thing to do, but nothing definite was decided. Now that they had come into money they did not feel so inclined to move their residence, though both felt that they might increase their scale of living, which had lately been at a distressingly low ebb. They spoke, too, about the advisability of a small car. Ralph knew of one—a second-hand Ford—to be had for a song. They ought not—he thought—to miss the chance. He would take occasion to meet the owner casually and throw out a feeler. It would not do to let the fellow know that there was any money coming to them, or he would put the price up for a certainty. In fact, it would be better to secure the car before the news got about. He secured it a few days later for eighty pounds, including repairs, which would take about a month. A letter from the lawyer next day informed them that he was attending to matters with all speed; and the next five weeks passed in slowly realising that at last they had turned the corner of their lives and were in smooth water. They ordered, among other things, the materials for a fowl-house, long desired, which Ralph helped to put up; and a considerable number of fowls, for feeding which he had a design which would enable them to lay a great many more eggs in the future than could reasonably be expected from the amount of food put into the fowls. He also caused an old stable to be converted into a garage. He still went to London two or three times a week, to attend to business which was not, as a rule, there. On his way from St. Pancras to Red Lion Square, where his office was, he had long been attracted by an emerald pendant with pearl clasp in a jeweller's shop window. He went in now to ask its price. Fifty-eight pounds—emeralds were a rising market. The expression rankled in him, and going to Hatton Garden to enquire into its truth, he found the statement confirmed. "The chief advantage of having money," he thought, "is to be able to buy at the right moment." He had not given Eileen anything for a long time, and this was an occasion which could hardly he passed over. He bought the pendant on his way back to St. Pancras, the draft in payment absorbing practically all his balance. Eileen was delighted with it. They spent that evening in the nearest approach to festivity that they had known for several years. It was, as it were, the crown of the long waiting for something out of nothing. All those little acerbities which creep into the manner of two married people who are always trying to round the corner fell away, and they sat together in one large chair, talking and laughing over the countless tricks which Providence—"that fat chough"—had played them. They carried their lightheartedness to bed.

They were awakened next morning by the sound of a car. The Ford was being delivered with a request for payment. Ralph did not pay; it would be "all right," he said. He stabled the car and wrote to the lawyer that he would be glad to have news and an advance of £100. On his return from town in the evening, two days later he found Eileen in the dining-room with her hair wild and an opened letter before her. She looked up with the word: "Here!" and Ralph took the letter.

> "Lodgers and Wayburn,
> "Solicitors, Ipswich.
> "Dear Mr. Wolchett,
> "In answer to yours of the fifteenth, I have obtained probate, paid all debts, and distributed the various legacies. The sale of furniture took place last Monday. I now have pleasure in enclosing you a complete and, I think, final account, by which you will see that there is a sum in hand of forty-three pounds due to you as residuary legatee. I am afraid this will seem a disappointing result, but as you were doubtless aware (though I was not when I had the pleasure of seeing you), the greater part of your aunt's property passed under a deed of settlement, and it seems she had been dipping heavily into the capital of the remainder for some years past.
> "Believe me,
> "Faithfully yours,
> "Edward Lodgers."

For a minute the only sounds were the snapping of Ralph's jaws and Eileen's rapid breathing. Then she said:

"You never said a word about a settlement. I suppose you got it muddled as usual!"

Ralph did not answer, too deep in his anger with the old woman who had left that "fat chough" a hundred pounds to provide him—Ralph—with forty-three.

"You always believe what you want to believe!" cried Eileen; "I never saw such a man."

Ralph went to Ipswich on the morrow. After going into everything with the lawyer, he succeeded in varying the account by fifteen shillings, considerably more than which was absorbed by the fee for this interview, his fare, and hotel bill. The conduct of his aunt, in having caused him to get it into his head that there was no settlement, and in living on her capital, gave him pain quite beyond the power of expression; and more than once he recalled with a shudder that slightly quizzical look on her dead face. He returned to Eileen the following day with his brain racing round and round. Getting up next morning, he said:

"I believe I can get a hundred for that car; I'll go up and see about it."

"Take this, too," said Eileen, handing him the emerald pendant. Ralph took it with a grunt.

"Lucky," he muttered; "emeralds are a rising market. I bought it on purpose."

He came back that night more cheerful. He had sold the car for sixty-five pounds, and the pendant for forty-two pounds—a good price, for emeralds were now on the fall! With the cheque for forty-three pounds, which represented his expectations, he proved that they would only be fourteen pounds out on the whole business when the fowls and fowlhouse had been paid for; and they would have the fowls—the price of eggs was going up. Eileen agreed that it was the moment to develop poultry-keeping. They might expect good returns. And holding up her face she said:

"Give me a kiss, dear Ralph!"

Ralph gave it, with his thirsty eyes fixed, expectant, on something round the corner of her head, and the smile, which never moved, on his cheeks.

After all, there was her reversion! They would come into it some day.

[*1919*]

A WOMAN

A TRAVELLER was writing to his friend: . . . "We were sitting on the *stoep*. Above the pines the long line of Table Mountain was like a violet shadow two shades deeper than the sky. We had no light except the 'Cross,' and a swarm of other stars; it was a rare night, dark crystal.

"There had been a dance, and the girls had gone to bed; all the shutters were closed, the old house against our backs looked very silent, and flat, and long. Only the door was open, and we sat round it. The sparks from our pipes writhed about in the air, or, falling on to the *stoep*, expired like the words dropping from our mouths. You know the kind of talk. In the morning we had played cricket amongst the trees—a hit into the vineyards, 'five and out'—girls and all. In the afternoon we had played tennis, on a half-made court—the girls too. In the evening we had danced. Some had hitched up, and departed. Some had gone to bed. We four were left, and old Juno, the pointer, with her head on her paws, and her nose wrinkling at the squeaking of some tiny beast in the darkness. Little Byng, with his waistcoat unbuttoned, was sitting quite square above his parted legs; round-faced little man, no neck to speak of, straw-coloured hair, and eyes without lashes, just like a dissipated egg. You know him, Billy Byng, best-hearted little man, they say, in Cape Colony. Young Sanley—married to one of the Detwell girls, sleeping a healthy sleep already indoors—such a neat, smooth chap; great Scott! yes, and how commonplace! with his pale moustache, and his high white forehead, and his slim nose, and his well-cut clothes, and his tidy made-up tie. And our host—you know him; a little too alert, a little too dark, a little too everything, but a right good fellow; engaged to the other Detwell girl, who was perhaps thinking of him, and perhaps wasn't, in her bed just over our heads. Well, we were talking; profaning things a bit; not much, you know, couldn't lay claim to original profanity; just tarbrushing the surface. We were all a bit bored, rather sleepy, and accordingly, just a little too jovial. Even Juno, who's at least as wise as any human, was pondering somewhat gloomily over her master's intention of taking us to shoot pheasants at daybreak—'before it was too hot.' We had been there before; we knew it—that pheasant shooting, up stony slopes in a tangle of cover, with the chance of a couple of shots, at most, producing one disembowelled bird. Every now and then one of us would get up, walk to the edge of the *stoep*, stare into the dark vineyard, stretch as if he were going to make a move, and after all yield to our host's: 'Just one more, boys!'

"All of a sudden young Sanley murmured:

"' I heard footsteps.'

"'Some nigger,' said our host.

"And then at the far end of the s a woman appeared, walked straight into our midst, and sat down. It was pretty startling and absurd. Little Byng seemed absolutely transfixed; he blinked his lashless eyes, and seemed to twitch all over his face. Sanley got very pale and nervously tapped the table. Our host alone kept the use of his tongue.

"'Corrie!' he said.

"'Why not? Give me a drink, Jack Allen.'

"Our host in a kind of surreptitious way poured brandy into a glass and added seltzer.

"The woman held out her hand for it, and as she tilted her chin to drink, the cloak fell from her shoulders, and we could see her neck and arms gleaming out of her evening dress.

"'Thanks!' she said; 'I wanted that.' Then she bent over the table and leaned her face on her hand. Well, no one spoke, and we all cast secret looks back at the house. Sanley reached out his hand quietly and drew the door to.

"The woman said:

"'I saw the bowls of your pipes, and heard your voices. You're not too lively now.'

"Her voice wasn't loud; but it sounded wilfully coarsened. Her lips were slightly parted above her forefinger crooked across her chin. Her nostrils seemed to broaden as she looked at us, in a sort of distrustful way. She wore no hat, and her hair was like a little black patch of the night over her brow. Her eyes; how can I describe them? They seemed to see everything, and to see nothing. They were so intent, and mournful, and defiant; hard, if you like, tragic, too. I remembered, now, where I had met her—though I hadn't been ten days in the Colony—at the supper party of a man called Brown, after the theatre; very vulgar and noisy.

"The most notorious woman in Cape Town! Her house had been pointed out to me, too, just at the corner of the Malay quarter; a little house, painted mauve, with large red flowers starring its front.

"The most notorious woman in Cape Town! I looked at our host. He was biting his fingers. At Byng. His mouth was a little open, as if he were about to make a very sage remark. Sanley struck me as looking altogether too pitiably decent.

"Our host broke the silence.

"'How? Where? Eh! What?'

"'Staying down there at Charlie Lennard's; what a beast! Oh! what a beast!'

"Her eyes rested, wistfully it seemed to me, on each of us in turn.

"'It's a beautiful night, isn't it?' she said.

"Little Byng kicked out his foot, as if he would have sent something sprawling, and began stuttering out:

"'I beg pardon—I beg pardon.' I saw the old pointer thrust her nose against the woman's knees. Something moved, back in the house; we all looked round with a start. Then the woman began to laugh, almost noiselessly, as though she had an unholy understanding of our minds, as if she would never leave off. I saw Sanley tear at his hair, and stealthily smooth it down again. Our host frowned horribly, and thrust his hands so deep into his pockets that it seemed to me they must go through the linings. Little Byng almost bounded up and down in his chair. Then, just as suddenly, the woman stopped laughing; there was dead silence. You could only hear the squeaking of the tiny beast. At last the woman said:

"'Doesn't it smell good to-night? It's quiet, too . . . Here let me have another drink!' She took the glass our host held out: 'Your very good health,' she said, 'my respectable friends!'

"Our host suddenly resumed his seat, crossed his arms, and sighed. A pitiful little noise he made of it.

"'I'm not going to hurt you,' she said; 'I wouldn't hurt a fly to-night—— It smells like home. Look!' She held out the edge of her skirts to us. 'Dew! I'm dripping; isn't it sweet?'

"Her voice had lost all coarseness—it might have been your mother or sister speaking; it was ever so queer, and little Byng sputtered out: 'Too bad! too bad!' but whether to her, or of her, or to us—no one knew.

"'I've walked miles to-night,' she said. 'Haven't had such a walk since I was a girl.' There was a kind of tone in her voice that hurt me horribly; and suddenly young Sanley rose.

"'Excuse me, Allen!' he stammered: 'it's very late. Going to turn in.' I caught the gleam of his eyes on the woman.

"'Oh! are you going?' she said. There was a sort of regret, a sort of something innocent and unconscious in her voice that seemed regularly to pierce a bag of venom in that smooth young man.

"'Madam, I am. My wife——' He stopped, groped for the door, pulled it open, smiled his mean tidy smile, and vanished.

"The woman had risen, and she gave a sort of laugh.

"'*His wife*! Oh! Well, I wish her happiness. Ah! my God! I *do* wish her happiness—I *do*; and yours, Jack Allen; and yours, if you have one. Billy Byng, you remember me—you remember when I first— to-night, I thought—I thought—' She hid her face. One by one we slunk off the *stoep*, and left her, sobbing her heart out before the house.

"God knows what she was thinking of! God knows what sort of things lurk round us, and leap out—thank Heaven! not often—from the darkness, as that did!

"I crept back later to the edge of the vineyard.

"There she was still, and, beside her, little Byng, with his toes turned out, bending over her fingers. Then I saw him draw them under his arm, pat them with his other hand, and, gazing up at the sky, lead her gently out into the darkness.

[*1900*]

A HEDONIST

RUPERT K. Vaness remains freshly in my mind because he was so fine and large, and because he summed up in his person and behaviour a philosophy which, budding before the war, hibernated during that distressing epoch, and is now again in bloom.

He was a New Yorker addicted to Italy. One often puzzled over the composition of his blood. From his appearance it was rich; and his name fortified the conclusion. What the K. stood for, however, I never learned; the three possibilities were equally intriguing. Had he a strain of Highlander with Kenneth or Keith; a drop of German or Scandinavian with Kurt or Knut; a blend of Syrian or Armenian with Khalil or Kassim? The blue in his fine eyes seemed to preclude the last, but there was an encouraging curve in his nostrils, and a raven gleam in his auburn hair, which by the way was beginning to grizzle and recede when I knew him. The flesh of his face, too, had sometimes a tired and pouchy appearance, and his tall body looked a trifle rebellious within his extremely well-cut clothes— but, after all, he was fifty-five. You felt that Vaness was a philosopher, yet he never bored you with his views, and was content to let you grasp his moving principle gradually, through watching what he ate, drank, smoked, wore, and how he encircled himself with the beautiful things and people of this life. One presumed him rich, for one was never conscious of money in his presence. Life moved round him with a certain noiseless ease or stood still at a perfect temperature, like the air in a conservatory round a choice blossom which a draught might shrivel.

This image of a flower in relation to Rupert K. Vaness pleases me, because of that little incident in Magnolia Garden, near Charleston, South Carolina.

Vaness was the sort of man of whom one could never say with safety whether he was revolving round a beautiful young woman or whether the beautiful young woman was revolving round him. His looks, his wealth, his taste, his reputation, invested him with a certain sun-like quality; but his age, the recession of his locks, and the advancement of his waist were beginning to dim his lustre; so that whether he was moth or candle was becoming a moot point. It was moot to me, watching him and Miss Sabine Monroy at Charleston throughout the month of March. The casual observer would have said that she was "playing him up" as a young poet of my acquaintance puts it; but I was not casual. For me Vaness had the attraction of a theorem, and I was looking rather deeply into him and Miss Monroy. That girl had charm. She came, I think, from Baltimore, with a strain in her, they said, of old Southern Creole blood. Tall and what is known as willowy, with dark chestnut hair, very broad dark eyebrows, very soft quick eyes, and a pretty mouth—when she did not accentuate it with lip-salve—she had more sheer quiet vitality than any girl I ever saw. It was delightful to watch her dance, ride, play tennis. She laughed with her eyes; she talked with a savouring vivacity. She never seemed tired or bored. She was—in one hackneyed word—"attractive." And Vaness, the connoisseur, was quite obviously attracted. Of men who professionally admire beauty one can never tell offhand whether they definitely design to add a pretty woman to their collection, or whether their dalliance is just matter of habit. But he stood and sat about her, he drove and rode, listened to music, and played cards with her; he did all but dance with her, and even at times trembled on the brink of that. And his eyes—those fine lustrous eyes of his—followed her about.

How she had remained unmarried to the age of twenty-six was a mystery, till one reflected that with her power of enjoying life she could not yet have had the time. Her perfect physique was at full stretch for eighteen hours out of the twenty-four each day. Her sleep must have been like that of a baby. One figured her sinking into dreamless rest the moment her head touched pillow, and never stirring till she sprang up into her bath.

As I say, for me, Vaness, or rather his philosophy, *erat demonstrandum* was philosophically in some distress just then. The microbe of fatalism, already present in the brains of artists before the War, had been considerably enlarged by that depressing occurrence. Could a civilisation basing itself on the production of material advantages, do anything but ensure the desire for more and more material advantages? Could it promote progress even of a material character except in countries whose resources were still much in excess of their population? The war had seemed to me to show that mankind was too combative an animal ever to recognise that the good of all was the good of one. The coarse-fibred, pugnacious, and self-seeking would, I had become sure, always carry too many guns for the refined and kindly. In short, there was not enough altruism to go round—not half, not a hundredth part enough. The simple heroism of mankind, disclosed or rather accentuated by the war, seemed to afford no hope—it was so exploitable by the rhinoceri and tigers of high life. The march of science appeared on the whole to be carrying us backward. I deeply suspected that there had been ages when the populations of this earth, though less numerous and comfortable, had been proportionately more healthy than they were at present. As for religion, I had never had the least faith in Providence rewarding the pitiable by giving them a future life of bliss; the theory seemed to me illogical, for even more pitiable in this life appeared to me the thick-skinned and successful, and these, as we know, in the saying about the camel and the needle's eye, our religion consigns wholesale to hell. Success, power, wealth—those aims of profiteers and premiers, pedagogues and Pandemoniacs, of all, in fact, who could not see God in a dew-drop, hear Him in distant goat-bells, and scent Him in a pepper tree—had, always appeared to me akin to dry rot. And yet every day one saw more distinctly that they were the pea in the thimble-rig of life, the hub of a universe which, to the approbation of the majority they represented, they were fast making uninhabitable. It did not even seem of any use to help one's neighbours; all efforts at relief just gilded the pill and encouraged our stubbornly contentious leaders to plunge us all into fresh miseries. So I was searching right and left for some thing to believe in, willing to accept even Rupert K.

Vaness and his basking philosophy. But could a man bask his life right out? Could just looking at fine pictures, tasting rare fruits and wines, the mere listening to good music, the scent of azaleas and the best tobacco, above all the society of pretty women, keep salt in my bread, and ideal in my brain? Could they? That's what I wanted to know.

Everyone who goes to Charleston in the Spring, soon or late, visits Magnolia Garden. A painter of flowers and trees, myself, I specialise in gardens, and freely assert that none in the world is so beautiful as this. Even before the magnolias come out, it consigns the Boboli at Florence, the Cinnamon Gardens of Colombo, Concepcion at Malaga, Versailles, Hampton Court, the Generaliffe at Granada, and La Mortola to the category of "also ran." Nothing so free, gracious, so lovely and wistful, nothing so richly coloured, yet so ghostlike, exists, planted by the sons of men. It is a kind of Paradise which has wandered down, a miraculously enchanted wilderness. Brilliant with azaleas, or magnolia-pale, it centres round a pool of water, overhung by tall trunks festooned with the grey Florida moss. Beyond anything I have ever seen, it is other-worldly. And I went there day after day, drawn as one is drawn in youth by visions of the Ionian Sea, of the East, or the Pacific Isles. I used to sit paralysed by the absurdity of putting brush to canvas, in front of that dream-pool. I wanted to paint, of it a picture like that of the fountain, by Helleu, which hangs in the Luxembourg. But I knew I never should.

I was sitting there one sunny afternoon with my back to a clump of azaleas, watching an old coloured gardener—so old that he had started life as an "owned" negro, they said, and certainly still retained the familiar suavity of the old-time darkie—I was watching him prune the shrubs when I heard the voice of Rupert K. Vaness say, quite close: "There's nothing for me but beauty, Miss Monroy."

The two were evidently just behind my azalea clump, perhaps four yards away, yet as invisible as if in China.

"Beauty is a wide, wide word. Define it, Mr. Vaness."

"An ounce of fact is worth a ton of theory—it stands before me."

"Come now, that's just a get-out. Is beauty of the flesh or of the spirit?"

"What is the spirit, as you call it? I'm a Pagan."

"Oh! so am I. But the Greeks were Pagans."

"Well, spirit is only the refined side of sensual appreciations."

"I wonder!"

"I have spent my life in finding that out."

"Then the feeling this garden rouses in me is purely sensuous?"

"Of course. If you were standing there blind and deaf, without the powers of scent and touch, where would your feeling be?"

"You are very discouraging, Mr. Vaness."

"No, Madam—I face facts. When I was a youngster I had plenty of fluffy aspiration towards I didn't know what—I even used to write poetry."

"Oh! Mr. Vaness, was it good?"

"It was not. I very soon learned that a genuine sensation was worth all the uplift in the world."

"What is going to happen when your senses strike work?"

"I shall sit in the sun and fade out."

"I certainly do like your frankness."

"You think me a cynic, of course; I am nothing so futile, Miss Sabine. A cynic is just a posing ass proud of his attitude. I see nothing to be proud of in my attitude, just as I see nothing to be proud of in the truths of existence."

"Suppose you had been poor?"

"My senses would be lasting better than they are; and when they at last failed, I should die quicker, from want of food and warmth—that's all."

"Have you ever been in love, Mr. Vaness?"

"I am in love now."

"And your love has no element of devotion, no finer side?"

"None. It wants."

"I have never been in love. But, if I were, I think I should want to lose myself, rather than to gain the other."

"Would you? Sabine, *I am in love with you.*"

"Oh! Shall we walk on?"

I heard their footsteps, and was alone again, with the old gardener lopping at his shrubs.

But what a perfect declaration of hedonism; how simple and how solid was this Vaness theory of existence! Almost Assyrian—worthy of Louis Quinze!

And just then the old negro came up.

"It's pleasant settin'," he said in his polite and hoarse half-whisper; "dar ain't no flies yet."

"It's perfect, Richard. This is the most beautiful spot in the world."

"Sure," he answered, softly drawling. "In de war time de Yanks nearly burn d'house heah. Sherman's Yanks. Sure dey did, po'ful angry wi' ole Massa dey was, 'cos he hid up d' silver plate afore he went away. My ole father was de factotalum den. De Yanks too'm, Suh; dey took'm; and de Major he tell my fader to show'm whar de plate was. My ole fader he look at 'm an' say: 'What yuh take me foh? Yuh take me for a sneakin' nigger? No, Suh, yuh kin do wot yuh like wid dis chile, he ain't goin' to act no Judas. No, Suh!' And de Yankee Major he put'm up against dat tall live oak dar, an' he say: 'Yu darn ungrateful nigger. I'se come all dis way to set yuh free. Now, whar's dat silver plate, or I shoot yuh up, sure!' 'No, Suh,' says my fader, 'shoot away. I'se never goin' t' tell.' So dey begin to shoot, and shot all roun'm to skeer'm up. I was a lil' boy den, an' I see my ole fader wid my own eyes, Suh, standin' thar's bold's Peter. No, Suh, dey didn't never got no word from him; he loved de folk heah; sure he did."

The old man smiled; and in that beatific smile I saw not only his perennial pleasure in the well-known story, but the fact that he too would have stood there with the bullets raining round him, sooner than betray the folk he loved.

"Fine story, Richard. But—very silly obstinate old man, your father, wasn't he?"

He looked at me with a sort of startled anger, which slowly broadened into a grin; then broke into soft hoarse laughter.

"Oh! yes, Suh, sure! Berry silly obstinacious ole man. Yes, Suh, indeed!" And he went off cackling to himself.

He had only just gone when I heard footsteps again behind my azalea clump, and Miss Monroy's voice:

"Your philosophy is that of faun and nymph. But can you play the part?"

"Only let me try." Those words had such a fevered ring that in imagination I could see Vaness all flushed, his fine eyes shining, his well-kept hands trembling, his lips a little protruded.

There came a laugh, high, gay, sweet.

"Very well, then; catch me!" I heard a swich of skirt against the shrubs, the sound of flight; an astonished gasp from Vaness, and the heavy thud thud of his feet, following on the path through the azalea maze. I hoped fervently that they would not suddenly come running past and see me sitting there. My straining ears caught another laugh far off, a panting sound, a muttered oath, a far-away Cooee! And then, staggering, winded, pale with heat and with vexation, Vaness appeared, caught sight of me, and stood a moment—baff! Sweat was running down his face, his hand was clutching at his side, his stomach heaved—a hunter beaten and undignified. He muttered, turned abruptly on his heel, and left me staring at where his fastidious dandyism and all that it stood for had so abruptly come undone.

I know not how he and Miss Monroy got home to Charleston; not in the same car, I guess. As for me, I travelled deep in thought, conscious of having witnessed something rather tragic, not looking forward to my next encounter with Vaness.

He was not at dinner, but the girl was there; radiant as ever; and though I was glad she had not been caught, I was almost angry at the signal triumph of her youth. She wore a black dress with a red flower in her hair, and another at her breast, and had never looked so vital and so pretty. Instead of dallying with my cigar beside cool waters in the lounge of the hotel, I strolled out afterwards on the Battery and sat down beside the statue of a tutelary personage. A lovely evening: from some tree or shrub close by emerged an adorable faint fragrance, and in the white electric light the acacia foliage was patterned out against a thrilling blue sky. If there were no fireflies abroad, there should have been. A night for hedonists indeed!

And, suddenly, in fancy, there came before me Vaness's well-dressed person, panting, pale, perplexed; and beside him, by a freak of vision, stood the old darkie's father, bound to the live oak, with the bullets whistling past, and his face transfigured. There they stood alongside—the creed of pleasure, which depended for fulfilment on its waist measurement; and the creed of love devoted unto death!

'Aha!' I thought; 'which of the two laughs last?'

And just then I saw Vaness himself beneath a lamp; cigar in mouth, and cape flung back so that its silk lining shone. Pale and heavy, in the cruel white light, his face had a bitter look. And I was sorry— very sorry, at that moment, for Rupert K. Vaness.

[*1920*]

A MILLER OF DEE

MacCreedy was respectable, but an outcast in his village.

There was nothing against him; on the contrary, he held the post of ferry-man to the people of the Manor, and nightly explained in the bar-parlour that if he had not looked sharp after his rights he would have been a salaried servant: "At a fixed wage, ye'll understand, without a chance to turn an honest penny."

He turned the honest pennies by exacting sixpenny ferry tolls from every person who was not a member of the Manor family. His doctrine, preached nightly, was that the gentry were banded to destroy the rights of the poor; yet, in spite of this, which should have conferred on him popularity, he was subtly and mysteriously felt to be a spiritual alien. No one ever heard him object to this unwritten, unspoken verdict; no one knew, in fact, whether he was aware of it. On still evenings he could be seen sitting in his boat in the Manor pool, under the high-wooded cliff, as if brooding over secret wrongs. He was a singer, too, with a single song, "The Miller of Dee," which he gave on all occasions; the effort of producing it lent his mouth a ludicrous twist under his whitey-brown moustache. People on the Manor terrace above could hear him sing it at night in an extraordinarily flat voice, as he crossed the river back to his cottage below.

No one knew quite where he came from, though some mentioned Ireland; others held a Scotch theory; and one man, who had an imagination, believed him to be of Icelandic origin. This mystery rankled in the breast of the village—the village of white cottages, with its soft, perpetual crown of smoke, and its hard north-country tongue. MacCreedy was close about money, too—no one knew whether he had much money or little.

Early one spring he petitioned for a holiday, and disappeared for a month. He returned with a wife, a young anæmic girl, speaking in a Southern accent. A rather interesting creature, this wife of MacCreedy, very silent, and with a manner that was unconsciously, and, as it were, ironically submissive.

On May mornings her slender figure, which looked as if it might suddenly snap off at the waist, might be seen in the garden, hanging clothes out to dry, or stooping above the vegetables, while MacCreedy watched her in a possessive manner from the cottage doorway. Perhaps she symbolised victory to him, a victory over his loneliness; perhaps he only looked on her as more money in his stocking. She made no friends, for she was MacCreedy's wife, and a Southerner; moreover, MacCreedy did not want her to make friends. When he was out it was she who would pull the ferry-boat over, and, after landing the passengers, remain motionless, bowed over her sculls, staring after them, as though loth to lose the sound of their footsteps; then she would pull slowly back across the swirl of silver-brown water, and, tying up the boat, stand with her hand shading her eyes. MacCreedy still went to the "public" at nights, but he never spoke of his wife, and it was noticed that he stared hard with his pug's eyes at anyone who asked after her. It was as though he suspected the village of wanting to take her from him. The same instinct that made him bury his money in a stocking bid him bury his wife. Nobody gave him anything, none should touch his property!

Summer ripened, flushed full, and passed; the fall began. The river came down ruddy with leaves, and often in the autumn damp the village was lost in its soft mist of smoke. MacCreedy became less and less garrulous, he came to the "public" seldom, and in the middle of his drink would put his glass down, and leave, as though he had forgotten something. People said that Mrs. MacCreedy looked unhappy; she ceased to attend church on Sundays. MacCreedy himself had never attended.

One day it was announced in the village that Mrs. MacCreedy's mother was ill—that Mrs. MacCreedy had gone away to nurse her; and, in fact, her figure was no more seen about the cottage garden beneath the cliff. It became usual to ask MacCreedy about his mother-in-law, for the question seemed to annoy him. He would turn his head, give a vicious tug at the sculls, and answer, "Oh! aye, a wee bit better!"

Tired perhaps of answering this question, he gave up going to the "public" altogether, and every evening, when the shadows of the woods were closing thick on the water, he could be seen staring over the side of his boat moored in the deep backwater below his cottage; the sound of his favourite song was heard no more. People said: "He misses his wife!" and for the first time since he had been amongst them a feeling for him almost amounting to warmth grew up in the village.

Early one morning, however, the underkeeper, who had an old-time grudge against MacCreedy, after an hour of patient toil, fished Mrs. MacCreedy up from the bottom of the backwater. She was neatly sewn in a sack, weighted with stones, and her face was black. They charged MacCreedy, who wept and said nothing. He was removed to the county gaol.

At his trial he remained dumb, and was found guilty. It was proved among other things that Mrs. MacCreedy had no mother.

While he was waiting to be hanged, he asked for the chaplain, and made the following statement:

"Parson," said he, "I'm not caring what ye have to say—ye will get plenty chance to talk when I'm gone. It's not to you I'm speaking, nor to anybody in particular—I'm just lonely here; it's a luxury to me to see a face that's not that gravy-eyed old warder's. I don't believe ye're any better than me, but if I did, what then? It's meself I've got to make me peace with. Man, d'ye think I'd have kept me independence if I'd ha' belived the likes of ye? They never had a good word for me down there, gentry as bad as the rest—the pack of fools! And why didn't they have a good word for me? Just because I'm an independent man. They'll tell ye that I was close; stingy they'll call it—and why was I close? Because I knew they were all against me. Why should I give 'em anything? They were all waitin' to take it from me! They'll say I set no store by my wife; but that's a lie parson—why, she was all I had! As sure as I'm speaking to ye, if I

hadn't done what I did I'd have lost her. I was for guessing it all the
autumn. I'm not one of those bodies that won't look a thing in the
face; ye can't hoodwink me with palaver. I put it to ye, if ye had a
diamond wouldn't ye a sight sooner pitch it into the sea than have it
stolen? Ye know ye would! Well, she's just dead; and so'll I be when
they squeeze the life out of me. Parson, don't ye go and blabber
about her doin' wrong. She never did wrong; hadn't the time to. I
wouldn't have ye take away her reputation when I'm gone and can't
defend her. But there was aye the certainty that she would 'a done
it; 'twas coming, d'ye see? Aye! but I was bound to lose her; and I'll
tell ye how I made sure.

"'Twas one day nigh the end of October; I emptied the ferry till,
and I said to my wife: 'Jenny,' I said, 'ye'll do the ferry work to-day;
I'm away to the town for a suit o' clothes. Ye will take care,' I said,
'that no one sneaks over without paying ye his proper saxpence.'

"'Very well, MacCreedy,' she says. With that I put some bread and
meat in a bit of paper, and had her ferry me across. Well, I went away
up the road till I thought she would have got back; and then I turned
round and came softly down again to the watter; but there she was,
still sitting where I'd left her. I was put aback by that, parson; ye
know what it is when your plans get upset. 'Jenny,' I said to her, as if
I came for that very purpose, 'ye'll look sharp after them fares?'

"'Yes,' she says, 'MacCreedy.' And with that she turns the boat
round. Well, presently I came down again and hid in some bushes on
the bank, and all day I stayed there watching. Have ye ever watched
a rabbit trap? She put four people across the river, and every time
I saw them pay her. But late in the afternoon that man—the devil
himself, the same I was lookin' after—came down and called out
'Ferry!' My wife she brought the ferry over, and I watched her close
when he stepped in. I saw them talking in the boat, and I saw him
take her hands when he left it. There was nothing more to see, for he
went away. I waited till evening, then out I crept and called 'Ferry!'
My wife came down—she was aye ready—and fetched me across.
The first thing I did was to go to the till and take out four saxpences.
'Oh,' I said, 'Jenny, ye've had four fares then?'

"'Yes,' she said, 'just four.'

"'Sure?' I said.

"'Sure,' she said, 'MacCreedy.'

"Have ye ever seen the eyes of a rabbit when the fox is nigh her?

"I asked her who they were, and when she told me the names of the first four, and never another name, I knew I'd lost her. She got to bed presently, and after she was in bed I waited, sitting by the fire. The question I put to meself was this: 'Will I let them have her? Will I let them tak' her away?' The sweat ran off me. I thought maybe she'd forgotten to name him, but there was her eyes; and then, where was his saxpence? In this life, parson, there's some things ye cannot get over.

"'No, I said to meself, 'either ye've took up with him or else ye're goin' to tak' up with him, or ye'd ha' had his saxpence.' I felt myself heavier than lead. 'Ye'd ha' had his saxpence,' I said to meself; 'ther's no gettin' over that.' I would have ye know that my wife was an obedient woman, she aye did what she was told, an' if it hadn't been for a vera good reason she'd ha' had his saxpence; there's no manner of doubt about it. I'm not one of those weak-minded bodies who believe that marriages are sacred; I'm an independent man. What I say is, every man for himself, an' every woman too, and the less of cant the better. I don't want ye to have the chance to take away me reputation when I'm gone, with any such foolish talk. 'Twasn't the marriage; 'twas just the notion of their stealing her. I never owed any man of them a penny, or a good turn—him least of all; and was I to see them steal her and leave me bare? Just as they'd ha' stolen my saxpences; the very money out of me pocket, if I'd ha' let them. I asked ye, was I to do that? Was I to see meself going back to loneliness before me own eyes? 'No,' I said to meself; 'keep yourselves to yourselves, I'll keep meself to mine!' I went and took a look at her asleep, and I could fancy her with a smile as if she were glad to ha' done with me—going off with him to those others up at the village to make a mock of me. I thought, 'Ye've got to do something, MacCreedy, or ye'll just be helping them to steal her from yerself.' But what could I do? I'm a man that looks things through and through, and sees what's logical. There was only one logic to this; but, parson, I cried while I was putting the pillow to her face. She struggled very little, poor thing—she was aye an obedient woman. I sewed her body up in a sack, and all the time I thought: 'There goes MacCreedy!' But I cannot say that I regretted it exactly. Human nature's no so very simple. 'Twas the hanging about the spot after, that was the ruin of me; if ye've got things valuable hidden up, ye're bound to hang around them, ye feel so lonely."

On the morning of his execution MacCreedy ate a good breakfast, and made a wan attempt to sing himself his favourite song:

> "I care for nobody—no, not I,
> And nobody cares for me!"

[*1903*]

LATE—299

I

1

IT was disconcerting to the governor. The man's smile was so peculiar. Of course these educated prisoners—doctors, solicitors, parsons—one could never say good-bye to them quite without awkwardness; couldn't dismiss them with the usual: "Shake hands! Hope you'll keep straight, and have luck." No! With the finish of his sentence a gentleman resumed a kind of equality, ceased to be a number, ceased even being a name with out prefix, to which the law and the newspapers with their unfailing sense of what was proper at once reduced a prisoner on, or even before, his conviction. No. 299 was once more Dr. Philip Raider, in a suit of dark-grey tweeds, lean and limber, with grey hair grown again in readiness for the outer world, with deep-set shining eyes, and that peculiar smile—a difficult subject. The governor decided suddenly to say only, "Well, good-bye, Dr. Raider," and, holding out his hand, he found it remain in: contact with nothing.

So the fellow was going out in defiant mood—was he! The governor felt it rather hard after more than two years, and his mind retracted his recollections of this prisoner: An illegal operation case! Not a good "mixer"—not that his prisoners were allowed to mix; still, always reassuring to know that they would if not strenuously prevented! Record—Exemplary. Chaplain's report—Nothing doing, or words to that effect. Work—Bookbinding. Quite! But chief memory that of a long loose figure loping round at exercise, rather like a wolf. And there he stood! The tall governor felt at the moment oddly short. He raised his hand from its posture of not too splendid isolation, and put the closure with a gesture. No. 299's lips moved:

"Is that all?"

Accustomed to being "sir'd" to the last, the governor reddened. But the accent was so refined that he decided not to mention it.

"Yes, that's all."

"Thank you. Good morning."

The eyes shone from under the brows, the smile curled the lips under the long, fine, slightly hooked nose; the man loped easily to the door. He carried his hands well. He made no noise going out. Damn! The fellow had looked so exactly as if he had been thinking: 'You poor devil!' The governor gazed round his office. Highly specialised life, no doubt! The windows had bars; it was here that he saw refractory prisoners in the morning, early. And, thrusting his hands into his pockets, he frowned.

Outside, the head warder, straight, blue-clothed, grizzled, walked ahead, with a bunch of keys.

"All in order," he said to the blue-clothed janitor, "No. 299—going out. Anyone waiting for him?"

"No, sir."

"Right. Open!"

The door clanged under the key.

"Good day to you," said the head warder.

The released prisoner turned his smiling face and nodded; turned it to the janitor, nodded again, and walked out between them, putting on a grey felt hat. The door clanged under the key.

"Smiling!" remarked the janitor.

"Ah! Cool customer," said the head warder. "Clever man though, I'm told."

His voice sounded resentful, a little surprised, as if he had missed the last word by saying it . . .

Hands in pockets, the released prisoner walked at leisure in the centre of the pavement. An October day of misty sunshine, and the streets full of people seeking the midday meal. Chancing to glance at this passer-by, their eyes glanced away at once, as a finger flies from a too-hot iron . . .

2

On the platform the prison chaplain, who had a day off and was going up to town, saw a face under a grey hat which seemed vaguely familiar.

"Yes," said a voice, "Late—299. Raider."

The chaplain felt surprise.

"Oh! Ah!" he stammered. "You went out to-day, I think. I hope you——"

"Thanks, very much."

The train came clattering in. The chaplain entered a third-class compartment; Late—299 followed. The chaplain experienced something of a shock. Extremely unlike a prisoner! And this prisoner, out of whom he had, so to speak, had no change whatever these two years past, had always made him feel uncomfortable. There he sat opposite, turning his paper, smoking a cigarette, as if on terms of perfect equality. Lowering his own journal, the chaplain looked out of the window, trying to select a course of conduct; then, conscious that he was being stared at, he took a flying look at his *vis-à-vis*. The man's face seemed saying: 'Feel a bit awkward, don't you? But don't worry. I've no ill-feeling. You have a devilish poor time.'

Unable to find the proper reply to this look, the chaplain remarked:

"Nice day. Country's looking beautiful."

Late—299 turned those shining eyes of his toward the landscape. The man had a hungry face in spite of his smile, and the chaplain asked:

"Will you have a sandwich?"

"Thanks . . ."

"Forgive my inquiring," said the chaplain presently, blowing crumbs off his knees, "but what will you do now? I hope you're going to——" How could he put it? "Turn over a new leaf"? "Make good"? "Get going"? He could not put it, and instead took the cigarette which Late—299 was offering him. The man was speaking too; his words seemed to come slowly through the smoke, as if not yet used to a tongue.

"These last two years have been priceless."

"Ah!" said the chaplain hopefully.

"I feel right on top."

The chaplain's spirit drooped.

"Do you mean," he said, "that you don't regret—that you aren't—
er——"

"Priceless!"

The man's face had a lamentable look—steely, strangely smiling.
No humility in it at all. He would find society did not tolerate such
an attitude. No, indeed! He would soon discover his place.

"I'm afraid," he said kindly, "that you'll find society very
unforgiving. Have you a family?"

"Wife, son, and daughter."

"How will they receive you?"

"Don't know, I'm sure."

"And your friends? I only want to prepare you a little."

"Fortunately I have private means."

The chaplain stared. What a piece of luck—or was it a
misfortune?

"If I'd been breakable, your prison would have broken me. Have
another cigarette?"

"No, thank you."

The chaplain felt too sad. He had always said nothing could be done
with them so long as their will-power was unbroken. Distressing to
see a man who had received this great lesson still so stiff-necked! And,
lifting his journal, he tried to read. But those eyes seemed boring
through the print. It was most uncomfortable. Oh! most! . . .

II

1

In the withdrawing-room of a small house near Kew Gardens, Mrs.
Philip Raider was gazing at a piece of pinkish paper in her hand, as
if it had been one of those spiders of which she had so constitutional

a horror. Opposite her chair her son had risen, and against the wall her daughter had ceased suddenly to play Brahm's Variations on a theme by Haydn.

"He says to-night!"

The girl dropped her hands from the keys. "To-night? I thought it was next month. Just like father—without a word of warning!"

The son mechanically took out his pipe, and began polishing its bowl. He was fresh-faced, fair, with a small head.

"Why didn't he tell us to meet him in London? He must know we've got to come to an arrangement."

The daughter, too, got up, leaning against the piano—a slight figure, with bushy, dark, short hair.

"What are we to do, Mother?"

"Jack must go round, and put Mabel and Roderick off for this evening."

"Yes, and what then, if he's going to stay here? Does he know that I'm engaged, and Beryl too?"

"I think I told him in my last letter."

"What are *you* going to do, Mother?"

"It's come so suddenly—I don't know."

"It's indecent!" said the boy violently.

His sister picked up the dropped telegram. "'Earl's Court, five four.' He may be here any minute. Jack, do hurry up! Doesn't he realise that nobody knows down, here?"

Mrs. Raider turned to the fire.

"Your father will only have realised his own feelings."

"Well, he's got to realise. I'll make him——!"

"Dr. Raider, ma'am."

Late—299 stood, smiling, in front of the door which the maid had closed behind him.

"Well, Bertha?" he said. "Ah, Beryl! Well, Jack!" His daughter alone replied.

"*Well*, Father, you might have let us know beforehand!"

Late—299 looked from one face to the other.

"Never tell children they're going to have a powder. How are you all?"

"Perfectly well, thank you. How are you?"

"Never better. Healthy life—prison!"

As if walking in her sleep, Mrs. Raider came across the room. She put out her hand with a groping gesture. Late—299 did not take it.

"Rather nice here," he said. "Can I have a wash?"

"Jack, show your father the lavatory."

"The bathroom, please."

The son crossed from the window, glanced at his father's smiling face, and led the way.

Mrs. Raider, thin, pale, dark, spoke first. "Poor Philip!"

"It's impossible to pity father, Mother; it always was. Except for his moustache being gone, I don't see much change, anyway. It's you I pity. He simply can't stay here. Why! everybody thinks you're a widow."

"People generally know more than they seem to, Beryl."

"Nobody's ever given us a hint. Why couldn't he have consulted us?"

"He didn't think of us when he did that horrible thing. And it was so gratuitous, unless——! Mother, sometimes I've thought he had to do it; that he was her—her lover as well as her doctor!"

Mrs. Raider shook her head.

"If it had been that, he'd have told me. Your father is always justified in his own eyes."

"What am I to do about Roddy?"

"We must just wait."

"Here's Jack! Well?"

"He's having a bath as hot as he can bear it. All he said was: 'This is the first thing you do when you go in, and the first thing you do when you come out—symmetrical, isn't it?' I've got to take him up a cup of coffee. It's really too thick! The servants can't help knowing that a Dr. Raider who gets into the bath the moment he comes to call must be our father."

"It's comic."

"Is it? He doesn't show a sign of shame. He'll call it from the housetops. I thought, of course, he'd go abroad."

"We all thought that."

"If he were down in the mouth, one could feel sorry for him. But he looks as pleased as Punch with himself. And it's such a beastly sort of crime—how am I to put it to Mabel? If I just say he's been in prison, she'll think it's something even worse. Mother, do insist on his going at once. We can tell the servants he's an uncle—who's been in contact with small pox."

"*You* take him the coffee, Mother—oh! you can't, if he's to be an uncle! Jack, tell him nobody here knows, and mother can't stand it, and hurry up! It's half-past six now."

The son passed his fingers through his brushed-back hair; his face looked youthful, desperate.

"Shall I?"

Mrs. Raider nodded.

"Tell him, Jack, that I'll come out to him, wherever he likes to go; that I always expected him to arrange that, that this is—too difficult—" She covered her lips with her hand.

"All right, Mother! I'll jolly well make him understand. But don't laugh out about it to the servants yet. Suppose it's we who have to go? It's his house!"

"Is it, Mother?"

"Yes; I bought it with his money under the power of attorney he left."

"Oh! Isn't that dreadful?"

"It's *all* dreadful, but we must consider him."

The girl shook back her fuzzy hair.

"It does seem rather a case of 'coldly received.' But father's always been shut up in himself. He can't expect us suddenly to slobber over him. If he's had a horrible time, so have we."

"Well, shall I go?"

"Yes, take him the coffee. Be quick, my dear boy, and be nice to him!"

The son said with youthful grimness, "Oh! I'll be nice!" and went.

"Mother, don't look like that!"

"How should I look? Smiling?"

"No, don't smile—it's like him. Cry it off your chest."

2

Late—299 was sitting in the bath, smiling through steam and the smoke of his cigarette, at his big toe. Raised just above the level of the water, it had a nail blackened by some weight that had dropped on it. He took the coffee-cup from his son's hand.

"For two years and nine months I've been looking forward to this—but it beats the band, Jack."

"Father—I ought to———"

"Good coffee, tobacco, hot water—greatest blessings earth affords. Half an hour in here, and—spotless, body and soul!"

"Father———!"

"Yes, is there anything you want to add?"

"We've been here two years."

"Not so long as I was there. Do you like it?"

"Yes."

"I didn't. Are you studying medicine?"

"No. Botany."

"Good. You won't have to do with human beings."

"I've got the promise of a job in the gardens here at the beginning of next year. I'm—I'm engaged."

"Excellent. I believe in marrying young."

"Beryl's engaged too."

"Your mother isn't by any chance?"

"Father!"

"My dear fellow, one expects to have been dropped. Why suppose one's family superior to other people's? *Pas si bête!*"

Gazing at that smiling face where prison pallor was yielding to the heat, above the neck whose sinews seemed unnaturally sharp and visible, the boy felt a spasm of remorse.

"We've never had a proper chance to tell you how frightfully sorry we've been for you. Only, we don't understand even now why you did such a thing."

"Should I have done it if I'd thought it would have been spotted? A woman going to the devil; a small risk to oneself—and there we were! Never save anyone at risk to yourself, Jack. I'm sure you agree."

The boy's face went very red. How could he ever get out what he had come to say?

"I have no intention of putting my tail between my legs. D'you mind taking this cup?"

"Will you have another, Father?"

"No, thanks. What time do you dine?"

"Half-past seven."

"You might lend me a razor. I was shaved this morning with a sort of bill-hook."

"I'll get you one."

Away from that smiling stranger in the bath, the boy shook himself. He must and would speak out!

When he came back with the shaving gear, his father was lying flat, deeply immersed, with closed eyes. And, setting his back against the door, he blurted out: "Nobody knows down here. They think mother's a widow."

The eyes opened, the smile resumed control.

"Do you really think that?"

"I do; I know that Mabel—the girl I'm engaged to—has no suspicion. She's coming to dinner; so is Roddy Blades—Beryl's *fiancé*."

"Mabel, and Roddy Blades—glad to know their names. Give me that big towel, there's a good fellow. I'm going to wash my head."

Handing him the towel, the boy turned. But at the door he stopped. "Father——!"

"Quite. These natural relationships are fixed beyond redemption."

The boy turned and fled.

His mother and sister stood waiting at the foot of the stairs.

"Well?"

"It's no good. I simply can't tell him we want him to go."

"No, my dear. I understand."

"Oh! but Mother——! Jack, you must."

"I can't, I'm going to put them off." Seizing his hat, he ran. He ran between small houses in the evening mist, trying to invent. At the corner of the long row of little villas, he rang a bell.

"Can I see Miss Mabel?"

"She's dressing, sir. Will you come in?"

"No. I'll wait here."

In the dark porch he tried hard to rehearse himself. Awfully sorry! Somebody had come—unexpectedly—on business! Yes! On what business?

"Hallo, Jack!"

A vision in the doorway—a fair head, a rosy, round, blue-eyed face above a swansdown collar.

"Look here, darling—shut the door."

"Why? What is it? Anything up?"

"Yes, something pretty badly up. You can't come tonight, Mabel."

"Don't squeeze so hard! Why not?"

"Oh! well—there—there's a reason!"

"I know. Your father's come out!"

"What? How——?"

"But of course. We all know about it. We must be awfully nice to him."

"D'you mean to say that Roddy and everybody——We thought nobody knew."

"Bless you, yes! Some people feel one way and some the other. I feel the other."

"Do you know what he did?"

"Yes; I got hold of the paper."

"Why didn't you tell me?"

"Why didn't *you*?"

"It was too beastly. Well?"

"I think it was a shame."

"But you can't have that sort of thing allowed."

"Why not?"

"Where would the population be?"

"Well, we're overpopulated. Everybody says so."

"That's quite another thing. This is the law."

"Look here! If you want to argue, come in. It's jolly cold."

"I don't want to argue; I must go and tell Roddy. It's an awful relief about you, darling. Only—you don't know my father."

"Then I can't come?"

"Not to-night. Mother——"

"Yes, I expect she's frightfully glad."

"Oh! yes—yes! She—yes!"

"Well, good-night. And look here—you go back. I'll tell Roddy. No! Don't rumple me!"

Running back between small houses, the boy thought: "Good God! How queer! How upside down! She—she——! It's awfully modern!"

3

Late—299 sat in the firelight, a glass beside him, a cigarette between his smiling lips. The cinders clicked; the clock struck. Eleven! He pitched the stump of his cigarette into the ashes, stretched himself, and rose. He went upstairs and opened the first door. The room was dark. A faint voice said:

"Philip?"

"Yes."

The light sprang out under his thumb. His wife was sitting up in bed, her face pale, her lips moving:

"To-night—must you?"

Late—299 moved to the foot of the bed; his lips, still smiled, his eyes gazed hungrily.

"Not at all. We learn to contain ourselves in prison. No vile contacts? Quite so. Good-night!"

The voice from the bed said faintly:

"Philip, I'm so sorry; it's the suddenness—I'm——"

"Don't mention it." The light failed under his thumb. The door fell to . . .

Three people lay awake, one sleeping. The three who lay awake were thinking: 'If only he made one feel sorry for him! If only one could love him! His self-control is forbidding—it's not human! He ought to want our sympathy. He ought to sympathise with us. He doesn't seem to feel—for himself, for us, for anything. And to-morrow what will happen? Is life possible here, now? Can we stand him in the house, about the place? He's frightening!'

The sleeper, in his first bed of one thousand and one nights, lay, with eyes pinched up between brows and bony cheeks of a face as if carved from ivory, and lips still smiling at the softness under him.

Past dawn the wakeful slept, the sleeper awoke. His eyes sought the familiar little pyramid of gear on the shelf in the corner, the bright tins below, the round port-hole, the line of distemper running along the walls, the closed and solid smallness of a cell. And the blood left his heart. They weren't there! His whole being struggled with such unreality. He was in a room staring at light coming through chintz curtains. His arms were not naked. This was a sheet! For a moment he shivered, uncertain of everything; then lay back, smiling at a papered ceiling.

III

1

"It can't go on, Mother. It simply can't. I feel an absolute worm whenever I'm with him. I shall have to clear out, like Beryl. He has just one object all the time—to make every one feel small and mean."

"Remember what he's been through!"

"I don't see why *we* should be part of his revenge. We've done nothing, except suffer through him."

"He doesn't want to hurt us or anyone."

"Well, whenever people talk to him, they dry up, at once, as if he'd skinned them. It's a disease."

"One can only pity him."

"He's perfectly happy, Mother. He's getting his own back."

"If only that first night———"

"We tried. It's no good. He's absolutely self-sufficient. What about to-morrow night?"

"We can't leave him on Christmas Day, Jack."

"Then we must take him to Beryl's. I can't stick it here. Look! There he goes!"

Late—299 passed the window where they stood, loping easily, a book under his arm.

"He must have seen us. We mightn't exist! . . ."

2

Late—299, with the book under his arm, entered Kew Gardens and sat down on a bench. A nursery governess with her charges came and settled down beside him.

"Peter, Joan, and Michael," said Late 299, "quite in the fashion."

The governess stirred uneasily; the gentleman looked funny, smiling there!

"And what are you teaching them?"

"Reading, writing, and arithmetic, sir, and Bible stories."

"Intelligent? . . . Ah! Not very. Truthful? . . . No! No children are."

The governess twisted her hands. "Peter!" she said, "where's your ball? We must go and look for it."

"But I've got it, Miss Somers."

"Oh! Well, it's too sharp, sitting here. Come along!"

She passed away, and Peter, Joan, and Michael trailed after. Late—299 smiled on; and a Pekinese, towing a stout old lady, smelled at his trousers.

"It's my cat," said Late—299. "Dogs and cats their pleasure is——"

Picking up the Pekinese, the stout old lady pressed it under her arm as though it were a bagpipe, and hurried on like a flustered goose.

Some minutes passed. A workman and his wife sat down to gaze at the pagoda.

"Queer building!" said Late—299.

"Ah!" said the workman. "Japanese, they say!"

"Chinese, my friend. Good people, the Chinese—no regard for human life."

"What's that? Good—did you say?"

"Quite!"

"Eh?"

The workman's wife peered round him.

"Come on, John! The sun gits in me eyes 'ere."

The workman rose. "'Good,' you said, didn't you? *Good* people?"

"Yes."

The workman's wife drew at his arm. "There, don't get arguin' with strangers. Come on!" The workman was drawn away . . .

A clock struck twelve. Late—299 got up and left the gardens. Walking between small houses, he rang at the side entrance of a little shop.

"If your father's still blind—I've come to read to him again."

"Please, sir, he'll always be."

"So I supposed."

On a horsehair sofa, below the dyed-red plumes of pampas-grass, a short and stocky man was sitting, whittling at a wooden figure. He sniffed, and turned his sightless eyes toward his visitor; his square face in every line and bump seemed saying:

"You don't down me."

"What are you making?" said Late—299.

"Christmas Eve. I'm cuttin' out our Lord. I make 'em rather nice. Would you like this one?"

"Thank you."

"Kep' I's end up well, our Lord, didn't He? 'Love your neighbour as yourself'—that means you got to love yourself. And He did, I think; not against Him, neither."

"Easier to love your neighbours when you can't see them, eh?"

"What's that? D'you mind lendin' me your face a minute? It'll help me a lot with this 'ere. I make 'em lifelike, you know."

Late—299 leaned forward, and the tips of the blind man's fingers explored his features.

"'Igh cheek-bones, eyes back in the 'ead, supraorbital ridges extra special, rather low forehead slopin' to thick hair. Comin' down, two 'ollers under the cheek-bones, thin nose a bit 'ooky, chin sharpish, no moustache. You've got a smile, 'aven't you? And your own teeth? I should say you'd make a very good model. I don't 'old with 'Im always 'avin' a beard. Would you like the figure 'anging', or carryin' the cross?"

"As you wish. D'you ever use your own face?"

"Not for 'Im—for statesmen, or 'eroes, I do. I done one of Captain Scott with my face. Rather pugnacious, my style; yours is sharp, bit acid, suitable to saints, martyrs, and that. I'll just go over you once more—then I'll 'ave it all 'ere. Sharp neck; bit 'unchy in one shoulder; ears stick up a bit; tallish thin man, ain't you, and throw your feet forward when you walk? Give us your 'and a minute. Bite your fingers, I see. Eyes blue, eh—with pin-points to 'em—yes? Hair a bit reddish before it went piebald—that right? Thank you, much obliged. Now, if you like to read, I'll get on with it."

Late—299 opened the book.

"'. . . But at last in the drift of time Hadleyburg had the ill luck to offend a passing stranger, possibly without knowing it, certainly without caring, for Hadleyburg was sufficient unto itself and cared not a rap for strangers and their opinions. Still, it would have been well to make an exception in this one's case, for he was a bitter man and revengeful.'"

"Ah!" interjected the blind man deeply, "there you 'ave it. Talkin' of feelin's, what gave you a fellow-feelin' for me, if I may ask?"

"I can look at you, my friend, without your seeing me."

"Eh! What about it with other people, then?"

"They can look at me without my seeing them."

"I see! Misanthropical. Any reason for that?"

" Prison."

"What oh! Outcast and rejected of men."

"No. The other way on."

The blind man ceased to whittle and scoop.

"I like independence," he said; "I like a man that can go his own way. Ever noticed cats? Men are like dogs mostly; only once in a way you get a man that's like a cat. What *were* you? if it's not a rude question. In the taxes?"

"Medico."

"What's a good thing for 'eartburn?"

"Which kind?"

"Wind, ain't it? But I see your meanin'. Losin' my sight used to burn my 'eart a lot; but I got over that. What's the use? You couldn't have any worse misfortune. It gives you a feelin' of bein' insured-like."

"You're right," said Late—299, rising to go.

The blind man lifted his face in unison. "Got your smile on?" he said. "Just let me 'ave another feel at it, will you?"

Late—299 bent to the outstretched fingers.

"Yes," said the blind man, "same with you—touched bottom. Next time you come I'll 'ave something on show that'll please you, I think; and thank you for readin'."

"Let me know if it bores you."

"I will," said the blind man, following without movement the footsteps of his visitor that died away.

3

Christmas night—wild and windy, a shower spattering down in the street; Late—299 walking two yards before his wife, their son walking two yards behind his mother. A light figure, furred to the ears, in a doorway watching for them.

"Come along, darling. Sorry we had to bring him."

"Of course you had to, Jack!"

"Look! He can't even walk with mother. It's a disease. He went to church to-day, and all through the sermon never took his eyes off—the poor old vicar nearly broke down."

"What was it about?"

"Brotherly love. Mother says he doesn't mean it—but it's like—what's that thing that stares?"

"A basilisk. I've been trying to put myself in his place, Jack. He must have swallowed blood and tears in there—ordered about like a dog, by common men, for three years nearly. If you don't go under, you must become inhuman. This is better than if he'd come out crawling."

"Perhaps. Look out—the rain! I'll turn your hood up, darling." A spattering shower, the whispering hushed . . .

A lighted open doorway, a red hall, a bunch of hanging mistletoe, a girl beneath, with bushy hair.

"Happy Christmas, Father!"

"Thanks. Do you want to be kissed?"

"As you like. Well, Mother darling! Hallo, you two! Come in! Roddy, take father's coat."

"How are you sir? Beastly weather!"

"That was the advantage we had in prison. Weather never troubled us. 'Peace and Goodwill' in holly-berries! —Very neat! They used to stick them up in there. Christianity is a really remarkable fraud, don't you think? . . ."

Once again those four in the street, and the bells chiming for midnight service.

"What an evening!"

"Let them get out of hearing, Jack."

"Worse than ever! My God, he'd turn the milk sour! And I thought liquor might make him possible. He drank quite a lot."

"Only a few days now, and then! . . ."

"Do you agree with mother that he doesn't mean it, Mabel?"

"Oh! yes, I do."

"The way he sits and smiles! Why doesn't he get himself a desert?"

"Perhaps he is . . ."

4

"'Ere you are!" said the blind man. "Best I can do under the circs. 'Ad a bit o' trouble with the cross; got it top 'eavy, I'm afraid; but thought you'd rather carry it."

"Quite a masterpiece!"

"Speaking serious?" said the blind man. "You could improve it with a box o' colours; make it more 'uman like."

"I'll do that."

"I wouldn't touch the face, nor the cross—leave 'em wooden; but the hair and the dress, and the blood from the crown a' thorns, might be all the better for a bit o' brightenin'. How's the man that corrupted 'Adleyburg?"

Late—299 opened the book.

"'. . . Goodson looked him over, like as if he was hunting for a place on him that he could despise the most; then he says: "So you are the Committee of Inquiry, are you?" Sawlsberry said that was about what he was. "H'm! Do they require particulars, or do you reckon a kind of *general* answer will do?" "If they require particulars I will come back, Mr. Goodson; I will take the general answer first." "Very well, then; tell them to go to hell—I reckon that's general enough. And I'll give you some advice, Sawlsberry; when you come back for the particulars, fetch a basket to carry what's left of yourself home in.""

The blind man chuckled.

"Ah! I like that Mark Twain. Nice sense o' humour—nothin' sickly."

"Bark and quinine, eh?"

"Bark and bite," said the blind man. "What do you think of 'uman nature yourself?"

"Little or nothing."

"And yet there's a bit of all right about it, too. Look at you and me; we got our troubles, and 'ere we are—jolly as sandboys! Be self-sufficient, or you've got to suffer. That's what you feel, ain't it? Am I mistook, or did you nod?"

"I did. Your eyes look as if they saw."

"Bright, are they? You and me could 'ave sat down and cried 'em out any time—couldn't we? But we didn't. That's why I say there's a bit of all right about us. Put the world from you, and keep your pecker up. When you can't think worse of things than what you do, you'll be 'appy—not before. That's right, ain't it?"

"Quite."

"Took me five years. 'Ow long were you about it?"

"Nearly three."

"Well, you 'ad the advantage of birth and edjucation. I can tell that from your voice—got a thin, mockin' sound. I started in a barber shop, got mine in an accident with some 'air-curlers What I miss most is not bein' able to go fishin'. No one to take me. Don't you miss cuttin' people up?"

"No."

"Well, I suppose a gent never gets a passion; I'd a perfect passion for fishin'. Never missed Sunday, wet or fine. That's why I learned this carvin'—must 'ave an 'obby to go on with. Are you goin' to write your 'istory? Am I wrong, or did you shake your 'ead?"

"I did. My hobby is watching the show go by."

"That might 'ave suited me at one time—always liked to see the river flowin' down. I'm a bit of a philosopher myself. You ain't, I should say."

"Why not?"

"Well, I've a fancy you want life to come to heel too much—misfortune of bein' a gent, perhaps. Am I right?"

Late—299 closed the book and rose. "Pride!" he said.

"Ah!" said the blind man, groping with his eyes, "that's meat and drink to you. Thought as much. Come again, if I don't worry you."

"And take you fishing?"

"Reelly? You will? Shake 'ands."

Late—299 put out his hand. The blind man's groped up and found it.

5

"Wednesday again, is it, partner, if I'm not troublin' you?"

"Wednesday it is."

At the door of his house, with the "catch" in a straw bag, the blind man stood a minute listening to his partner's foot steps, then felt his way to his horsehair sofa under the pampas-grass. Putting his cold feet up under the rug, he heaved a sigh of satisfaction, and fell asleep.

Between the bare acacias and lilac-bushes of the little villas, Late—299 passed on. Entering his house, he sought his study, and stretched his feet toward the fire, and the cat, smelling him fishy, sprang on to his knee.

"Philip, may I come in?"

"You may."

"The servants have given notice. I wanted to say, wouldn't you like to give this up and go abroad with me?"

"Why this sudden sacrifice?"

"Oh, Philip! You make it so hard for me. What do you really want me to do?"

"Take half my income and go away."

"What will you do, here, alone?"

"Get me a char. The cat and I love chars."

"Philip!"

"Yes?"

"Won't you tell me what's in your heart? Do you want always to be lonely like this?"

Late—299 looked up.

"Reality means nothing to those who haven't lived with it. I do."

"But why?"

"My dear Bertha—that is your name, I think?"

"Oh, God! You *are* terrible!"

"What would you have me—a whining worm? Crawling to people I despise—squirming from false position to false position? Do you want humility? What is it you want?"

"I want you to be human."

"Then you want what you have got. I *am* so human that I'll see the world damned before I take its pity, or eat its salt. Leave me alone. I am content."

"Is there nothing I can do?"

"Yes, stand out of my firelight . . ."

6

Two figures, in the dark outside, before the uncurtained window.

"Look, Mabel!"

"Be careful! He may see. Whisper!"

"The window's shut."

"Oh! Why doesn't he draw the blinds—if he must sit like that!

"'A desert dark without a sound
And not a drop to eat or drink
And a dark desert all around!'

Jack, I pity him."

"He doesn't suffer. It's being fond of people makes you suffer. He's got all he wants. Look at him."

The firelight on the face—its points and hollows, its shining eyes, its stillness and intensity, its smile; and on the cat, hunched and settled in the curve of the warm body. And the two young people, shrinking back, pass on between small houses, clutching each other's hands.

[*1923*]

THE SILENCE

In a car of the Naples express a mining expert was diving into a bag for papers. The strong sunlight showed the fine wrinkles on his brown face and the shabbiness of his short, rough beard. A newspaper cutting slipped from his fingers; he picked it up, thinking: 'How the dickens did that get in here?' It was from a colonial print of three years back; and he sat staring, as if in that forlorn slip of yellow paper he had encountered some ghost from his past.

These were the words he read: "We hope that the set-back to civilisation, the check to commerce and development, in this promising centre of our colony may be but temporary; and that capital may again come to the rescue. Where one man was successful, others should surely not fail? We are convinced that it only needs——" . . . And the last words: "For what can be sadder than to see the forest spreading its lengthening shadows, like symbols of defeat, over the untenanted dwellings of men; and where was once the merry chatter of human voices, to pass by in the silence——" . . .

On an afternoon, thirteen years before, he had been in the city of London, at one of those emporia where mining experts perch, before fresh flights, like sea-gulls on some favourite rock. A clerk said to him: "Mr. Scorrier, they are asking for you downstairs—Mr. Hemmings of the New Colliery Company."

Scorrier took up the speaking tube. "Is that you, Mr. Scorrier? I hope you are very well, sir. I am—Hemmings—I am—coming up."

In two minutes he appeared, Christopher Hemmings, secretary of the New Colliery Company, known in the City—behind his back—as "Down-by-the-starn" Hemmings. He grasped Scorrier's hand—the gesture was deferential, yet distinguished. Too handsome, too capable, too important, his figure, the cut of his iron-grey beard, and his intrusively fine eyes conveyed a continual courteous invitation to inspect their infallibilities. He stood, like a City "Atlas," with his legs apart, his coat tails gathered in his hands, a whole globe of financial matters deftly balanced on his nose. "Look at me!" he seemed to say. "It's heavy, but how easily I carry it. Not the man to let it down, sir!"

"I hope I see you well, Mr. Scorrier," he began. "I have come round about our mine. There is a question of a fresh field being opened up—between ourselves, not before it's wanted. I find it difficult to get my Board to take a comprehensive view. In short, the question is: Are you prepared to go out for us, and report on it? The fees will be all right." His left eye closed. "Things have been very—er—dicky; we are going to change our superintendent. I have got little Pippin—you know little Pippin?"

Scorrier murmured, with a feeling of vague resentment: "Oh yes. He's not a mining man!"

Hemmings replied: "We think that he will do." 'Do you?' thought Scorrier; 'that's good of you!'

He had not altogether shaken off a worship he had felt for Pippin—"King" Pippin he was always called, when they had been boys at the Camborne Grammar-school. "King" Pippin! the boy with the bright colour, very bright hair, bright, subtle, elusive eyes, broad shoulders, little stoop in the neck, and a way of moving it quickly like a bird; the boy who was always at the top of everything, and held his head as if looking for something further to be the top of. He remembered how one day "King" Pippin had said to him in his soft way, "Young Scorrie, I'll do your sums for you"; and in answer to his dubious, "Is that all right?" had replied, "Of course—I don't want you to get behind that beast Blake, he's not a Cornishman" (the beast Blake was an Irishman not yet twelve). He remembered, too, an occasion when "King" Pippin with two other boys fought six louts and got a licking, and how Pippin sat for half an hour afterwards, all bloody, his head in his hands, rocking to and fro, and weeping tears of mortification; and how the next day he had sneaked off by himself, and, attacking the same gang, got frightfully mauled a second time.

Thinking of these things he answered curtly: "When shall I start?"

"Down-by-the-starn" Hemmings replied with a sort of fearful sprightliness: "There's a good fellow! I will send instructions; so glad to see you well." Conferring on Scorrier a look—fine to the verge of vulgarity—he withdrew. Scorrier remained seated; heavy with insignificance and vague oppression, as if he had drunk a tumbler of sweet port.

A week later, in company with Pippin, he was on board a liner.

The "King" Pippin of his school-days was now a man of forty-four. He awakened in Scorrier the uncertain wonder with which men look backward at their uncomplicated teens; and staggering up and down the decks in the long Atlantic roll, he would steal glances at his companion, as if he expected to find out from them something about himself. Pippin had still "King" Pippin's bright, fine hair, and dazzling streaks in his short beard; he had still a bright colour and suave voice, and what there were of wrinkles suggested only subtleties of humour and ironic sympathy. From the first, and apparently without negotiation, he had his seat at the captain's table, to which on the second day Scorrier too found himself translated, and had to sit, as he expressed it ruefully, "among the big-wigs."

During the voyage only one incident impressed itself on Scorrier's memory, and that for a disconcerting reason. In the forecastle were the usual complement of emigrants. One evening, leaning across the rail to watch them, he felt a touch on his arm; and, looking round, saw Pippin's face and beard quivering in the lamplight. "Poor people!" he said. The idea flashed on Scorrier that he was like some fine wire sound recording instrument.

'Suppose he were to snap!' he thought. Impelled to justify this fancy, he blurted out: "You're a nervous chap. The way you look at those poor devils!"

Pippin hustled him along the deck. "Come, come, you took me off my guard," he murmured, with a sly, gentle smile, "that's not fair."

He found it a continual source of wonder that Pippin, at his age, should cut himself adrift from the associations and security of London life to begin a new career in a new country with dubious prospect of success. 'I always heard he was doing well all round,' he thought; 'thinks he'll better himself, perhaps. He's a true Cornishman.'

The morning of arrival at the mines was grey and cheerless; a cloud of smoke, beaten down by drizzle, clung above the forest; the wooden houses straggled dismally in the unkempt semblance of a street, against a background of endless, silent woods. An air of blank discouragement brooded over everything; cranes jutted idly over empty trucks; the long jetty oozed black slime; miners with listless faces stood in the rain; dogs fought under their very legs. On the way to the hotel they met no one busy or serene except a Chinee who was polishing a dish-cover.

The late superintendent, a cowed man, regaled them at lunch with his forebodings; his attitude toward the situation was like the food, which was greasy and uninspiring. Alone together once more, the two new-comers eyed each other sadly.

"Oh dear!" sighed Pippin. "We must change all this, Scorrier; it will never do to go back beaten. I shall not go back beaten; you will have to carry me on my shield," and slyly: "Too heavy, eh? Poor fellow!" Then for a long time he was silent, moving his lips as if adding up the cost. Suddenly he sighed, and grasping Scorrier's arm said: "Dull, aren't I? What will you do? Put me in your report, 'New Superintendent—sad, dull dog—not a word to throw at a cat!'" And as if the new task were too much for him, he sank back in thought. The last words he said to Scorrier that night were:

"Very silent here. It's hard to believe one's here for life. But I feel I am. Mustn't be a coward, though!" and brushing his forehead, as though to clear from it a cobweb of faint thoughts, he hurried off.

Scorrier stayed on the verandah smoking. The rain had ceased, a few stars were burning dimly; even above the squalor of the township the scent of the forests, the interminable forests, brooded. There sprang into his mind the memory of a picture from one of his children's fairy books—the picture of a little bearded man on tiptoe, with poised head and a great sword, slashing at the castle of a giant.

It reminded him of Pippin. And suddenly, even to Scorrier—whose existence was one long encounter with strange places—the unseen presence of those woods, their heavy, healthy scent, the little sounds, like squeaks from tiny toys, issuing out of the gloomy silence, seemed intolerable, to be shunned, from the mere instinct of self-preservation. He thought of the evening he had spent in the bosom of "Down-by-the-starn" Hemmings' family, receiving his last instructions—the security of that suburban villa, its discouraging gentility; the superior acidity of the Miss Hemmings; the noble names of large contractors, of company promoters, of a peer, dragged with the lightness of gun-carriages across the conversation; the autocracy of Hemmings, rasped up here and there, by some domestic contradiction. It was all so nice and safe—as if the whole thing had been fastened to an anchor sunk beneath the pink cabbages of the drawing-room carpet! Hemmings, seeing him off the premises, had said with secrecy: "Little Pippin will have a good thing. We shall make his salary £—. He'll be a great man—quite a king. Ha-ha!"

Scorrier shook the ashes from his pipe. 'Salary!' he thought, straining his ears; 'I wouldn't take the place for five thousand pounds a year. And yet it's a fine country,' and with ironic violence he repeated, 'a dashed fine country!'

Ten days later, having finished his report on the new mine, he stood on the jetty waiting to go aboard the steamer for home.

"God bless you!" said Pippin. "Tell them they needn't be afraid; and sometimes when you're at home think of me, eh?"

Scorrier, scrambling on board, had a confused memory of tears in his eyes, and a convulsive handshake.

II

It was eight years before the wheels of life carried Scorrier back to that disenchanted spot, and this time not on the business of the New Colliery Company. He went for another company with a mine some thirty miles away. Before starting, however, he visited

Hemmings. The secretary was surrounded by pigeon-holes and finer than ever; Scorrier blinked in the full radiance of his courtesy. A little man with eyebrows full of questions, and a grizzled beard, was seated in an arm-chair by the fire.

"You know Mr. Booker," said Hemmings—"one of my directors. This is Mr. Scorrier, sir—who went out for us."

These sentences were murmured in a way suggestive of their uncommon value. The director uncrossed his legs, and bowed. Scorrier also bowed, and Hemmings, leaning back, slowly developed the full resources of his waistcoat.

"So you are going out again, Scorrier, for the other side. I tell Mr. Scorrier, sir, that he is going out for the enemy. Don't find them a mine as good as you found us, there's a good man."

The little director asked explosively: "See our last dividend? Twenty per cent.; eh, what?"

Hemmings moved a finger, as if reproving his director. "I will not disguise from you," he murmured, "that there is friction between us and—the enemy; you know our position too well—just a little too well, eh? 'A nod's as good as a wink.'"

His diplomatic eyes flattered Scorrier, who passed a hand over his brow—and said: "Of course."

"Pippin doesn't hit it off with them. Between ourselves, he's a leetle too big for his boots. You know what it is when a man in his position gets a sudden rise!"

Scorrier caught himself searching on the floor for a sight of Hemmings' boots; he raised his eyes guiltily. The secretary continued: "We don't hear from him quite as often as we should like, in fact."

To his own surprise Scorrier murmured: "It's a silent place!"

The secretary smiled. "Very good! Mr. Scorrier says, sir, it's a silent place; ha—ha! I call that very good!" But suddenly a secret irritation seemed to bubble in him; he burst forth almost violently: "He's no business to let it affect him; now, has he? I put it to you, Mr. Scorrier, I put it to you, sir!"

But Scorrier made no reply, and soon after took his leave: he had been asked to convey a friendly hint to Pippin that more frequent letters would be welcomed. Standing in the shadow of the Royal

Exchange, waiting to thread his way across, he thought: 'So you must have noise, must you—you've got some here, and to spare.' . . .

On his arrival in the new world he wired to Pippin asking if he might stay with him on the way up country, and received the answer: "Be sure and come."

A week later he arrived (there was now a railway) and found Pippin waiting for him in a phaeton. Scorrier would not have known the place again; there was a glitter over everything, as if some one had touched it with a wand. The tracks had given place to roads, running firm, straight, and black between the trees under brilliant sunshine; the wooden houses were all painted; out in the gleaming harbour amongst the green of islands lay three steamers, each with a fleet of busy boats; and here and there a tiny yacht floated, like a sea-bird on the water. Pippin drove his long-tailed horses furiously; his eyes brimmed with subtle kindness, as if according Scorrier a continual welcome. During the two days of his stay Scorrier never lost that sense of glamour. He had every opportunity for observing the grip Pippin had over everything. The wooden doors and walls of his bungalow kept out no sounds. He listened to interviews between his host and all kinds and conditions of men. The voices of the visitors would rise at first—angry, discontented, matter-of-fact, with nasal twang, or guttural drawl; then would come the soft patter of the superintendent's feet crossing and recrossing the room. Then a pause, the sound of hard breathing, and quick questions— the visitor's voice again, again the patter, and Pippin's ingratiating but decisive murmurs. Presently out would come the visitor with an expression on his face which Scorrier soon began to know by heart, a kind of pleased, puzzled, helpless look, which seemed to say, "I've been done, I know—I'll give it to myself when I'm round the corner."

Pippin was full of wistful questions about "home." He wanted to talk of music, pictures, plays, of how London looked, what new streets there were, and, above all, whether Scorrier had been lately in the West Country. He talked of getting leave next winter, asked whether Scorrier thought they would "put up with him at home"; then, with the agitation which had alarmed Scorrier before, he added: "Ah! but I'm not fit for home now. One gets spoiled; it's big and silent here. What should I go back to? I don't seem to realise."

Scorrier thought of Hemmings. "'Tis a bit cramped there, certainly," he muttered.

Pippin went on as if divining his thoughts. "I suppose our friend Hemmings would call me foolish; he's above the little weaknesses of imagination, eh? Yes; it's silent here. Sometimes in the evening I would give my head for somebody to talk to—Hemmings would never give his head for anything, I think. But all the same, I couldn't face them at home. Spoiled!" And slyly he murmured: "What would the Board say if they could hear that?"

Scorrier blurted out: "To tell you the truth, they complain a little of *not* hearing from you."

Pippin put out a hand, as if to push something away. "Let them try the life here!" he broke out; "it's like sitting on a live volcano—what with our friends, 'the enemy,' over there; the men; the American competition. I keep it going, Scorrier, but at what a cost—at what a cost!"

"But surely—letters?"

Pippin only answered: "I try—I try!"

Scorrier felt with remorse and wonder that he had spoken the truth. The following day he left for his inspection, and while in the camp of "the enemy" much was the talk he heard of Pippin.

"Why!" said his host, the superintendent, a little man with a face somewhat like an owl's, "d'you know the name they've given him down in the capital—'the King'—good, eh? He's made them 'sit up' all along this coast. I like him well enough—good-hearted man, shocking nervous; but my people down there can't stand him at any price. Sir, he runs this colony. You'd think butter wouldn't melt in that mouth of his; but he always gets his way; that's what riles 'em so; that and the success he's making of his mine. It puzzles me; you'd think he'd only be too glad of a quiet life, a man with his nerves. But no, he's never happy unless he's fighting, something where he's got a chance to score a victory. I won't say he likes it, but, by Jove, it seems he's got to do it. Now that's funny! I'll tell you one thing, though—shouldn't be a bit surprised if he broke down some day;

and I'll tell you another," he added darkly, "he's sailing very near the wind, with those large contracts that he makes. I wouldn't care to take his risks. Just let them have a strike, or something that shuts them down for a spell—and mark my words, sir—it'll be all up with them. But," he concluded confidentially, "I wish I had his hold on the men; it's a great thing in this country. Not like home, where you can go round a corner and get another gang. You have to make the best you can out of the lot you have; you won't get another man for love or money without you ship him a few hundred miles." And with a frown he waved his arm over the forests to indicate the barrenness of the land.

III

Scorrier finished his inspection and went on a shooting trip into the forest. His host met him on his return. "Just look at this!" he said, holding out a telegram. "Awful, isn't it?" His face expressed a profound commiseration, almost ludicrously mixed with the ashamed contentment that men experience at the misfortunes of an enemy.

The telegram, dated the day before, ran thus: "Frightful explosion New Colliery this morning, great loss of life feared."

Scorrier had the bewildered thought: 'Pippin will want me now.'

He took leave of his host, who called after him: "You'd better wait for a steamer! It's a beastly drive!"

Scorrier shook his head. All night, jolting along a rough track cut through the forest, he thought of Pippin. The other miseries of this calamity at present left him cold; he barely thought of the smothered men; but Pippin's struggle, his lonely struggle with this hydra-headed monster, touched him very nearly. He fell asleep and dreamed of watching Pippin slowly strangled by a snake; the agonised, kindly, ironic face peeping out between two gleaming coils was so horribly real, that he awoke. It was the moment before dawn: pitch-black branches barred the sky; with every jolt of the wheels the gleams from the lamps danced, fantastic and intrusive, round ferns and tree-stems, into the cold heart of the forest. For an hour or more Scorrier tried to feign sleep, and hide from the stillness and overmastering gloom of these great woods. Then softly a whisper of noises stole forth, a stir of light, and the whole slow radiance of the morning glory. But it brought no warmth; and Scorrier wrapped himself closer in his cloak, feeling as though old age had touched him.

Close on noon he reached the township. Glamour seemed still to hover over it. He drove on to the mine. The winding-engine was turning, the pulley at the top of the head-gear whizzing round; nothing looked unusual. 'Some mistake!' he thought. He drove to the mine buildings, alighted, and climbed to the shaft head. Instead of the usual rumbling of the trolleys, the rattle of coal discharged over the screens, there was silence. Close by, Pippin himself was standing, smirched with dirt. The cage, coming swift and silent from below, shot open its doors with a sharp rattle. Scorrier bent forward to look. There lay a dead man, with a smile on his face.

"How many?" he whispered.

Pippin answered: "Eighty-four brought up—forty-seven still below," and entered the man's name in a pocket-book.

An older man was taken out next: he too was smiling—there had been vouchsafed to him, it seemed, a taste of more than earthly joy. The sight of those strange smiles affected Scorrier more than all the anguish or despair he had seen scored on the faces of other dead men. He asked an old miner how long Pippin had been at work.

"Thirty hours. Yesterday he wer' below; we had to nigh carry mun up at last. He's for goin' down again, but the chaps won't lower mun;" the old man gave a sigh. "I'm waiting for my boy to come up, I am."

Scorrier waited too—there was fascination about those dead, smiling faces. The rescuing of these men who would never again breathe went on and on. Scorrier grew sleepy in the sun. The old miner woke him, saying: "Rummy stuff this here choke-damp; see, they all dies drunk! "The very next to be brought up was the chief engineer. Scorrier had known him quite well, one of those Scotsmen who are born at the age of forty and remain so all their lives. His face—the only one that wore no smile—seemed grieving that duty had deprived it of that last luxury. With wide eyes and drawn lips he had died protesting.

Late in the afternoon the old miner touched Scorrier's arm, and said: "There he is—there's my boy!" And he departed slowly, wheeling the body on a trolley.

As the sun set, the gang below came up. No further search was possible till the fumes had cleared. Scorrier heard one man say: "There's some we'll never get; they've had sure burial."

Another answered him: "'Tis a gude enough bag for me!" They passed him, the whites of their eyes gleaming out of faces black as ink.

Pippin drove him home at a furious pace, not uttering a single word. As they turned into the main street, a young woman starting out before the horses obliged Pippin to pull up. The glance he bent on Scorrier was ludicrously prescient of suffering. The woman asked for her husband. Several times they were stopped thus by women asking for their husbands or sons. "This is what I have to go through," Pippin whispered.

When they had eaten, he said to Scorrier: "It was kind of you to come and stand by me! They take me for a good, poor creature that I am. But shall I ever get the men down again? Their nerve's shaken. I wish I were one of those poor lads, to die with a smile like that!"

Scorrier felt the futility of his presence. On Pippin alone must be the heat and burden. Would he stand under it, or would the whole thing come crashing to the ground? He urged him again and again to rest, but Pippin only gave him one of his queer smiles. "You don't know how strong. I am!" he said.

IV

He himself slept heavily; and, waking at dawn, went down. Pippin was still at his desk; his pen had dropped; he was asleep. The ink was wet; Scorrier's eye caught the opening words:

"Gentlemen,—since this happened I have not slept." . . .

He stole away again with a sense of indignation that no one could be dragged in to share that fight. The London Boardroom rose before his mind. He imagined the portentous gravity of Hemmings; his face and voice and manner conveying the impression that he alone could save the situation; the six directors; all men of commonsense and certainly humane, seated behind large turret-shaped inkpots; the concern and irritation in their voices, asking how it could have happened; their comments: "An awful thing!" "I suppose Pippin is doing the best he can!" "Wire him on no account to leave the mine idle!" "Poor devils!" "A fund? Of course, what ought we to give?" He had a strong conviction that nothing of all this would disturb the commonsense with which they would go home and eat their mutton. A good thing too; the less it was taken to heart the better! But Scorrier felt angry. The fight was so unfair! A fellow all nerves—with not a soul to help him! Well, it was his own lookout! He had chosen to centre it all in himself, to make himself its very soul. If he gave way now, the ship must go down! By a thin thread, Scorrier's hero-worship still held. 'Man against nature,' he thought, 'I back the man.' The struggle in which he was so powerless to give aid, became intensely personal to him, as if he had engaged his own good faith therein.

The next day they went down again to the pithead; and Scorrier himself descended. The fumes had almost cleared, but there were some places which would never be reached. At the end of the day all but four bodies had been recovered. "In the day o' judgment," a miner said, "they four'll come out of here." Those unclaimed bodies haunted Scorrier. He came on sentences of writing, where men waiting to be suffocated had written down their feelings. In one place, the hour, the word "Sleepy," and a signature. In another, "A.F.—done for." When he came up at last Pippin was still waiting, pocket-book in hand; they again departed at a furious pace.

Two days later Scorrier, visiting the shaft, found its neighbourhood deserted—not a living thing of any sort was there except one Chinaman poking his stick into the rubbish. Pippin was away down the coast engaging an engineer; and on his return, Scorrier had not the heart to tell him of the desertion. He was spared the effort, for Pippin said: "Don't be afraid—you've got bad news? The men have gone on strike."

Scorrier sighed. "Lock, stock and barrel."

"I thought so—see what I have here!" He put before Scorrier a telegram:

"At all costs keep working—fatal to stop—manage this somehow.—HEMMINGS."

Breathing quickly, he added: "As if I didn't know! 'Manage this somehow'—a little hard!"

"What's to be done?" asked Scorrier.

"You see I am commanded!" Pippin answered bitterly. "And they're quite right; we *must* keep working—our contracts! Now I'm down—not a soul will spare me!"

The miners' meeting was held the following day on the outskirts of the town. Pippin had cleared the place to make a public recreation ground—a sort of feather in the company's cap; it was now to be the spot whereon should be decided the question of the company's life or death.

The sky to the west was crossed by a single line of cloud like a bar of beaten gold; tree shadows crept towards the groups of men; the evening savour, that strong fragrance of the forest, sweetened the air. The miners stood all round amongst the burnt tree-stumps, cowed and sullen. They looked incapable of movement or expression. It was this dumb paralysis that frightened Scorrier. He watched Pippin speaking from his phaeton, the butt of all those sullen, restless eyes. Would he last out? Would the wires hold? It was like the finish of a race. He caught a baffled look on Pippin's face, as if he despaired of piercing that terrible paralysis. The men's eyes had begun to wander. 'He's lost his hold,' thought Scorrier; 'it's all up!'

A miner close beside him muttered: "Look out!"

Pippin was leaning forward, his voice had risen, the words fell like a whiplash on the faces of the crowd: "You shan't throw me over; do you think I'll give up all I've done for you? I'll make you the first power in the colony! Are you turning tail at the first shot? You're a set of cowards, my lads!"

Each man round Scorrier was listening with a different motion of the hands—one rubbed them, one clenched them, another moved his closed fist, as if stabbing some one in the back. A grisly-bearded, beetle-browed, twinkling-eyed old Cornishman muttered: "Ah'm not troublin' about that." It seemed almost as if Pippin's object was to get the men to kill him; they had gathered closer, crouching for a rush. Suddenly Pippin's voice dropped to a whisper: "I'm disgraced! Men, are you going back on me?"

The old miner next Scorrier called out suddenly: "Anny that's Cornishmen here to stand by the superintendent?" A group drew together, and with murmurs and gesticulation the meeting broke up.

In the evening a deputation came to visit Pippin; and all night long their voices and the superintendent's footsteps could be heard. In the morning, Pippin went early to the mine. Before supper the deputation came again; and again Scorrier had to listen hour after hour to the sound of voices and footsteps till he fell asleep. Just before dawn he was awakened by a light. Pippin stood at his bedside. "The men go down to-morrow," he said: "What did I tell you? Carry me home on my shield, eh?"

In a week the mine was in full work.

V

Two years later, Scorrier heard once more of Pippin. A note from Hemmings reached him asking if he could make it convenient to attend their Board meeting the following Thursday. He arrived rather before the appointed time. The secretary received him, and, in answer to inquiry, said: "Thank you, we are doing well—between ourselves, we are doing very well."

"And Pippin?"

The secretary frowned. "Ah, Pippin! We asked you to come on his account. Pippin is giving us a lot of trouble. We have not had a single line from him for just two years!" He spoke with such a sense of personal grievance that Scorrier felt quite sorry for him. "Not a single line," said Hemmings, "since that explosion—you were there at the time, I remember! It makes it very awkward; I call it personal to *me*."

"But how——" Scorrier began.

"We get—telegrams. He writes to no one, not even to his family. And why? Just tell me why? We hear of him; he's a great nob out there. Nothing's done in the colony without his finger being in the pie. He turned out the last Government because they wouldn't grant us an extension for our railway—shows he can't be a fool. Besides, look at our balance-sheet!"

It turned out that the question on which Scorrier's opinion was desired was, whether Hemmings should be sent out to see what was the matter with the superintendent. During the discussion which ensued, he was an unwilling listener to strictures on Pippin's silence. "The explosion," he muttered at last, "a very trying time!"

Mr. Booker pounced on him. "A very trying time! So it was—to all of us. But what excuse is that?"

Scorrier was obliged to admit that it was none.

"Business is business—eh, what?"

Scorrier, gazing round that neat Board-room, nodded. A deaf director, who had not spoken for some months, said with sudden fierceness: "It's disgraceful!" He was obviously letting off the fume of long-unuttered disapprovals. One perfectly neat, benevolent old fellow, however, who had kept his hat on, and had a single vice— that of coming to the Board-room with a brown paper parcel tied up with string—murmured: "We must make allowances," and started an anecdote about his youth. He was gently called to order by his secretary. Scorrier was asked for his opinion. He looked at Hemmings. "My importance is concerned," was written all over the secretary's face. Moved by an impulse of loyalty to Pippin, Scorrier answered, as if it were all settled: "Well, let me know when you are starting, Hemmings—I should like the trip myself."

As he was going out, the chairman, old Jolyon Forsyte, with a grave, twinkling look at Hemmings, took him aside. "Glad to hear you say that about going too, Mr. Scorrier; we must be careful—Pippin's such a good fellow, and so sensitive; and our friend there—a bit heavy in the hand, um?"

Scorrier did in fact go out with Hemmings. The secretary was sea-sick, and his prostration, dignified but noisy, remained a memory for ever; it was sonorous and fine—the prostration of superiority; and the way in which he spoke of it, taking casual acquaintances into the caves of his experience, was truly interesting.

Pippin came down to the capital to escort them, provided for their comforts as if they had been royalty, and had a special train to take them to the mines.

He was a little stouter, brighter of colour, greyer of beard, more nervous perhaps in voice and breathing. His manner to Hemmings was full of flattering courtesy; but his sly, ironical glances played on the secretary's armour like a fountain on a hippopotamus. To Scorrier, however, he could not show enough affection.

The first evening, when Hemmings had gone to his room, he jumped up like a boy out of school. "So I'm going to get a wigging," he said: "I suppose I deserve it; but if you knew—if you *only* knew! . . . Out here they've nicknamed me 'the King'—they say I rule the colony. It's myself that I can't rule"; and with a sudden burst of passion such as Scorrier had never seen in him: "Why did they send this man here? What can he know about the things that I've been through?" In a moment he calmed down again: "There! this is very stupid; worrying you like this!" and with a long, kind look into Scorrier's face, he hustled him off to bed.

Pippin did not break out again, though fire seemed to smoulder behind the bars of his courteous irony. Intuition of danger had evidently smitten Hemmings, for he made no allusion to the object of his visit. There were moments when Scorrier's common-sense sided with Hemmings—these were moments when the secretary was not present.

'After all,' he told himself, 'it's a little thing to ask—one letter a month. I never heard of such a case.' It was wonderful indeed how they stood it! It showed how much they valued Pippin! What was the matter with him? What was the nature of his trouble? One glimpse Scorrier had when even Hemmings, as he phrased it, received "quite a turn." It was during a drive back from the most outlying of the company's trial mines, eight miles through the forest. The track led through a belt of trees blackened by a forest fire. Pippin was driving. The secretary seated beside him wore an expression of faint alarm, such as Pippin's driving was warranted to evoke from almost any face. The sky had darkened strangely, but pale streaks of light, coming from one knew not where, filtered through the trees. No breath was stirring; the wheels and horses' hoofs made no sound on the deep fern mould. All around, the burnt tree-trunks, leafless and jagged, rose like withered giants, the passages between them were black, the sky black, and black the silence. No one spoke, and literally the only sound was Pippin's breathing. What was it that was so terrifying? Scorrier had a feeling of entombment; that nobody could help him; the feeling of being face to face with Nature; a sensation as if all the comfort and security of words and rules had dropped away from him. And—nothing happened. They reached home and dined.

During dinner he had again that old remembrance of a little man chopping at a castle with his sword. It came at a moment when Pippin had raised his hand with the carving-knife grasped in it to answer some remark of Hemmings' about the future of the company. The optimism in his uplifted chin, the strenuous energy in his whispering voice, gave Scorrier a more vivid glimpse of Pippin's nature than he had perhaps ever had before. This new country, where nothing but himself could help a man—that was the castle! No wonder Pippin was impatient of control, no wonder he was out of hand, no wonder he was silent—chopping away at that! And suddenly he thought: 'Yes, and all the time one knows, Nature must beat him in the end!'

That very evening Hemmings delivered himself of his reproof. He had sat unusually silent; Scorrier, indeed, had thought him a little drunk, so portentous was his gravity; suddenly, however, he rose. It was hard on a man, he said, in his position, with a Board (he spoke as of a family of small children), to be kept so short of information.

He was actually compelled to use his imagination to answer the shareholders' questions. This was painful and humiliating; he had never heard of any secretary having to use his imagination! He went further—it was insulting! He had grown grey in the service of the company. Mr. Scorrier would bear him out when he said he had a position to maintain—his name in the City was a high one; and, by George! he was going to keep it a high one; he would allow nobody to drag it in the dust—that ought clearly to be understood. His directors felt they were being treated like children; however that might be, it was absurd to suppose that he (Hemmings) could be treated like a child! . . . The secretary paused; his eyes seemed to bully the room.

"If there were no London office," murmured Pippin, "the shareholders would get the same dividends."

Hemmings gasped. "Come!" he said, "this is monstrous!"

"What help did I get from London when I first came here? What help have I ever had?"

Hemmings swayed, recovered, and with a forced smile replied that, if this were true, he had been standing on his head for years; he did not believe the attitude possible for such a length of time; personally he would have thought that he too had a little something to say to the company's position, but no matter! . . . His irony was crushing . . . It was possible that Mr. Pippin hoped to reverse the existing laws of the universe with regard to limited companies; he would merely say that he must not begin with a company of which he (Hemmings) happened to be secretary. Mr. Scorrier had hinted at excuses; for his part, with the best intentions in the world, he had great difficulty in seeing them. He would go further—he did *not* see them! The explosion! . . . Pippin shrank so visibly that Hemmings seemed troubled by a suspicion that he had gone too far.

"We know," he said, "that it was trying for you——"

"Trying!" burst out Pippin.

"No one can say," Hemmings resumed soothingly, "that we have not dealt liberally." Pippin made a motion of the head. "We think we have a good superintendent; I go further, an excellent superintendent. What I say is: Let's be pleasant! I am not making an unreasonable request!" He ended on a fitting note of jocularity; and, as if by consent, all three withdrew, each to his own room, without another word.

In the course of the next day Pippin said to Scorrier: "It seems I have been very wicked. I must try to do better;" and with a touch of bitter humour, "They are kind enough to think me a good superintendent, you see! After that I must try hard."

Scorrier broke in: "No man could have done so much for them;" and, carried away by an impulse to put things absolutely straight, went on: "But, after all, a letter now and then—what does it amount to?"

Pippin besieged him with a subtle glance. "You too?" he said—"I must indeed have been a wicked man!" and turned away.

Scorrier felt as if he had been guilty of brutality; sorry for Pippin, angry with himself; angry with Pippin, sorry for himself. He earnestly desired to see the back of Hemmings. The secretary gratified the wish a few days later, departing by steamer with ponderous expressions of regard and the assurance of his goodwill.

Pippin gave vent to no outburst of relief, maintaining a courteous silence, making only one allusion to his late guest, in answer to a remark of Scorrier:

"Ah! don't tempt me! mustn't speak behind his back."

VI

A month passed, and Scorrier still remained Pippin's guest. As each mail-day approached he experienced a queer suppressed excitement. On one of these occasions Pippin had withdrawn to his room; and when Scorrier went to fetch him to dinner he found him with his head leaning on his hands, amid a perfect litter of torn paper. He looked up at Scorrier.

"I can't do it," he said, "I feel such a hypocrite; I can't put myself into leading-strings again. Why should I ask these people, when I've settled everything already? If it were a vital matter they wouldn't want to hear—they'd simply wire, 'Manage this somehow!'"

Scorrier said nothing, but thought privately: 'This is mad business!' What was a letter? Why make a fuss about a letter? The approach of mail-day seemed like a nightmare to the superintendent; he became feverishly nervous like a man under a spell; and, when the mail had gone, behaved like a respited criminal. And this had been going on two years! Ever since that explosion. Why, it was monomania!

One day, a month after Hemmings' departure, Pippin rose early from dinner; his face was flushed, he had been drinking wine. "I won't be beaten this time," he said, as he passed Scorrier. The latter could hear him writing in the next room, and looked in presently to say that he was going for a walk. Pippin gave him a kindly nod.

It was a cool, still evening: innumerable stars swarmed in clusters over the forests, forming bright hieroglyphics in the middle heavens, showering over the dark harbour into the sea. Scorrier walked slowly. A weight seemed lifted from his mind,
so entangled had he become in that uncanny silence. At last Pippin had broken through the spell. To get that letter sent would be the laying of a phantom, the rehabilitation of commonsense. Now that this silence was in the throes of being broken, he felt curiously tender towards Pippin, without the hero-worship of old days, but with a queer protective feeling. After all, he was different from other men. In spite of his, feverish, tenacious energy, in spite of his ironic humour, there was something of the woman in him! And as for this silence, this horror of control—all geniuses had "bees in their bonnets," and Pippin was a genius in his way!

He looked back at the town. Brilliantly lighted it had a thriving air—difficult to believe of the place he remembered ten years back; the sounds of drinking, gambling, laughter, and dancing floated to his ears. 'Quite a city!' he thought. With this queer elation on him he walked slowly back along the street, forgetting that he was simply an oldish mining expert, with a look of shabbiness, such as clings to men who are always travelling, as if their "nap" were for ever being rubbed off. And he thought of Pippin, creator of this glory.

He had passed the boundaries of the town, and had entered the forest. A feeling of discouragement instantly beset him. The scents and silence, after the festive cries and odours of the town, were undefinably oppressive. Notwithstanding, he walked a long time, saying to himself that he would give the letter every chance. At last, when he thought that Pippin must have finished, he went back to the house.

Pippin had finished. His forehead rested on the table, his arms hung at his sides; he was stone-dead! His face wore a smile, and by his side lay an empty laudanum bottle.

The letter, closely, beautifully written, lay before him. It was a fine document, clear, masterly, detailed, nothing slurred, nothing concealed, nothing omitted; a complete review of the company's position; it ended with the words: "Your humble servant, RICHARD PIPPIN."

Scorrier took possession of it. He dimly understood that with those last words a wire had snapped. The border-line had been overpassed; the point reached where that sense of proportion, which alone makes life possible, is lost. He was certain that at the moment of his death Pippin could have discussed bimetallism, or any intellectual problem, except the one problem of his own heart; *that*, for some mysterious reason, had been too much for him. His death had been the work of a moment of supreme revolt—a single instant of madness on a single subject! He found on the blotting-paper, scrawled across the impress of the signature, "Can't stand it!" The completion of that letter had been to him a struggle ungraspable by Scorrier. Slavery? Defeat? A violation of Nature? The death of justice? It were better not to think of it! Pippin could have told—but he would never speak again. Nature, at whom, unaided, he had dealt so many blows, had taken her revenge! . . .

In the night Scorrier stole down, and, with an ashamed face, cut off a lock of the fine grey hair. 'His daughter might like it!' he thought.

He waited till Pippin was buried, then, with the letter in his pocket, started for England.

He arrived at Liverpool on a Thursday morning, and travelling to town, drove straight to the office of the company. The Board were sitting. Pippin's successor was already being interviewed. He passed out as Scorrier came in, a middle-aged man with a large, red beard, and a foxy, compromising face. He also was a Cornishman. Scorrier wished him luck with a very heavy heart.

As an unsentimental man, who had a proper horror of emotion, whose living depended on his good sense, to look back on that interview with the Board was painful. It had excited in him a rage of which he was now heartily ashamed. Old Jolyon Forsyte, the chairman, was not there for once, guessing perhaps that the Board's view of this death would be too small for him; and little Mr. Booker sat in his place. Every one had risen, shaken hands with Scorrier, and expressed themselves indebted for his coming. Scorrier placed Pippin's letter on the table, and gravely the secretary read out to his Board the last words of their superintendent. When he had finished, a director said, "That's not the letter of a madman!" Another answered: "Mad as a hatter; nobody but a madman would have thrown up such a post." Scorrier suddenly withdrew. He heard Hemmings calling after him. "Aren't you well, Mr. Scorrier? aren't you well, sir?"

He shouted back: "Quite sane, I thank you." . . .

The Naples "express" rolled round the outskirts of the town. Vesuvius shone in the sun, uncrowned by smoke. But even as Scorrier looked, a white puff went soaring up. It was the footnote to his memories.

[*February, 1901*]

A FEUD

I

ITs psychic origin, like that of most human loves and hates, was obscure, and yet, like most human hates and loves, had a definite point of physical departure—the moment when Bowden's yellow dog bit Steer's ungaitered leg. Even then it might not have "got going," as they say, but for the village sense of justice which caused Steer to bring his gun next day and solemnly execute the dog. He was the third person the dog had bitten; not even Bowden, who was fond of his whippet, opposed the execution, but the shot left him with an obscure feeling of lost property, a dim sense of disloyalty to his dog. Steer was a Northerner, an Easterner, a man from a part called Lincolnshire, outlandish, like the Frisian cattle he mixed with the Devons on his farm—this, Bowden could not help feeling in the bottom of his soul, was what had moved his dog. Snip had not liked, any more than his master, that thin, spry, red grey-bearded chap's experimental ways of farming, his habit of always being an hour, a week, a month earlier than Bowden; had not liked his lean, dry activity, his thin legs, his east-wind air. Bowden knew that he would have shot Steer's dog if he himself had been the third person Steer's dog had bitten; but then Steer's dog had *not* bitten Bowden, and Bowden's dog *had* bitten Steer; and this seemed to Bowden to show that his dog knew what was what. And while he was burying the poor brute, he had muttered: "Darn the man! What did he want trapesin' about my yard in his Sunday breeks—seein' what he could get, I suppose!" And with each shovel of earth he threw on the limp yellow body, a sticky resentment had oozed from his spirit and clung, undissolving, round the springs of its action. To inter the dog properly was a long hot job.

'He comes and shoots my dog—of a Sunday too, and leaves me to bury 'un,' he thought, wiping his round, well-coloured face; and he spat as if the ground in front of him were Steer. When he had finished and rolled a big stone on to the little mound, he went in, and, sitting down moodily in the kitchen, said:

"Girl, draw me a glass o' cider." Having drunk it, he looked up and added: "I've a-burried she up to Crossovers." The dog was male, a lissome whippet unconnected with the business of the farm, and Bowden had called him "she" from puppy-hood. The dark-haired, broad-faced, rather sullen-looking girl whom he addressed flushed, and her grey eyes widened with pain. "'Twas a shame!" she muttered.

"Ah!" said Bowden.

Bowden farmed about a hundred acres of half-and-half sort of land, some good, some poor, just under the down. He was a widower, with a mother and an only son. A broad, easy man, with a dark round head, a rosy face, and immense capacity for living in the moment. Looking at him, you would have said not a man in whom things would rankle. But then to look at a West Countryman you would say so many things that have their lurking negations. He was a native of the natives—his family went back in the parish to times beyond the opening of the register; his ancestors had been churchwardens in remote days. His father, "Daddy Bowden," an easy-going, handsome old fellow, and a bit of a rip, had died at ninety. He himself was well over fifty, but had no grey hair as yet. He took life easy, and let his farm off lightly, keeping it nearly all to pasture, with a conservative grin (Bowden was a Liberal) at the outlandish efforts of his neighbour Steer (a Tory) to grow wheat, bring in Frisian stock, and use new-fangled machines. Steer had originally come to that part of the country as a gentleman's bailiff, and this induced a sort of secret contempt in Bowden, whose forefathers in old days had farmed their own land here round about. Bowden's mother, eighty-eight years old, was a little pocket-woman almost past speech, with dark bright eyes and innumerable wrinkles, who sat all day long in any warmth there was, conserving energy. His son Ned, a youth of twenty-four, bullet-headed like all the Bowdens, was of a lighter colour in hair and eyes. At the moment of history when Steer shot Bowden's dog, he was keeping company with Steer's niece, Molly Winch, who kept house for the confirmed bachelor that Steer was. The other member of Bowden's household, the girl Pansy, was an orphan, some said born under a rose, who came from the other side of the moor and earned fourteen pounds a year. She kept to herself, had dark fine hair, grey eyes, a pale broad face; "broody" she was given somewhat to the "tantrums"; now she would look quite plain; now, when moved or excited, quite pretty. Hers was all the housework, and much of the poultry-feeding, wood-cutting and water-drawing. She was hard-worked, and often sullen because of it.

Having finished his cider, Bowden stood in the kitchen porch looking idly at a dance of gnats. The weather was fine, and the hay was in. It was one of those intervals between harvests which he was wont to take easy, and it would amuse him to think of his neighbour always "puzzivanting" over some "improvement" or other. But it did not amuse him this evening. That chap was for ever trying to sneak ahead of his neighbours! Young Bowden had just milked the cows, and was turning them down the lane. The lad would "slick himself up" and go courting that niece of Steers! The courtship seemed to Bowden suddenly unnatural. A cough made him conscious of the girl Pansy standing behind him with her sleeves rolled up.

"Butiful evenin'," he said—"gude for the corn." When Bowden indulged his sense of the æsthetic he would apologise with some comment that implied commercial benefit or loss; while Steer would pass on with only a dry "Fine evenin'." In talking with Steer one never lost consciousness of his keen "on-the-makeness," as of a progressive individualist who has no means of covering his nature from one's eyes. Bowden one might meet for weeks without realising that beneath his uncontradictious pleasantry was a self-preservative individualism quite as stubborn. To the casual eye, Steer was much more up to date and "civilised"; to one looking deeper, Bowden had been "civilised" much longer. He had grown protective covering in a softer climate, or drawn it outward from an older strain of blood.

"The gnats are dancin'," he said; "fine weather," and the girl Pansy nodded. Watching her turn the handle of the separator, he marked her glance straying down the yard to where Ned was shutting the

lane gate. She was a likely-looking wench, with her shapely browned arms, and her black hair fine as silk, which she kept brushing back from her eyes with her free hand, and it gave him a kind of farmyard amusement to see those eyes of hers following his son about. "She's Ned's if he wants her—young hussy!" he thought. "Begad, but it would put Steer's nose out of joint properly, if that girl got in front of his precious niece." To say that this thought was father to a wish would too definitely express the circumambulatory mind of Bowden
—a lazy and unprecise thinker; but it lurked and hovered while he took his ash-plant and browsed his way out of the yard, to have a look at the young bull before supper. At the meadow of the coarse water-weed and pasture, where the young red bull was grazing, he stood leaning over the gate, with the swallows flying high. The young bull was "lukin'-up bravely—in another year he would lay over that bull of Steers—ah, he would that! And a dim savagery stirred in Bowden, then passed in the sensuous enjoyment—which a farmer never admits—at the scent, sight, sounds of his fields in fine weather; at the blue above and the green beneath him, the gleam of that thread of water, half-smothered in bulrushes, "daggers," and monkey-flower under the slowly sinking sun; at the song of a lark and the murmuring in the ash trees; at the glistening ruddy coat of the young bull and the sound of his cropping. Three rabbits ran into the hedge. So that fellow had shot his dog—his dog that had nipped up more rabbits out of corn than any dog he ever owned! He tapped his stick on the gate. The young bull raised a lazy head, gazed at his master, and, flicking his tail at the flies, resumed his pasturing.

"Shot my dog!" thought Bowden. "Shot my dog! Yu wait a bit!"

II

The girl Pansy turned the handle of the separator, and its whining drone mixed with the thoughts and feelings, poignant yet formless, of one who had little say in her own career. There was an ache in her loins, for hay harvest was ever a hard week; and an ache in her heart, because she had no leisure, like Molly Winch and other girls who could find time for the piano and to make their dresses. She touched her hard frieze skirt. She was sick of the ugly thing! And she hastened the separator. She had to feed the calves, and set the supper, before she could change into her Sunday frock and go to evening church—her one weekly festivity. Ned Bowden! Her fancy soared to the monstrous extravagance of herself and Ned walking across the fields to church together, singing out of one hymn-book; Ned, who had given her a look when he passed just now as if he realised at last that she had been thinking of him for weeks. A dusky flush crept up in her pale cheeks. A girl must think of somebody—she wasn't old Mother Bowden, with her hands on her lap all day, in sunlight or fire-shine, content just to be warm! And she turned the handle with a sort of frenzy. Would the milk never finish running through? Ned never saw her in her frock—her frock sprigged with cornflowers; he went off too early to his courting, Sunday evenings. In this old skirt she looked so thick and muddy! And her arms——! Gazing despairingly at arms browned and roughened, her fancy took another monstrous flight. She saw herself and Molly Winch side by side ungarbed. Ah, she would make two of that

Molly Winch! The thought at once pained and pleased her. It was genteel to be thin and elegant; and yet—instinct told her—strength and firmness of flesh had been desirable before ever gentility existed. She let the handle go, and, lifting the pail of

"waste," hurried down with it to the dark byre, whence the young calves were thrusting their red muzzles. She pushed them back in turn—greedy little things; smacking their wet noses, scolding them. Ugh! How mucky it was in there—they ought to give that byre a good clean-up! She could barely wait for them to finish their drink, one by one—little slow, eager things—such was the longing in her to be in time this evening; then, banging down the empty pail, she ran to set out supper on the long deal table. In the last of the sunlight old Mother Bowden's bright eyes seemed to watch her inhumanly. She would never be done in time—never be done in time!

The beef, the cider, the cheese, the bread, the pickles—what else? Lettuce! Yes, and it wasn't washed, and Bowden loved his lettuce!

But she couldn't wait—she couldn't! Perhaps he'd forget it—if she put some cream out! From the cool, dark dairy, down the little stone passage, she fetched the remains of the scalded cream.

"Watch the cat, Missis Bowden!" And she ran up the wriggling narrow stairs.

The room she slept in was like a ship's cabin—no bigger. She drew the curtain over the porthole-like window, tore off her things and flung them on the narrow bed. This was her weekly change. There was a hole in her undergarment, and she tore it wider in her hurry. "I won't have time for a good wash," she thought. Taking her one towel, she damped it, rubbed it over her, and began to dress furiously. The church bell had begun its dull, hard single chime. The little room was fiery hot, and beads of sweat stood on the girl's brow. Savagely she thought: 'Why can't I have time to be cool, like Molly Winch?' A large spider, a little way out from one corner of the ceiling, seemed watching her, and she shuddered. She couldn't bear spiders—great hairy things! But she had no time to stretch up her hand and kill it. Glancing through a chink left by the drawn curtain, to see whether Ned had come down into the yard, she snatched up her powder-puff—precious possession, nearest approach to gentility—and solemnly rubbed it over face and neck. Now she wouldn't shine, anyway! She fastened on her Sunday hat, a broad-brimmed straw, trimmed with wide-eyed artificial daisies, and stood a moment contemplating her image in a mirror the size of her two hands. The scent of the powder, as of gone-off violets, soothed her nerves. But why was her hair so fine that it wouldn't stay in place?—and why black, instead of goldeny-brown like Molly Winch's hair? Her lip drooped—her eyes looked wide and mournful in the glass. She snatched up her pair of dirty white cotton gloves, took her prayer-book, threw open the door, and stood listening. Dead silence in the house! Ned Bowden's room, with his father's and his old grandmother's, were up the other stairs. She would have liked him to see her coming down—like what the young men did in the magazines, looking up at the young ladies, beautiful and cool, descending slowly. But would he look at her when he had his best on, going to Molly Winch? She went down the wriggling staircase. Gnats were still dancing outside the porch, ducks bathing and preening their feathers in sunlight which had lost all sting. She did not sit down, for fear of being caught too obviously waiting, but stood changing from tired foot to foot, while the scent of powder mingled queerly with the homely odour of the farmyard and the lingering perfume of the hay stacked up close by. The bell stopped ringing. Should she wait? Perhaps he wasn't going to church at all: just going to sit with Molly Winch, or to walk in the lanes with her. Oh no, that Molly Winch was too prim and proper; she wouldn't miss church! And suddenly something stirred within the girl. What would *she* not miss for a walk in the lanes with Ned? It wasn't fair! Some people had everything! The sound of heavy boots from stair to stair came to her ears, and, more swiftly than one would have thought natural to that firm body, she sped through the yard and passed through the door in its high wall to the field path. Scarcely more than a rut, it was strewn with wisps of hay, for they had not yet raked this last field, and the air smelled very sweet. She dawdled, every sense throbbing, aware of his approach behind her, and its measured dwelling on either foot which no Bowden could abandon, even when late for church. He ranged up; his hair was greased, his square figure stuffed handsome into boardlike Sunday dittos. His red face shone from soap, his grey eyes shone from surplus energy. From head to foot—he was wonderful! Would he pass her, or fall in alongside? He fell into step. The girl's heart thumped, her cheeks burned under the powder, so that the scent thereof was released. Young Bowden's arm, that felt like iron, bumped her own, and at the thrill which went through her, she half-closed her eyes.

"I reckon we're tu late," he said.

Her widened eyes challenged his stare.

"Don't you want to see Molly Winch, then?"

"No, I don't want any words about that dog."

Quick to see her chance, the girl exclaimed:

"'Twas a shame—it was; but she'd think more of her uncle's leg than of 'im, I know."

Again his arm pressed hers; he said: "Let's go down into the brake."

The bit of common land below the field was high with furze, where a few brown-gold blossoms were still clinging. A late cuckoo called shrilly from an ash tree below. The breeze stirred a faint rustling out of the hedgerow trees. Young Bowden sat down among the knee-high bracken that smelled of sap, and put his arm about her.

III

IN parishes whose farms are scattered and there is no real village, gossip has not quite its proper wings; and the first intimation Steer had that his niece was being slighted came from Bowden himself. Steer was wont to drive the seven miles to market in a small spring cart filled with produce on the journey in, and with groceries on the journey out. He held his eastwind face steadily, with eyes fixed on the ears of his mare. His niece sometimes sat beside him—one of those girls whose china is a little too thin for farm life. She was educated, and played the piano. Steer was proud of her, in spite of his low opinion of her father, who had died of consumption and left Steer's sister in poor circumstances and health. Molly Winch's face, indeed, had refinement; it coloured easily a faint rose-pink, was pointed in the chin, had a slightly tip-tilted nose, and pretty, truthful eyes—a nice face.

Steer's mare usually did the seven miles in just under forty minutes, and he was proud of her, especially when she overhauled Bowden's mare. The two spring carts travelled abreast of each other just long enough for these words to be exchanged:

"Mornin', Bowden!"

"Mornin'!—mornin', Miss Molly, 'aven't seen yu lately; thought yu were visitin'!"

"No, Mr. Bowden."

"Glad to see yu lukin' up s'well. Reckon Ned's tu busy elsewhere just now."

It was then that Steer's mare drew well ahead.

"My old mare's worth two of his," Steer thought.

Bowden's cart was distant dust before he turned to his niece and said:

"What's the matter with Ned Bowden? When did you see him last?"

His shrewd light eyes noted her lips quivering, and the stain on her cheeks.

"It's—it's a month now."

"It is—is it?" was all Steer said. But he flicked the mare sharply with his whip, thinking: "What's this? Didn't like that fellow's face—was he makin' game of us?"

Steer was an abstemious man; a tot of sloe gin before he embarked for home was the extent of his usual potations at "The Drake." But that day he took two tots, because of the grin on the face of Bowden, who would sit an hour and more after he had gone, absorbing gin and cider. Was that grin meant for him and for his niece?

A discreet man, too, he let a fortnight pass while he watched out. Ned Bowden did not come to church, nor was he seen at Steer's. Molly looked pale and peaky. And something deep stirred in Steer. "If he don't mean to keep his word to her," he thought, "I'll have the law of him, young pup!"

People talked no more freely to Steer than he to them; and another week had passed before he had fresh evidence. It came, after a parish meeting, from the schoolmistress, a grey-haired single lady much respected.

"I don't like Molly looking so pale and daverdy, Mr. Steer; I'm grieved about Ned Bowden—I thought he was a steady boy."

"What about him?"

"That girl at Bowden's."

Steer flopped into the depths of consciousness. So everybody round had known, maybe for weeks, that his niece was being jilted for that cross-bred slut; known, and been grinning up their sleeves, had they? He announced to his niece that evening:

"I'm goin' round to Bowden's."

She, coloured, then went pale.

"They shan't put it up on you," he said, "I'll see to that. Give me that ring of his—I may want it."

Molly Winch silently slipped off her amethyst engagement ring and gave it to him.

Steer put on his best hat, breeches and gaiters, took a thin stick and set out.

Corn harvest was coming near, and he crossed a field of his own wheat into a field of Bowden's oats. Steer was the only farmer round about who grew wheat. Wheat! In Bowden's view it was all his politics! But Steer was thinking: 'My wheat's lookin' well—don't think much of these oats' (another of his foreign expressions, for oats were "corn" to Bowden); 'he'll have no straw.'

He had not been in Bowden's yard since the day he executed the yellow whippet dog, and his calf twitched—the brute had given it a shrewd nip.

The girl Pansy opened the door to him. And, seeing the flush rise into her pale cheeks, he thought, 'If I were to lay my stick across your back, you'd know it, my girl.'

Bowden had just finished his supper of bacon, beans, and cider, and was smoking his pipe before the embers of a wood fire. He did not get up, and there seemed to Steer something studied and insulting in the way he nodded to a chair. He sat down with his stick across his knees, while the girl went quickly out.

"Butiful evenin'," said Bowden. "Fine weather for the corn. Have a drink o' cider?"

Steer shook his head. The cautious man was making sure of his surroundings before he opened fire. Old Mrs. Bowden sat in her chair by the recessed fire, with her little old back turned to the room. Bowden's white-headed bobtail was stretched out with his chin on his paws; a yellow cat crouched, still as the Sphinx, with half-closed eyes; nothing else was alive, except the slow-ticking clock.

Steer held up the amethyst ring.

"See this!"

Undisturbed by meaning or emotion, Bowden turned his face slowly towards the ring.

"Ah! What about it?"

"'Twas given to my niece for a purpose. Is that purpose goin' to be fulfilled?"

"Tidden for me to say. Ask Ned."

Steer closed his hand, slightly covered with reddish hairs.

"I've heard tales," he said, "and if he don' mean to keep his word I'll have the law of him. I've always thought my niece a sight too good for him; but if he thinks he can put a slight on her he's reckoning without the cost—that's all."

Bowden blew out a cloud of smoke.

"Ned's a man grown."

"Do you abet him?"

Bowden turned his head lazily.

"Don't you come here bullying me." And again he puffed out a cloud of smoke. Its scent increased the resentment in Steer, who was no smoker.

"Like father, like son," he said. "We know what your father was like."

Bowden took his pipe from his mouth with a fist the size of a beefsteak.

"With the old lady settin' there! Get out o' my house!" A wave of exasperated blood flooded Steer's thin cheeks.

"You know right well that she hears naught."

Bowden replaced his pipe. "'Tes no yuse tachin' yu manners," he muttered.

Something twitched in Steer's lean throat, where the reddish-grey hair covered his Adam's apple.

"I'll give your son a week, and then look out." A chuckle pursued him to the door.

"All right!" he thought. "We'll see who'll laugh last."

IV

Difficult to say whether morality exists in a man like Bowden, whose blood is racy of the soil, and whose farmyard is so adjacent. That his son should run riot with the girl Pansy would have struck him more, perhaps, if Steer had not shot his dog—the affair so providentially put that fellow's nose out of joint. It went far, in fact, to assuage his outraged sense of property, and to dull the feeling that he had betrayed his dog by not actively opposing village justice. As for the "Law," the Bowdens had lived for too many generations in a parish where no constable was resident to have any belief in its powers. He often broke the law himself in a quiet way—shooting stray pheasants and calling them pigeons, not inspecting his rabbit-traps morning and evening, not keeping quite to date in dipping his sheep, and so forth. "The Law" could always be evaded. Besides, what law was Ned breaking? That was Steer's talk!

He was contemptuously surprised, therefore, when, three weeks later, Ned received a document headed "High Courts of Justice. Winch *versus* Bowden," claiming five hundred pounds for breach of promise of marriage. An outlandish trick—with the war on too! Couldn't Ned please himself as to what girl he'd take? He was for putting it in the fire. But the more the two examined the document the more hypnotised they became. Lawyers were no use except to charge money—but, perhaps a lawyer ought to have a look at it.

On market day, therefore, they took it to Applewhite, of Applewhite and Carter, who subjected them to a prolonged catechism. Had Ned engaged himself to the girl? Well, yes, he supposed he had. How had he broken off the engagement—he had written to the girl? No! Well, he had received letters from her asking him what was the matter? Yes, two. Had he answered them? No. Had he seen the girl and done it by word of mouth? No! He had not seen the girl for ten weeks. Was he prepared to see the girl or write to her? He was not. Was he ready to marry her? No! Why was that?

Ned looked at his father; and Bowden looked at Ned. The girl Pansy had never been mentioned between them.

Mr. Applewhite repeated his question. Ned did not know.

According to the lawyer, if Ned did not know, nobody did. What had caused the change in his feelings?

It was Bowden who answered——

"He shot my dog."

"Who?"

"Steer."

Mr. Applewhite was unable to see the connection. If that was all, he was afraid young Mr. Bowden would either have to marry the girl or "stand to be shot at" himself. And suddenly he looked at Ned. "Is there anything against this girl?" No, there was nothing against her.

"Then why not marry her?"

Again Ned shook his bullet head.

The lawyer smoothed his chin—he was a pleasant fellow—and a good fisherman.

"About this young lady, Miss Winch; excuse my asking, but I suppose you haven't been putting the cart before the horse?"

For the third time Ned shook his head.

No, there had been nothing of that sort. He did not add that if there had he might not have been overmastered by the propinquity of the girl Pansy.

"There's another girl in this, I suppose," said the lawyer suddenly. "Well, I don't want to hear. It's for you to decide what you'll do—marry the girl or defend the action and get the damages reduced—it's a stiff claim. You and your father had better go away, talk it over again, and let me know. If you defend, you'll have to go up to London. In the box, least said is soonest mended. You'll simply say you found you were mistaken, and thought it more honourable to break off at once than to go on. That sometimes goes down rather well with juries, if the man looks straight-forward."

The Bowdens went away. Steer passed them on the journey home. He was alone, driving that mare of his. The Bowdens grinned faintly as he went by. Then Bowden called out two words——

"Stickin' plaster!"

If Steer heard, he gave no sign, but his ears looked very red.

When his hurrying cart was a speck at the top of the steep rise, Bowden turned a little towards his son.

"I want to make that chap sweat," he said.

"Ah!" answered Ned.

But how to make Steer sweat without sweating themselves? That was what exercised the Bowdens, each according to his lights and circumstances, which, of course, were very different. Even in this quandary they did not mention the girl Pansy. To do so would have been to touch on feeling; both felt it better to keep to facts and to devices. It was Bowden who put the finishing touch to a long and devious silence.

"If yu don' du nothin', Ned, I don' see how they can 'ave yu. Yu've not putt nothin' on paper. How'm they to tell yu don' mean to marry her? I'd let 'em stew in their own juice. Don't yu never admit it. Drop word to that lawyer chap that yu'm not guilty."

Ned nodded, but underneath his stolidity he could not help feeling that it was not so simple as all that. To him, though not quite tired of the girl Pansy, his first choice had begun to be faintly desirable again—her refinement "in the distance enchanted," was regaining some of its attraction to his cooling blood. What would have been the course of events but for Steer's next action is, indeed, uncertain.

V

In having the law of "those two fellows," Steer had passed through an experience with his niece which had considerably embittered feelings already acid. The girl had shown a "lady like" shrinking from pressing a man who had ceased to want her. There was an absolute difference between her wishes and her uncle's. He would not have young Bowden marry her for anything; he just wanted revenge on the Bowdens. She wanted young Bowden still; but if she couldn't get him, would cry quietly and leave it at that. The two points of view had been irreconcilable, till Steer, taking the bit between his teeth, assured his niece that to bring the action was the only way of inducing young Bowden to come back to her. This gave him a bad conscience, for he was fond of his niece, and he really felt that to bring the action would make that fellow Bowden stick his toes in all the more, and refuse to budge. He thought always of Bowden first and of the five hundred that would come out of his pocket, not out of Ned's.

Steer owned the local weed-sprayer, which by village custom was at the service of his neighbours in rotation. This year he fetched the sprayer back from Pethick's farm just as it was on the point of going on to Bowden's, without reason given. Bowden, who would not have been above using "that chap's sprayer" so long as it came to him from Pethick, in ordinary rotation, was above sending to Steer's for it. He took the action as a public proclamation of enmity, and in the Three Stars Inn, where he went nearly every evening for a glass of cider with a drop of gin and a clove in it, he said out loud that Steer was a "colley," and Ned wouldn't be seen dead with that niece of his.

By those words, soon repeated far and wide, he committed his son just when Ned was cooling rapidly towards the girl Pansy, and beginning to think of going to church once more and seeing whether Molly wouldn't look at him again. After all, it was he, not his father, who would have to go into the witness-box; moreover, he had nothing against Molly Winch.

Now that the feud was openly recognised by village tongues, its origin was already lost. No one—hardly even the Bowdens—remembered that Bowden's dog had bitten Steer, and Steer had shot it; so much spicier on the palate was Ned's aberration with the girl Pansy, and its questionable consequences. Corn harvest passed, and bracken harvest; the autumn gales, sweeping in from the Atlantic, spent their rain on the moor; the birch-trees goldened and the beech-trees grew fox-red, and, save that Molly Winch was never seen, that Bowden and Steer passed each other as if they were stocks or stones, and for the interest taken in the girl Pansy's appearance by anyone who had a glimpse of her (not often now, for she was seldom out of the farmyard), the affair might have been considered at an end.

Steer was too secretive and too deadly in earnest to mention the breach-of-promise suit; the Bowdens, at once too defiant of the law and too anxious to forget it. By never mentioning it, even to each other, and by such occasional remarks as: "Reckon that chap's bit off more than he can chu," they consigned it to a future which to certain temperaments never exists until it is the present. They

had, indeed, one or two legal reminders, and Ned had twice to
see Mr. Applewhite on market days, but between all this and real
apprehension was always the slow and stolid confidence that "the
Law" could be avoided if you "sat tight and did'n du nothin'."

When, therefore, in late November, Ned received a letter from the
lawyer telling him to be at the High Courts of Justice in the Strand,
London, at ten-thirty in the morning on the next day but one,
prepared to give his evidence, a most peculiar change took place in
that bullet-headed youth. His appetite abandoned him; sweat stood
on his brow at moments unconnected with honest toil. He gave the
girl Pansy black looks; and sat with his prepared evidence before
him, wiping the palms of his hands stealthily on his breeches. That
which he had never really thought would spring was upon him after
all, and panic, such as nothing physical could have caused in him,
tweaked his nerves and paralysed his brain. But for his father he
would never have come up to the scratch. Born before the halfpenny
Press, and unable to ride a bicycle, unthreatened, moreover, by the
witness-box, Bowden—after a long pipe—gave out his opinion that
it "widden never du to let that chap 'ave it all his own way. There
wasn't nothin' to it, if Ned kept a stiff upper lip. 'Twid be an 'oliday-
like in London for them both."

So, dressed in their darkest and most board-like tweeds, with black
bowler hats, they drove in next day to catch the London train, with
a small boy bobbing on a board behind them to drive the mare back
home. Deep within each was a resentful feeling that this came of
women; and they gave no thought to the feelings of the girl who was
the plaintiff in the suit, or of the girl who watched them drive out of
the yard. While the train swiftly bore them, stolid and red-faced, side
by side, the feeling grew within them that to make a holiday of this
would spite that chap Steer. He wanted to make them sweat; if they
did not choose to sweat—it was one in the eye for him.

They put up at an hotel with a Devonshire name in Covent
Garden, and in the evening visited a music-hall where was a show
called the "Rooshian Ballet." They sat a little forward with their
hands on their thighs, their ruddy faces, expressionless as waxworks,
directed towards the stage, whereon "Les Sylphides" were floating

white and ethereal. When the leading *danseuse* was held upside down, Bowden's mouth opened slightly. He was afterwards heard to say that she had "got some legs on her." Unable to obtain refreshment after the performance, owing to the war, they sought the large flasks in their bedroom, and slept, snoring soundly, as though to express even in their slumbers a contempt for the machinations of "that chap, Steer."

VI

Though sorely tried by the "pernickety" nature of his niece, Steer had been borne up by the thought that he had only to hold on a little longer to obtain justice. How he had got her to the starting-post he really did not know, so pitiably had she "jibbed." The conviction that good solid damages would in the end be better for her than anything else had salved and soothed a conscience really affected by her nervous distress. Her pale face and reddened eyes on the way to the court disturbed him, and yet he knew they were valuable—she was looking her best for the occasion. It would be all over—he told her—in an hour, and then she should go to the seaside—what did she say to Weston-super-Mare (with one syllable)? She said nothing, and he had entered the Law Courts with his arm through hers, and his upper lip very long. The sight of the two Bowdens seated on a bench in the corridor restored the burning in his heart. He marked his niece's eyes slide round when they passed young Bowden. Yes! She would take him even now! He saw Ned shuffle his feet, and Bowden grin, and he hurried her on—not for anything would he forego the five hundred out of that fellow's pocket! At that moment the feud between him and his neighbour showed naked—those young people were but the catspaws of it. The custom of the court compelled them all presently to be sitting in a row, divided faction from faction by not more than the breadth of a pig. Steer's thin face, racked by effort to follow the patter of the chap in a wig, acquired a sort of maniacal fixity; but he kept hold of his niece's arm, squeezing it half-consciously now and again, and aware of her shrinking faint look. As for "Those two fellows," they sat as they might have at an auction, giving nothing away, putting the whole business in its proper place—monkey tricks that must fail if they "sat tight and didn't du nothin'." It seemed unjust to Steer that they should seem unmoved while his niece was wilting beside him. When she went up, trembling, into the "dock," a strong scent of camphor floated from Steer, stirred from his clothes by the heat within him. He could hardly hear, and they kept telling her to speak up. He saw tears roll down her cheeks; and the ginger in the greying hair and beard brightened the while he stared at the Bowdens, who never moved. They didn't ask her much—not even Bowden's counsel—afraid to, he could see! And, vaguely through his anger and discomfort, Steer felt that, with her "ladylikeness," her tears, her shrinking, she was making a good impression on judge and jury. It enraged him to see her made to shrink and weep, but it delighted him too.

She came back to his side and sat down, all shrunk into herself. Bowden's counsel began outlining the defence, and Steer listened with his mouth a little open—an outrageous defence, for what did it amount to but a confession that the fellow had played fast, and loose! His client—said counsel—came into court not to defend this action, but to express his regret as an honourable man for having caused the plaintiff distress, though not, he would submit, any material damage, for, now that they had seen her in the box, it would be absurd to suppose that what was called her "value in the marriage market" had deteriorated. His client had come there to tell them the simple truth that, finding his feelings towards the plaintiff changed, he had considered it more honourable, wise and merciful, to renounce his engagement before it was too late, rather than to enter into a union from the start doomed to unhappiness, which the gentlemen of the jury must remember, would, in the nature of men and things, fall far more heavily on the plaintiff than on the defendant himself. Though fully admitting his responsibility for the mistake he had made and the hastiness of which he had been guilty, the defendant believed they would give him credit for his moral courage in stopping before it was too late, and saving the plaintiff from a miserable fiasco.

At the words "moral courage," Steer had righted himself in his seat so suddenly that the judge was seen to blink. "Moral courage!" Wasn't anybody going to tell those dodos there that the fellow had been playing the rip with that cross-bred girl? Wasn't anybody going to tell them that Bowden had put his son up to this to spite him— Steer? A sense of mystification and falsity muddled and enraged him; it was all bluff and blarney, like selling a horse.

With the robust common-sense characteristic—counsel went on—of plain and honest men, the jury would realise that one could not have things both ways in this world—however it might be in the next. The sad records of the Divorce Court showed what was the outcome of hasty and ill-considered marriages. They gave one to think furiously, indeed, whether these actions for breach of promise, with their threat of publicity, were not responsible for much of the work of that dismal tribunal. He would submit that where you had, as here, a young man admitting his error and regretting it, yet manly enough to face this ordeal in order to save the plaintiff—and in less degree himself, of course—from a life of misery, that young man was entitled, if not to credit, at least to just and considerate treatment at the hands of his fellow-citizens, who had themselves all been young, and, perhaps, not always as wise as Solomon. Let them remember what young blood was—a sunny lane in that beautiful Western county, the scent of honeysuckle, a pretty girl—and then let them lay their hands on their hearts and say that they themselves might not have mistaken the emotions of a moment for a lifelong feeling.

"Don't let us be hypocrites, gentlemen, and pretend that we always carry out that to which in moments of mid-summer madness we commit ourselves. My client will tell you quite simply, for he is a simple country youth, that he just made a mistake, which no one regrets more than he, and then I shall leave it in your hands— confident that, sorry as we all are for the disappointment of this charming girl, you will assess the real values of the case with the instinct of shrewd and understanding men."

"Well, I'm darned!"

"H'sh! Silence in the Court!"

The mutter, which had been riven from Steer by counsel's closing words, by no means adequately expressed feelings which grew with every monosyllable from that "young ruffian" answering the cunning questions of his advocate.

With his sleek bullet-head he looked sheepish enough, but the thing was being made so easy for him—that was what seemed villainous to Steer, that and the sight of Bowden's face unmoved, the breadth of two pigs away. When his own counsel began to cross-examine, Steer became conscious that he had made a hideous mistake. Why had he not caused his lawyer to drag in the girl Pansy? What on earth had he been about to let his natural secretiveness, his pride in his niece, prevent him using the weapon which would have alienated every sympathy from that young rascal ? He tingled with disappointed anger. So the fellow was not to be shown up properly! It was outrageous. And then suddenly his ears pricked. "Now, young man," counsel was saying, "don't you think that in days like these you can serve your country better than by going about breaking girls' hearts? . . . Kindly answer that question! . . . Don't waste his Lordship's time. Yes? Speak up, please."

"I'm workin' the land—I'm growin' food for you to eat!"

"Indeed! The jury will draw their own conclusions as to what sort of leniency they can extend to a young man in your position."

Steer's lips relaxed. That was a nasty one!

Then came the speeches from counsel on both sides, and everything was said over again, but Steer had lost interest; disappointment nagged at him, as at a man who has meant to play a fine innings—and gets out for seven. Now the Judge was saying everything that everybody had said and a little more besides. The jury must not let themselves this, and let themselves that. Defendant's counsel had alluded to the Divorce Court—they must not allow any such consideration to weigh with them. While the law was what it was, breach-of-promise actions must be decided on their merits. They would consider this, and they would consider that, and return a verdict, and give damages according to their consciences. And out the jury filed. Steer felt lonely while they were absent. On one side of him were those Bowdens, whom he wanted to make sweat; on the other his niece, whom, to judge from her face, he *had* made sweat. He was not a lover of animals, but a dog against his legs would have been a comfort during that long quarter of an hour, while those two enemies of his so stolidly stared before them. Then the jury came back, and the sentiment in his heart stuttered into a form he could have sent through the post. "Oh, Lord, make them sweat! Your humble servant, J. Steer."

"We find for the plaintiff, with damages—three hundred pounds."

Three hundred! And costs—with costs it would come to five! And Bowden had no capital; he was always on the edge of borrowing to get through—yes, it would push him, hard! And, grasping his niece's arm, Steer rose and led her out by the right-hand door, while the Bowdens sought the left. In the corridor his lawyer came up. The fellow hadn't half done his job! And Steer was about to say so, when those two passed, walking as though over turnips, and he heard Bowden say:

"Think he'll get that stickin'-plaster—let 'im wait an' see!

He was about to answer, when the lawyer laid hold of his lapel.

"Get your niece away, Mr. Steer; she's had enough."

And, without sense of conquest, with nothing but a dull, irritable aching in his heart, Steer took her arm and walked her out of the precincts of the law.

VII

The news that Ned Bowden had "joined up" reached the village simultaneously with the report that Steer had "shot" him in London for three hundred pounds and costs for breaking his promise to Molly Winch. The double sensation was delicious. Honours seemed so easy that no one could see which had come off best. It was fairly clear, however, that Molly Winch and the girl Pansy had come off worst. And there was great curiosity to see them. This was not found possible, for Molly Winch was at Weston-super-Mare and the girl Pansy invisible, even by those whose business took them to Bowden's yard. Bowden himself put in his customary appearance at The Three Stars, where he said quite openly that Steer would never see a penny of that money; Steer his customary appearances at church, where he was a warden, and could naturally say nothing. Christmas passed, and the New Year wore on through colourless February and March, when every tree was bare, the bracken's russet had gone dark-dun, and the hedgerows were songless.

Steer's victory had lost him his niece; she had displayed invincible reluctance to return as a conquering heroine, and had gone into an office. Bowden's victory had lost him his son, whose training would soon be over now, and whose battalion was in Flanders. Neither of the neighbouring enemies showed by word or sign that they saw any connection between victory and loss; but the schoolmistress met them one afternoon at the end of March seated in their carts face to face in a lane so narrow that some compromise was essential to the passage of either. They had been there without movement long enough for their mares to begin grazing in the hedge on either hand. Bowden was sitting with folded arms and an expression as of his own bull on his face. Steer's teeth and eyes were bared very much like a dog's when it is going to bite.

The schoolmistress, who had courage, took hold of Bowden's mare and backed her.

"Now, Mr. Steer," she said, "pull in to your left, please. You can't stay here all day, blocking the lane for everybody."

Steer, who, after all, prized his reputation in the parish, jerked the reins and pulled into the hedge. And the schoolmistress, without more ado, led Bowden's mare past, foot by foot. The wheels scraped, both carts jolted slightly; the two farmers' faces, so close together, moved no muscle, but when the carts had drawn clear, each, as if by agreement, expectorated to his right. The schoolmistress loosed the head of Bowden's mare and said:

"You ought to be ashamed of yourself, Mr. Bowden; you and Mr. Steer."

"How's that?" said Bowden.

"How's that, indeed? Everybody knows the state of things between you. No good can come of it. In war-time, too, when we ought all to be united. Why can't you shake hands and be friends?"

Bowden laughed.

"Shake 'ands with that chap? I'd suner shake 'ands with a dead pig. Let 'im get my son back out o' the Army."

The schoolmistress looked up at him.

"Ah! I hope you're going to look after that poor girl when her time comes," she said.

Bowden nodded.

"Never fear! I suner my grandchild was hers than that niece of Steers."

The schoolmistress was silent.

"Well," she said at last, "it's an unchristian state of mind."

"Yu go to Steer, Ma'am, an' see whether he'll be more Christianlike. He 'olds the plate out, Sundays."

This was precisely what the good lady did. More, perhaps, from curiosity than in a proselytising mood.

"What!" said Steer, who was installing a beehive. "When that God-darned fellow put his son up to jilting my niece!"

"And you a Christian, Mr. Steer!"

"There's a limit to that, Ma'am," said Steer drily. "In my opinion, not even our Lord could have put up with that chap. Don't you waste your breath trying to persuade me."

"Dear me!" murmured the schoolmistress; "I don't know which of you is worst."

The only people, in fact, who did know were Steer and Bowden, whose convictions about each other increased as the spring came in with song and leaf and sunshine, and there was no son to attend to the sowing and the calving, and no niece to make the best butter in the parish.

Towards the end of May, on a "brave" day, when the wind was lively in ash-trees, and the buttercups bright gold, the girl Pansy had her hour; and on the following morning Bowden received this letter from his son:

"DEAR FATHER,

"They don't let us tell where we are, so all I can
say is there's some crumps come over that stop
at nothing, and you could bury a waggon where
they hit. The grub is nothing to complain of. Hope
you have done well with calves. The green there is
within sight of here wouldn't keep a rabbit going
half a day. The thing I wish to say is: If I have a son
by you know who—call it Edward, after you and
me. It makes you think out here. She would like to
hear perhaps that I will marry her if I come back,
so as not to have it on my mind. There is some
German prisoners in our section—big fellows, and
proper swine with their machine-guns, I can tell
you. Hope you are well, as this leaves me. Has that
swine Steer given over asking for his money? I
would like to see the old farm again. Tell Granma to
keep warm. No more now from your loving son,
"NED."

After standing for some minutes by the weighing-machine trying
to make head or tail of his own sensations, Bowden took the letter
up to the girl Pansy, lying beside her offspring in her narrow cabin
of a room. In countrymen who never observe themselves, a letter
or event which ploughs up fallow land of feeling, or blasts the rock
of some prejudice, causes a prolonged mental stammer or hiatus. So
Ned wanted to marry the girl if he came home! The Bowdens were
an old family, the girl cross-bred. It wasn't fitting! And the news
that Ned had it on his mind brought home to Bowden as never
before, the danger his son was in. With profound instinct he knew
that compunction did not seriously visit those who felt life sure and
strong within them; so that there was a kind of superstition in the
way he took the letter up to the girl. After all, the child was as much
bone of Ned's bone and of his own as if the girl had been married in
church—a boy too. He gave it her with the words: "Here's a present
for yu and Edward the Seventh."

The village widow, accustomed to attend these simple cases, stepped outside, and while the girl was reading, Bowden sat down on the low seat beneath the little window. The ceiling just touched his head, so that he did not care to remain standing. Her coarse nightgown fell back from her strong arms and neck, her hair showed black and lustreless on the coarse pillow; he could not see her face for the letter, but he heard her sigh. Somehow he felt sorry.

"Shud ought to du yu good," he said.

Dropping the letter, so that her eyes met his, the girl spoke.

"'Tisn' nothin' to me; Ned don't care for me no more."

Something inexpressibly cheerless in the tone of her voice and uncannily searching in her dark gaze, disturbed Bowden.

"Cheer up!" he murmured; "yu've got a monstrous baby there, all to yureself."

Going up to the bed, he clucked his tongue and held his finger out to the baby. He did it softly, and with a sort of native aptitude.

"He'm a proper little man." Then he took up the letter, for there "wasn't," he felt, "no yuse in leavin' it there against Ned if an' in case he should change his mind when he came safe 'ome." But, as he went out, he saw the girl Pansy put the baby to her breast, and again he felt that disturbance, as of pity. With a nod to the village widow, who was sitting on an empty grocery-box reading an old paper by the light coming through half a skylight, Bowden descended the twisting stairs to the kitchen. His mother was seated where the sunlight fell, her bright little dark eyes moving among their mass of wrinkles. Bowden stood a moment watching her.

"Well, Granny," he said, "y'um a great-granny now."

The old lady nodded, mumbled her lips a little in a smile, and rubbed one hand on the other. Bowden experienced a shock.

"There ain't no sense in et," he muttered to himself, without knowing too well what he meant.

VIII

Bowden did not attend when, three weeks later, the baby was christened Edward Bowden. He spent the June morning in his cart with a bull calf, taking it to market. The cart did not run well, because the weight of the calf made it jerk and dip. Though used to it all his life, he had never become quite case-hardened to separating calves from their mothers. Bowden had a queer feeling for cattle—more feeling, indeed, than he had for human beings. He always sat sulky when there was a little red beast tied up and swaying there behind him. Somehow he felt for it, as if in some previous existence he might himself have been a red bull calf.

Passing through a village someone called:

"'Eard the nus? They beat the Germans up proper yest'day mornin'."

Bowden nodded. News from the war was now nothing but a reminder of how that fellow Steer had deprived him of Ned's help and company. The war would be over some day, he supposed, but they didn't seem to get on with it, gaining ground one day and losing it the next, and all the time passing this law and that law interfering with the land. Didn't they know the land couldn't be interfered with—the cuckoos? Steer, of course, was all part of this interference with the land—the fellow grew wheat where anybody could have told him it couldn't be grown!

The day was hot, the road dusty, and that chap Steer hanging about the market like the colley he was—so that Bowden imbibed, freely at "The Drake" before making a start for home.

When he entered his kitchen the newly christened baby was lying in a grocery box, padded with a pillow and shawl, just out of the sunlight in which old Mrs. Bowden sat moving her hands as if weaving a spell. Bowden's sheepdog had lodged its nose on the edge of the box, and was sniffing as if to ascertain the difference in the baby. In the background the girl Pansy moved on her varying business; she looked strong again, but pale still, and "daverdy," Bowden thought. He stood beside the box contemplating the "monstrous" baby. It wasn't like Ned, nor anything, so far as he could see. It opened its large grey eyes while he stood there. That colley Steer would never have a grandchild, not even one born like this! The thought pleased him. He clucked to the baby with his tongue, and his sheepdog jealously thrust its head with mass of brushed-back snowy hair under his hand.

"Hullo!" said Bowden. "What's matter wi' yu?"

He went out presently, in the slanting sunlight, to look at some beasts he had on the rough grounds below his fields, and the dog followed. Among the young bracken and the furze not yet in bloom again, he sat down on a stone. The afternoon was glorious beyond all words, now that the sun was low and its glamour had motion, as it were, and flight across the ash-trees, the hawthorn, and the fern. One Maytree close beside him was still freakishly in delicate flower, with a sweet and heavy scent; in the hedge the round, cream-coloured heads of the elder-flower flashed, flat against the glistening air, while the rowans up the gully had passed already from blossom to brown unrounded berries.

There was all the magic of transition from season to season, even in the song of the cuckoo, which flighted arrowlike to a thorn-tree up the rocky dingle, and started a shrill calling. Bowden counted his beasts, and marked the fine sheen on their red coats. He was drowsy from his hot day, from the cider he had drunk, and the hum of the flies in the fern. Unconsciously he enjoyed a deep and sensuous peace of warmth and beauty. Ned had said there was no green out there! It was unimaginable! No green—not the keep of a rabbit; not a curling young caterpillar-frond of fern; no green tree for a bird to light on! And Steer had sent him out there! Through his drowsiness that thought came flapping its black wings. Steer! who had no son to fight, who was making money hand over fist. It seemed to Bowden that a malevolent fortune protected that stingy chap, who couldn't even take his glass.

There were little blue flowers, speedwell and milkwort, growing, plentifully in the rough grass around; Bowden noted, perhaps for the first time, that small natural luxury of which Steer had deprived his son by sending him to where no grass grew.

He rose at length, retracing his slow-lifted tread up the lane, deep-soiled with the dried dung of his cows, where innumerable gnats danced level with the elder-blossom and the ash-leaves. He entered the yard as the village postman was leaving it. The man stopped in the doorway, and turned his red face, white head, and dark eyes blinking in the level sunlight.

"There's a talegram for yu, Mist Bowden," he said, and vanished.

"What's that?" said Bowden dully, and passed in under the porch.

The "talegram" lay unopened on the kitchen table, and Bowden stared at it. Very few such missives had come his way, perhaps not half-a-dozen in his fifty odd years. He took it up—handling it rather as he might have handled a fowl that would peck—and broke it open with his thumb.

"Greatly regret inform you your son killed in action on seventh instant.—War Office."

He read it through again and again before he sat down heavily, dropping it on the table. His round solid face looked still and blind, its mouth just a little open. The girl Pansy came up and stood beside him.

"Here!" he said; "read that."

The girl read it and put her hands up to her ears.

"That idn' no yuse," he said, with surprising quickness.

The girl's pale face crimsoned; she uttered a little wail and ran from the room.

In the whitewashed kitchen the only moving things were the clock's swinging pendulum and old Mrs. Bowden's restless eyes, close to the geranium on the window sill, where the last of the sunlight fell before passing behind the house. Minute after minute ticked away before Bowden made a movement—his head bowed, his shoulders rounded, his knees apart. Then he got up.

"God for ever darn the blasted colley!" he said slowly, gathering up the telegram. "Where's my stick?"

Lurching blindly he walked round the room, watched by the old woman's little dark bright eyes, and went out. He went at his unvaried gait on the path towards Steer's, slowly climbing the two stiles, and emerging from the field into Steer's farmyard.

"Master in?" he said to the boy who stood by the cowbyre.

"No."

"Where is he then?"

"Not 'ome from market yet."

"Oh, he idden, idden he!"

And Bowden turned up into the lane. There was a dull buzzing in his ears, but his nostrils moved, savouring the evening scents, of grass, of cow-dung, dried earth, and hedgerow weeds. His nose was alive, the rest within him all knotted into a sort of bitter tangle round his heart. The blood beat in his temples, and he dwelled heavily on foot and foot. Along this road Steer must come in his cart—God for ever darn him! Beyond his own top pasture he reached the Inn abutting on the road. From the bench in there under the window he could see anyone who passed. The innkeeper and two labourers were all the company as yet. Bowden took, his usual mug and sat down on the window seat. He did not speak of his loss, and they did not seem to know of it. He just sat with his eyes on the road. Now and then he responded to some question, now and then got up and had his mug refilled. Someone came in; he noted the lowering of voices. They were looking at him. They knew. But he sat on silent till the inn closed. It was still daylight when he lurched back up the road towards home, intent on not missing Steer. The sun had gone down; it was very still. He leaned against the wicket-gate of his top field. Nobody passed. Twilight crept up. The moon rose. An owl began hooting. Behind him in the field from a group of beech-trees the shadows stole out ever so faint in the flowery grass and darkened slowly in the brightening moonlight.

Bowden leaned his weight against the wood—one knee crooked, and then the other—in dogged stupefaction. He had begun imagining things, but not very much. No grass, no trees, where his son had been killed, no birds, no animals; what could it be like—all mucky grey in the moonlight—and Ned's face all grey! So he would never see Ned's face any more! That colley, Steer—that colley, Steer! His dead son would never see and hear and smell his home again. Vicarious home-sickness for this native soil and scent and sound—this nest of his fathers from time beyond measuring—swept over Bowden. He thought of the old time when his wife was alive and Ned was born. His wife—why! she had brought him six, and of the lot he had only "saved" Ned, and he was a twin. He remembered how he had told the doctor that he wasn't to worry about the "maiden" so long as he saved the boy. He had wanted the boy to come after him here; and now he was dead, and that—that colley, Steer!

He heard the sound of wheels—a long way off, but coming steadily. Gripping his stick he stood up straight, staring down the road all barred with moonlight and the dusk. Closer came the rumble, the clop-clop of hoofs, till the shape of horse and cart came out of darkness into a bright patch. Steer's right enough! Bowden opened his wicket-gate and waited. The cart came slowly; Bowden saw that the mare was lame, and Steer was leading her. He lurched a yard out from the gate.

"'Ere," he said, "I want to speak to yu. Come in 'ere! "

The moonlight fell on Steer's thin, bearded face.

"What's that?" he answered.

Bowden turned towards the gate.

"Hitch the mare up; I want to settle my account.'"

He saw Steer stand quite still, as if debating, then pass the reins over the gate. His voice came sharp and firm:

"Have you got that money, then?"

"Ah!" said Bowden, and drew back under the trees. He saw Steer coming cautiously—the colley—with a stick in his hand. He raised his own.

"That's for Ned," he said, and struck with all his might.

The blow fell short a little; Steer staggered back, raising his stick.

He struck again, but the sticks clashed, and, dropping his own, Bowden lurched at his enemy's throat. He had twice Steer's strength and bulk; half his lean quickness and sobriety. They swayed between the beech-trunks, now in shadow, now in moonlight which greyed their faces, and showed the expression in their eyes of men out to kill. They struggled chest against chest, striving to throw each other, with short, hard gruntings. They reeled against a trunk, staggered and unclinched, and stood, breathing hard, glaring at each other. All those months of hatred looked out of their eyes, and their hands twitched convulsively. Suddenly Steer went on his knees, and gripping Bowden's legs, strained at them till the heavy, unsteady bulk pitched forward and fell over Steer's back with stunning weight. They rolled on the grass then, all mixed up, till they came apart, and sat facing each other, dazed—Bowden from the drink shaken up within him, Steer from the weight which had pitched upon his spine. They sat as if each knew there was no hurry and they were there to finish this; watching each other, bent a little forward, their legs stuck out in the moonlight, their mouths open, breathing in hard gasps, ridiculous—to each other! And suddenly the church bell began to toll. Its measured sound at first reached only the surface of Bowden's muddled brain, dully devising the next attack; then slid into the chambers of his consciousness. Tolling? Tolling! For whom? His hands fell by his sides. Impulse and inhibition, action and superstition, revenge and mourning gripped each other and rolled about within him. A long minute passed. The bell tolled on. A whinny came from Steer's lame mare outside the gate. Suddenly Bowden staggered up, turned his back on his enemy, and, lurching in the moonlight, walked down the field for home. The clover among the wild grasses smelled sweet; he heard the sound of wheels—Steer had started again! Let him go! 'Twasn't no use—'twidden bring Ned back! He reached the yard door and stood leaning against it. Cold streaming moonlight filled the air, covered the fields; the pollarded aspens shivered above him; on the low rock-wall the striped roses were all strangely coloured; and a moth went by brushing his cheek.

Bowden lowered his head, as if butting at the beauty of the night. The bell had ceased to toll—no sound now but the shiver of the aspens and the murmur of a stream. 'Twas monstrous peaceful—surely!

And in Bowden something went out. He had not the heart to hate.

[*1921*]

A FISHER OF MEN

LONG ago it is, now, that I used to see him issue from the rectory, followed by his dogs, an Irish and a fox terrier. He would cross to the churchyard, and, at the gate, stand looking over the Cornish upland of his cure of souls, towards the sea, distant nearly a mile. About his black thin figure there was one bright spot, a little gold cross, dangling on his vest. His eyes at such moments were like the eyes of fishermen watching from the cliffs for pilchards to come by; but as this fisher of men marked the grey roofs covered with yellow lichen where his human fishes dwelt, red stains would come into his meagre cheeks. His lips would move and he would turn abruptly in at the gate over which was written: "This is the Gate of Heaven."

A certain green spot within that churchyard was kept clear of grave-stones, which thickly covered all the rest of the ground. He never—I believe—failed to look at it, and think: "I will keep that corner free. I will not be buried amongst men who refuse their God!"

For this was his misfortune, which, like a creeping fate, had come on him year by year throughout his twenty years of rectorship. It had eaten into his heart, as is the way with troubles which a man cannot understand. In plain words, his catch of souls had dwindled season by season till, from three hundred when he was first presented to the living, it barely numbered forty. Sunday after Sunday he had conducted his three services. Twice a week from the old pulpit, scanning through the church twilight that ever scantier flock of faces, he had in his dry, spasmodic voice—whose harsh tones, no doubt, were music to himself—pronounced this conduct blessed, and that accursed, in accordance with his creed. Week after week he had told us all the sinfulness of not attending God's House, of not observing the Lord's Day. He had respected every proper ritual and ceremony; never refusing baptism even to the illegitimate, nor burial to any but such as took their own lives; joining in marriage with a certain exceptional alacrity those whose conduct had caused scandal in the village. His face had been set, too, against irreverence; no one, I remember, might come to his church in flannel trousers.

Yet his flock had slowly diminished! Living, unmarried, in the neglected rectory, with his dogs, an old housekeeper, and a canary, he seemed to have no interests, such as shooting, or fishing, to take him away from his parish duties; he asked nothing better than to enter the houses and lives of his parishioners; and as he passed their doors—spare, black, and clean-shaven—he could often be seen to stop, make, as it were, a minatory gesture, and walk on with his hungry eyes fixed straight before him. Year by year, to encourage them, he printed privately and distributed documents containing phrases such as these: "It were better for him that a mill-stone were hanged about his neck, and he were cast into the sea." "But the fearful and unbelieving shall have their part in the lake which burneth with fire and brimstone." When he wrote them, his eyes—I fancy—flared, as though watching such penalties in process of infliction. Had not his parishioners in justice merited those fates?

If, in his walks, he came across a truant, some fisherman or farmer, he would always stop, with his eyes fastened on the culprit's face:

"You don't come to church now; how's that?"

Like true Cornishmen, hoping to avoid unpleasantness, they would offer some polite excuse: They didn't knaw ezactly, zur—the missus 'ad been ailin'; there was always somethin'—like—that! This temporising with the devil never failed to make the rector's eyes blaze, or to elicit from him a short dry laugh: "You don't know what you're saying, man! You must be mad to think you can save your soul that way! This is a Christian country!

Yet never after one of these encounters did he see the face of that parishioner in his church again. "Let un wait!" they would murmur, "tidden likely we'm gwine to his church t'be spoke to like dogs!"

But, indeed, had they been dogs, the rector would not have spoken to them like that. To dogs his conduct was invariably gentle. He might be seen sometimes beside a field of standing corn, where the heads of his two terriers could be marked spasmodically emerging above the golden stalks, as they hunted a covey of partridges or brood of young pheasants which they had scented. His harsh voice could be heard calling them:

"Jim, Jim! Pat, Pat! To heel, you rascals!" But when they came out, their tongues lolling ecstatically, he only stooped and shook his finger at them, and they would lick his hand, or rub themselves against his trousers, confident that he would never strike them. With every animal, with every bird and insect he was like this, so gentle that they trusted him completely. He could often be surprised sitting on a high slate stile, or standing in a dip of the wide road between banks of gorse and bramble, with his head, in its wide hat, rather to one side, while a bullfinch or hedge-sparrow on a branch, not three feet off, would be telling him its little tale. Before going for a walk he would sweep his field-glass over the pale-gold landscape of cornfield, scorched pasturage and sand-dune, to see if any horse seemed needing water, or sheep were lying on its back. He was an avowed enemy, too, of traps and gins, and whenever he met with one, took pains to ensure its catching nothing. Such consistent tenderness to dumb animals was perhaps due to a desire to take their side against farmers who would not come to church; but more, I think, to the feeling that the poor things had no souls, that they were here to-day and gone to-morrow—they could not be saved and must be treated with compassion, unlike those men with immortal spirits entrusted by God specially to his care, for whose wanton disobedience no punishment, perhaps, could be too harsh. It was as if, by endowing him with her authority over other men, the Church had divided him into two.

For the view he took of life was very simple, undisturbed by any sense of irony, unspoiled by curiosity, or desire to link effect with cause, or, indeed, to admit the necessity of cause at all. At some fixed date God had made the earth of matter; this matter He had divided into the inanimate and the animate, unconnected with each other; animate matter He had again divided into men, and animals; in men He had placed souls, making them in His own image. Men again He had divided into the Church and other men; and for the government and improvement of these other men, God had passed Himself into His Church. That Church again had passed herself into her ministers. Thus, on the Church's minister—placed by Providence beyond the fear of being in the wrong—there had been enjoined the bounden duty of instructing, ruling, and saving at all costs the souls of men.

This was why, I think, when he encountered in the simple folk committed to his charge a strange dumb democratic spirit, a wayward feeling that the universe was indivisible, that power had not devolved, but had evolved, that things were relative, not absolute, and so forth—expressed in their simple way, he had experienced from the first a gnawing irritation which, like a worm, seemed to have cankered his heart. Gradually one had seen this canker stealing out into his face and body, into his eyes and voice, into the very gestures of his lean arms and hands. His whole form gave the impression of a dark tree withered and eaten by some desiccating wind, like the stiff oaks of his Cornish upland, gnarled and riven by the Atlantic gales.

Night and day in the worn old rectory, with its red conservatory, he must have brooded over the wrong done him by his people, in depriving him of his just due, the power to save their souls. It was as though an officer, gagged and bound at the head of his company, should have been forced to watch them manœuvring without him. He was like a schoolmaster tied to his desk amongst the pandemonium of his scholars. His failure was a fact strange and intolerable to him, inexplicable, tragic—a fact mured up in the mystery which each man's blindness to the nature of his own spirit wraps round his relations with his fellow beings. He could not doubt that, bereaved by their own wilful conduct of his ministrations, of the Church in fact, and, through the Church, of God, his parishioners were given up to damnation. If they were thus given up to damnation, he, their proper pastor—their rightful leader, the symbol of the Church, that is of God—was but a barren, withered thing. This thought he could not bear. Unable to see himself as others saw him, he searched to find excuses for them. He found none; for he knew that he had preached no narrow doctrines cursed with the bigotry which he recognised in

the Romish or Nonconformist faiths. The doctrines and dogmas he
was appointed to administer were of the due and necessary breadth,
no more, no less. He was scrupulous, even against his own personal
feeling, to observe the letter of the encyclicals. Thus, nothing in the
matter of his teaching could account for the gradual defection of his
flock. Nor in the manner of it could he detect anything that seemed
to himself unjustified. Yet, as the tide ebbed from the base of the grey
cliffs, so, without haste, with deadly certainty, the tide ebbed from his
church. What could he, then, believe but that his parishioners meant
to be personally offensive to himself?

In the school-house, at the post office, on the green, at choir
practice or on the way to service, wherever he met them, one could
see that he was perpetually detecting small slights or incivilities.
He had come, I think, almost to imagine that these people, who
never came to church, fixed the hours of their births and deaths and
marriages maliciously; that they might mock at the inconvenience
caused to one who neither could, nor would, refuse to do his duty.
It was blasphemy they were committing. In avoiding God's church,
yet requiring such services of His minister, they were making God
their servant.

One could find him any evening in his study, his chin resting on
his hand, the oil-lamp flaring slightly, his dogs curled up beside him,
and the cloth cover drawn over the cage of his canary so that the
little creature should not suffer from the light. Almost the first words
he spoke would show how ceaselessly he brooded. "Nothing," he
would say, "ever prospers in this village; I've started this and that!
Look at the football club, look at the Bible class—all no good! With
people such as these, wanting in all reverence, humility, and love of
discipline! You have not had the dealings with them that I have!"

In truth his dealings with them had become notorious throughout
the district. A petition, privately subscribed, and presented to the
Bishop for his removal, had, of course, met with failure. A rector
could not be removed from his living for any reason—it had
been purchased for him by his father. Nor could his position as
minister be interfered with on any such excuse as that of the mere
personal dislike of his parishioners—as well, indeed, seek by petition

to remove the Church herself. The knowledge of his unassailable position found expression among his parishioners in dogged looks, and the words: "Well, we don't trouble!"

It was in the twentieth year of his rectorship that a slight collision with the parish council drew from him this letter: "It is my duty to record my intention to attend no more meetings, for I cannot, as a Christian, continue to meet those who obstinately refuse to come to church."

It was then late September, and the harvest festival had been appointed for the following Sunday. The week passed, but the farmers had provided no offerings for the decoration of the church; the fishermen, too, accustomed by an old tradition in that parish to supply some purchased fruit in lieu of their shining fishes, sent nothing. The boycott had obviously been preconcerted.

But when the rector stepped that Sunday into the pulpit the church was fuller than it had been for many years. Men and women who had long ceased to attend had come, possessed evidently by an itch to see how "th' old man" would take it. The eyes of the farmers and fishermen, hardened by the elements, had in them a grim humorous curiosity, such as one may remark in the eyes of a ring of men round some poor wretch, whom, moved by a crude sense of justice, they have baited into the loss of dignity. Their faces, with hardly an exception, seemed to say: "Sir, we were given neither hand nor voice in the choosing of you. From the first day you showed us the cloven hoof. We have never wanted you. If we must have you, let us at all events get some sport out of you!"

The rector's white figure rising from the dark pulpit received without movement the shafts of all our glances; his own deep-set hungering eyes were fixed on the Bible in his hand. He gave out his text: "The kindly fruits of the earth, in due season——"

His voice—strangely smooth and low that morning, I remember— began discoursing of the beneficence and kindliness of God, who had allowed the earth to provide men year by year with food, according to their needs. It was as though the mellow sentiment of that season of fruition had fallen on his exiled spirit. But presently he paused, and, leaning forward, looked man by man, woman by woman, at us all. Those eyes now had in them the peculiar flare which we knew so well. His voice rose again: "And how have you met this benefaction, my brethren, how have you shown your gratitude to God, embodied in His Church and in me, her appointed representative? Do you think, then, that God will let you insult Him with impunity? Do you think in your foolish pride that God will suffer you unpunished to place this conspired slight on Him? If you imagine this, you are woefully mistaken. I know the depths of your rebellious hearts; I read them like this Book. You seek, you have always sought, to set my authority at defiance—a wayward and disobedient generation. But let me tell you: God, who has set His Holy Church over you, is a just and strong God; as a kind master chastises his dogs for their own good, so will He chastise you. You have sought to drive me out from among you"—and from his pale twisting lips, through the hush, there came a sound like a laugh—"to drive the Church, to drive God Himself, away! You could not have made a grosser error. Do you think that we, in solemn charge of your salvation, are to be moved by such puerile rebellion? Not so! God has appointed us—to God alone we are accountable. Not if every man and woman in the parish, aye, and every child, deserted this church, would I recoil one step from my duty, or resign my charge! As well imagine, forsooth, that your great Church is some poor man-elected leader, subject to your whims, and to be deposed as the fancy takes you! Do you conceive the nature of the Church and of my office to be so mean and petty that I am to feed you with the food you wish me to feed you with, to lead you into such fields as you dictate? No! my brethren, you have not that power! Is the shepherd elected by the sheep? Listen, then, to the truth, or to your peril be it! The Church is a rock set up by God amongst the shifting sands of life. It comes from Heaven, not from this miserable earth. Its mission is to command, yours to obey. If the last man in this Christian country proved a rebel and a traitor, the Church and her ministers would stand immovable, as I stand here, firm in my sacred resolve to save your souls. Go down on your knees, and beg God to forgive you for the wanton insult you have offered Him! ... Hymn 266: 'Lead, kindly Light, amid the encircling gloom!'"

Through the grey aisles, where so great a silence reigned, the notes of the organ rose. The first verse of that hymn was sung only by the choir and a few women's voices; then one by one the men joined in. Our voices swelled into a shout louder than we had ever heard in the little church before—a mutinous, harsh, roaring sound, as though, in the words of that gentle hymn, each one of this grim congregation were pouring out all the resentment in his heart. The roar emerging through the open door must have startled the passing tourists, and the geese in the neighbouring farm-yard. It ended with a groan like the long-drawn sob of a wave sucking back.

In the village all the next week little except this sermon was discussed. Farmers and fishermen are men of the world. The conditions of their lives, which are guarded only by their own unremitting efforts, which are backed by no authority save their own courage in the long struggle with land and sea, gives them a certain deep philosophy. Amongst the fishermen there was one white-bearded old fellow who even seemed to see a deep significance in the rector's sermon. "Mun putts hissel' above us, like the Czar o' Roossia," he said, "'tes the sperrit o' the thing that's wrong. Talk o' lovin' kindness, there's none 'bout the Church, 'sfar's I can see, 'tes all: 'Du this, or ye'll be blasted!' This man—he's a regular chip o' the old block!" He spoke, indeed, as though the rector's attitude towards them were a symbol of the Church's attitude to men. Among the farmers such analogies were veiled by the expression of simpler thoughts:

"Yu med ta' a 'arse to the watter, yu can't mak' un drink!"

"Whu wants mun, savin' our souls! Let mun save's own!"

"We'm not gude enough to listen to his prachin', I rackon!"

It was before a congregation consisting of his clerk, two tourists, three old women, one of them stone deaf, and four little girls, that the unfortunate man stood next Sunday morning.

Late that same wild and windy afternoon a jeering rumour spread down in the village: "Th' old man's up to Tresellyn 'Igh Cliff, talkin' to the watters!"

A crowd soon gathered, eager for the least sensation that should break the monotony. Beyond the combe, above the grey roofs of the fishing village, Tresellyn High Cliff rises abruptly. At the top, on the very edge, the tiny black shape of a man could be seen standing with his arms raised above his head. Now he kneeled, then stood motionless for many minutes with hands outstretched; while behind him the white and brown specks of his two terriers were visible, couched along the short grass. Suddenly he could be seen gesticulating wildly, and the speck shapes of the dogs leaping up, and cowering again as if terrified at their master's conduct.

For two hours this fantastic show was witnessed by the villagers with gloating gravity. The general verdict was: "Th' old man's carryin' on praaperly." But very gradually the sight of that tiny black figure appealing to his God—the God of his Church militant which lived by domination—roused the superstition of men who themselves were living in primitive conflict with the elements. They could not but appreciate what was so in keeping with the vengeful spirit of a fighting race. One could see that they even began to be afraid. Then a great burst of rain, sweeping from the sea, smothered all sight of him.

Early next morning the news spread that the rector had been found in his armchair, the two dogs at his feet, and the canary perched on his dead hand. His clothes were unchanged and wet, as if he had sunk into that chair, and passed away, from sheer exhaustion. The body of "the poor unfortunate gentleman"—the old housekeeper told me—was huddled and shrunk together; his chin rested on the little gold cross dangling on his vest.

They buried him in that green spot, apart from his parishioners, which he had selected for his grave, placing on the tomb stone these words:

HIC JACET

P———— W————

PASTOR ECCLESIÆ BRITANNICÆ

"GOD IS LOVE"

[*1908*]

MANNA

I

THE Petty Sessions Court at Linstowe was crowded. Miracles do not happen every day, nor are rectors frequently charged with larceny. The interest roused would have relieved all those who doubt the vitality of our ancient church. People who never went outside their farms or plots of garden had walked as much as three miles to see the show. Mrs. Gloyn, the sandy-haired little keeper of the shop where soap and herrings, cheese, matches, boot-laces, bull's-eyes, and the other luxuries of a countryside could be procured, remarked to Mrs. Redland, the farmer's wife, "'Tis quite a gatherin', like." To which Mrs. Redland replied, "'Most like church of a Sunday."

More women, it is true, than men were present, because of their greater piety, and because most of them had parted with pounds of butter, chickens, ducks, potatoes, or some such offertory in kind during the past two years, at the instance of the rector. They had a vested interest in this matter, and were present, accompanied by their grief at value unreceived. From Trover, their little village on the top of the hill two miles from Linstowe, with the squat church-tower, beautifully untouched, and the body of the building ruined by perfect restoration, they had trooped in; some even coming from the shore of the Atlantic, a mile beyond, across the Downs, whence other upland square church-towers could be viewed on the sky-line against the grey January heavens. The occasion was in a sense unique, and its piquancy strengthened by that rivalry which is the essence of religion.

For there was no love lost between church and chapel in Trover, and the rector's flock had long been fortified in their power of "parting" by fear lest "chapel" (also present that day in court) should mock at his impecuniosity. Not that his flock approved of his poverty. It had seemed "silly-like" ever since the news had spread that his difficulties had been caused by a faith in shares. To improve a secure if moderate position by speculation would not have seemed wrong if he had succeeded, but failure had made him dependent on their butter, their potatoes, their eggs and chickens. In that parish, as in others, the saying "Nothing succeeds like success" was true, nor had the villagers any abnormal disposition to question the title-deeds of affluence.

But it is equally true that nothing irritates so much as finding that one of whom you have the right to beg is begging of you. This was why the rector's tall, thin, black figure, down which a ramrod surely had been passed at birth; his narrow, hairless, white and wasted face, with red eye-brows over eyes that seemed now burning and now melting; his grizzled red hair under a hat almost green with age; his abrupt and dictatorial voice; his abrupt and mirthless laugh—all were on their nerves. His barked-out utterances, "I want a pound of butter—pay you Monday!" "I want some potatoes—pay you soon!" had sounded too often in the ears of those who had found his repayments so far purely spiritual. Now and then one of the more cynical would remark, "Ah! I told un *my* butter was all to market." Or, "The man can't 'ave no principles—he didn't get no chicken out o' me." And yet it was impossible to let him and his old mother die on them—it would give too much pleasure "over the way." And they never dreamed of losing him in any other manner, because they knew his living had been purchased. Money had passed in that transaction; the whole fabric of the Church and of society was involved. His professional conduct, too, was flawless; his sermons long and fiery; he was always ready to perform those supernumerary duties—weddings, baptisms, and burials—which yielded him what revenue he had, now that his income from the living was mortgaged up to the hilt. Their loyalty held as the loyalty of people will when some great institution of which they are members is endangered.

Gossip said that things were in a dreadful way at the Rectory; the external prosperity of that red-brick building surrounded by laurels which did not flower, heightened ironically the conditions within. The old lady, his mother, eighty years of age, was reported never to leave her bed this winter, because they had no coal. She lay there, with her three birds flying about dirtying the room, for neither she nor her son would ever let a cage-door be shut—deplorable state of things! The one servant was supposed never to be paid. The tradesmen would no longer leave goods because they could not get their money. Most of the furniture had been sold; and the dust made you sneeze "fit to bust yourself, like."

With a little basket on his arm the rector collected for his household three times a week, pursuing a kind of method, always in the apparent belief that he would pay on Monday, and observing the Sabbath as a day of rest. His mind seemed ever to cherish the faith that his shares were on the point of recovery; his spirit never to lose belief in his divine right to be supported. It was extremely difficult to refuse him; the postman had twice seen him standing on the railway line that ran past just below the village, "with 'is 'at off, as if he was in two minds—like!" This vision of him close to the shining metals had powerfully impressed many good, souls who loved to make flesh creep. They would say, "I wouldn' never be surprised if someat' 'appened to 'im one of these days!" Others, less romantic, shook their heads, insisting that "he wouldn' never do nothin' while his old mother lived." Others again, more devout, maintained that "he wouldn' never go against the scriptures, settin' an example like that!"

II

The Petty Sessions Court that morning resembled church on the occasion of a wedding, for the villagers of Trover had put on their black clothes and grouped themselves according to their religious faiths—"Church" in the right, "Chapel" in the left-hand aisle. They presented all that rich variety of type and monotony which the remoter country still affords to the observer; their mouths were almost all a little open and their eyes fixed with intensity on the Bench. The three magistrates—Squire Pleydell in the chair, Dr. Becket on his left, and "the Honble" Calmady on his right—were by most seen for the first time in their judicial capacity; and curiosity was divided between their proceedings and observation of the rector's prosecutor, a small baker from the town whence the village of Trover derived its necessaries. The face of this fellow, like that of a white walrus, and the back of his bald head were of interest to everyone until the case was called and the rector himself entered. In his thin black overcoat he advanced and stood as if a little dazed. Then, turning his ravaged face to the Bench, he jerked out:

"Good morning! Lot of people!"

A constable behind him murmured:

"Into the dock, sir, please."

Moving across, he entered the wooden edifice.

"Quite like a pulpit," he said, and uttered his barking laugh. Through the court ran a stir and shuffle, as it might be of sympathy with his lost divinity, and every eye was fixed on that tall, lean figure, with the red, grey-streaked hair.

Entering the witness-box, the prosecutor deposed as follows:

"Last Tuesday afternoon, your Honours, I 'appened. to be drivin' my cart meself up through Trover on to the cottages just above the dip, and I'd gone in to Mrs. 'Oney's, the laundress, leavin' my cart standin', same as I always do. I 'ad a bit o' gossip, an' when I come out, I see this gentleman walkin' away in front towards the village street. It so 'appens I 'appened to look in the back o' my cart, and I thinks to meself: 'That's funny! There's only two flat rounds—'ave I left two 'ere by mistake?' I call to Mrs. 'Oney an' I says, 'I 'aven't been absent, 'ave I, an' left ye two?' 'No,' she says, 'only one—'ere 'tis! Why?' she says. 'Well,' I says, 'I 'ad four when I come in to you; there's only two now. 'Tis funny!' I says. "Ave you dropped one?' she says. 'No,' I says, 'I counted 'em.' 'That's funny,' she says; 'perhaps a dog's 'ad it.' ''E may 'ave,' I says, 'but the only thing I see on the road is that there.' An' I pointed to this gentleman. 'Oh!' she says, 'that's the rector.' 'Yes,' I says, 'I ought to know that, seein' 'e's owed me money a matter of eighteen months. I think I'll drive on,' I says. Well, I drove on, and come up to this gentleman. 'E turns 'is 'ead and looks at me. 'Good-afternoon!' he says—like that. 'Good-afternoon, sir,' I says. 'You 'aven't seen a loaf, 'ave you?' 'E pulls the loaf out of 'is pocket. 'On the ground,' 'e says; 'dirty,' 'e says. 'Do for my birds! Ha! ha!' like that. 'Oh!' I says, 'indeed! Now I know!' I says. I kept my 'ead, but I thinks: 'That's a bit too light 'earted. You owes me one pound, eight and tuppence; I've whistled for it gettin' on for two years, but you ain't content with that, it seems! Very well,' I thinks; 'we'll see. An' I don't give a darn whether you're a parson or not!' I charge 'im with takin' my bread."

Passing a dirty handkerchief over his white face and huge gingery moustache, the baker was silent. Suddenly from the dock the rector called out: "Bit of dirty bread—feed my birds. Ha, ha!"

There was a deathly little silence. Then the baker said slowly:

"What's more, I say he ate it 'imself. I call two witnesses to that."

The chairman, passing his hand over his hard, alert face, that of a master of hounds, asked:

"Did you see any dirt on the loaf? Be careful!"

The baker answered stolidly:

"Not a speck."

Dr. Becket, a slight man with a short grey beard and eyes restive from having to notice painful things, spoke:

"Had your horse moved?"

"'E never moves."

"Ha, ha!" came the rector's laugh.

The chairman said sharply:

"Well, stand down; call the next witness—Charles Stodder, carpenter. Very well! Go on, and tell us what you know."

But before he could speak the rector called out in a loud voice, "Chapel!"

"Hsssh, sir!" But through the body of the court had passed a murmur of challenge, at it were, from one aisle to the other.

The witness, a square man with a red face, grey hair, whiskers, and moustache, and lively, excitable, dark eyes, watering with anxiety, spoke in a fast, soft voice.

"Tuesday afternoon, your worships, it might be about four o'clock, I was passin' up the village, an' I saw the rector at his gate with a loaf in 'is 'and."

"Show us how."

The witness held his black hat to his side, with the rounded top outwards.

"Was the loaf clean or dirty?"

Sweetening his little eyes, the witness answered:

"I should say 'twas clean."

"Lie!"

The chairman said sternly:

"You mustn't interrupt, sir. You didn't see the bottom of the loaf?"

The witness's little eyes snapped.

"Not eggzactly."

"Did the rector speak to you?"

The witness smiled. "The rector wouldn' never stop me if I was passin'. I collects the rates."

The rector's laugh, so like a desolate dog's bark, killed the bubble of gaity rising in the court; and again that deathly little silence followed.

Then the chairman said:

"Do you want to ask him anything?"

The rector turned. "Why d'you tell lies?"

The witness, screwing up his eyes, said excitedly:

"What lies 'ave I told, please?"

"You said the loaf was clean."

"So 'twas clean, so far as I see."

"Come to church and you won't tell lies."

"Reckon I can learn truth faster in chapel."

The chairman rapped his desk.

"That'll do, that'll do! Stand down! Next witness—Emily Bleaker. Yes? What are you? Cook at the rectory? Very well. What do you know about the affair of this loaf last Tuesday afternoon?"

The witness, a broad-faced, brown-eyed girl, answered stolidly, "Nothin', zurr."

"Ha, ha!"

"Hssh! Did you see the loaf?"

"Noa."

"What are you here for, then?"

"Master asked for a plate and a knaife. He an' old missus ate et for dinner. I see the plate after; there wasn't on'y crumbs on et."

"If you never saw the loaf, how do you know they ate it?"

"Because ther warn't nothin' else in the 'ouse."

The rector's voice barked out:

"Quite right!"

The chairman looked at him fixedly.

"Do you want to ask her anything?"

The rector nodded.

"You, been paid your wages?"

"Noa, I 'asn't."

"D'you know why?"

"Noa."

"Very sorry—no money to pay you. That's all."

This closed the prosecutor's case and there followed a pause, during which the Bench consulted together and the rector eyed the congregation, nodding to one here and there. Then the chairman, turning to him, said:

"Now, sir, do you call any witnesses?"

"Yes. My bell-ringer. He's a good man. You can believe him."

The bell-ringer, Samuel Bevis, who took his place in the witness-box, was a kind of elderly Bacchus, with permanently trembling hands. He deposed as follows:

"When I passed rector Tuesday arternoon, he calls after me: 'See this!' 'e says, and up 'e held it. 'Bit o' dirrty bread,' 'e says: 'do for my burrds.' Then on he goes walkin'."

"Did you see whether the loaf was dirty?"

"Yaas, I think 'twas dirrty."

"Don't *think*! Do you *know*?"

"Yaas; 'twas dirrty."

"Which side?"

"Which saide? I think 'twas dirrty on the bottom."

"Are you sure?"

"Yaas; 'twas dirrty on the bottom, for zartain."

"Very well. Stand down. Now, sir, will you give us your version of this matter?"

The rector, pointing at the prosecutor and the left-hand aisle, jerked out the words:

"All chapel—want to see me down."

The chairman said stonily:

"Never mind that. Come to the facts, please."

"Certainly! Out for a walk—passed the baker's cart—saw a loaf fallen in the mud—picked it up—do for my birds."

"What birds?"

"Magpie and two starlings; quite free—never shut the cage door; well fed."

"The baker charges you with taking it from his cart."

"Lie! Underneath the cart in a puddle."

"You heard what your cook said about your eating it. Did you?"

"Yes, birds couldn't eat all—nothing in the house—mother and I—hungry."

"Hungry?"

"No money. Hard up—very! Often hungry. Ha, ha!"

Again through the court that queer rustle passed. The three magistrates gazed at the accused. Then "the Honble" Calmady said:

"You say you found the loaf under the cart. Didn't it occur to you to put it back? You could see it had fallen. How else could it have come there?"

The rector's burning eyes seemed to melt.

"From the sky—manna." Staring round the court, he added, "Hungry—God's elect—to the manna born!" And, throwing back his head, he laughed. It was the only sound in a silence as of the grave.

The magistrates spoke together in low tones. The rector stood motionless, gazing at them fixedly. The people in the court sat as if at a play. Then the chairman said:

"Case dismissed."

"Thank you."

Jerking out that short thanksgiving, the rector descended from
the dock and passed down the centre aisle, followed by every eye.

III

From the Petty Sessions Court the congregation wended its way
back to Trover, by the muddy lane, "Church" and "Chapel," arguing
the case. To dim the triumph of the "Church" the fact remained that
the baker had lost his loaf and had not been compensated. The loaf
was worth money; no money had passed. It was hard to be victorious
and yet reduced to silence and dark looks at girding adversaries. The
nearer they came to home, the more angry with "Chapel" did they
grow. Then the bell-ringer had his inspiration. Assembling his three
assistants, he hurried to the belfry, and in two minutes the little old
tower was belching forth the merriest and maddest peal those bells
had ever furnished. Out it swung in the still air of the grey winter
day, away to the very sea.

A stranger, issuing from the inn, hearing that triumphant sound,
and seeing so many black-clothed people about, said to his driver:

"What is it—a wedding?"

"No, zurr, they say 'tis for the rector, like; he've a just been
acquitted for larceny."

On the Tuesday following, the rector's ravaged hairless face appeared
in Mrs. Gloyn's doorway, and his voice, creaking like a saw, said:

"Can you let me have a pound of butter? Pay you soon."

What else could he do? Not even to God's elect does the sky
always send down manna.

[*1916*]

"CAFARD"

THE soldier, Jean Liotard, lay, face to the earth, by the bank of the River Drôme. He lay where the grass and trees ended, and between him and the shrivelled green current was much sandy foreshore, for summer was at height, and the snows had long finished melting and passing down. The burning sun had sucked up all moisture, the earth was parched, but to-day a cool breeze blew, willow and aspen leaves were fluttering and hissing as if millions of tiny kisses were being given up there; and a few swathes of white cloud were drawn, it seemed—not driven—along the blue. The soldier, Jean Liotard, had fixed his eyes on the ground, where was nothing to see but a few dry herbs. He had "*cafard*," for he was due to leave the hospital to-morrow and go up before the military authorities, for "*prolongation*." There he would answer perfunctory questions, and be told at once: *Au dépôt* or have to lie naked before them that some "*major*" might prod his ribs, to find out whether his heart, displaced by shellshock, had gone back sufficiently to normal position. He had received one "*prolongation*," and so, wherever his heart now was, he felt sure he would not get another. "*Au dépôt*" was the fate before him, fixed as that river flowing down to its death in the sea. He had "*cafard*"—the little black beetle in the brain, which gnaws and eats and destroys all hope and heaven in a man. It had been working at him all last week, and now he was at a monstrous depth of evil and despair. To begin again the cursed barrack-round, the driven life, until in a month perhaps, packed like bleating sheep in the troop-train, he made that journey to the fighting line again—"*A la hachette—à la hachette!*"

He had stripped off his flannel jacket, and lay with shirt opened to the waist, to get the breeze against his heart. In his brown good-looking face, the hazel eyes, which in these three God-deserted years had acquired a sort of startled gloom, stared out like a dog's, rather prominent, seeing only the thoughts within him—thoughts and images swirling round in a dark whirlpool, drawing his whole being deeper and deeper. He was unconscious of all the summer hum and rustle—the cooing of the dove up in that willow tree, the winged enamelled fairies floating past, the chirr of the cicadas, that little brown lizard among the pebbles, almost within reach, seeming to listen to the beating of summer's heart, so motionless it lay; unconscious, as though in verity he were again deep in some stifling trench, with German shells whining over him, and the smell of muck and blood making fœtid the air. He was in the mood which curses God and dies; for he was devout—a Catholic, and still went to Mass. And God had betrayed the earth, and Jean Liotard. All the enormities he had seen in his two years at the front—the mouthless, mangled faces, the human ribs whence rats would steal; the frenzied, tortured horses, with leg or quarter rent away, still living; the rotted farms, the dazed and hopeless peasants; his innumerable suffering comrades; the desert of no-man's land; and all the thunder and moaning of war; and the reek and the freezing of war; and the driving—the callous, perpetual driving by some great Force which shovelled warm human hearts and bodies, warm human hopes and loves by the million into the furnace; and over all, dark sky without a break, without a gleam of blue or lift anywhere—all this enclosed him, lying in the golden heat, so that not a glimmer of life or hope could get at him. Back into it all again! Back into it, he who had been through forty times the hell that the "*majors*" ever endured, five hundred times the hell ever glimpsed at by those *deputes*, safe with their fat salaries and their gabble about victory and the lost provinces and the future of the world—the *Canaille*! Let them allow the soldiers, whose lives they spent like water—"*les camarades*" on both sides—poor devils who bled, and froze, and starved, and sweated—let them suffer these to make the peace! Ah! what a peace that would be—its first condition, all the sacred politicians and pressmen hanging in rows in every country; the mouth fighters, the pen fighters, the fighters with other men's blood! Those comfortable citizens would never rest while there was a young man with whole limbs left in France! Had he not

killed enough Boches that they might leave him and his tired heart
in peace? He thought of his first charge; of how queer and soft that
Boche body felt when his bayonet went through; and another, and
another. Ah! he had "*joliment*" done his duty that day! And something
wrenched at his ribs. They were only Boches, but their wives and
children, their mothers—faces questioning, faces pleading for
them—pleading with whom? Ah! not with him! Who was he that
had taken those lives, and others since, but a poor devil without a life
himself, without the right to breathe or move except to the orders
of a Force which had no mind, which had no heart, had nothing
but a blind will to go on, it knew not why. If only he survived—it
was not possible—but if only he survived, and with his millions of
comrades could come back and hold the reckoning! Some scare-
the-crows then would waggle in the wind. The butterflies would
perch on a few mouths empty at last; the flies enjoy a few silent
tongues! Then slowly his fierce unreasoning rancour vanished into
a mere awful pity for himself. Was a fellow never again to look at
the sky, and the good soil, the fruit, the wheat, without this dreadful
black cloud above him; never again make love among the trees, or
saunter down a lighted boulevard, or sit before a *café*; never again
attend Mass without this black dog of disgust and dread sitting on
his shoulders, riding him to death? Angels of pity! Was there never
to be an end? One was going mad under it—yes, mad! And the face
of his mother came before him, just as he had seen her last, three
years ago, when he left his home in the now invaded country to join
his regiment—his mother who, with all his family, was in the power
of the Boche. He had gone gaily, and she had stood like stone, her
hand held over her eyes, in the sunlight, watching him while the
train ran out. Usually the thought of the cursed Boches holding in
their heavy hands all that was dear to him was enough to sweep his
soul to a clear, definite hate, which made all this nightmare of war
seem natural and even right; but now it was not enough—he had
"*cafard*." He turned on his back. The sky above the mountains might
have been black for all the joy its blue gave him. The butterflies,
those drifting flakes of joy, passed unseen. He was thinking: No rest,
no end, except by walking over bodies, dead, mangled bodies of

poor devils like himself, poor hunted devils, who wanted nothing but never to lift a hand in combat again so long as they lived, who wanted—as he wanted—nothing but laughter and love and rest! *Quelle vie*! A carnival of leaping demonry! A dream—unutterably bad! 'And when I go back to it all,' he thought, 'I shall go all shaven and smart, and wave my hand as if I were going to a wedding, as we all do. *Vive la France*! Ah! what mockery! Can't a poor devil have a dreamless sleep!' He closed his eyes, but the sun struck hot on them through the lids, and he turned over on his face again and looked longingly at the river—they said it was deep in mid-stream; it still ran fast there! What was that down by the water? Was he really mad? And he uttered a queer laugh. There was his black dog—the black dog off his shoulders, the black dog which rode him, yea, which had be come his very self, just going to wade in! And he called out:

"Hé! le copain!" It was not his dog, for it stopped drinking, tucked its tail in, and cowered at the sound of his voice. Then it came from the water and sat down on its base among the stones and looked at him. A real dog. But what a guy! What a thin wretch of a little black dog! It sat and stared—a mongrel who might once have been pretty. It stared at Jean Liotard with the pathetic gaze of a dog so thin and hungry that it earnestly desires to go to men and get fed once more, but has been so kicked and beaten that it dare not. It seemed held in suspense by the equal overmastering impulses, fear and. hunger. And Jean Liotard stared back. The lost, as it were despairing, look of the dog began to penetrate his brain. He held out his hand, and said: "*Viens*!" But at the sound the little dog only squirmed away a few paces, then again sat down and resumed its stare. Again Jean Liotard uttered that queer laugh. If the good God were to hold out His hand and say to him, "*Viens*!" he would do exactly as that little beast; he would not come, not he! What was he too but a starved and beaten dog—a driven wretch, kicked to hell! And again, as if experimenting with himself, he held out his hand and said: "*Viens*!" and again the beast squirmed a little further away, and again sat down and stared. Jean Liotard lost patience. His head drooped till his forehead touched the ground. He smelt the parched herbs, and a faint sensation of comfort stole through his nerves. He lay unmoving, trying to fancy himself dead and out of it all. The hum of summer, the smell of grasses, the caress of the breeze going over! He pressed the palms of his outstretched hands on the warm soil, as one might on a woman's breast. If only it were really death, how much better than life in this butcher's shop! But death—his death, was waiting for him away over there, under the moaning shells, under the whining bullets, at the end of a steel spike—a mangled, fœtid death. Death—his death, had no sweet scent and no caress—save the kisses of rats and crows. Life and death, what were they? Nothing but the preying of creatures the one on the other—nothing but that; and love, the blind instinct which made these birds and beasts of prey. *Bon sang de bon sang*! The Christ hid his head finely nowadays! That cross up there on the mountain top, with the sun gleaming on it—they had been right to put it up where no man lived, and not even a dog roamed to be pitied! 'Fairy tales!' he thought: 'Those who drive and those who are driven, those who eat and those who are eaten—we are all poor devils together. There is no pity, no God!' And the flies drummed their wings above him. And the sun, boring into his spine through his thin shirt, made him reach for his jacket. The little dog, still sitting on its base twenty yards away, cowered and dropped its ears when he moved; and he thought: 'Poor beast! Someone has been doing the devil's work on you not badly!' There were some biscuits in the pocket of his jacket, and he held one out. The dog shivered, and its thin pink tongue bled out, panting with desire and fear. Jean Liotard tossed the biscuit gently about half-way. The dog cowered back a step or two, crept forward three, and again squatted. Then very gradually it crept up to the biscuit, bolted it, and regained its distance. The soldier took out another. This time he threw it five paces only in front of him. Again the little beast cowered, slunk forward, seized the biscuit, devoured it; but this time it only recoiled a pace or two, and seemed, with panting mouth and faint wagging of the tail, to beg for more. Jean Liotard held a third biscuit as far out in front of him as he could, and waited. The creature crept forward and squatted just out of reach. There it sat, with saliva dripping from its mouth; seemingly it could not make up its mind to that awful venture. The soldier sat motionless; his outstretched hand began to tire, but he did not budge—he meant to conquer its fear. At last it snatched the biscuit. Jean Liotard instantly held out a fourth. That too was snatched, but at the fifth he was able to touch the dog. It cowered almost into the ground at touch of his fingers, and then lay, still trembling violently, while the soldier continued to stroke its head and ears. And suddenly his heart gave a twitter, the creature had licked his hand. He took out his last biscuit, broke it up, and fed the dog slowly with the bits, talking all the time; when the last crumb was gone he continued to murmur and crumple its ears softly. He had become aware of something happening within the dog—something in the nature of conversion, as if it were saying: "My master, my new master—I worship, I love you!" The creature came gradually closer, quite close; then put up its sharp black nose and began to lick his face. Its little hot rough tongue licked and licked, and with each lick the soldier's heart relaxed, just as if the licks were being given there and something licked away. He put his arms round the thin body and hugged it, and still the creature went on feverishly licking at his face and neck and chest, as if trying to creep inside him. The sun poured down, the lizards rustled and whisked among the pebbles; the kissing never ceased up there among the willow and aspen leaves, and every kind of flying thing went past drumming its wings. There was no change in the summer afternoon. God might not be there, but pity had come back; Jean Liotard no longer had "*cafard.*" He put the little dog gently off his lap, got up, and stretched himself. "*Voyons, mon brave, faut aller voir les copains! Tu es à moi.*" The little dog stood up on its hind legs, scratching with its forepaws at the soldier's thigh; as if trying to get at his face again; as if begging not to be left; and its tail waved feverishly, half in petition, half in rapture. The soldier caught the paws, set them down, and turned his face for home, making the noises that a man makes to his dog; and the little dog followed, close as he could get to those moving ankles, lifting his snout and panting with anxiety and love.

[*1917*]

THE RECRUIT

SEVERAL times since that fateful fourth of August he had said: "I sh'll 'ave to go."

And the farmer and his wife would look at him, he with a sort of amusement, she with a queer compassion in her heart, and one or the other would reply smiling: "That's all right, Tom; there's plenty Germans yet. Yu wait a bit."

His mother, too, who came daily from the lonely cottage in the little combe on the very edge of the big hill to work in the kitchen and farm dairy, would turn her dark, taciturn head, with still plentiful black hair, towards his face, which for all its tan was so weirdly reminiscent of a withered baby, pinkish and light-lashed with forelock and fair hair thin and rumpled, and small blue eyes; and she would mutter:

"Don't yu never fret, boy. They'll come for 'ee fast enough when they want 'ee." No one, least of all perhaps his mother, could take quite seriously that little square, short-footed man, born when she was just seventeen. Sure of work because he was first-rate with every kind of beast, he was not yet looked on as being quite "all there." He could neither read nor write, had scarcely ever been outside the parish, and then only in a shandrydan on a club treat, and knew no more of the world than the native of a small South Sea Island. His life from school age on had been passed, year in, year out, from dawn till dark, with the cattle and their calves, the sheep, the horses and the wild moor ponies; except when hay or corn harvest, or any exceptionally exacting festival absorbed him for the moment. From shyness he never went into the bar of the inn, and so had missed the greater part of village education. He could, of course, read no papers; a map was to him but a mystic mass of marks and colours; he had

never seen the sea, never a ship; no water broader than the parish
streams; until the war had never met anything more like a soldier
than the constable of the neighbouring village. But he had once seen
a Royal Marine in uniform. What sort of creatures these Germans
were to him, who knows? They were cruel—he had grasped that.
Something noxious, perhaps, like the adders whose backs he broke
with his stick; something dangerous, like the chained dog at Shapton
Farm, or the bull at Vannacombe. When the war first broke out, and
they had called the younger blacksmith (a reservist and noted village
marksman) back to his regiment, the little cowman had smiled and
said: "Wait till regiment gets to front; Fred'll soon shoot 'em up."

But weeks and months went by, and it was always the Germans,
the Germans; Fred had clearly not yet shot them up. And now one
and now another went off from the village, and two from the farm
itself; and the great Fred returned slightly injured for a few weeks'
rest, and, full of whisky from morning till night, made the village
ring; and finally went off again in a mood of manifest reluctance. All
this weighed dumbly on the mind of the little cowman, the more
heavily that because of his inarticulate shyness he could never talk
that weight away, nor could anyone by talk relieve him, no premises
of knowledge or vision being there. From sheer physical contagion
he felt the grizzly menace in the air, and a sense of being left behind
when others were going to meet that menace with their fists, as
it were. There was something proud and sturdy in the little man,
even in the look of him, for all that he was "poor old Tom," who
brought a smile to the lips of all. He was passionate, too, if rubbed
up the wrong way; but it needed the malevolence and ingenuity
of human beings to annoy him—with his beasts he never lost his
temper, so that they had perfect confidence in him. He resembled
herdsmen of the Alps, whom one may see in dumb communion
with their creatures up in those high solitudes; for he too dwelt in
a high solitude cut off from real fellowship with men and women
by lack of knowledge, and by the supercilious pity in them. Living
in such a remote world his talk—when he did say something— had
ever the surprising quality attaching to the thoughts of those by
whom the normal proportions of things are quite unknown. His

short square figure, hatless and rarely coated in any weather, dotting from foot to foot, a bit of stick in one hand. and often a straw in the mouth—he did not smoke—was familiar in the yard where he turned the handle of the separator, or in the fields and cowsheds, from daybreak to dusk, save for the hours of dinner and tea, which he ate in the farm kitchen, making sparse and surprising comments. To his peculiar whistles and calls the cattle and calves, for all their rumination and stubborn shyness, were amazingly responsive. It was a pretty sight to see them pushing against each other round him—for, after all, he was as much the source of their persistence, especially through the scanty winter months, as a mother starling to her unfledged young.

When the Government issued their request to householders to return the names of those of military age ready to serve if called on, he heard of it, and stopped munching to say in his abrupt fashion: "I'll go—fight the Germans." But the farmer did not put his name down, saying to his wife:

"Poor old Tom! 'Twidden be 'ardly fair—they'd be makin' game of 'un."

And his wife, her eyes shining with motherliness, answered: "Poor lad, he's not fit-like."

The months went on—winter passing to spring, and the slow decking of the trees and fields began with leaves and flowers, with butterflies and the songs of birds. How far the little cowman would notice such a thing as that no one could ever have said, devoid as he was of the vocabulary of beauty, but like all the world his heart must have felt warmer and lighter under his old waistcoat, and perhaps more than most hearts, for he could often be seen standing stock-still in the fields, his browning face turned to the sun.

Less and less he heard talk of Germans—dogged acceptance of the state of war having settled on that far countryside—the beggars were not beaten and killed off yet, but they would be in good time. It was unpleasant to think of them more than could be helped. Once in a way a youth went off and "listed," but, though the parish had given more perhaps than the average, a good few of military age still clung to life as they had known it. Then some bright spirit conceived the notion that a county regiment should march through the remoter districts to rouse them up.

The cuckoo had been singing five days; the lanes and fields, the woods and the village green were as Joseph's coat, so varied and so bright the foliage, from golden oak-buds to the brilliant little lime-tree leaves, the feathery green shoots of larches, and the already darkening bunches of the sycamores. The earth was dry—no rain for a fortnight—when the cars containing the brown-clad men and a recruiting band drew up before the inn. Here were clustered the farmers, the innkeeper, the grey-haired postman; by the church gate and before the schoolyard were knots of girls and children, schoolmistress, schoolmaster, parson; and down on the lower green a group of likely youths, an old labourer or two, and apart from human beings, as was his wont, the little cowman in brown corduroys tied below the knee and an old waistcoat, the sleeves of his blue shirt dotted with pink rolled up to the elbows of his brown arms; so he stood, his brown neck and shaven-looking head quite bare, with his bit of stick wedged between his waist and the ground, staring with all his light-lashed water-blue eyes under the thatch of his forelock.

The speeches rolled forth glib; the khaki-clad men drank their second fill that morning of coffee and cider; the little cowman stood straight and still, his head drawn back. Two figures—officers, men who had been at the front—detached themselves and came towards the group of likely youths. These wavered a little, were silent, sniggered, stood their ground—the khaki-clad figures passed among them. Hackneyed words, jests, the touch of flattery changing swiftly to chaff—all the customary performance, hollow and pathetic; and then the two figures re-emerged, their hands clenched, their eyes shifting here and there, their lips drawn back in fixed smiles. They had failed and were trying to hide it. They must not show contempt—the young slackers might yet come in when the band played.

The cars were filled again, the band struck up: "It's a long, long way to Tipperary."

And at the edge of the green, within two yards of the car's dusty passage, the little cowman stood apart and stared. His face was red. Behind him they were cheering—the parson and farmers, schoolchildren, girls, even the group of youths. He alone did not cheer, but his face grew still more red. When the dust above the road and the distant blare of "Tipperary" had dispersed and died he walked back to the farm, dotting from one to other of his short feet. All that afternoon and evening he spoke no word; but that flush seemed to have settled in his face for good and all. He milked some cows, but forgot to bring the pails up. Two of his precious cows he left unmilked till their distressful lowing caused the farmer's wife to go down and see. There he was, standing against a gate moving his brown neck from side to side like an animal in pain, oblivious, seemingly, of everything. She spoke to him:

"What's matter, Tom?" All he could answer was:

"I'se goin', I'se goin'." She milked the cows herself.

For the next three days he could settle to nothing, leaving his jobs half done, speaking to no one save to say:

"I'se goin'; I'se got to go." Even the beasts looked at him surprised.

On the Saturday the farmer, having consulted with his wife, said quietly:

"Well, Tom, ef yu want to go, yu shall. I'll drive 'ee down Monday. Us won't du nothin' to keep yu back."

The little cowman nodded. But he was restless as ever all through that Sunday, eating nothing.

On Monday morning, arrayed in his best clothes, he got into the dog-cart. There, without good-bye to anyone, not even to his beasts, he sat staring straight before him, square, and jolting up and down beside the farmer, who turned on him now and then a dubious, almost anxious eye.

So they drove the eleven miles to the recruiting station. He got down, entered, the farmer with him.

"Well, my lad," they asked him, "what d'you want to join?"

"Royal Marines."

It was a shock, coming from the short square figure of such an obvious landsman. The farmer took him by the arm.

"Why, yu'm a Devon man, Tom; better take county regiment. An't they gude enough for yu?"

Shaking his head he answered: "Royal Marines."

Was it the glamour of the words or the Royal Marine he had once seen that moved him to wish to join that outlandish corps? They took him to the recruiting station for the Royal Marines.

Stretching up his short square body and blowing out his cheeks to increase his height, he was put before the reading board. His eyes were splendid; little that passed in hedgerows, or the heavens, in woods, or on the hillsides, could escape them. They asked him to read the print.

Staring, he answered: "L."

"No, my lad, you're guessing."

"L."

The farmer plucked at the recruiting officer's sleeve, his face was twitching, and he whispered hoarsely:

"'E don't know 'is alphabet."

The officer turned and contemplated that short square figure with the browned face so reminiscent of a withered baby, and the little blue eyes staring out under the dusty forelock. Then he grunted, and going up to him, laid a hand on his shoulder.

"*Your* heart's all right, my lad, but you can't pass."

The little cowman looked at him, turned, and went straight out. An hour later he sat again beside the farmer on the way home, staring before him and jolting up and down.

"They won't get me," he said suddenly: "I can fight, but I'se not goin'." A fire of resentment seemed to have been lit within him. That evening he ate his tea, and next day settled down again among his beasts. But whenever, now, the war was mentioned he would look up with his puckered smile which seemed to have in it a resentful amusement, and say:

"They ain't got me yet."

His dumb sacrifice passing their comprehension had been rejected—or so it seemed to him. He could not understand why they had spurned him—he was as good as they! His pride was hurt. No! They should not get him now!

[*1917*]

COMPENSATION

IF, as you say (said Ferrand), there is compensation in this life for everything, do tell me where it comes in here.

Two years ago I was interpreter to an hotel in Ostend, and spent many hours on the Plage waiting for the steamers to bring sheep to my slaughter. There was a young man about that year who had a stall of cheap jewellery; I don't know his name, for among us he was called Tchuk-Tchuk; but I knew *him*—for we interpreters know everybody. He came from Southern Italy and called himself an Italian, but by birth he was probably an Algerian Jew; an intelligent boy, who knew that, except in England, it is far from profitable to be a Jew in these days. After seeing his nose and his beautiful head of frizzly hair, however, there was little more to be said on the subject. His clothes had been given him by an English tourist—a pair of flannel trousers, an old frock coat, a bowler hat. Incongruous? Yes, but think, how cheap! The only thing that looked natural to him was his tie; he had unsewn the ends and wore it without a collar. He was little and thin, which was not surprising, for all he ate a day was half a pound of bread, or its equivalent in macaroni, with a little piece of cheese, and on a feast day a bit of sausage. In those clothes, which were made for a fat man, he had the appearance of a scarecrow with a fine, large head. These "Italians" are the Chinese of the West. The conditions of life down there being impossible, they are driven out like locusts or the old inhabitants of Central Asia—a regular invasion. In every country they have a kind of Society which helps them to make a start. When once provided with organs, jewellery, or whatever their profession, they live on nothing, drink nothing, spend no money. Smoke? Yes, they smoke; but you have to give them the tobacco. Sometimes they bring their women; more often they come alone—they make money more quickly without. The end they have in view is to scrape together a treasure of two or three hundred pounds and go back to Italy rich men. If you're accustomed to the Italian at home, it will astonish you to see how he works when he's out of his own country, and how provident he is—a regular Chinaman. Tchuk-Tchuk was alone, and he worked like a slave. He was at his stand, day in, day out; if the sun burned, if there was a gale; he was often wet through, but no one could pass without receiving a smile from his teeth and a hand stretched out with some gimcrack or other. He always tried to impress the women, with whom he did most of his business—especially the *cocotterie*. Ah! how he looked at them with his great eyes! Temperamentally, I dare say, he was vicious enough; but, as you know, it costs money to be vicious, and he spent no money. His expenses were twopence a day for food and fourpence for his bed in a *café* full of other birds of his feather— sixpence a day, three shillings and sixpence a week. No other sort of human creature can keep this up long. My minimum is tenpence, which is not a bed of roses; but, then, I can't do without tobacco (to a man in extreme poverty a single vice is indispensable). But these "Italians" do without even that. Tchuk-Tchuk sold; not very hard work, you say? Try it for half an hour; try and sell something good— and Tchuk-Tchuk's things were rubbish—flash coral jewellery, Italian enamels made up into pins and brooches, celluloid gimcracks. In the evenings I've often seen him doze off from sheer fatigue, but always with his eyes half-open, like a cat. His soul was in his stall; he watched everything—but only to sell his precious goods, for nothing interested him; he despised all the world around him—the people, the sea, the amusements; they were ridiculous and foreign. He had his stall, and he lived to sell. He was like a man shut up in a box—with not a pleasure, not a sympathy, nothing wherewith to touch this strange world in which he found himself.

"I'm of the South," he would say to me, jerking his head at the sea; "it's hard there. Over there I got a girl. She wouldn't be sorry to see me again; not too sorry! Over there one starves; name of a Saint" (he chose this form of oath, no doubt, because it sounded Christian), "it's hard there!"

I am not sentimental about Tchuk-Tchuk; he was an egoist to the bottom of his soul, but that did not in the least prevent his suffering for the want of his South, for the want of his sunshine, and his girl—the greater the egoism the greater the suffering. He craved like a dumb animal; but, as he remarked, "Over there one starves!" Naturally he had not waited for that. He had his hopes. "Wait a bit!" he used to say. "Last year I was in Brussels. Bad business! At the end they take away all my money for the Society, and give me this stall. This is all right—I make some money this season."

He had many clients among "women of morals," who had an eye for his beautiful head of hair, who know, too, that life is not all roses; and there was something pathetic in the persistency of Tchuk-Tchuk and the way his clothes hung about him like sacks; nor was he bad-looking, with his great black eyes and his slim, dirty hands.

One wet day I came on the Estacade when hardly a soul was there. Tchuk-Tchuk had covered his stall with a piece of old. tarpaulin. He was smoking a long cigar.

"Aha! Tchuk-Tchuk," I said, "smoking?"

"Yes," says he, "it's good!"

"Why not smoke every day, you miser? It would comfort you when you're hungry."

He shook his head. "Costs money," says he. "This one cost me nothing. A kind of an individual gave it me—a red-faced Englishman—said he couldn't smoke it. He knew nothing, the idiot—this is good, I tell you!"

But it was Tchuk-Tchuk who knew nothing—he had been too long without the means of knowledge. It was interesting to see the way he ate, drank, inhaled, and soaked up that rank cigar—a true revel of sensuality.

The end of the season came, and all of us birds who prey on the visitors were getting ready to fly; but I stayed on, because I liked the place—the gay-coloured houses, the smell of fish in the port, the good air, the long green seas, the dunes; there's something of it all in my blood, and I'm always sorry to leave. But after the season is over—as Tchuk-Tchuk would say "Name of a saint—one starves over there!"

One evening, at the very end, when there were scarcely twenty visitors in the place, I went as usual to a certain *café*, with two compartments, where everyone comes whose way of living is dubious—bullies, comedians, off-colour actresses, women of morals, "Turks," "Italians," "Greeks"—all such, in fact, as play the game of stealing—a regular rag-shop of cheats and gentlemen of industry—very interesting people, with whom I am well acquainted. Nearly everyone had gone so that evening there were but few of us in the restaurant, and in the inner room three Italians only. I passed into that.

Presently in came Tchuk-Tchuk, the first time I had ever seen him in a place where one could spend a little money. How thin he was, with his little body and his great head! One would have said he hadn't eaten for a week. A week? A year! Down he sat, and called for a bottle of wine; and at once he began to chatter and snap his fingers. "Ha, ha!" says one of the Italians; "look at Tchuk-Tchuk. What a nightingale he has become all of a sudden. Come, Tchuk-Tchuk, give us some of your wine, seeing you're in luck!"

Tchuk-Tchuk gave us of his wine, and ordered another bottle. "Ho, ho!" says another Italian, "must have buried his family, this companion!" We drank—Tchuk-Tchuk faster than all. Do you know that sort of thirst, when you drink just to give you the feeling of having blood in the veins at all? Most people in that state can't stop—they drink themselves dead drunk. Tchuk-Tchuk was not like that. He was careful, as always, looking to his future. Oh! he kept his heart in hand; but in such cases a little goes a long way; he became cheerful—it doesn't take much to make an Italian cheerful who has been living for months on water and half-rations of bread and macaroni. It was evident, too, that he had reason to feel gay. He sang and laughed, and the other Italians sang and laughed with him. One of them said: "It seems our Tchuk-Tchuk has been doing good business. Come, Tchuk-Tchuk, tell us what you have made this season!"

But Tchuk-Tchuk only shook his head.

"Eh!" said the Italian, "the shy bird. It ought to be something good. As for me, comrades, honestly, five hundred francs is all I've made—not a centime more—and the half of that goes to the patron."

And each of them began talking of his gains, except Tchuk-Tchuk, who showed his teeth, and kept silence.

"Come, Tchuk-Tchuk," said one, "don't be a bandit—a little frankness!"

"He won't beat my sixteen hundred!" said another.

"Name of a Saint!" said Tchuk-Tchuk suddenly, "what do you say to four thousand?"

But we all laughed.

"La la!" said one, "he mocks us!"

Tchuk-Tchuk opened the front of his old frockcoat.

"Look!" he cried, and he pulled out four bills—each for a thousand francs. How we stared!

"See," said he, "what it is to be careful—I spend nothing—every cent is here! Now I go home—I get my girl; wish me good journey!" He set to work again to snap his fingers.

We stayed some time and drank another bottle. Tchuk-Tchuk paying. When we parted nobody was helpless, only, as I say, Tchuk-Tchuk on the road to the stars, as one is after a six months' fast. The next morning I was drinking a "bock" in the same *café*, for there was nothing else to do, when all of a sudden who should come running in but this same Tchuk-Tchuk! Ah! but he was no longer on the road to the stars. He flung himself down at the table, with his head between his hands, and the tears rolled down his cheeks.

"They've robbed me," he cried, "robbed me of every sou; robbed me while I slept. I had it here, under my pillow; I slept on it; it's gone—every sou!" He beat his breast.

"Come, Tchuk-Tchuk," said I, "from under your pillow? That's not possible!"

"How do I know?" he groaned; "it's gone, I tell you—all my money, all my money. I was heavy with the wine——" All he could do was to repeat again and again: "All my money, all my money!"

"Have you been to the police?"

He had been to the police. I tried to console him, but with out much effect, as you may imagine. The boy was beside himself.

The police did nothing—why should they? If he had been a Rothschild it would have been different but seeing he was only a poor devil of an Italian who had lost his all——!

Tchuk-Tchuk had sold his stall, his stock, everything he had, the day before, so he had not even the money for a ticket to Brussels. He was obliged to walk. He started—and to this day I see him starting, with his little hard hat on his beautiful black hair, and the unsewn ends of his tie. His face was like the face of the Devil thrown out of Eden!

What became of him I cannot say, but I do not see too clearly in all this the compensation of which you have been speaking.

And Ferrand was silent.

[*1904*]

CONSCIENCE

Taggart sat up. The scoop under the ranger's fence, cannily selected for his sleeping-place, was overhung by branches, and the birds of Hyde Park were at matins already. His watch had gone the way of his other belongings during the last three months, and he could only assume from the meagre light that it was but little after dawn. He was not grateful to the birds; he would be hungry long before a breakfast coming from he hardly knew where. But he listened to them with interest. This was the first night he had passed in the open, and, like all amateurs, he felt a kind of triumph at having achieved vagrancy in spite of the law, the ranger, and the dew. He was a Northumbrian too, and his "tail still up," as he expressed it. Born in a town, Taggart had not much country lore—at sparrows, blackbirds, thrushes, his knowledge stopped; but he enjoyed the bobbery the little beggars were kicking up, and, though a trifle stiff perhaps, he felt "fine."

He lit his pipe, and almost at once his brain began to revolve the daily problem of how to get a job, and of why he had lost the one he had.

Walking, three months ago, burly, upright, secure and. jolly, into the room of his chief at the offices of "Conglomerated Journals Ltd.," he had been greeted with:

"Morning, Taggart. Georgie Grebe is to give us an article for *The Lighthouse*. He won't have time to write it, of course. I want you just to do us a column he could sign—something Grebeish. I'm anxious for a feature of that sort every week now in *The Lighthouse*; got half a dozen really good names. We must get it on its legs with the big Public?"

Taggart smiled. Georgie Grebe! The name was a household word—tophole idea to get him!

"Did he ever write a line in his life, sir?"

"Don't suppose so—but you know the sort of thing he *would* write; he gets nothing for it but the Ad. The week after I've got Sir Cutman Kane—you'll want to be a bit careful there; but you can get his manner from that book of his on murder trials. He hasn't got a minute—must have it devilled; but he'll sign anything decently done. I'm going to *make* 'em buy *The Lighthouse*, Taggart. Get on to the Grebe article at once, will you?"

Taggart nodded, and drawing from his pocket some type written sheets of paper, laid them on the bureau.

"Here's your signed leader, sir; I've gingered it a bit too much, perhaps."

"Haven't time to look at it; got to catch the boat train, Taggart."

"Shall I tone it down a little?"

"Better perhaps; use your judgment. Sit here, and do it right now. Good-bye; back on Friday."

Reaching for his soft hat, assisted into his coat by Taggart, the chief was gone.

Taggart sat down to pencil the signed leader.

"Good leader," he thought, "pity nobody knows I write 'em."

This devilling was quite an art, and, not unlike art, poorly enough paid—still, not bad fun feeling you were the pea and the chief only the shell—the chief, with his great name and controlling influence. He finished pencilling; O.K.'d the sheets; thought: 'Georgie Grebe! What the deuce shall I write about?' and went back to his room.

It was not much of a room, and there was not much in it except Jimmy Counter, smoking a pipe and writing furiously. Taggart sat down too, lit his own pipe, took a sheet of paper and scrawled the words: "Georgie Grebe Article" across the top.

Georgie Grebe! It *was* a scoop! The chief had a wonderful flair for just the names that got the Public. There was some thing rather beautifully simple about writing an article for a man who had never written a line—something virginal in the conception. And when you came to think of it, something virginal in the Public's buying of the article to read the thoughts of their idol, Georgie Grebe. Yes, and what were the thoughts of their idol, Georgie Grebe? If he, Taggart, didn't know, nobody would, not even Georgie Grebe! Taggart smiled, then felt a little nervous. Georgie Grebe—celebrated clown—probably he hadn't any thoughts! Really, there was something very trustful about the Public! He dipped his pen in ink and sat staring at the nib. Trustful! The word had disturbed the transparency of his mental process, as a crystal of peroxide will disturb and colour a basinful of water. Trustful! The Public would pay their pennies to read what they thought were the thoughts of Georgie Grebe. But Georgie Grebe had no thoughts! Taggart bit into the pipe stem. Steady! He was getting on too fast. Of course Georgie Grebe had thoughts if he signed! By writing his name he adopted them—didn't he? His name would be reproduced in autograph, with the indispensable portrait. People would see by his features that Georgie Grebe must have had those thoughts. Trustful! Was the Public so very trustful—when there was such evidence? Besides, Grebe would read his thoughts— fraudulent! Bosh! This was just devilling; there was nothing fraudulent about "devilling"—everybody did it! Fraudulent! You might as well say those signed leaders written for the chief were fraudulent. Of course they weren't—they were only devilled. The Public paid for the thoughts of the chief, and they were the thoughts of the chief, since he signed them. Devilled thoughts! And yet! Would the Public pay if those leaders were signed A. F. Taggart? The thoughts would be the same—very good thoughts. They ought to pay—but—would they? He struck another match, and wrote:

"I am no writer, ladies and gentlemen. I am—believe me—a simple clown. In balancing this new pole upon my nose I am conscious of a certain sense of fraud——"

He crossed out the paragraph. That word again—must keep it from buzzing senselessly round his brain like this! He was only devilling; hold on to the word devilling; it was his living to devil—more or less—just earning his living—getting nothing out of it! Neither was Georgie Grebe—only the Ad! Then who was getting something out of it? "Conglomerated Journals"! out of Georgie Grebe's name; out of the chief's name below the devilled leaders—a pretty penny! But was there any harm in making the most of a big name? Taggart frowned. Suppose a man went into a shop and bought a box of pills, marked

"Holloway," made up from a recipe of "Tompkins"—did it matter that the man thought they were Holloway's, if they were just as good pills, perhaps better? Taggart laid down his pen and took his pipe out of his mouth. 'Gosh!' he thought; 'never looked at it this way before! I believe it does matter. A man ought to get the exact article he pays for. If not, any fraud is possible. New Zealand mutton can be sold as English. Jaeger stuffs can have cotton in them. This Grebe article's a fraud.' He relit his pipe. With the first puff his English hatred of a moral attitude, or "swank" of any sort beset him. Who was he to take stand against a custom? Didn't secretaries write the speeches of Parliamentary "big-bugs"? Weren't the opinions of eminent lawyers often written by their juniors, read over and signed? Weren't briefs and pleadings devilled? Yes; but all that was different. In such cases the Public weren't paying for expression, they were paying for knowledge; the big lawyer put his imprimatur on the knowledge, not on the expression of it; the Cabinet Minister endorsed his views, whether he had written them out or not, and it was his views the Public paid for, not the expression of them. But in this Grebe article the Public would not be paying for any knowledge it contained, nor for any serious views; it would pay for a peep into the mind of their idol. 'And his mind will be mine!' thought Taggart; 'but who'd spend his money to peep into my mind, if he *knew* it was my mind?' He got up, and sat down again.

With a Public so gullible—what did it matter? They lapped up anything and asked for more. Yes! But weren't the gullible the very people who oughtn't to be gulled? He rose again and toured the dishevelled room. The man at the other table raised his head.

"You seem a bit on your toes."

Taggart stared down at him.

"I've got to write some drivel in *The Lighthouse* for Georgie Grebe to sign. It's just struck me that it's a fraud on the Public. What do you say, Jimmy?"

"In a way. What about it?"

"If it is, I don't want to do it—that's all."

His colleague whistled.

"My dear chap, here am I writing a racing article, 'From the Man in the Paddock'—I haven't been on a race-course for years."

"Oh! well—that's venial."

"All's venial in our game. Shut your eyes and swallow. You're only devilling."

"Ga!" said Taggart. "Give a thing a decent label, and it is decent."

"I say, old man, what did you have for breakfast?"

"Look here, Jimmy, I'm inclined to think I've struck a snag. It never occurred to me before."

"Well, don't let it occur to you again. Think of old Dumas. I've heard he put his name to sixty volumes in one year. Has that done him any harm?"

Taggart rumpled his hair, reddish and rather stiff.

"Damn!" he said.

Counter laughed.

"You get a fixed screw for doing what you're told. Why worry? Papers must be sold. Georgie Grebe—that's some stunt."

"Blast Georgie Grebe!"

He took his hat and went out; a prolonged whistle followed him. All next day he spent doing other jobs, trying to persuade himself that he was a crank, and gingerly feeling the mouths of journalists. All he got was: Fuss about nothing! What was the matter with devilling? With life at such pressure, what else could you have? But for the life of him he could not persuade himself to go on with the thoughts of Georgie Grebe. He remembered suddenly that his father had changed the dogmas of his religion at forty-five, and thereby lost a cure of souls. He was very unhappy; it was like discovering that he had inherited tuberculosis. On Friday he was sent for by the chief.

"Morning, Taggart; I'm just back. Look here, this leader for to-morrow—it's nothing but a string of statements. Where's my style?"

Taggart shifted his considerable weight from foot to foot.

"Well, sir," he said, "I thought perhaps you'd like to put that in yourself, for a change. The facts are all right."

The chief stared.

"My good fellow, do you suppose I've got time for that? Anybody could have written this; I can't sign it as it stands. Tone it up."

Taggart took the article from the chief's hand.

"I don't know that I can," he said; "I'm——" and stopped. The chief said kindly:

"Are you ill?"

Taggart disclaimed.

"Private trouble?"

"No."

"Well, get on with it, then. How's the Grebe article turned out?"

"It hasn't."

"How d'you mean?"

Taggart felt his body stiffening.

"Fact is I can't write it."

"Good gracious, man, any drivel will do, so long as it's got a flavour of some sort to carry the name."

Taggart swallowed.

"That's it. Is it quite playing the game with the Public, sir?

The chief seemed to loom larger suddenly.

"I don't follow you, Taggart."

Taggart blurted out: "I don't want to write anyone else's stuff in future, unless it's just news or facts."

The chief's face grew very red.

"I pay you to do certain work. If you don't care to carry out instructions, we can dispense with your services. What's the matter with you, Taggart?"

Taggart replied with a wry smile:

"Suffering from a fit of conscience, sir. Isn't it a matter of commercial honesty?"

The chief sat back in his swivel chair and gazed at him for quite twenty seconds.

"Well," he said at last in an icy voice, "I have never been so insulted. Good-morning! You are at liberty."

Taggart laid down the sheets of paper, walked stiffly to the door, and turned.

"Awfully sorry, sir; can't help it."

The chief bowed distantly, and Taggart went out.

For three months he had enjoyed liberty. Journalism was overstocked; his name not well known. Too shy and proud to ask for recommendation from "Conglomerated Journals," he could never bring himself to explain why he had "got the hoof." Claim a higher standard of morality than his fellows—not he. For two months he had carried on pretty well, but the last few weeks had brought him low indeed. Yet the more he brooded, the more he felt he had been right, and the less inclined he was to speak of it. Loyalty to the chief he had insulted by taking such an attitude, dislike of being thought a fool, beyond all, dread of "swanking" kept him silent. When asked why he had left "Conglomerated Journals" he returned the answer always: "Disagreement on a point of principle," and refused to enter into details. But a feeling had got about that he was a bit of a crank; for though no one at "Conglomerated Journals" knew exactly why he had vanished, Counter had spread the news that he had blasted Georgie Grebe, and refused to write his article. Someone else had done it. Taggart read the production with irritation. It was jolly bad. Inefficient devilling still hurt one who had devilled long and efficiently without a qualm. When the article which had not been written by Sir Cutman Kane appeared—he swore aloud. It was no more like the one Sir Cutman would have signed if Taggart had written it, than the boots of Taggart were like the boots of the chief, who seemed to wear a fresh pair every day, with cloth tops. He read the chief's new leaders with melancholy, spotting the many deficiencies of style supplied to the chief by—whoever it was now wrote them. His square red cheerful face had a bitter look while he was reading; and when he had finished, he would rumple his stiff hair. But he was sturdy, and never got so far as calling himself a fool for his pains, though week by week he felt more certain that his protest had been vain.

Sitting against the ranger's paling, listening to the birds, he had a dreamy feeling about it all. Queer creatures, human beings! So damned uncritical! Had he not been like that himself for years and years? The power of a label—that was what struck him, sitting there. Label a thing decently, and it *was* decent! Ah! but, "Rue by any other name would smell as sour!" Conscience!—it was the devil!

[*1922*]

ONCE MORE

Awakened by the tiny kicks of her baby, she straightened his limbs on her breast, and lay staring up at the dirty ceiling. The first light of the March morning, through a window which had but a ragged piece of muslin over the lower half, spread its pale glimmer in the little room. It was, like all the little back rooms of that street, deserted by Hope; neither was there anything in it of beauty or value except the remains of her stock of violets in the round brown-wicker basket.

Soothed by the warmth of her chest and arms, the baby was sleeping again, with his down-covered tiny head snuggled into the hollow of her neck; and, just above that head, the mother's face was like that of a little sphinx.

Two days before, her husband had left her, saying that he was not coming back, but this had not dismayed her, for with the strange wisdom of those who begin to suffer young, she had long ago measured her chances with and without him. She made more than he did in their profession of flower-selling, because sometimes a "toff" gave her a fancy price, touched perhaps by the sight of her tired, pretty face, and young figure bent side ways by the weight of her baby. Yes, he took more money off her than she did off him; besides, he had left her twice before in the same way, and twice come back. The feeling in her heart was due to another discovery. Last evening, going home dead-tired, she had seen him on an omnibus with his arm round a woman's waist. At that sight a flame had leaped up in her; burdened with baby and basket, she had run after the bus; but it went too fast for her; she was soon left behind. And long, huddled over her fire, she had sat, seeing him with that other woman. And when the fire went out, getting into bed, had lain sleepless, still seeing, and hearing, and shivering with the cold. So, that was where he went! Was she going to put up with it any more? Thus she lay brooding, avoiding all extravagance, matter-of-fact, sphinx-like, even in thought.

The room grew light; she got up, went to the little cracked mirror, and looked long at her face. If she had ever known that she was pretty, the life she led with her boy-husband, sometimes ill-treated, always scantily clothed, and more or less in want, had bereft her of this knowledge. The woman round whose waist she had seen his arm looked well-fed and had feathers in her hat. And in that mirror she tried desperately to find something which might weigh against those full cheeks and those feathers. But she seemed to herself all eyes, there was no colour in her cheeks; she seemed sad to herself. Turning from that glass of little comfort, she lit the fire, and, taking up her baby, sat down to feed it. With her bare feet to the flame, and feeling the movement of the baby's lips against her, she had the first sensation of warmth since the omnibus had passed her. To her, striving so hard but so unconsciously for any thought that would assuage her jealousy, there came a recollection that was almost pleasant. Last evening a "toff," entering his garden gate, had bought from her a single bunch of violets for half-a-crown. Why had he smiled, and given her that half-crown? With each tug of the baby's lips the sensation of warmth grew, and with it began to be mingled a feeling of excitement. He would not have looked at her so long, would not have smiled—unless he had thought her pretty! But suddenly the baby's lips ceased to move; the feeling of excitement died. Wrapping the little thing in her shawl, she laid him back on the bed; then, heating a little water, began to wash with unwonted care. She had a passionate desire to make herself finer than that woman with feathers in her hat. No "toff" would have smiled at her, even though she had not had to pawn her clothes. Her little brain, frozen with brooding, flaming with jealousy, ran riot amongst clothes. There hung on two nails driven into the wall—all her wardrobe—a ragged skirt, torn jersey, and black straw hat. She put on her one undergarment, and went up to them. Looking at those dim clothes, she was vaguely conscious of the irony in things. Three weeks ago she had "put away" her best suit for four

shillings and sixpence, to renew her husband's stock of flowers, which
rain had ruined. She had pawned her attractions to give him the
chance to go after that woman! From the secret place where she kept
her wealth, from those many pawn-tickets, she selected one, and put
it between her teeth; then, from a broken cup, where, under a ragged
cloth, she stored her money, she took the "toffs" half-crown, and five
pennies. It was all she had, and the week's rent was owing. She looked
round the room; her blankets were in pawn; there was nothing left
except her shawl. It was a thick shawl, good for eighteenpence. With
interest threepence, she would still need fourpence to redeem her
suit. She went to her flower-basket and lifted the piece of dirty
sacking. The bunches were withered. In her rage and disturbance
over night, she had forgotten to damp them. She sat down on her
bed, and for full quarter of an hour stayed there unmoving, more like
a little sphinx than ever, with her short, ivory-coloured face, black
eyes, straight brows and closed, red lips. Suddenly she got up; took off
her undergarment and examined it. There were no holes!' Wrapping
it tightly in her shawl, she put on skirt and jersey, pinned her hat to
her black hair, took pawn-ticket and her money, and went down the
dirty stairs, out into the cold.

She made her way to the small shop which was the centre of her
universe. No one was there, for the door had only just been opened;
and she waited, stolid, amongst those innumerable goods, each one
of which had been brought there wrapped in the stuff of human life.
The proprietor caught sight of her presently through the glass of the
inner door. He was a dark, strong man, and his quick eye, which had
in it a sort of cringing hardness instantly marked her shawl.

"I've had that. before, I think, eighteenpence, ain't it?" From its
recesses he took the undergarment. He looked at this critically; it was
very plain, thick, and had no frills, but it was strangely new. "Sixpence
on that, 'alfpenny off for the washing." Then, as if something in the
nature of this transaction had moved him, he added: "Let you off the
washing." She silently held out to him her small rough hand, with
her money and the pawn-ticket. He scrutinised both, and said: "I see;
that'll be tuppence I owe you on the deal."

With the twopence and her suit, she journeyed home. She put

on the suit over her skirt and jersey, for the sake of the warmth, and because that woman had full cheeks; stood for some minutes smoothing her hair and rubbing her face, goose-fleshed with the cold; then, leaving her baby with the woman on the ground floor, she went out towards the road where the omnibus had passed. Her heart was dry with longing to meet that woman; to be avenged on her, and *him*. All the morning she walked up and down. Now and again a youth stopped her, and tried to enter into conversation; but he soon desisted, as if something in her face had withered his good intentions. With the twopence she bought a sausage-roll, ate it, went home, fed her baby, and again came out. It was now afternoon, but she still wandered up and down, always driven on by that longing; and every now and then smiling up at some man. What she thought to gain by these smiles cannot be told, for no one could have answered them, so mirthless were they; and yet they gave her a queer dead pleasure, as if she felt that they ministered to her vengeance. A strong wind drove the clouds over a clear blue sky, and in this wind the buds and few crocuses in the gardens were trembling. In some of the Squares, too, pigeons were cooing; and all the people seemed hurrying with happiness. But for that young wife, for ever walking and loitering down the long road where the omnibus had passed, spring travelled the air in vain.

At five o'clock, moved by yet another obscure impulse of her longing for revenge, she branched off her beat to the white house where she had seen the "toff" enter last evening. She hesitated long before ringing the bell, and then very stolidly asked to see "the gentleman," in a voice a little thick and hoarse from the many colds she caught selling her flowers. While the maid went to see if this were possible, she waited in the hall. There was a mirror there; but she did not look at herself, standing quite still with her eyes fixed on the ground.

She was shown into a room, lighter, warmer, more strange than any room she had ever been in; giving her a feeling as though a plateful of Christmas pudding, soft, dark, and rich, had been placed before her. The walls were white and the wood work white, and there were brown velvet curtains, and gold frames round the pictures. She went in smiling, as at the men in the street. But the smile faded from her lips at once. On a sofa was a lady in a white dress; and she wished to turn and go away, for she felt at once that they must know she had no undergarment beneath her new suit. The gentleman asked her to sit down. She sat down, therefore; and in answer to questions, told them that her stock was spoiled, that she owed a week's rent, that her husband had left her and the baby! But even while speaking, she felt that this was not what she had come to say. They seemed to ask the questions over and over again, as if they did not understand her. And she told them suddenly that her husband had gone with another woman. When she said that, the lady made soft sounds, as if she understood and was sorry. She noticed what pretty small ears the lady had. The gentleman was afraid he did not know what could be done for her: Did she wish to leave her husband? She answered quickly: "I couldn't stay with him now, of course." And the lady murmured: "No, no; of course not." What then—the gentleman said—did she propose to do? She remained silent, staring at the carpet. It seemed to her suddenly that they were thinking: 'She's come for money.' The gentleman took out a sovereign, and said:

"Will that be any good to you?" She made a little bob, and took the sovereign, clutching it very tight. It seemed to her that they wanted her to go away. She got up, therefore, and went to the door. The gentleman went with her; and as he opened the front door he smiled. She did not smile back, for she saw that he had only meant to be kind, yesterday. And this hurt her, as if suddenly there had slipped away from her part of her revenge.

She went home, still clutching the unchanged sovereign; so weak and faint that she could hardly feed her baby. She made up her fire and sat down beside it. It was past six, and nearly dark. Twice before, he had come back on the third day, about this time. If he were to come back now!

She crouched nearer to the fire. It grew quite dark. She looked at her baby; he was asleep, with his tiny fists crumpled against his cheeks. She made up the fire, and went back to her beat along the road where the omnibus had passed.

Two or three men stopped her, but she no longer smiled at them, and they soon sheered off. It was very clear, very cold; but she did not feel the cold. Her eyes were fastened on those great vans of warmth, the motor omnibuses. Long before each had borne its burden close, her eyes had begun searching. Long after they had rumbled by, her gaze followed them from under the brim of her black straw hat. But that for which she was looking never appeared. In the midst of the roar and the sudden hushes, of the stir and confusion of lamplight and shadow, the stir and confusion and blackness in her own heart, she thought of her baby, and hurried away. He was still sleeping, the fire still alight. Without undressing, she crept into bed, exhausted. If she was like a little sphinx awake, she was more so than ever under the mystery of sleep, with her black lashes resting on her cheeks, and her lips just parted. In her dreams she twisted her hands and moaned. She woke at midnight.

By the light of the still live fire she saw her husband moving past the foot of the bed. He neither spoke, nor looked at her, but sat down before the fire, and began to take off his boots. The sight of that domestic act roused her to fury. So he could come in when he liked—after going where he had gone, after being what he had been, the——! But no fierce sound came; she could form no word bad enough to call him by. After three days—after what she had seen—after all her waiting—and walking—and suffering—taking off his boots! Stealthily she raised herself in bed, the better to watch that act. If she had opened her mouth it would have been to utter a scream; no lesser cry could have relieved her heart. And still he neither spoke nor looked at her. She saw him slide down off the wooden chair, as if he would creep right into the fire. And she thought: 'Let him burn, the——!' A vile word clung in her brain and would not come forth. She could just see his figure hunched now all in a heap; she could hear his teeth chattering, and the sound gave her pleasure. Then he was quite silent, and she, too, held her breath. Was he asleep? The thought of this sleep, while she lay there consumed with rage, was too much for her. She uttered a little furious sound. He did not look up, but his foot moved, and a loosened cinder fell; there was again silence. She began creeping to the foot of the bed. Crouching there, with loins curved, and her face bent down between her stretched-out arms, she was close above his huddled figure; so close that with her hands she could have seized and twisted back his head. In fancy she was already doing this, putting her eyes close to his, setting her teeth in his forehead—so vividly that she had the taste of blood in her mouth. Suddenly she recoiled, burying her face between her arms, on the ragged bed coverlet. For some minutes she stayed thus, crouched like a wild cat on a branch. There was a dreadful sore feeling within her. She was thinking of the first night they had come home to that room; she was remembering his kisses. Something clicked in her throat. She no longer wished to tear and bite, and she raised her face. He had not stirred. She could just see the outline of his cheeks and chin; beardless, of a boy, utterly still, as if dead. She felt cold, and afraid. What was this silence? She could not even hear him breathe. She slid down on the floor. His eyes were open, very colourless, staring at the dying fire; his cheeks were hollow, his lips seemed to have no blood in them. But they moved, shivering desperately. So he was not dead! Only frozen and starved as he had been when he came back to her those two other times. The mask of her face let nothing be seen of her thoughts and feelings, but her teeth bit into her lower lip. So this was how he had come back to her once more!

The last of the fuel in the grate suddenly flickered into flame. He turned his head towards her. By the light of that feeble fire his eyes were like the eyes of her baby; they seemed to ask her for something; they looked so helpless; all his shuddering form seemed helpless. He muttered something; but his shivering choked the words, so that all that came to her was a sound such as her baby made. And at that sound something in her heart gave way; she pulled his head down on her breast, and with all her strength clutched him to her. And as the fire died, she still held him there, rocking him and sobbing, and once more trying to give him of the warmth of her little body.

[*1910*]

BLACKMAIL

I

THE affectionate if rather mocking friend who had said of Charles Granter: "*Ce n'est pas un homme, c'est un bâtiment,*" seemed justified, to the thin dark man following him down Oakley Street, Chelsea, that early October afternoon. From the square foundations of his feet to his square fair beard and the top of his head under a square black bowler, he looked very big, solid as granite, indestructible—steel-clad, too, for his grey clothes increased his bulk in the mild sunlight; too big to be taken by the board—only fit to be submarined. And the man, dodging in his wake right down to the Embankment, ran up once or twice under his counter and fell behind again, as if appalled by the vessel's size and unconsciousness. Considering the heat of the past summer, the plane-trees were still very green, and few of their twittering leaves had dropped or turned yellow—just enough to confirm the glamorous melancholy of early Fall. Granter, though he lived with his wife in some mansions close by, went out of his way to pass under those trees and look at the river. This seeming disclosure of sensibility, perhaps, determined the shadowy man to dodge up again and become stationary close behind. Ravaged and streaked, as if he had lived submerged, he stood carefully noting with his darting dark eyes that they two were quite alone; then, swallowing violently so that the strings of his lean neck writhed, he moved stealthily up beside Granter, and said in a hurried, hoarse voice: "Beg pardon, Mister—ten pounds, and I'll say nothin'."

The face which Granter turned towards that surprising utterance was a good illustration of the saying, "And things are not what they seem." Above that big building of a body it quivered, ridiculously alive, and complex, as of a man full of nerves, humours, sarcasms; and a deep continuous chinking sound arose—of Charles Granter jingling coins in his trouser pocket. The quiver settled into raised eyebrows, into crows' feet running out on to the broad cheekbones, into a sarcastic smile drooping the corners of the lips between moustache and beard. He said in his rather high voice:

"What's the matter with you, my friend?"

"There's a lot the matter with me, Mister. Down and out I am. I know where you live, I know your lady; but—ten pound and I'll say nothin'."

"About what?"

"About your visitin' that gell, where you've just come from. Ten pound. It's cheap—I'm a man of me word."

With lips still sarcastically drooped, Granter made a little derisive sound.

Blackmail, by George!

"Come on, Guv'nor—I'm desperate; I mean to have that ten pounds. You give it me here at six o'clock this evenin', if you 'aven't got it on you." His eyes flared suddenly in his hungry face. "But no tricks! I ain't killed Huns for nothin'."

Granter surveyed him for a moment, then turned his back and looked at the water.

"Well, you've got two hours to get it in—six o'clock, Mister; and no tricks—I warn you."

The hoarse voice ceased, the sound of footsteps died away; Granter was alone. The smile still clung to his lips, but he was not amused; he was annoyed, with the measured indignation of a big man highly civilised and innocent. Where had this ruffian sprung from? To be spied on, without knowing it, like this! His ears grew red. The damned scoundrel!

The thing was too absurd to pay attention to. And, instantly, his highly-sophisticated consciousness began to pay attention. How many visits had he made to this distressed flower-girl? Three? And all because he didn't like handing over the case to that Society which always found out the worst. They said private charity was dangerous.

Apparently it was! Blackmail! A consideration came, perching like a crow on the branches of his mind: why hadn't he mentioned the flower-girl to his wife, and made *her* do the visiting? Why! Because Olga would have said the girl was a fraud. And perhaps she was! A put-up job! Would the scoundrel have ventured on this threat at all if the girl were not behind him? She might support him with lies! His wife might believe them——She—she had such a vein of cynicism! How sordid, how domestically unpleasant!

Granter felt quite sick. Every decent human value seemed suddenly in question. And a second crow came croaking. Could one leave a scoundrel like this to play his tricks with impunity? Oughtn't one to go to the police? He stood extraordinarily still—a dappled leaf dropped from a plane-tree and lodged on his bowler hat; at the other end of him a little dog mistook him for a lamp-post. This was no joke! For a man with a reputation for humanity, integrity and commonsense—no joke at all! A Police Court meant the prosecution of a fellow-creature; getting him perhaps a year's imprisonment, when one had always felt that punishment practically never fitted crime! Staring at the river, he seemed to see cruelty hovering over himself, his wife, Society, the flower-girl, even over that scoundrel—naked cruelty, waiting to pounce on one or all. Whichever way one turned, the thing was dirty, cruel. No wonder blackmail was accounted such a heinous crime. No other human act was so cold-blooded, spider-like, and slimy; none plunged so deadly a dagger into the bowels of compassion; so eviscerated humanity, so murdered faith! And it would have been worse, if his conscience had not been clear. But was it so extremely clear? Would he have taken the trouble to go to that flower-girl's dwelling, not once, but three times, unless she had been attractive, unless her dark brown eyes had been pretty, and her common voice so soft? Would he have visited the blowsy old flower-woman at that other corner, in circumstances, no doubt, just as strenuous? His honesty answered: No. But his sense of justice added that, if he did like a pretty face, he was not vicious— he was fastidious and detested subterfuge. But then Olga was so cynical; she would certainly ask him why he hadn't visited the old flower-woman as well, and the lame man who sold matches, and

all the other stray unfortunates of the neighbourhood. Well, there
it was; and a bold course always the best! But what was the bold
course? To go to the police? To his wife? To that girl, and find out if
she were in this ramp? To wait till six o'clock, meet the ruffian, and
shake the teeth out of him? Granter could not decide. All seemed
equally bold—would do equally well. And a fifth course presented
itself which seemed even bolder: Ignore the thing!

The tide had just turned, and the full waters below him were
in suspense, of a sunlit soft grey colour. This stillness of the river
restored to Charles Granter something of the impersonal mood
in which he had crossed the Embankment to look at it. Here, by
the mother stream of this great town, was he, tall, strong, well-fed,
and, if not rich, quite comfortable; and here, too, were hundreds of
thousands like that needy flower-girl and this shadowy scoundrel,
skating on the edge of destitution. And here this water was—to him
a source of æsthetic enjoyment—to them a possible last refuge. The
girl had talked of it—beggar's patter, perhaps, like the blackmailer's
words: "I'm desperate—I'm down and out."

One wanted to be just! If he had known all about them—but
there it was, he knew nothing!

'I can't believe she's such an ungrateful little wretch!' he thought;
'I'll go back and see her again.'

He retraced his way up Oakley Street to the Mews which she
inhabited, and, ascending a stairway scented with petrol, knocked on a
half-open door, whence he could see her baby, of doubtful authorship,
seated in an empty flower-basket—a yellow baby, who stared up at
him with the placidity of one recently fed. That stare seemed to
Granter to be saying: "You look out that you're not taken for my
author. Have you got an alibi, old man?" And almost unconsciously
he began to calculate where he had been about fourteen or fifteen
months ago. Not in London—thank goodness! in Brittany with his
wife—all that July, August, and September. Jingling his money, he
contemplated the baby. It seemed more, but it *might* be only four
months old! The baby opened its mouth in a toothless smile. "Ga!"
it said, and stretched out a tiny hand. Granter ceased to jingle the
coins and gazed round the room. The first time he came, a month

ago, to test her street-corner story, its condition had been deplorable. His theory that people were never better than their environments had prompted the second visit, and that of this afternoon. He had, he told himself, wanted to know that he was not throwing away his money. And there certainly was some appearance of comfort now in a room so small that he and the baby and a bed almost filled it. But the longer he contemplated them, the greater fool he felt for ever having come there even with those best intentions which were the devil. And, turning to go, he saw the girl herself coming up the stairs, with a paper bag in her hand and an evident bull's-eye in her mouth, for a scent of peppermint preceded her. Surely her cheekbones were higher than he had thought, her eyebrows more oblique—a gipsy look! Her eyes, dark and lustrous as a hound puppy's, smiled at him, and he said in his rather high voice:

"I came back to ask you something."

"Yes, sir."

"Do you know a dark man with a thin face and a slight squint, who's been in the Army?"

"What's his name, sir?"

"I don't know; but he followed me from here, and tried to blackmail me on the Embankment. You know what blackmail is?"

"No, sir."

Feline, swift, furtive, she had passed him and taken up her baby, slanting her dark glance at him from behind it.. Granter's eyes were very round just then, the corners of his mouth very drawn down. He was experiencing a most queer sensation. Really it was as if—though he disliked poetic emphasis—as if he had suddenly seen something pre-civilised, pre-human, snake-like, cat-like, monkey-like too, in those dark sliding eyes and that yellow baby. Sure, as he stood there, she was in it; or, if not in it, she knew of it!

"A dangerous game, that," he said. "Tell him—for his own good—he had better drop it."

And, while he went, very square, downstairs, he thought: 'This is one of the finest opportunities you ever had for getting to the bottom of human nature, and you're running away from it.' So strongly did this thought obsess him that he halted, in two minds, outside. A chauffeur, who was cleaning his car, looked at him curiously. Charles Granter moved away.

II

When he reached the little drawing-room of their flat, his wife was making tea. She was rather short, with a good figure, and brown eyes in a flattish face, powdered and by no means unattractive. She had Slav blood in her—Polish; and Granter never now confided to her the finer shades of his thoughts and conduct because she had long made him feel he was her superior in moral sensibility. He had no wish to feel superior—it was often very awkward; but he could not help it. In view of this attempt at blackmail, it was more than awkward. For it is extraordinarily unpleasant to fall from a pedestal on which you do not wish to be.

He sat down, very large, in a lacquered chair with black cushions, spoke of the leaves turning, saw her look at him and smile, and felt that she knew he was disturbed.

"Do you ever wonder," he said, tinkling his tea-spoon, "about the lives that other people live?"

"What sort of people, Charles?"

"Oh—not our sort; matchsellers, don't you know, flower-sellers, people down and out?"

"No, I don't think I do."

If only he could tell her of this monstrous incident without slipping from his pedestal!

"It interests me enormously; there are such queer depths to reach, don't you know."

Her smile seemed to answer: "You don't reach the depths in me." And it was true. She was very Slav, with the warm gleam in her eyes and the opaque powdered skin of her flat comely face. An enigma—flatly an enigma! There were deep waters below the pedestal, like—like Phylæ, with columns still standing in the middle of the Nile Dam. Absurd!

"I've often wondered," he said, "how I should feel if I were down and out."

"You? You're too large, Charles, and too dignified, my dear; you'd be on the Civil List before you could turn round." Granter rose from the lacquered chair, jingling his. coins. The most vivid pictures at that moment were, like a film, unrolled before his mind—of the grey sunlit river, and that accosting blackguard with his twisted murky face, and lips uttering hoarse sounds; of the yellow baby, and the girl's gipsy-dark glance from behind it; of a Police Court, and himself standing there and letting the whole cartload of the Law fall on them. And he said suddenly:

"I was blackmailed this afternoon, on the Embankment."

She did not answer, and turning with irritation, he saw that her fingers were in her ears.

"I do wish you wouldn't jingle your money so!" she said.

Confound it! She had not heard him.

"I've had an adventure," he began again. "You know the flower-girl who stands at that corner in Tite Street?"

"Yes; a gipsy baggage."

"H'm! Well, I bought a flower from her one day, and she told me such a pathetic story that I went to her den to see if it was true. It seemed all right, so I gave her some money, don't you know. Then I thought I'd better see how she was spending it, so I went to see her again, don't you know."

A faint "Oh! Charles!" caused him to hurry on.

"And—what d'you think—a blackguard followed me to-day and tried to blackmail me for ten pounds on the Embankment."

A sound brought his face round to attention. His wife was lying back on the cushions of her chair in paroxysms of soft laughter.

It was clear to Granter, then, that what he had really been afraid of was just this. His wife would laugh at him—laugh at him slipping from the pedestal! Yes! it was that he had dreaded—not any disbelief in his fidelity. Somehow he felt too large to be laughed at. He *was* too large! Nature had set a size beyond which husbands——!

"I don't see what there is to laugh at!" he said frigidly; "there's no more odious crime than blackmail."

His wife was silent; two tears were trickling down her cheeks.

"Did you give it him?" she said in an extinguished voice.

"Of course not."

"What was he threatening?"

"To tell you."

"But what?"

"His beastly interpretation of my harmless visits."

The tears had made runlets in her powder, and he added viciously: "He doesn't know you, of course."

His wife dabbed her eyes, and a scent of geranium arose.

"It seems to me," said Granter, "that you'd be even more amused if there were something in it!"

"Oh! no, Charles, but—perhaps there is."

Granter looked at her fixedly.

"I'm sorry to disappoint you, there is not."

He saw her cover her lips with that rag of handkerchief, and abruptly left the room.

He went into his study and sat down before the fire. So it was funny to be a faithful husband? And suddenly he thought: 'If my wife can treat this as a joke, what—what about herself?' A nasty thought! An unconscionable thought! Really, it was as though that blackmailing scoundrel had dirtied human nature, till it seemed to function only from low motives. A church clock chimed. Six already! The ruffian would be back there on the Embankment, waiting for his ten pounds. Granter rose. His duty was to go out and hand him over to the police.

'No!' he thought viciously, 'let him come here! I'd very much like him to come here I'd teach him!'

But a sort of shame beset him. Like most very big men, he was quite unaccustomed to violence—had never struck a blow in his life, not even in his school-days—had never had occasion to. He went across to the window. From there he could just see the Embankment parapet through the trees, in the failing light, and presently—sure enough—made out the fellow's figure slinking up and down like a hungry dog. And he stood, watching, jingling his money—nervous, sarcastic, angry, very interested. What would the rascal do now? Would he beard this great block of flats? And was the girl down there too—the girl, with her yellow baby? He saw the slinking figure cross from the far side and vanish under the loom of the mansions. In that interesting moment Granter burst through the bottom of one of his trousers pockets: several coins jingled on to the floor and rolled away. He was still looking for the last when he heard the door-bell ring—he had never really believed the ruffian would come up! Straightening himself abruptly, he went out into the hall. Service was performed by the mansions staff, so there was no one in the flat but himself and his wife. The bell rang again, and she, too, appeared.

"This is my Embankment friend who amuses you so much. I should like you to see him," he said grimly. He noted a quizzical apology on her face and opened the hall door.

Yes! there stood the man! By electric light in upholstered surroundings, more "down and out" than ever. A bad lot, but a miserable poor wretch, with his broken boots, his thin, twisted, twitching face, his pinched shabby figure—only his hungry eyes looked dangerous.

"Come in," said Granter. "You want to see my wife, I think."

The man recoiled.

"I don't want to see 'er," he muttered, "unless you force me to. Give us *five* pound, Guv'nor, and I won't worry you again. I don't want to cause trouble between man and wife."

"Come in," repeated Granter; "she's expecting you."

The man stood, silently passing a pale tongue over a pale upper lip, as though conjuring some new resolution from his embarrassment.

"Now, see 'ere, Mister," he said suddenly, "you'll regret it if I come in—you will, straight."

"I shall regret it if you don't. You're a very interesting fellow; and an awful scoundrel."

"Well, who made me one?" the man burst out; "you answer me that."

"Are you coming in?"

"Yes, I am."

He came, and Granter shut the door behind him. It was like inviting a snake or a mad dog into one's parlour; but the memory of having been laughed at was so fresh within him that he rather welcomed the sensation.

"Now," he said, "have the kindness!" and opened the drawing-room door.

The man slunk in, blinking in the stronger light.

Granter went towards his wife, who was standing before the fire.

"This gentleman has an important communication to make to you, it seems."

The expression of her face struck him as peculiar—surely she was not frightened! And he experienced a kind of pleasure in seeing them both look so exquisitely uncomfortable.

"Well," he said ironically, "perhaps you'd like me not to listen." And, going back to the door, he stood leaning against it with his hands up to his ears. He saw the fellow give him a furtive look and go nearer to her; his lips moved rapidly, hers answered, and he thought: 'What on earth am I covering my ears for?' As he took his hands away, the man turned round and said:

"I'm goin' now, Mister; a little mistake—sorry to 'ave troubled you."

His wife had turned to the fire again; and with a puzzled feeling Granter opened the door. As the fellow passed, he took him by the arm, twisted him around into the study, and, locking the door, put the key into his pocket.

"Now, then," he said, "you precious scoundrel!"

The man shifted on his broken boots. "Don't. you hit me, Guv'nor. I got a knife here."

"I'm not going to hit you. I'm going to hand you over to the police."

The than's eyes roved, looking for a way of escape, then rested, as if fascinated, on the glowing hearth.

"What's ten pound?" he said suddenly. "You'd never ha' missed it."

Granter smiled.

"You don't seem to realise, my friend, that blackmail is the most devilish crime a man can commit." And he crossed over to the telephone.

The man's eyes, dark, restless, violent, and yet hungry, began to shift up and down the building of a man before him.

"No," he said suddenly, with a sort of pathos, "don't do that, Guv'nor!"

Something—the look of his eyes or the tone of his voice—affected Granter.

"But if I don't," he said slowly, "you'll be blackmailing the next person you meet. You're as dangerous as a viper."

The man's lips quivered; he covered them with his hand, and said from behind it:

"I'm a man like yourself. I'm down and out—that's all. Look at me!"

Granter's glance dwelt on the trembling hand. "Yes, but you fellows destroy all belief in human nature," he said vehemently.

"See 'ere, Guv'nor; you try livin' like me—you try it! My Gawd! You try my life these last six months—cadgin' and crawlin' for a job!" He made a deep sound. "A man 'oo's done 'is bit, too. Wot life is it? A stinkin' life, not fit for a dawg, let alone a 'uman bein'. An' when I see a great big chap like you, beggin' your pardon, Mister—well fed, with everything to 'is 'and—it was regular askin' for it. It come over me, it did."

"No, no," said Granter grimly; "that won't do. It couldn't have been sudden. You calculated—you concocted this. Blackmail is sheer filthy cold-blooded blackguardism. You don't care two straws whom you hurt, whose lives you wreck, what faiths you destroy." And he put his hand on the receiver.

The man squirmed.

"Steady on, Guv'nor! I've gotta find food. I've gotta find clothes. I can't live on air. I can't go naked."

Granter stood motionless, while the man's voice continued to travel to him across the cosy room.

"Give us a chawnce, Guv'nor! Ah! give us a chawnce! You can't understand my temptations. Don't 'ave the police to me. I won't do this again—give you me word—so 'elp me! I've got it in the neck. Let me go, Guv'nor!"

In Granter, motionless as the flats he lived in, a really heavy struggle was in progress—not between duty and pity, but between revengeful anger and a sort of horror at using the strength of prosperity against so broken a wretch.

"Let me go, Mister!" came the hoarse voice again. "Be a sport!"

Granter dropped the receiver, and unlocked the door.

"All right; you can go."

The man crossed swiftly.

"Christ!" he said; "good luck! And as to the lady—I take it back. I never see 'er. It's all me eye."

He was across the hall and gone before Granter could say a word; the scurrying shuffle of his footsteps down the stairs died away. "And as to the lady—I take it back—I never see her. It's all me eye!" Good God! The scoundrel, having failed with him, had been trying to blackmail his wife—his wife, who had laughed at his fidelity!—his wife who had looked—frightened! "All me eye!" Her face started up before Granter—scared under its powder, with a mask drawn over it. And he had let that scoundrel go! Scared! That was the meaning! ... Blackmail—of all poisonous human actions! ... His wife! ... But ... what now ...!

[*1921*]

TWO LOOKS

THE old director of the "Yew Trees" Cemetery walked slowly across from his house to see that all was ready.

He had seen pass into the square of earth committed to his charge so many to whom he had been in the habit of nodding, so many whose faces even he had not known. To him it was the everyday event; yet this funeral, one more in the countless tale, disturbed him—a sharp reminder of the passage of time.

For twenty years had gone by since the death of Septimus Godwin, the cynical, romantic doctor who had been his greatest friend; by whose cleverness all had sworn, of whose powers of fascination all had gossiped! And now they were burying his son!

He had not seen the widow since, for she had left the town at once; but he recollected her distinctly—a tall, dark woman with bright brown eyes, much younger than her husband, and only married to him eighteen months before he died. He remembered her slim figure standing by the grave at that long-past funeral, and the look on her face which had puzzled him so terribly—a look of—a most peculiar look!

He thought of it even now, walking along the narrow path toward his old friend's grave—the handsomest in the cemetery, commanding from the topmost point the whitened slope and river that lay beyond. He came to its little private garden. Spring flowers were blossoming; the railings had been freshly painted; and by the door of the grave wreaths awaited the new arrival. All was in order.

The old director opened the mausoleum with his key. Below, seen through a thick glass floor, lay the shining coffin of the father; beneath, on the lower tier, would rest the coffin of the son.

A gentle voice, close behind him, said:

"Can you tell me, sir, what they are doing to my old doctor's grave?"

The old director turned and saw before him a lady well past middle age. He did not know her face, but it was pleasant, with faded rose-leaf cheeks, and silvered hair under a shady hat.

"Madam, there is a funeral here, this afternoon."

"Ah! Can it be his wife?"

"Madam, his son; a young man of only twenty."

"His son! At what time did you say?"

"At two o'clock."

"Thank you; you are very kind."

With uplifted hat he watched her walk away. It worried him to see a face he did not know.

All went off beautifully; but, dining that same evening with his friend, a certain doctor, the old director asked:

"Did you see a lady with grey hair hovering about this afternoon?"

The doctor, a tall man, with a beard still yellow, drew his guest's chair nearer to the fire.

"I did," he answered.

"Did you remark her face? A very odd expression—a sort of—what shall I call it? Very odd indeed! Who is she? I saw her at the grave this morning."

The doctor shook his head.

"Not so very odd, I think."

"Come! What do you mean by that?"

The doctor hesitated. Then, taking the decanter, he filled his old friend's glass, and answered:

"Well, sir, you were Godwin's greatest chum—I will tell you, if you like, the story of his death. You were away at the time, if you remember."

"It is safe with me," said the old director.

"Septimus Godwin," began the doctor slowly, "died on a Thursday about three o'clock, and I was only called in to see him at two. I found him far gone, but conscious now and then. It was a case of—but you know the details, so I needn't go into that. His wife was in the room, and on the bed at his feet lay his pet dog—a terrier; you may recollect, perhaps, he had a special breed. I hadn't been there ten minutes, when a maid came in and whispered something to her mistress. Mrs. Godwin answered angrily, 'See him? Go down and say she ought to know better than to come here at such a time!' The maid went, but soon came back. Could the lady see Mrs. Godwin for just a moment? Mrs. Godwin answered that she could not leave her husband. The maid looked frightened and went away again. She came back for the third time. The lady had said she must see Dr. Godwin; it was a matter of life and death! 'Death—indeed!' exclaimed Mrs. Godwin. 'Shameful! Go down and tell her, if she doesn't go immediately I will send for the police!'

"The poor maid looked at me. I offered to go down and see the visitor myself. I found her in the dining-room, and knew her at once. Never mind her name, but she belongs to a county family not a hundred miles from here. A beautiful woman, she was then; but her face that day was quite distorted.

"'For God's sake, doctor,' she said, 'is there any hope?'

"I was obliged to tell her there was none.

"'Then I must see him,' she said.

"I begged her to consider what she was asking. But she held me out a signet ring. Just like Godwin—wasn't it—that sort of Byronism, eh!

"'He sent me this,' she said, 'an hour ago. It was agreed between us that if ever he sent that, I must come. If it were only myself I could bear it—a woman can bear anything; but he'll die thinking I wouldn't come, thinking I didn't care—and I would give my life for him this minute!'

"Now, a dying man's request is sacred. I told her she should see him. I made her follow me upstairs and wait outside his room. I promised to let her know if he recovered consciousness. I have never been thanked like that, before or since.

"I went back into the bedroom. He was still unconscious and the terrier whining. In the next room a child was crying—the very same young man we buried to-day. Mrs. Godwin was still standing by the bed.

"'Have you sent her away?'

"I had to say that Godwin really wished to see her. At that she broke out: I won't have her here—the wretch!'

"I begged her to control herself, and remember that her husband was a dying man.

"'But I'm his wife,' she said, and flew out of the room."

The doctor paused, staring at the fire. He shrugged his shoulders, and went on: "I'd have stopped her fury, if I could! A dying man is not the same as the live animal, that he must needs be wrangled over. And suffering's sacred, even to us doctors. I could hear their voices outside. Heaven knows what they said to each other. And there lay Godwin with his white face and his black hair—deathly still—fine-looking fellow he always was! Then I saw that he was coming to! The women had begun again outside—first the wife, sharp and scornful; then the other, hushed and slow. I saw Godwin lift his finger and point it at the door. I went out and said to the woman, 'Dr. Godwin wishes to see you; please control yourself.'

"We went back into the room. The wife followed. But Godwin had lost conciousness again. They sat down, those two, and hid their faces. I can see them now, one on each side of the bed, their eyes covered with their hands, each with her claim on him, all murdered by the other's presence; each with her torn love. H'm! What they must have suffered, then! And all the time the child crying—the child of one of them that might have been the other's!"

The doctor was silent, and the old director turned towards him his white-bearded, ruddy face, with a look as if he were groping in the dark.

"Just then, I remember," the doctor went on suddenly, "the bells of St. Jude's close by began to peal out for the finish of a wedding. That brought Godwin back to life. He just looked from one woman to the other with a queer, miserable sort of smile, enough to make your heart break. And they both looked at him. The face of the wife—poor thing!—was as bitter hard as a cut stone, but she sat there, without ever stirring a finger. As for the other woman—I couldn't look at her. Godwin beckoned to me; but I couldn't catch his words, the bells drowned them. A minute later he was dead.

"Life's a funny thing! You wake in the morning with your foot firm on the ladder—one touch, and down you go! You snuff out like a candle. And it's lucky when your flame goes out if only one woman's flame goes out too.

"Neither of those women cried. The wife stayed there by the bed. I got the other one away to her carriage, down the street. And so she was there to-day! That explains, I think, the look you saw."

The doctor ceased; and in silence the old director nodded. Yes! That explained the look he had seen on the face of that unknown woman, the deep, unseizable, weird look. That explained the look he had seen on the wife's face: at the funeral twenty years ago!

And peering wistfully, he said:

"They looked—they looked—almost triumphant!"

Then, slowly, he rubbed his hands over his knees, with the secret craving of the old for warmth.

[*1904*]

A LONG-AGO AFFAIR

HUBERT Marsland, the landscape painter, returning from a day's sketching on the river in the summer of 1921, had occasion to stay the progress of his two-seater about ten miles from London for a minor repair, and while his car was being seen to, strolled away from the garage to have a look at a house where he had often spent his holidays as a boy. Walking through a gateway and passing a large gravel-pit on his left, he was soon opposite the house, which stood back a little in its grounds. Very much changed! More pretentious, not so homely as when his Uncle and Aunt lived there, and he used to play cricket on this warren opposite, where the cricket ground, it seemed, had been turned into a golf course. It was late—the dinner-hour, nobody playing, and passing on to the links he stood digesting the geography. Here must have been where the old pavilion was. And there—still turfed—where he had made that particularly nice stroke to leg, when he went in last and carried his bat for thirteen. Thirty-nine years ago—his sixteenth birthday. How vividly he remembered his new pads! A. P. Lucas had played against them and only made thirty-two—one founded one's style on A. P. Lucas in those days—feet in front of the bat, and pointed a little forward, elegant; you never saw it now, and a good thing too—one could sacrifice too much to style! Still, the tendency was all the other way; style was too much "off," perhaps!

He stepped back into the sun and sat down on the grass. Peaceful—very still! The haze of the distant downs was visible between his Uncle's old house and the next; and there was the clump of elms on the far side behind which the sun would be going down just as it used to then. He pressed the palms of his hands to the turf. A glorious summer—something like that summer of long ago. And warmth from the turf, or perhaps from the past, crept into his heart and made it ache a little. Just here he must have sat, after his innings, at Mrs. Monteith's feet peeping out of a flounced dress. Lord! The fools boys were! How headlong and uncalculating their devotions! A softness in voice and eyes, a smile, a touch or two—and they were slaves! Young fools, but good young fools. And, standing behind her chair—he could see him now—that other idol Captain MacKay, with his face of browned ivory—just the colour of that elephant's tusk his Uncle had, which had gone so yellow—and his perfect black moustache, his white tie, check suit, carnation, spats, Malacca cane—all so fascinating! Mrs. Monteith, "the grass widow" they had called her! He remembered the look in people's eyes, the tone in their voices. Such a pretty woman! He had "fallen for her" at first sight, as the Yanks put it—her special scent, her daintiness, her voice! And that day on the river, when she made much of him, and Captain MacKay attended Evelyn Curtiss so assiduously that he was expected to propose. Quaint period! They used the word courting then, wore full skirts, high stays; and himself a blue elastic belt round his white-flannelled waist. And in the evening afterwards, his Aunt had said with an arch smile: "Good-night, *silly* boy!" Silly boy indeed, with a flower the grass widow had dropped pressed by his cheek into his pillow! What folly! And that next Sunday—looking forward to Church—passionately brushing his top hat; all through the service spying at her creamy profile, two pews in front on the left, between goat-bearded old Hallgrave her Uncle, and her pink, broad, white-haired Aunt; scheming to get near her when she came out, lingering, lurking, getting just a smile and the rustle of her flounces. Ah, ha! A little went a long way then! And the last day of his holidays and its night with the first introduction to reality. Who said the Victorian Age was innocent?

Marsland put his palm up to his cheek. No! the dew was not yet falling! And his mind lightly turned and tossed his memories of women, as a man turns and tosses hay to air it; but nothing remembered gave him quite the feeling of that first experience.

His Aunt's dance! His first white waistcoat, bought *ad hoc*, from the local tailor, his tie laboriously imitating the hero—Captain MacKay's.

All came back with such freshness in the quiet of the warren—the expectancy, the humble shy excitement, the breathless asking for a dance, the writing "Mrs. Monteith" twice on his little gilt-edged programme with its tiny tasselled white pencil; her slow-moving fan, her smile. And the first dance when it came; what infinite care not to tread on her white satin toes; what a thrill when her arm pressed his in the crush—holy rapture, about all the first part of that evening, with yet another dance to come! If only he could have twirled her and "reversed" like his pattern, Captain MacKay! Then delirium growing as the second dance came near, making him cut his partner—the cool grass-scented air out on the dark terrace, with the chafers booming by, and in the starshine the poplars wondrously tall; the careful adjustment of his tie and waistcoat, the careful polishing of his hot face! A long breath then, and into the house to find her! Ballroom, supper-room, stairs, library, billiard-room, all drawn blank—"Estudiantina" going on and on, and he a wandering, white-waistcoated young ghost. Ah! The conservatory—and the hurrying there! And then the moment which had always been, was even now, such a blurred confused impression. Smothered voices from between a clump of flowers: "I saw her." "Who was the man?" A glimpse, gone past in a flash, of an ivory face, a black moustache! And then her voice: "Hubert"; and her hot hand clasping his, drawing him to her; her scent, her face smiling, very set! A rustling behind the flowers, those people spying; and suddenly her lips on his cheek, the kiss sounding in his ears, her voice saying, very softly: "Hubert, dear boy!" The rustle receded, ceased. What a long silent minute, then, among the ferns and blossoms in the dusk with her face close to his, pale, perturbed, before she led him out into the light, while he was slowly realising that she had made use of him to shelter her. A boy—not old enough to be her lover, but old enough to save her name and that of Captain MacKay! Her kiss—the last of many—but not upon *his* lips, *his* cheeks! Hard work realising that! A boy—of no account—a boy, who in a day would be at school again, kissed that *he* and *she* might renew their intrigue unsuspected!

How had he behaved the rest of that evening of romance bedrabbled? He hardly knew. Betrayed with a kiss! Two idols in the dust! And did they care what he was feeling? Not they! All they cared for was to cover up their tracks with him! But somehow—somehow—he had never shown her that he knew. Only, when their dance was over, and someone came and took her for the next, he escaped up to his little room, tore off his gloves, his waistcoat; lay on his bed, thought bitter thoughts. A boy! There he had stayed, with the thrum of the music in his ears, till at last it died away for good and the carriages were gone, and the night was quiet.

Squatting on the warren grass, still warm and dewless, Marsland rubbed his knees. Nothing like boys for generosity! And, with a little smile, he thought of his Aunt next morning, half-arch and half-concerned: "It isn't nice, dear, to sit out in dark corners, and—well, perhaps, it wasn't your fault, but still, it isn't nice—not—quite——" and of how suddenly she had stopped, looking in his face, where his lips were curling in his first ironic laugh. She had never forgiven him that laugh—thinking him a cynical young Lothario? And Marsland thought: 'Live and learn! Wonder what became of those two? Victorian Age! Hatches were battened down in those days! But, innocent—my hat!'

Ah! The sun was off, dew falling! He got up, rubbing his knees to take the stiffness out of them. Pigeons in the wood beyond were calling. A window in his Uncle's old home blazed like a jewel in the sun's last rays between the poplar trees. Heh! dear—a little long-ago affair!

[1922]

THE FIRST AND THE LAST

I

"So the last shall be first, and the first last."—Holy Writ.

It was a dark room at that hour of six in the evening, when just the single oil reading-lamp under its green shade let fall a dapple of light over the Turkey carpet; over the covers of books taken out of the book-shelves, and the open pages of the one selected; over the deep blue and gold of the coffee service on the little old stool with its Oriental embroidery. Very dark in the winter, with drawn curtains, many rows of leather-bound volumes, oak-pannelled walls and ceiling. So large, too, that the lighted spot before the fire where he sat was just an oasis. But that was what Keith Darrant liked, after his day's work—the hard early morning study of his "cases," the fret and strain of the day in court; it was his rest, these two hours before dinner, with books, coffee, a pipe, and sometimes a nap. In red Turkish slippers and his old brown velvet coat, he was well suited to that framing of glow and darkness. A painter would have seized avidly on his clear-cut, yellowish face, with its black eyebrows twisting up over eyes—grey or brown, one could hardly tell, and its dark grizzling hair still plentiful, in spite of those daily hours of wig. He seldom thought of his work while he sat there, throwing off with practised ease the strain of that long attention to the multiple threads of argument and evidence to be disentangled—work profoundly interesting, as a rule, to his clear intellect, trained to almost instinctive rejection of all but the essential, to selection of what was legally vital out of the mass of confused tactical and human detail presented to his scrutiny; yet sometimes tedious and wearing. As for instance to-day, when he had suspected his client of perjury, and was almost convinced that he must throw up his brief. He had disliked the weak-looking, white-faced fellow from the first, and his nervous, shifty answers, his prominent startled eyes—a type too common in these days of canting tolerations and weak humanitarianism; no good, no good!

Of the three books he had taken down, a volume of Voltaire—curious fascination that Frenchman had, for all his destructive irony!—a volume of Burton's travels, and Stevenson's "New Arabian Nights", he had pitched upon the last. He felt, that evening, the want of something sedative, a desire to rest from thought of any kind. The court had been crowded, stuffy; the air, as he walked home, soft, sou'-westerly, charged with coming moisture, no quality of vigour in it; he felt relaxed, tired, even nervy, and for once the loneliness of his house seemed strange and comfortless.

Lowering the lamp, he turned his face towards the fire. Perhaps he would get a sleep before that boring dinner at the Tellassons'. He wished it were vacation, and Maisie back from school. A widower for many years, he had lost the habit of a woman about him; yet to-night he had a positive yearning for the society of his young daughter, with her quick ways, and bright, dark eyes. Curious what perpetual need of a woman some men had! His brother Laurence—wasted—all through women—atrophy of willpower! A man on the edge of things; living from hand to mouth; his gifts all down at heel! One would have thought the Scottish strain might have saved him; and yet, when a Scotsman did begin to go downhill, who could go faster? Curious that their mother's blood should have worked so differently in her two sons. He himself had always felt he owed all his success to it.

His thoughts went off at a tangent to a certain issue troubling his legal conscience. He had not wavered in the usual assumption of omniscience, but he was by no means sure that he had given right advice. Well! without that power to decide and hold to decision in spite of misgiving, one would never have been fit for one's position at the Bar, never have been fit for anything. The longer he lived, the more certain he became of the prime necessity of virile and decisive action in all the affairs of life. A word and a blow—and the blow first! Doubts, hesitation, sentiment—the muling and puking of this twilight age———! And there welled up on his handsome face a smile that was almost devilish—the tricks of firelight are so many! It faded again in sheer drowsiness; he slept …

He woke with a start, having a feeling of something out beyond the light, and without turning his head said: "What's that?" There came a sound as if somebody had caught his breath. He turned up the lamp.

"Who's there?"

A voice over by the door answered:

"Only I—Larry."

Something in the tone, or perhaps just being startled out of sleep like this, made him shiver. He said:

"I was asleep. Come in!"

It was noticeable that he did not get up, or even turn his head, now that he knew who it was, but waited, his half-closed eyes fixed on the fire, for his brother to come forward. A visit from Laurence was not an unmixed blessing. He could hear him breathing, and became conscious of a scent of whisky. Why could not the fellow at least abstain when he was coming here! It was so childish, so lacking in any sense of proportion or of decency! And he said sharply:

"Well, Larry, what is it?"

It was always something. He often wondered at the strength of that sense of trusteeship, which kept him still tolerant of the troubles, amenable to the petitions of this brother of his; or was it just "blood" feeling, a Highland sense of loyalty to kith and kin; an old-time quality which judgment and half his instincts told him was weakness, but which, in spite of all, bound him to the distressful fellow? Was he drunk now, that he kept lurking out there by the door? And he said less sharply:

"Why don't you come and sit down?"

He was coming now, avoiding the light, skirting along the walls just beyond the radiance of the lamp, his feet and legs to the waist brightly lighted, but his face disintegrated in shadow, like the face of a dark ghost.

"Are you ill, man?"

Still no answer, save a shake of that head, and the passing up of a hand, out of the light, to the ghostly forehead under the dishevelled hair. The scent of whisky was stronger now; and Keith thought:

"He really is drunk. Nice thing for the new butler to see! If he can't behave——"

The figure against the wall heaved a sigh—so truly from an overburdened heart that Keith was conscious with a certain dismay of not having yet fathomed the cause of this uncanny silence. He got up, and, back to the fire, said with a brutality born of nerves rather than design:

"What is it, man? Have you committed a murder, that you stand there dumb as a fish?"

For a second no answer at all, not even of breathing; then, just the whisper:

"Yes."

The sense of unreality which so helps one at moments of disaster enabled Keith to say vigorously:

"By Jove! You have been drinking!"

But it passed at once into deadly apprehension.

"What do you mean? Come here, where I can see you. What's the matter with you, Larry?"

With a sudden lurch and dive, his brother left the shelter of the shadow, and sank into a chair in the circle of light. And another long, broken sigh escaped him.

"There's nothing the matter with me, Keith! It's true!"

Keith stepped quickly forward, and stared down into his brother's face; and instantly he saw that it was true. No one could have simulated the look in those eyes—of horrified wonder, as if they would never again get on terms with the face to which they belonged. To see them squeezed the heart—only real misery could look like that. Then that sudden pity became angry bewilderment.

"What in God's name is this nonsense?"

But it was significant that he lowered his voice; went over to the door, too, to see if it were shut. Laurence had drawn his chair forward, huddling over the fire—a thin figure, a worn, highcheek-boned face with deep-sunk blue eyes, and wavy hair all ruffled, a face that still had a certain beauty. Putting a hand on that lean shoulder, Keith said:

"Come, Larry! Pull yourself together, and drop exaggeration."

"It's true, I tell you; I've killed a man."

The noisy violence of that outburst acted like a douche. What was the fellow about—shouting out such words! But suddenly Laurence lifted his hands and wrung them. The gesture was so utterly painful that it drew a quiver from Keith's face.

"Why did you come here," he said, "and tell *me* this?"

Larry's face was really unearthly sometimes, such strange gleams passed up on to it!

"Whom else should I tell? I came to know what I'm to do, Keith? Give myself up, or what?"

At that sudden introduction of the practical, Keith felt his heart twitch. Was it then as real as all that? But he said, very quietly:

"Just tell me——How did it come about, this—affair?"

That question linked the dark, gruesome, fantastic nightmare on to actuality.

"When did it happen?"

"Last night."

In Larry's face there was—there had always been—something childishly truthful. He would never stand a chance in court! And Keith said:

"How? Where? You'd better tell me quietly from the beginning. Drink this coffee; it'll clear your head."

Laurence took the little blue cup and drained it.

"Yes," he said. "It's like this, Keith. There's a girl I've known for some months now——"

Women! And Keith said between his teeth: "Well?"

"Her father was a Pole who died over here when she was sixteen, and left her all alone. A man called Walenn, a mongrel American, living in the same house, married her, or pretended to—she's very pretty, Keith—he left her with a baby six months old, and another coming. That one died, and she did nearly. Then she starved till another fellow took her on. She lived with him two years; then Walenn turned up again, and made her go back to him. The brute used to beat her black and blue, all for nothing. Then he left her again. When I met her she'd lost her elder child, too, and was taking any body who came along."

He suddenly looked up into Keith's face.

"But I've never met a sweeter woman, nor a truer, that I swear. Woman! She's only twenty now! When I went to her last night that brute—that Walenn—had found her out again; and when he came for me, swaggering and bullying—Look!" he touched a dark mark on his forehead—"I took his throat in my hands, and when I let go——"

"Yes?"

"Dead. I never knew till afterwards that she was hanging on to him behind."

Again he made that gesture—wringing his hands.

In a hard voice Keith said:

"What did you do then?"

"We sat by it a long time. Then I carried it on my back down the street, round a corner to an archway."

"How far?"

"About fifty yards."

"Was anyone—did anyone see?"

"No."

"What time?"

"Three."

"And then?"

"Went back to her."

"Why—in Heaven's name?"

"She was lonely and afraid; so was I, Keith."

"Where is this place?"

"Forty-two, Borrow Street, Soho."

"And the archway?"

"Corner of Glove Lane."

"Good God! Why—I saw it in the paper!"

And seizing the journal that lay on his bureau, Keith read again that paragraph: "The body of a man was found this morning under an archway in Glove Lane, Soho. From marks about the throat suspicions of foul play are entertained. The body had apparently been robbed, and nothing was discovered leading to identification."

It was real earnest, then. Murder! His own brother! He faced round and said:

"You saw this in the paper, and dreamed it. Understand—you dreamed it!"

The wistful answer came:

"If only I had, Keith—if only I had!"

In his turn, Keith very nearly wrung his hands.

"Did you take anything from the—body?"

"This dropped while we were struggling."

It was an empty envelope with a South American post-mark addressed: "Patrick Walenn, Simon's Hotel, Farrier Street, London." Again with that twitching in his heart, Keith said:

"Put it in the fire."

Then suddenly he stooped to pluck it out. By that command—he had—identified himself with this—this—— But he did not pluck it out. It blackened, writhed, and vanished. And once more he said:

"What in God's name made you come here and tell *me*?"

"You know about these things. I didn't mean to kill him. I love the girl. What shall I do, Keith?"

Simple! How simple To ask what he was to do! It was like Larry! And he said:

"You were not seen, you think?"

"It's a dark street. There was no one about."

"When did you leave this girl the second time?"

"About seven o'clock."

"Where did you go?"

"To my rooms."

"In Fitzroy Street?"

"Yes."

"Did anyone see you come in?"

"No."

"What have you done since?"

" Sat there."

"Not been out?"

"No."

"Not seen the girl?"

"No."

"You don't know, then, what she's done since?"

"No."

"Would she give you away?"

"Never."

"Would she give herself away—hysteria?"

"No."

"Who knows of your relations with her?"

"No one."

"No one?"

"I don't know who should, Keith."

"Did anyone see you going in last night, when you first went to her?"

"No. She lives on the ground floor. I've got keys."

"Give them to me. What else have you that connects you with her?"

"Nothing."

"In your rooms?"

"No."

"No photographs. No letters?"

"No."

"Be careful."

"Nothing."

"No one saw you going back to her the second time?"

"No."

"No one saw you leave her in the morning?"

"No."

"You were fortunate. Sit down again, man. I must think."

Think! Think out this accursed thing—so beyond all thought, and all belief. But he could not think. Not a coherent thought would come. And he began again:

"Was it his first reappearance with her?"

"Yes."

"She told you so?"

"Yes."

"How did he find out where she was?"

"I don't know."

"How drunk were you?"

"I was not drunk."

"How much had you drunk?"

"About a bottle of claret—nothing."

"You say you didn't mean to kill him?"

"No—God knows!"

"That's something. What made you choose the arch?"

"It was the first dark place."

"Did his face look as if he had been strangled?"

"Don't!"

"Did it?"

"Yes."

"Very disfigured?"

"Yes."

"Did you look to see if his clothes were marked?"

"No."

"Why not?"

"Why not? My God! If you had done it——!"

"You say he was disfigured. Would he be recognisable?"

"I don't know."

"When she lived with him last—where was that?"

"I don't know for certain. Pimlico, I think."

"Not Soho?"

"No."

"How long has she been at the Soho place?"

"Nearly a year."

"Always the same rooms?"

"Yes."

"Is there anyone living in that house or street who would be likely to know her as his wife?"

"I don't think so."

"What was he?"

"I should think he was a professional 'bully.'"

"I see. Spending most of his time abroad, then?"

"Yes."

"Do you know if he was known to the police?"

"I haven't heard of it."

"Now listen, Larry. When you leave here go straight home, and don't go out till I come to you, to-morrow morning. Promise that!"

"I promise."

"I've got a dinner engagement. I'll think this out. Don't drink. Don't talk! Pull yourself together."

"Don't keep me longer than you can help, Keith!"

That white face, those eyes, that shaking hand! With a twinge of pity in the midst of all the turbulence of his revolt, and fear, and disgust, Keith put his hand on his brother's shoulder, and said:

"Courage!"

And suddenly he thought: 'My God! Courage! I shall want it all myself!'

II

Laurence Darrant, leaving his brother's house in the Adeiphi, walked northwards, rapidly, slowly, rapidly again. For, if there are men who by force of will do one thing only at a time, there are men who from lack of will do now one thing, now another, with equal intensity. To such natures, to be gripped by the Nemesis which attends the lack of self-control is no reason for being more self-controlled. Rather does it foster their pet feeling: "What matter? To-morrow we die!" The effort of will required to go to Keith had relieved, exhausted and exasperated him. In accordance with those three feelings was the progress of his walk. He started from the door with the fixed resolve to go home and stay there quietly till Keith came. He was in Keith's hands; Keith would know what was to he done. But he had not gone three hundred yards before he felt so utterly weary, body and soul, that if he had but had a pistol in his pocket he would have shot himself in the street. Not even the thought of the girl—this young unfortunate with her strange devotion, who had kept him straight these last five months, who had roused in him a depth of feeling he had never known before—would have availed against that sudden black dejection. Why go on—a waif at the mercy of his own nature, a straw blown here and there by every gust which rose in him? Why not have done with it for ever, and take it out in sleep?

He was approaching the fatal street, where he and the girl, that early morning, had spent the hours clutched together, trying in the refuge of love to forget for a moment their horror and fear. Should he go in? He had promised Keith not to. Why had he promised? He caught sight of himself in a chemist's lighted window. Miserable, shadowy brute! And he remembered suddenly a dog he had picked up once in the streets of Pera, a black-and-white creature—different from the other dogs, not one of their breed, a pariah of pariahs, who had strayed there somehow. He had taken it home to the house where he was staying, contrary to all custom of the country; had got fond of it; had shot it himself, sooner than leave it behind again to the mercies of its own kind in the streets. Twelve years ago! And those sleeve-links made of little Turkish coins he had brought back for the girl at the hairdresser's in Chancery Lane where he used to get shaved—pretty creature, like a wild rose. He had asked of her a kiss for payment. What queer emotion when she put her face forward to his lips—a sort of passionate tenderness and shame, at the softness and warmth of that flushed cheek, at her beauty and trustful gratitude. She would soon have given herself to him—that one! He had never gone there again! And to this day he did not know why he had abstained; to this day he did not know whether he were glad or sorry not to have plucked that rose. He must surely have been very different then! Queer business, life—queer, queer business!—to go through it never knowing what you would do next. Ah! to be like Keith, steady, buttoned-up in success; a brass pot, a pillar of society! Once, as a boy, he had been within an ace of killing Keith, for sneering at him. Once in Southern Italy he had been near killing a driver who was flogging his horse. And now, that dark-faced, swinish bully who had ruined the girl he had grown to love—he had done it! Killed him! Killed a man!

He who did not want to hurt a fly. The chemist's window confronted him with the sudden thought that he had at home that which made him safe, in case they should arrest him. He would never again go out without some of those little white tablets sewn into the lining of his coat. Restful, even exhilarating thought! They said a man should not take his own life. Let *them* taste horror—those glib citizens! Let them live as that girl had lived, as millions lived all the world over, under their canting dogmas! A man might rather even take his life than watch their cursed inhumanities.

He went into the chemist's for a bromide; and, while the man was mixing it, stood resting one foot like a tired horse. The "life" he had squeezed out of that fellow! After all, a billion living creatures gave up life each day, had it squeezed out of them, mostly. And perhaps not one a day deserved death so much as that loathly fellow. Life! a breath—a flame! Nothing! Why, then, this icy clutching at his heart?

The chemist brought the draught.

"Not sleeping, sir?"

"No."

The man's eyes seemed to say: "Yes! Burning the candle at both ends—I know!" Odd life, a chemist's; pills and powders all day long, to hold the machinery of men together! Devilish odd trade!

In going out he caught the reflection of his face in a mirror; it seemed too good altogether for a man who had committed murder. There was a sort of brightness underneath, an amiability lurking about its shadows; how—how could it be the face of a man who had done what he had done? His head felt lighter now, his feet lighter; he walked rapidly again.

Curious feeling of relief and oppression all at once! Frightful—to long for company, for talk, for distraction; and—to be afraid of it! The girl—the girl and Keith were now the only persons who would not give him that feeling of dread. And, of those two—Keith was not——! Who could consort with one who was never wrong, a successful, righteous fellow; a chap built so that he knew nothing about himself, wanted to know nothing, a chap all solid actions? To be a quicksand swallowing up one's own resolutions was bad enough! But to be like Keith—all will-power, marching along, treading down his own feelings and weaknesses!—No! One could not make a comrade of a man like Keith, even if he were one's brother? The only creature in all the world was the girl. She alone knew and felt what he was feeling; would put up with him and love him whatever he did, or was done to him. He stopped and took shelter in a doorway, to light a cigarette.

He had suddenly a fearful wish to pass the archway where he had placed the body; a fearful wish that had no sense, no end in view, no anything; just an insensate craving to see the dark place again. He crossed Borrow Street to the little lane. There was only one person visible, a man on the far side with his shoulders hunched against the wind; a short, dark figure which crossed and came towards him in the flickering lamplight. What a face! Yellow, ravaged, clothed almost to the eyes in a stubbly greyish growth of beard, with blackish teeth, and haunting bloodshot eyes. And what a figure of rags—one shoulder higher than the other, one leg a little lame, and thin! A surge of feeling came up in Laurence for this creature, more unfortunate than himself. There were lower depths than his!

"Well, brother," he said, "*you* don't look too prosperous!"

The smile which gleamed out on the man's face seemed as unlikely as a smile on a scarecrow.

"Prosperity doesn't come my way," he said in a rusty voice. "I'm a failure—always been a failure. And yet—you wouldn't think it, would you?—I was a minister of religion once."

Laurence held out a shilling. But the man shook his head. "Keep your money," he said. "I've got more than you today, I daresay. But thank you for taking a little interest. That's worth more than money to a man that's down."

"You're right."

"Yes," the rusty voice went on; "I'd as soon die as go on living as I do. And now I've lost my self-respect. Often wondered how long a starving man could go without losing his self-respect. Not so very long. You take my word for that." And without the slightest change in the monotony of that creaking voice he added:

"Did you read of the murder? Just here. I've been looking at the place."

The words, "So have I!" leaped up to Laurence's lips; he choked them down with a sort of terror.

"I wish you better luck," he said. "Good-night!" and hurried away. A sort of ghastly laughter was forcing its way up in his throat. Was everyone talking of the murder he had committed? Even the very scarecrows?

III

There are some natures so constituted that, due to be hung at ten o'clock, they will play chess at eight. Such men invariably rise. They make especially good bishops, editors, judges, impresarios, Prime Ministers, money-lenders, and generals; in fact, fill with exceptional credit any position of power over their fellow-men. They have spiritual cold storage, in which are preserved their nervous systems. In such men there is little or none of that fluid sense and continuity of feeling known under those vague terms, speculation, poetry, philosophy. Men of facts and of decision switching imagination on and off at will, subordinating sentiment to reason ... one does not think of them when watching wind ripple over cornfields, or swallows flying.

Keith Darrant had need for being of that breed during his dinner at the Tellasson's. It was just eleven when he issued from the big house in Portland Place and refrained from taking a cab. He wanted to walk that he might better think. What crude and wanton irony there was in his situation! To have been made father-confessor to a murderer, he—well on towards a judgeship! With his contempt for the kind of weakness which landed men in such abysses, he felt it all so sordid, so "impossible," that he could hardly bring his mind to bear on it at all. And yet he must, because of two powerful instincts—self-preservation and blood-loyalty.

The wind had still the sapping softness of the afternoon, but rain had held off so far. It was warm, and he unbuttoned his fur overcoat. The nature of his thoughts deepened the dark austerity of his face, whose thin, well-cut lips were always pressing together, as if, by meeting, to dispose of each thought as it came up. He moved along the crowded pavements glumly. That air of festive conspiracy, which drops with the darkness on to lighted streets, galled him. He turned off on a darker route.

This ghastly business! Convinced of its reality, he yet could not see it. The thing existed in his mind, not as a picture, but as a piece of irrefutable evidence. Larry had not meant to do it, of course. But it was murder, all the same. Men like Larry—weak, impulsive, sentimental, introspective creatures—did they ever mean what they did? This man, this Walenn, was, by all accounts, better dead than alive; no need to waste a thought on him! But, crime—the ugliness—Justice unsatisfied! Crime concealed—and his own share in the concealment! And yet—brother to brother! Surely no one could demand action from him! It was only a question of what he was going to advise Larry to do. To keep silent, and disappear? Had that a chance of success? Perhaps—if the answers to his questions had been correct. But this girl! Suppose the dead man's relationship to her were ferreted out, could she be relied on not to endanger Larry? These women were all the same, unstable as water, emotional, shiftless—pests of society. Then, too, a crime untracked, dogging all his brother's after life; a secret following him wherever he might vanish to; hanging over him, watching for some drunken moment, to slip out of his lips. It was bad to think of. A clean breast of it? But his heart twitched within him. "Brother of Mr. Keith Darrant, the well-known King's Counsel"—visiting a woman of the town, strangling with his bare hands the woman's husband! No intention to murder, but—a dead man! A dead man carried out of the house, laid under a dark archway! Provocation! Recommended to mercy— penal servitude for life! Was that the advice he was going to give Larry to-morrow morning?

And he had a sudden vision of shaven men with clay-coloured features, run, as it were, to seed, as he had seen them once in Pentonville, when he had gone there to visit a prisoner. Larry! whom, as a baby creature, he had watched straddling; whom, as a little fellow, he had fagged; whom he had seen through scrapes at college; to whom he had lent money time and again, and time and again admonished in his courses. Larry! Five years younger than himself; and committed to his charge by their mother when she died. To become for life one of those men with faces like diseased plants; with no hair but a bushy stubble; with arrows marked on their yellow clothes! Larry! One of those men herded like sheep; at the beck and call of common men! A gentleman, his own brother, to live that slave's life, to be ordered here and there, year after year, day in, day out. Something snapped within him. He could not give that advice. Impossible! But, if not, he must make sure of his ground, must verify, must know. This Glove Lane—this archway? It would not be far from where he was that very moment. He looked for someone of whom to make enquiry. A policeman was standing at the corner, his stolid face illumined by a lamp; capable and watchful—an excellent officer, no doubt; but, turning his head away, Keith passed him without a word. Strange to feel that cold, uneasy feeling in presence of the law! A grim little driving home of what it all meant! Then, suddenly, he saw that the turning to his left was Borrow Street itself. He walked up one side, crossed over, and returned. He passed Number Forty-two, a small house with business names printed on the lifeless windows of the first and second floors; with dark-curtained windows on the ground floor, or was there just a slink of light in one corner? Which way had Larry turned? Which way under that grisly burden? Fifty paces of this squalid street—narrow, and dark, and empty, thank heaven! Glove Lane! Here it was! A tiny runlet of a street. And here——! He had run right on to the arch, a brick bridge connecting two portions of a ware house, and dark indeed.

"That's right, gov'nor! That's the place!" He needed all his self-control to turn leisurely to the speaker. "'Ere's where they found the body—very spot—leanin' up 'ere. They ain't got 'im yet. Lytest—me lord!"

It was a ragged boy holding out a tattered yellowish journal. His lynx eyes peered up from under lanky wisps of hair, and his voice had the proprietary note of one making "a corner" in his news. Keith took the paper and gave him twopence. He even found a sort of comfort in the young ghoul's hanging about there; it meant that others besides himself had come morbidly to look. By the dim lamplight he read: "Glove Lane garrotting mystery. Nothing has yet been discovered of the murdered man's identity; from the cut of his clothes he is supposed to be a foreigner." The boy had vanished, and Keith saw the figure of a policeman coming slowly down this gutter of a street. A second's hesitation, and he stood firm. Nothing obviously could have brought him here save this "mystery," and he stayed quietly staring at the arch. The policeman moved up abreast. Keith saw that he was the one whom he had passed just now. He noted the cold offensive question die out of the man's eyes when they caught the gleam of white shirt-front under the opened fur collar. And holding up the paper, he said:

"Is this where the man was found?"

"Yes, sir."

"Still a mystery, I see?"

"Well, we can't always go by the papers. But I don't fancy they do know much about it, yet."

"Dark spot. Do fellows sleep under here?"

The policeman nodded. "There's not an arch in London where we don't get 'em sometimes."

"Nothing found on him—I think I read?"

"Not a copper. Pockets inside out. There's some funny characters about this quarter. Greeks, Hitahans—all sorts."

Queer sensation this, of being glad of a policeman's confidential tone!

"Well, good-night!"

"Good-night, sir. Good-night!"

He looked back from Borrow Street. The policeman was still standing there holding up his lantern, so that its light fell into the archway, as if trying to read its secret.

Now that he had seen this dark, deserted spot, the chances seemed to him much better. "Pockets inside out!" Either Larry had had presence of mind to do a very clever thing, or someone had been at the body before the police found it. That was the more likely. A dead backwater of a place. At three o'clock—loneliest of all hours—Larry's five minutes' grim excursion to and fro might well have passed unseen! Now, it all depended on the girl; on whether Laurence had been seen coming to her or going away; on whether, if the man's relationship to her were discovered, she could be relied on to say nothing. There was not a soul in Borrow Street now; hardly even a lighted window; and he took one of those rather desperate decisions only possible to men daily accustomed to the instant taking of responsibility. He would go to her, and see for himself. He came to the door of Forty-two, obviously one of those which are only shut at night, and tried the larger key. It fitted, and he was in a gaslighted passage, with an oil-clothed floor, and a single door to his left. He stood there undecided. She must be made to understand that he knew everything. She must not be told more than that he was a friend of Larry's. She must not be frightened, yet must be forced to give her very soul away. A hostile witness—not to be treated as hostile

—a matter for delicate handling! But his knock was not answered.

Should he give up this nerve-racking, bizarre effort to come at a basis of judgment; go away, and just tell Laurence that he could not advise him? And then—what? Something *must* be done. He knocked again. Still no answer. And with that impatience of being thwarted, natural to him, and fostered to the full by the conditions of his life, he tried the other key. It worked, and he opened the door. Inside all was dark, but a voice from some way off, with a sort of breathless relief in its foreign tones, said:

"Oh! then it's you, Larry! Why did you knock? I was so frightened. Turn up the light, dear. Come in!"

Feeling by the door for a switch in the pitch blackness, he was conscious of arms round his neck, a warm thinly clad body pressed to his own; then withdrawn as quickly, with a gasp, and the most awful terror-stricken whisper:

"Oh! Who is it?"

With a glacial shiver down his own spine, Keith answered:

"A friend of Laurence. Don't be frightened!"

There was such silence that he could hear a clock ticking, and the sound of his own hand passing over the surface of the wall, trying to find the switch. He found it, and in the light which leaped up he saw, stiffened against a dark curtain evidently screening off a bedroom, a girl standing, holding a long black coat together at her throat, so that her face with its pale brown hair, short and square-cut and curling up underneath, had an uncanny look of being detached from any body. Her face was so alabaster pale that the staring, startled eyes, dark blue or brown, and the faint rose of the parted lips, were like colour stainings on a white mask; and it had a strange delicacy, truth, and pathos, such as only suffering brings. Though not susceptible to æsthetic emotion, Keith was curiously affected. He said gently:

"You needn't be afraid. I haven't come to do you harm—quite the contrary. May I sit down and talk?" And, holding up the keys, he added: "Laurence wouldn't have given me these, would he, if he hadn't trusted me?"

Still she did not move, and he had the impression that he was looking at a spirit—a spirit startled out of its flesh. Nor at the moment did it seem in the least strange that he should conceive such an odd thought. He stared round the room—clean and tawdry, with its tarnished gilt mirror, marble-topped side-table, and plush-covered sofa. Twenty years and more since he had been in such a place. And he said:

"Won't you sit down? I'm sorry to have startled you."

But still she did not move, whispering:

"Who are you, please?"

And, moved suddenly beyond the realm of caution by the terror in that whisper, he answered:

"Larry's brother."

She uttered a little sigh of relief which went to Keith's heart, and, still holding the dark coat together at her throat, came forward and sat down on the sofa. He could see that her feet, thrust, into slippers, were bare; with her short hair, and those candid startled eyes, she looked like a tall child. He drew up a chair and said:

"You must forgive me coming at such an hour; he's told me, you see."

He expected her to flinch and gasp; but she only clasped her hands together on her knees, and said:

"Yes?"

Then horror and discomfort rose up in him afresh.

"An awful business!"

Her whisper echoed him:

"Yes, oh! yes! Awful—it is awful!"

And suddenly realising that the man must have fallen dead just where he was sitting, Keith became stock silent, staring at the floor.

"Yes," she whispered; "just there. I see him now always falling!"

How she said that! With what a strange gentle despair! In this girl of evil life, who had brought on them this tragedy, what was it which moved him to a sort of unwilling compassion?

"You look very young," he said.

"I am twenty."

"And you are fond of—my brother?"

"I would die for him."

Impossible to mistake the tone of her voice, or the look in her eyes, true deep Slav eyes; dark brown, not blue as he had thought at first. It was a very pretty face—either her life had not eaten into it yet, or the suffering of these last hours had purged away those marks; or perhaps this devotion of hers to Larry. He felt strangely at sea, sitting there with this child of twenty; he, over forty, a man of the world, professionally used to every side of human nature. But he said, stammering a little:

"I—I have come to see how far you can save him. Listen, and just answer the questions I put to you."

She raised her hands, squeezed them together, and murmured:

"Oh! I will answer anything."

"This man, then—your—husband—was he a bad man?"

"A dreadful man."

"Before he came here last night, how long since you saw him?"

"Eighteen months."

"Where did you live when you saw him last?"

"In Pimlico."

"Does anybody about here know you as Mrs. Walenn?"

"No. When. I came here, after my little girl died, I came to live a bad life. Nobody knows me at all. I am quite alone."

"If they discover who he was, they will look for his wife?"

"I do not know. He did not let people think I was married to him. I was very young; he treated many, I think, like me."

"Do you think he was known to the police?"

She shook her head. "He was very clever."

"What is your name now?"

"Wanda Livinska."

"Were you known by that name before you were married?"

"Wanda is my Christian name. Livinska—I just call myself."

"I see; since you came here."

"Yes."

"Did my brother ever see this man before last night?"

"Never."

"You had told him about his treatment of you?"

"Yes. And that man first went for him."

"I saw the mark. Do you think anyone saw my brother come to you?"

"I do not know. He says not."

"Can you tell if anyone saw him carrying the—the thing away?"

"No one in this street—I was looking."

"Nor coming back?"

"No one."

"Nor going out in the morning?"

"I do not think it."

"Have you a servant?"

"Only a woman who comes at nine in the morning for an hour."

"Does she know Larry?"

"No."

"Friends, acquaintances?"

"No; I am very quiet. And since I knew your brother, I see no one. Nobody comes here but him for a long time now."

"How long?"

"Five months."

"Have you, been out to-day?"

"No."

"What have you been doing?"

"Crying."

It was said with a certain dreadful simplicity, and pressing her hands together she went on:

"He is in danger because of me. I am so afraid for him."

Holding up his hand to check that emotion, he said:

"Look at me!"

She fixed those dark eyes on him, and in her bare throat, from which the coat had fallen back, he could see her resolutely swallowing down her agitation.

"If the worst comes to the worst, and this man is traced to you, can you trust yourself not to give my brother away?"

Her eyes shone. She got up and went to the fireplace:

"Look! I have burned all the things he has given me—even his picture. Now I have nothing from him."

Keith, too, got up.

"Good! One more question: Do the police know you, because—because of your life?"

She shook her head, looking at him intently with those mournfully true eyes. And he felt a sort of shame.

"I was obliged to ask. Do you know where he lives?"

"Yes."

"You must not go there. And he must not come to you here."

Her lips quivered; but she bowed her head. Suddenly he found her quite close to him, speaking almost in a whisper:

"Please do not take him from me altogether. I will be so careful. I will not do anything to hurt him; but if I cannot see him sometimes I shall die. Please do not take him from me." And catching his hand between her own she pressed it desperately. It was several seconds before Keith said:

"Leave that to me. I will see him. I shall arrange. You must leave that to me."

"But you will be kind?"

He felt her lips kissing his hand. And the soft moist touch sent a queer feeling through him, protective, yet just a little brutal, having in it a shiver of sensuality. He withdrew his hand. And as if warned that she had been too pressing, she recoiled humbly. But suddenly she turned, and stood absolutely rigid; then almost inaudibly whispered: "Listen! Someone out—out there!" And darting past him she turned out the light.

Almost at once came a knock on the door. He could feel—actually feel the terror of this girl beside him in the dark. And he, too, felt terror. Who could it be? No one came but Larry, she had said. Who else then could it be? Again came the knock, louder! He felt the breath of her whisper on his cheek; "If it is Larry! I must open." He shrank back against the wall, heard her open the door and say faintly: "Yes. Please! Who?"

Light painted a thin moving line on the wall opposite, and a voice which Keith recognised answered:

"All right, miss. Your outer door's open here. You ought to keep it shut after dark."

God! That policeman! And it had been his own doing, not shutting the outer door behind when he came in. He heard her say timidly in her foreign voice: "Thank you, sir!" the policeman's retreating steps, the outer door being shut, and felt her close to him again. That something in her youth and strange prettiness had touched and kept him gentle, no longer blunted the edge of his exasperation, now that he could not see her. They were all the same, these women; could not speak the truth! And he said brusquely:

"You told me they didn't know you!"

Her voice answered like a sigh:

"I did not think they did, sir. It is so long I was not out in the town, not since I had Larry."

The repulsion which all the time seethed deep in Keith welled up at those words. His brother—son of *his* mother, a gentleman—the property of this girl, bound to her, body and soul, by this unspeakable event! But she had turned up the light. Had she some intuition that darkness was against her? Yes, she was pretty with that soft face, colourless save for its lips and dark eyes, with that face somehow so touching, so unaccountably good, and like a child's.

"I am going now," he said. "Remember! He mustn't come here; you mustn't go to him. I shall see him to-morrow. If you are as fond as him as you say—take care, take care!"

She sighed out, "Yes! oh, yes!" and Keith went to the door. She was standing with her back to the wall, and to follow him she only moved her head—that dove-like face with all its life in eyes which seemed saying: "Look into us; nothing we hide; all—all is there!"

And he went out.

In the passage he paused before opening the outer door. He did not want to meet that policeman again; the fellow's round should have taken him well out of the street by now, and, turning the handle cautiously, he looked out. No one in sight. He stood a moment, wondering if he should turn to right or left, then briskly crossed the street. A voice to his right hand said:

"Good-night, sir."

There in the shadow of a doorway the policeman was standing. The fellow must have seen him coming out! Utterly unable to restrain a start, and muttering "Good-night!" Keith walked on rapidly.

He went full quarter of a mile before he lost that startled and uneasy feeling in sardonic exasperation that he, Keith Darrant, had been taken for a frequenter of a lady of the town. The whole thing—the whole thing!—a vile and disgusting business! His very mind felt dirty and breathless; his spirit, drawn out of sheath, had slowly to slide back before he could at all focus and readjust his reasoning faculty. Certainly, he had got the knowledge he wanted. There was less danger than he thought. That girl's eyes! No mistaking her devotion. She would not give Larry away. Yes! Larry must clear out—South America—the East—it did not matter. But he felt no relief. The cheap, tawdry room had wrapped itself round his fancy with its atmosphere of murky love, with the feeling it inspired, of emotion caged within those yellowish walls and the red stuff of its furniture. That girl's face! Devotion; truth, too, and beauty, rare and moving, in its setting of darkness and horror, in that nest of vice and of disorder! … The dark archway; the street arab, with his gleeful: "They 'ain't got 'im yet!"; the feel of those bare arms round his neck; that whisper of horror in the darkness; above all,

again, her child face looking into his, so truthful! And suddenly he stood quite still in the street. What in God's name was he about? What grotesque juggling amongst shadows, what strange and ghastly eccentricity was all this? The forces of order and routine, all the actualities of his daily life, marched on him at that moment and swept everything before them. It was a dream, a nightmare—not real! It was ridiculous! That he—*he* should thus be bound up with things so black and bizarre!

He had come by now to the Strand, that street down which every day he moved to the Law Courts, to his daily work; his work so dignified and regular, so irreproachable and solid. No! The thing was all a monstrous nightmare! It would go, if he fixed his mind on the familiar objects around, read the names on the shops, looked at the faces passing. Far down the thoroughfare he caught the outline of the old church, and beyond, the loom of the Law Courts themselves. The bell of a fire-engine sounded, and the horses came galloping by, with the shining metal, rattle of hoofs, and hoarse shouting. Here was a sensation, real and harmless, dignified and customary! A woman flaunting round the corner looked up at him and leered out: "Good-night!" Even that was customary, tolerable. Two policemen passed, supporting between them a man the worse for liquor, full of fight and expletives; the sight was soothing, an ordinary thing which brought passing annoyance, interest, disgust. It had begun to rain; he felt it on his face with pleasure—an actual thing, not eccentric, a thing which happened every day!

He began to cross the street. Cabs were going at furious speed now that the last omnibus had ceased to run; it distracted him to take this actual, ordinary risk run so often every day. During that crossing of the Strand, with the rain in his face and the cabs shooting past, he regained for the first time his assurance, shook off this unreal sense of being in the grip of something, and walked resolutely to the corner of his home turning. But passing into that darker stretch, he again stood still. A policeman had also turned into that street on the other side. Not—surely not—! Absurd! They were all alike to look at—those fellows! Absurd! He walked on sharply, and let himself into his house. But on his way upstairs he could not for the life of him help raising a corner of a curtain and looking from the staircase window. The policeman was marching solemnly, about twenty-five yards away, paying apparently no attention to anything whatever.

IV

Keith woke at five o'clock, his usual hour, without remembrance. But the grisly shadow started up when he entered his study, where the lamp burned, and the fire shone, and the coffee was set ready, just as when yesterday afternoon Larry had stood out there against the wall. For a moment he fought against realisation; then, drinking off his coffee, sat down sullenly at the bureau to his customary three hours' study of the day's cases.

Not one word of his brief could he take in. It was all jumbled with murky images and apprehensions, and for full half an hour he suffered mental paralysis. Then the sheer necessity of knowing something of the case which he had to open at half-past ten that morning forced him to a concentration which never quite subdued the malaise at the bottom of his heart. Nevertheless, when he rose at half-past eight and went into the bathroom, he had earned his grim satisfaction in this victory of will-power. By half-past nine he must be at Larry's. A boat left London for the Argentine to-morrow. If Larry was to get away at once, money must be arranged for. And then at breakfast he came on this paragraph in the paper:

"SOHO MURDER
"Enquiry late last night established the fact that the police have discovered the identity of the man found strangled yesterday morning under an archway in Glove Lane. An arrest has been made."

By good fortune he had finished eating, for the words made him feel physically sick. At this very minute Larry might be locked up, waiting to be charged—might even have been arrested before his own visit to the girl last night. If Larry were arrested she must be implicated. What, then, would be his own position? Idiot to go and look at that archway, to go and see the girl! Had that policeman really followed him home? Accessory after the fact! Keith Darrant, King's Counsel, man of mark! He forced himself by an effort, which had something of the heroic, to drop this panicky feeling. Panic never did good. He must face it and see. He refused even to hurry, calmly collected the papers wanted for the day, and attended to a letter or two before he set out in a taxi-cab to Fitzroy Street.

Waiting outside there in the grey morning for his ring to be answered, he looked the very picture of a man who knew his mind, a man of resolution. But it needed all his will-power to ask without tremor: "Mr. Darrant in?" to hear without sign of any kind the answer: "He's not up yet, sir."

"Never mind; I'll go in and see him. Mr. Keith Darrant."

On his way to Laurence's bedroom, in the midst of utter relief, he had the self-possession to think: 'This arrest is the best thing that could have happened. It'll keep their noses on a wrong scent till Larry's got away. The girl must be sent off too, but not with him.' Panic had ended in quite hardening his resolution. He entered the bedroom with a feeling of disgust. The fellow was lying there, his bare arms crossed behind his tousled head, staring at the ceiling, and smoking one of many cigarettes whose ends littered a chair beside him, whose sickly reek tainted the air. That pale face, with its jutting cheek bones and chin, its hollow cheeks and blue eyes far sunk back—what a wreck of goodness!

He looked up at Keith through the haze of smoke and said quietly: "Well, brother, what's the sentence? 'Transportation for life, and then to be fined forty pounds'?"

The flippancy revolted Keith. It was Larry all over! Last night horrified and humble, this morning, "Don't care" and feather-headed. He said sourly:

"Oh! You can joke about it now?"

Laurence turned his face to the wall.

"Must."

Fatalism! How detestable were natures like that!

"I've been to see her," he said.

"You?"

"Last night. She can be trusted."

Laurence laughed.

"That I told you."

"I had to see for myself. You must clear out at once, Larry. She can come out to you by the next boat; but you can't go together. Have you any money?"

"No."

"I can foot your expenses, and lend you a year's income in advance. But it must be a clean cut; after you get out there your whereabouts must only be known to me."

A long sigh answered him.

"You're very good to me, Keith; you've always been very good. I don't know why."

Keith answered drily:

"Nor I. There's a boat to the Argentine to-morrow. You're in luck; they've made an arrest. It's in the paper."

"What?"

The cigarette end dropped, the thin pyjama'd figure writhed up and stood clutching at the bedrail.

"What?"

The disturbing thought flitted through Keith's brain: "I was a fool. He takes it queerly; what now?"

Laurence passed his hand over his forehead and sat down on the bed.

"I hadn't thought of that," he said. "It does me!"

Keith stared. In his relief that the arrested man was not Laurence, this had not occurred to him. What folly!

"Why?" he said quickly; "an innocent man's in no danger. They always get the wrong man first. It's a piece of luck, that's all. It gives us time."

How often had he not seen that expression on Larry's face, wistful, questioning, as if trying to see the thing with his—Keith's—eyes, trying to submit to better judgment? And he said, almost gently:

"Now, look here, Larry; this is too serious to trifle with. Don't worry about that. Leave it to me. Just get ready to be off. I'll take your berth and make arrangements. Here's some money for kit. I can come round between five and six and let you know. Pull yourself together, man. As soon as the girl's joined you out there, you'd better get across to Chile, the further the better. You must simply lose yourself. I must go now, if I'm to get to the Bank before I go down to the courts." And looking very steadily at his brother, he added:

"Come! You've got to think of me in this matter as well as of yourself. No playing fast and loose with the arrangements. Understand?"

But still Larry gazed up at him with that wistful questioning, and not till he had repeated, "Understand?" did he receive "Yes" for answer.

Driving away, he thought: 'Queer fellow! I don't know him, shall never know him!' and at once began to concentrate on the practical arrangements. At his bank he drew out £400; but waiting for the notes to be counted he suffered qualms. A clumsy way of doing things! If there had been more time! The thought 'Accessory after the fact!' now infected everything. Notes were traceable. No other way of getting him away at once, though. One must take lesser risks to avoid greater. From the bank he drove to the office of the steamship line. He had told Larry he would book his passage. But that would not do! He must only ask anonymously if there were accommodation. Having discovered that there were vacant berths, he drove on to the Law Courts. If he could have taken a morning off, he would have gone down to the police court and seen them charge this man. But even that was not too safe, with a face so well known as his. What would come of this arrest? Nothing, surely! The police always took somebody up to keep the public quiet. Then, suddenly, he had again the feeling that it was all a nightmare; Larry had never done it; the police had got the right man! But instantly the memory of the girl's awe-stricken face, her figure huddling on the sofa, her words: "I see him always falling!" came back. God! What a business!

He felt he had never been more clear-headed and forcible than that morning in court. When he came out for lunch he bought the most sensational of the evening papers. But it was yet too early for news, and he had to go back into court no whit wiser concerning the arrest. When at last he threw off wig and gown, and had got through a conference and other necessary work, he went out to Chancery Lane, buying a paper on the way. Then he hailed a cab and drove once more to Fitzroy Street.

V

Laurence had remained sitting on his bed for many minutes. An innocent man in no danger! Keith had said it—the celebrated lawyer! Could he rely on that? Go out 8,000 miles, he and the girl, and leave a fellow-creature perhaps in mortal peril for an act committed by himself?

In the past night he had touched bottom, as he thought: become ready to face anything. When Keith came in he would without murmur have accepted the advice: "Give yourself up!" He was prepared to pitch away the end of his life as he pitched from him the fag-ends of his cigarettes. And the long sigh he had heaved, hearing of reprieve, had been only half relief. Then, with incredible swiftness there had rushed through him a feeling of unutterable joy and hope. Clean away—into a new country, a new life! The girl and he! Out there he wouldn't care, would rejoice even to have squashed the life out of such a noisome beetle of a man. Out there! Under a new sun, where blood ran quicker than in this foggy land, and people took justice into their own hands. For it had been justice on that brute even though he had not meant to kill him. And then to hear of this arrest! They would be charging the man to-day. He could go and see the poor creature accused of the murder he himself had committed! And he laughed. Go and see how likely it was that they might hang a fellow-man in place of himself? He dressed, but too shaky to shave himself, went out to a barber's shop. While there he read the news which Keith had seen. In this paper the name of the arrested man was given: "John Evan, no address." To be brought up on the charge at Bow Street. Yes! He must go. Once, twice, three times he walked past the entrance of the court before at last he entered and screwed himself away among the tag and bob tail.

The court was crowded; and from the murmurs round he could tell that it was his particular case which had brought so many there. In a dazed way he watched charge after charge disposed of with lightning quickness. But were they never going to reach his business? And then suddenly he saw the little scarecrow man of last night advancing to the dock between two policemen, more ragged and miserable than ever by light of day, like some shaggy, wan, grey animal surrounded by sleek hounds.

A sort of satisfied purr was rising all round; and with horror Laurence perceived that this—this was the man accused of what he himself had done—this queer, battered unfortunate to whom he had shown a passing friendliness. Then all feeling merged in the appalling interest of listening. The evidence was very short. Testimony of the hotelkeeper where Walenn had been staying, the identification of his body, and of a snake-shaped ring he had been wearing at dinner that evening. Testimony of a pawnbroker, that this same ring was pawned with him the first thing yesterday morning by the prisoner. Testimony of a policeman that he had noticed the man Evan several times in Glove Lane, and twice moved him on from sleeping under that arch. Testimony of another policeman that, when arrested at midnight, Evan had said: "Yes; I took the ring off his finger. I found him there dead. ... I know I oughtn't to have done it. ... I'm an educated man; it was stupid to pawn the ring. I found him with his pockets turned inside out."

Fascinating and terrible to sit staring at the man in whose place he should have been; to wonder when those small bright-grey bloodshot eyes would spy him out, and how he would meet that glance. Like a baited raccoon the little man stood, screwed back into a corner, mournful, cynical, fierce, with his ridged, obtuse yellow face, and his stubbly grey beard and hair, and his eyes wandering now and again amongst the crowd. But with all his might Laurence kept his face unmoved. Then came the word "Remanded"; and, more like a baited beast than ever, the man was led away.

Laurence sat on, a cold perspiration thick on his forehead. Someone else, then, had come on the body and turned the pockets inside out before John Evan took the ring. A man such as Walenn would not be out at night without money. Besides, if Evan had found money on the body he would never have run the risk of taking that ring. Yes, someone else had come on the body first. It was for that one to come forward and prove that the ring was still on the dead man's finger when he left him, and thus clear Evan. He clung to that thought; it seemed to make him less responsible for the little man's position; to remove him and his own deed one step further back. If they found the person who had taken the money, it would prove Evan's innocence. He came out of the court in a sort of trance. And a craving to get drunk attacked him. One could not go on like this without the relief of some oblivion. If he could only get drunk, keep drunk till this business was decided and he knew whether he must give himself up or no. He had now no fear at all of people suspecting him; only fear of himself—fear that he might go and give himself up. Now he could see the girl; the danger from that was as nothing compared with the danger from his own conscience. He had promised Keith not to see her. Keith had been decent and loyal to him—good old Keith! But he would never understand that this girl was now all he cared about in life; that he would rather be cut off from life itself than be cut off from her. Instead of becoming less and less, she was becoming more and more to him—experience strange and thrilling! Out of deep misery she had grown happy—through him; out of a sordid, shifting life recovered coherence and bloom, through devotion to him—him, of all people in the world! It was a miracle. She demanded nothing of him, adored him, as no other woman ever had—it was this which had anchored his drifting barque; this—and her truthful mild intelligence, and that burning warmth of a woman who, long treated by men as but a sack of sex, now loves at last.

And suddenly, mastering his craving to get drunk, he made towards Soho. He had been a fool to give those keys to Keith. She must have been frightened by his visit; and, perhaps, doubly miserable since, knowing nothing, imagining everything! Keith was sure to have terrified her. Poor little thing!

Down the street where he had stolen in the dark with the dead body on his back, he almost ran for the cover of her house. The door was opened to him before he knocked, her arms were round his neck, her lips pressed to his. The fire was out, as if she had been unable to remember to keep warm. A stool had been drawn to the window, and there she had evidently been sitting, like a bird in a cage, looking out into the grey street. Though she had been told that he was not to come, instinct had kept her there; or the pathetic, aching hope against hope which lovers never part with.

Now that he was there, her first thoughts were for his comfort. The fire was lighted. He must eat, drink, smoke. There was never in her doings any of the "I am doing this for you, but you ought to be doing that for me" which belongs to so many marriages and *liaisons*. She was like a devoted slave, so in love with the chains that she never knew she wore them. And to Laurence, who had so little sense of property, this only served to deepen tenderness, and the hold she had on him. He had resolved not to tell her of the new danger he ran from his own conscience. But resolutions with him were but the opposite of what was sure to come; and at last the words, "They've arrested someone," escaped him.

From her face he knew she had grasped the danger at once; had divined it, perhaps, before he spoke. But she only twined her arms round him and kissed his lips. And he knew that she was begging him to put his love for her above his conscience. Who would ever have thought that he could feel as he did to this girl who had been in the arms of so many! The stained and suffering past of a loved woman awakens in some men only chivalry; in others, more respectable, it rouses a tigerish itch, a rancorous jealousy of what in the past was given to others. Sometimes it will do both. When he had her in his arms he felt no remorse for killing the coarse, handsome brute who had ruined her. He savagely rejoiced in it. But when she laid her head in the hollow of his shoulder, turning to him her white face with the faint colour-staining on the parted lips, the cheeks, the eyelids; when her dark, wide-apart, brown eyes gazed up in the happiness of her abandonment—he felt only tenderness and protection.

He left her at five o'clock, and had not gone two streets' length before the memory of the little grey vagabond, screwed back in the far corner of the dock like a baited raccoon, of his dreary, creaking voice, took possession of him again; and a kind of savagery mounted in his brain against a world where one could be so tortured without having meant harm to anyone.

At the door of his lodgings Keith was getting out of a cab. They went in together, but neither of them sat down; Keith standing with his back to the carefully shut door, Laurence with his back to the table, as if they knew there was a tug coming. And Keith said:

"There's room on that boat. Go down and book your berth before they shut. Here's the money!"

"I'm going to stick it, Keith."

Keith stepped forward and put a roll of notes on the table.

"Now look here, Larry. I've read the police-court proceedings. There's nothing in that. Out of prison, or in prison for a few weeks, it's all the same to a night-bird of that sort. Dismiss it from your mind—there's not nearly enough evidence to convict. This gives you your chance. Take it like a man, and make a new life for yourself."

Laurence smiled; but the smile had a touch of madness and a touch of malice. He took up the notes.

"Clear out, and save the honour of brother Keith. Put them back in your pocket, Keith, or I'll put them in the fire. Come, take them!" And, crossing to the fire, he held them to the bars. "Take them, or in they go!"

Keith took back the notes.

"I've still got some kind of honour; Keith; if I clear out I shall have none, not the rag of any, left. It may be worth more to me than that—I can't tell yet—I can't tell."

There was a long silence before Keith answered:

"I tell you you're mistaken; no jury will convict. If they did, a judge would never hang on it. A ghoul who can rob a dead body *ought* to be in prison. What he did is worse than what you did, if you come to that!"

Laurence lifted his face.

"Judge not, brother," he said; "the heart is a dark well."

Keith's yellowish face grew red and swollen, as though he were mastering the tickle of a bronchial cough.

"What are you going to do, then? I suppose I may ask you not to be entirely oblivious of our name; or is such a consideration unworthy of your honour?"

Laurence bent his head. The gesture said more clearly than words: "Don't kick a man when he's down!"

"I don't know what I'm going to do—nothing at present. I'm awfully sorry, Keith; awfully sorry."

Keith looked at him, and without another word went out.

VI

To any, save philosophers, reputation may be threatened almost as much by disgrace to name and family as by the disgrace of self. Keith's instinct was always to deal actively with danger. But this blow, whether it fell on him by discovery or by confession, could not be countered. As blight falls on a rose from who knows where, the scandalous murk would light on him. No repulse possible! Not even a wriggling from under! Brother of a murderer hung or sent to penal servitude! His daughter niece to a murderer! His dead mother— a murderer's mother! And to wait day after day, week after week, not knowing whether the blow would fall, was an extraordinary atrocious penance, the injustice of which, to a man of rectitude, seemed daily the more monstrous.

The remand had produced evidence that the murdered man had been drinking heavily on the night of his death, and further evidence of the accused's professional vagabondage and destitution; it was shown, too, that for some time the archway in Glove Lane had been his favourite night haunt. He had been committed for trial in January. This time, despite misgivings, Keith had attended the police court. To his great relief Larry was not there. But the policeman who had come up while he was looking at the archway, and given him afterwards that scare in the girl's rooms, was chief witness to the way the accused man haunted Glove Lane. Though Keith held his silk hat high, he still had the uncomfortable feeling that the man had recognised him.

His conscience suffered few, if any, twinges for letting this man rest under the shadow of the murder. He genuinely believed that there was not evidence enough to convict; nor was it in him to appreciate the tortures of a vagabond shut up. The scamp deserved what he had got for robbing a dead body; and in any case such a scarecrow was better off in prison than sleeping out under archways in December. Sentiment was foreign to Keith's character, and his justice that of those who subordinate the fates of the weak and shiftless to the needful paramountcy of the strong and well established.

His daughter came back from school for the Christmas holidays. It. was hard to look up from her bright eyes and rosy cheeks and see this shadow hanging above his calm and ordered life, as in a glowing room one's eye may catch an impending patch of darkness drawn like a spider's web across a corner of the ceiling.

On the afternoon of Christmas Eve they went, by her desire, to a church in Soho, where the Christmas Oratorio was being given; and coming away passed, by chance of a wrong turning, down Borrow Street. Ugh! How that startled moment, when the girl had pressed herself against him in the dark, and her terror-stricken whisper: "Oh! Who is it?" leaped out before him! Always that business—that ghastly business! After the trial he would have another try to get them both away. And he thrust his arm within his young daughter's, hurrying her on, out of this street where shadows filled all the winter air.

But that evening when she had gone to bed he felt uncontrollably restless. He had not seen Larry for weeks. What was he about? What desperations were hatching in his disorderly brain? Was he very miserable; had he perhaps sunk into a stupor of debauchery? And the old feeling of protectiveness rose up in him; a warmth born of long ago Christmas Eves, when they had stockings hung out in the night stuffed by a Santa Claus whose hand never failed to tuck them up, whose kiss was their nightly waft into sleep.

Stars were sparkling out there over the river; the sky frosty clear, and black. Bells had not begun to ring as yet. And obeying an obscure, deep impulse, Keith wrapped himself once more into his fur coat, pulled a motoring cap over his eyes, and sallied forth.

In the Strand he took a cab to Fitzroy Street. There was no light in Larry's windows, and on a card he saw the words "To Let." Gone! Had he after all cleared out for good? But how—without money? And the girl? Bells were ringing now in the silent frostiness. Christmas Eve! And Keith thought: 'If only this wretched business were off my mind! Monstrous that one should suffer for the faults of others!'

He took a route which led him past Borrow Street Solitude brooded there, and he walked resolutely down on the far side, looking hard at the girl's window. There was a light. The curtains just failed to meet, so that a thin gleam shone through. He crossed; and after glancing swiftly up and down, deliberately peered in.

He only stood there perhaps twenty seconds but visual records gleaned in a moment sometimes outlast the visions of hours and days. The electric light was not burning; but, in the centre of the room the girl was kneeling in her night-gown before a little table on which were four lighted candles Her arms were crossed on her breast; the candle-light shone on her fair cropped hair, on the profile of cheek and chin, on her bowed white neck. For a moment he thought her alone; then behind her saw his brother in a sleeping suit, leaning against the wall, with arms crossed, watching. It was the expression on his face which burned the whole thing in, so that always afterwards he was able to see that little scene—such an expression as could never have been on the face of one even faintly conscious that he was watched by any living thing on earth. The whole of Larry's heart and feeling seemed to have come up out of him. Yearning, mockery, love, despair! The depth of his feeling for this girl, his stress of mind, fears, hopes; the flotsam good and evil of his soul, all transfigured there, exposed and unforgettable. The candle-light shone upward on to his face, twisted by the strangest smile; his eyes, darker and more wistful than mortal eyes should be, seemed to beseech and mock the white-clad girl, who, all unconscious, knelt without movement, like a carved figure of devotion. The words seemed coming from his lips: "Pray for us! Bravo! Yes! Pray for us!" And suddenly Keith saw her stretch out her arms and lift her face with a look of ecstasy, and Laurence starting forward. What had she seen beyond the candle flames? It is the unexpected which invests visions with poignancy. Nothing more strange could Keith have seen in this nest of the murky and illicit. But in sheer panic lest he might be caught thus spying he drew back and hurried on.

So Larry was living there with her! When the moment came he could still find him. Before going in, he stood full five minutes leaning on the terrace parapet before his house, gazing at the star-frosted sky, and the river cut by the trees into black pools, oiled over by gleams from the Embankment lamps. And, deep down, behind his mere thoughts, he ached—somehow, somewhere ached. Beyond the cage of all that he saw and heard and thought, he had perceived something he could not reach. But the night was cold, the bells silent, for it had struck twelve. Entering his house, he stole upstairs.

VII

If for Keith those six weeks before the Glove Lane murder trial came on were fraught with uneasiness and gloom, they were for Laurence almost the happiest since his youth. From the moment when he left his rooms and went to the girl's to live, a kind of peace and exaltation took possession of him. Not by any effort of will did he throw off the nightmare hanging over him. Nor was he drugged by love. He was in a sort of spiritual catalepsy. In face of fate too powerful for his will, his turmoil, anxiety, and even restlessness had ceased; his life floated in the ether of "what must come, will." Out of this catalepsy, his spirit sometimes fell headlong into black waters. In one such whirlpool he was struggling on the night of Christmas Eve. When the girl rose from her knees he asked her:

"What did you see?"

Pressing close to him, she drew him down on to the floor before the fire; and they sat, knees drawn up, hands clasped, like two children trying to see over the edge of the world.

"It was the Virgin I saw. She stood against the wall and smiled. We shall be happy soon."

"When we die, Wanda," he said, suddenly, "let it be together. We shall keep each other warm out there."

Huddling to him she whispered: "Yes, oh, yes! If you die, I could not go on living."

It was this utter dependence on him, the feeling that he had rescued something, which gave him sense of anchorage. That, and his buried life in the retreat of these two rooms. Just for an hour in the morning, from nine to ten, the charwoman would come, but not another soul all day. They never went out together. He would stay in bed late, while Wanda bought what they needed for the day's meals; lying on his back, hands clasped behind his head, recalling her face, the movements of her slim, rounded, supple figure, robing itself before his gaze; feeling again the kiss she had left on his lips, the gleam of her soft eyes, so strangely dark in so fair a face. In a sort of trance he would lie still till she came back. Then get up to breakfast about noon off things she had cooked, drinking coffee. In the afternoon he would go out alone and walk for hours, anywhere, so long as it was East. To the East there was always suffering to be seen, always that which soothed him with the feeling that he and his troubles were only a tiny part of trouble; that while so many other sorrowing and shadowy creatures lived he was not cut off. To go West was to encourage dejection. In the West all was like Keith, successful, immaculate, ordered, resolute. He would come back tired out, and sit watching her cook their little dinner. The evenings were given up to love. Queer trance of an existence, which both were afraid to break. No sign from her of wanting those excitements which girls who have lived her life, even for a few months, are supposed to need. She never asked him to take her anywhere; never, in word, deed, look, seemed anything but almost rapturously content. And yet he knew, and she knew, that they were only waiting to see whether Fate would turn her thumb down on them. In these days he did not drink. Out of his quarter's money, when it came in, he had paid his debts—their expenses were very small. He never went to see Keith, never wrote to him, hardly thought of him. And from those dread apparitions—Walenn lying with the breath choked out of him, and the little grey, driven animal in the dock—he hid, as only a man can who must hide or be destroyed. But daily he bought a newspaper, and feverishly, furtively scanned its columns.

VIII

Coming out of the Law Courts on the afternoon of January 28, at the triumphant end of a desperately fought will case, Keith saw on a poster the words: "Glove Lane Murder: Trial and Verdict"; and with a rush of dismay he thought: 'Good God! I never looked at the paper this morning!' The elation which had filled him a second before, the absorption he had felt for two days now in the case so hardly won, seemed suddenly quite sickeningly trivial. What on earth had he been doing to forget that horrible business even for an instant? He stood quite still on the crowded pavement, unable, really unable, to buy a paper. But his face was like a piece of iron when he did step forward and hold his penny out. There it was in the "Stop Press"! "Glove Lane Murder. The jury returned a verdict of Guilty. Sentence of death was passed."

His first sensation was simple irritation. How had they come to commit such an imbecility? Monstrous! The evidence——! Then the futility of even reading the report, of even considering how they had come to record such a verdict struck him with savage suddenness. There it was, and nothing he could do or say would alter it; no condemnation of this idiotic verdict would help reverse it. The situation was desperate, indeed! That five minutes' walk from the Law Courts to his chambers was the longest he had ever taken.

Men of decided character little know beforehand what they will do in certain contingencies. For the imaginations of decided people do not endow mere contingencies with sufficient actuality. Keith had never really settled what he was going to do if this man were condemned. Often in those past weeks he had said to himself: 'Of course, if they bring him in guilty, that's another thing!' But, now that they had, he was beset by exactly the same old arguments and feelings, the same instincts of loyalty and protection towards Laurence and himself, intensified by the fearful imminence of the danger. And yet, here was this man about to be hung for a thing he had not done! Nothing could get over that! But then he was such a worthless vagabond, a ghoul who had robbed a dead body. If Larry were condemned in his stead, would there be any less miscarriage of justice? To strangle a brute who had struck you, by the accident of keeping your hands on his throat a few seconds too long, was there any more guilt in that—was there even as much as in deliberate theft from a dead man? Reverence for order, for justice, and established fact, will often march shoulder to shoulder with Jesuitry in natures to whom success is vital.

In the narrow stone passage leading to his staircase a friend called out: "Bravo, Darrant! That was a squeak! Congratulations!" And with a bitter little smile Keith thought: 'Congratulations! I!'

At the first possible moment he hurried back to the Strand, and, hailing a cab, he told the man to put him down at a turning near to Borrow Street.

It was the girl who opened to his knock. Startled, clasping her hands, she looked strange to Keith in her black skirt and blouse of some soft velvety stuff the colour of faded roses. Her round, rather long throat was bare; and Keith noticed fretfully that she wore gold earrings. Her eyes, so pitch dark against her white face, and the short fair hair which curled into her neck, seemed both to search and to plead.

"My brother?"

"He is not in, sir, yet."

"Do you know where he is?"

"No."

"He is living with you here now?"

"Yes."

"Are you still as fond of him as ever, then?"

With a movement, as though she despaired of words, she clasped her hands over her heart. And he said:

"I see."

He had the same strange feeling as on his first visit to her, and when through the chink in the curtains he had watched her kneeling—of pity mingled with some faint sexual emotion. And crossing to the fire he asked:

"May I wait for him?"

"Oh! Please! Will you sit down?"

But Keith shook his head. And with a catch in her breath she said:

"You will not take him from me. I should die."

He turned round on her sharply.

"*I* don't want him taken from you. I want to help you keep him. Are you ready to go away at any time?"

"Yes. Oh, yes!"

"And he?"

She answered almost in a whisper:

"Yes; but there is that poor man."

"That poor man is a graveyard thief; a hyena; a ghoul—not worth consideration." And the rasp in his own voice surprised him.

"Ah!" she sighed. "But I am sorry for him. Perhaps he was hungry. I have been hungry—you do things then that you would not. And perhaps he has no one to love; if you have no one to love you can be very bad. I think of him often—in prison."

Between his teeth Keith muttered: "And Laurence?"

"We do never speak of it; we are afraid."

"He's not told you, then, about the trial?"

Her eyes dilated.

"The trial! Oh! He was strange last night. This morning, too, he got up early. Is it—is it over?"

"Yes."

"What has come?"

"Guilty."

For a moment Keith thought she was going to faint. She had closed her eyes, and swayed so that he took a step and put his hands on her arms.

"Listen!" he said. "Help me, don't let Laurence out of your sight. We must have time. I must see what they intend to do. They can't be going to hang this man. I must have time, I tell you. You must prevent his giving himself up."

She stood, staring in his face, while he still held her arms, gripping into her soft flesh through the velvety sleeves.

"Do you understand?"

"Yes—but if he has already!"

Keith felt the shiver which ran through her. And the thought rushed into his mind: 'My God! Suppose the police come round while I'm here!' If Larry had indeed gone to them! If that policeman who had seen him here the night after the murder should find him here again just after the verdict! He said almost fiercely:

"Can I trust you not to let Larry out of your sight? Quick! Answer!"

Clasping her hands to her breast, she answered humbly:

"I will try."

"If he hasn't already done this, watch him like a lynx! Don't let him go out without you. I'll come to-morrow morning early. You're a Catholic, aren't you? Swear to me that you won't let him do anything till he's seen me again."

She did not answer, looking past him at the door; and Keith heard a key in the latch. There was Laurence himself, holding in his hand a great bunch of pink lilies and white narcissi. His face was pale and haggard. He said quietly :

"Hallo, Keith!"

The girl's eyes were fastened on Larry's face; and Keith looking from one to the other, knew that he had never had more need for wariness.

"Have you seen?" he said.

Laurence nodded. His expression, as a rule so tell-tale of his emotions, baffled Keith utterly.

"I've been expecting it."

"The thing can't stand—that's certain. But I must have time to look into the report. I must have time to see what I can do. D'you understand me, Larry?—I must have time." He knew he was talking at random. The only thing was to get them away at once out of reach of confession; but he dared not say so.

"Promise me that you'll do nothing, that you won't go out even till I've seen you tomorrow morning."

Again Laurence nodded. And Keith looked at the girl. Would she see that he did not break that promise? Her eyes were still fixed immovably on Larry's face. And with the feeling that he could get no further, Keith turned to go.

"Promise me," he said.

Laurence answered: "I promise."

He was smiling. Keith could make nothing of that smile, nor of the expression in the girl's eyes. And saying: "I have your promise, I rely on it!" he went.

IX

To keep from any woman who loves, knowledge of her lover's mood, is as hard as to keep music from moving the heart. But when that woman has lived in suffering, and for the first time knows the comfort of love, then let the lover try as he may to disguise his heart—no use! Yet by virtue of subtler abnegation she will often succeed in keeping it fro him that she knows.

When Keith was gone the girl made no outcry, asked no questions, managed that Larry should not suspect her intuition; all that evening she acted as if she knew of nothing preparing within him, and through him, within herself.

His words, caresses, the very zest with which he helped her to prepare the feast, the flowers he had brought, the wine he made her drink, the avoidance of any word which could spoil their happiness, all—all told her. He was too inexorably gay and loving. Not for her—to whom every word and every kiss had uncannily the desperate value of a last word and kiss—not for her to deprive herself of these by any sign or gesture which might betray her prescience. She took all, and would have taken more, a hundredfold. She did not want to drink the wine he kept tilting into her glass, but, with the acceptance learned by women who have lived her life, she did not refuse. She had never refused him anything.

Laurence drank deeply. The wine gave an edge to these few hours of pleasure, an exaltation of energy. It dulled his sense of pity, too. It was pity he was afraid of—for himself and for this girl. To make even this tawdry room look beautiful, with firelight and candlelight, dark amber wine in the glasses, tall pink lilies spilling their saffron, exuding their hot perfume—she and even himself must look their best. Not even music was lacking to their feast. Someone was playing a pianola across the street, and the sound, very faint, came stealing—swelling, sinking, festive, mournful; having a far-off life of its own, like the flickering fire-flames before which they lay embraced, or the lilies delicate between the candles. Listening to that music, tracing with his finger the tiny veins on her breast, he lay like one recovering from a swoon. No parting. None! But sleep, as the firelight sleeps when flames die; as music sleeps on its deserted strings!

And the girl watched him.

It was nearly ten when he bade her go to bed. And after she had gone obedient into the bedroom, he brought ink and paper down by the fire. The drifter, the unstable, the good-for- nothing—did not falter. He had thought, when it came to the point, he would fail himself; but a sort of rage bore him forward. If he lived on and confessed, they would shut him up, take from him the one thing he loved, cut him off from her; sand up his only well in the desert. Curse them! And he wrote by firelight which mellowed the white sheets of paper; while, against the dark curtain, the girl, in her nightgown, unconscious of the cold, stood watching.

A man, when he drowns, remembers his past. Like the lost poet he had "gone with the wind." Now it was for him to be true in his fashion. A man may falter for weeks and weeks, consciously, subconsciously, even in his dreams, till there comes that moment when the only thing impossible is to go on faltering. The black cap, the little driven grey man looking up at it with a sort of wonder— faltering had ceased!

He had finished now, and was but staring into the fire.

The fire, the candles, and the fire—no more the flame and flicker!

And, by the dark curtain, the girl watched.

X

Keith went, not home, but to his club; and in the room devoted to the reception of guests, empty at this hour, he sat down and read the report of the trial. The fools had made out a case that looked black enough. And for a long time, on the thick soft carpet which let out no sound of footfall, he paced up and down, thinking. He might see the defending counsel, might surely do that as an expert who thought there had been miscarriage of justice. They must appeal; a

petition, too, might be started in the last event. The thing could—
must be put right yet, if only Larry and that girl did nothing!

He had no appetite, but the custom of dining is too strong. And
while he ate, he glanced with irritation at his fellow members. They
looked so at their ease. Unjust—that this black cloud should hang
over one blameless as any of them! Friends, connoisseurs of such
things—a judge among them—came specially to his table to express
their admiration of his conduct of that will case. To-night he had real
excuse for pride, but he felt none. Yet, in this well-warmed quietly
glowing room, filled with decorously eating, decorously talking
men, he gained insensibly some comfort. This surely was reality; that
shadowy business out there only the drear sound of a wind one must
and did keep out—like the poverty and grime which had no real
existence for the secure and prosperous. He drank champagne. It
helped to fortify reality, to make shadows seem more shadowy. And
down in the smoking-room he sat before the fire, in one of those
chairs which embalm after-dinner dreams. He grew sleepy there, and
at eleven o'clock rose to go home. But when he had once passed
down the shallow marble steps, out through the revolving door which
let in no draughts, he was visited by fear, as if he had drawn it in with
the breath of the January wind. Larry's face; and the girl watching it!
Why had she watched like that? Larry's smile; the flowers in his hand?
Buying flowers at such a moment! The girl was his slave—whatever
he told her, she would do. But she would never be able to stop him. At
this very moment he might be rushing to give himself up!

His hand, thrust deep into the pocket of his fur coat, came in
contact suddenly with something cold. The keys Larry had given
him all that time ago. There they had lain forgotten ever since. The
chance touch decided him. He turned off towards Borrow Street,
walking at full speed. He could but go again and see. He would sleep
better if he knew that he had left no stone unturned. At the corner
of that dismal street he had to wait for solitude before he made for
the house which he now loathed with a deadly loathing. He opened
the outer door and shut it to behind him. He knocked, but no one
came. Perhaps they had gone to bed. Again and again he knocked,
then opened the door, stepped in, and closed it carefully. Candles

lighted, the fire burning; cushions thrown on the floor in front of
it and strewn with flowers! The table, too, covered with flowers and
with the remnants of a meal. Through the half-drawn curtain he
could see that the inner room was also lighted. Had they gone out,
leaving everything like this? Gone out! His heart beat. Bottles! Larry
had been drinking!

Had it really come? Must he go back home with this murk
on him; knowing that his brother was a confessed and branded
murderer? He went quickly to the half-drawn curtains and looked
in. Against the wall he saw a bed, and those two in it. He recoiled
in sheer amazement and relief. Asleep with curtains undrawn, lights
left on? Asleep through all his knocking! They must both be drunk.
The blood rushed up in his neck. Asleep! And rushing forward
again, he called out: "Larry!" Then, with a gasp he went towards
the bed. "Larry!" No answer! No movement! Seizing his brother's
shoulder, he shook it violently. It felt cold. They were lying in each
other's arms, breast to breast, lips to lips, their faces white in the light
shining above the dressing-table. And such a shudder shook Keith
that he had to grasp the brass rail above their heads. Then he bent
down, and, wetting his finger, placed it close to their joined lips. No
two could ever swoon so utterly as that; not even a drunken sleep
could be so fast. His wet finger felt not the faintest stir of air, nor
was there any movement in the pulses of their hands. No breath! No
life! The eyes of the girl were closed. How strangely innocent she
looked! Larry's open eyes seemed to be gazing at her shut eyes; but
Keith saw that they were sightless. With a sort of sob he drew down
the lids. Then, by an impulse that he could never have explained,
he laid a hand on his brother's head, and a hand on the girl's fair
hair. The clothes had fallen down a little from her bare shoulder; he
pulled them up, as if to keep her warm, and caught the glint of metal;
a tiny gilt crucifix no longer than a thumb nail, on a thread of steel
chain, had slipped down from her breast into the hollow of the arm
which lay round Larry's neck. Keith buried it beneath the clothes
and noticed an envelope pinned to the coverlet; bending down he
read: "Please give this at once to the police.—Laurence Darrant." He
thrust it into his pocket. Like elastic stretched beyond its uttermost,

his reason, will, faculties of calculation and resolve snapped to within him. He thought with incredible swiftness: 'I must know nothing of this. I must go!' And, almost before he knew that he had moved, he was out again in the street.

He could never have told of what he thought while he was walking home. He did not really come to himself till he was in his study. There, with a trembling hand, he poured himself out whisky and drank it off! If he had not chanced to go there, the charwoman would have found them when she came in the morning, and given that envelope to the police! He took it out. He had a right—a right to know what was in it! He broke it open.

> "I, Laurence Darrant, about to die by my own hand, declare that this is a solemn and true confession. I committed what is known as the Glove Lane Murder on the night of November the 27th last in the following way"—on and on to the last words—"We didn't want to die; but we could not bear separation, and I couldn't face letting an innocent man be hung for me. I do not see any other way. I beg that there may be no *post-mortem* on our bodies. The stuff we have taken is some of that which will be found on the dressing-table. Please bury us together.
>
> "Laurence Darrant.
> *January the 28th*, about ten o'clock p.m."

Full five minutes Keith stood with those sheets of paper in his hand, while the clock ticked, the wind moaned a little in the trees outside, the flames licked the logs with the quiet click and ruffle of their intense far-away life down there on the hearth. Then he roused himself, and sat down to read the whole again.

There it was, just as Larry had told it to him—nothing left out, very clear; even to the addresses of people who could identify the girl as having once been Walenn's wife or mistress. It would convince. Yes! It would convince.

The sheets dropped from his hand. Very slowly he was grasping the appalling fact that on the floor beside his chair lay the life or death of yet another man; that by taking this confession he had taken into his own hands the fate of the vagabond lying under sentence of death; that he could not give him back his life without incurring the smirch of this disgrace, without even endangering himself. If he let this confession reach the authorities he could never escape the gravest suspicion that he had known of the whole affair during these two months. He would have to attend the inquest, be recognised by that policeman as having come to the archway to see where the body had lain, as having visited the girl the very evening after the murder. Who would believe in the mere coincidence of such visits on the part of the murderer's brother? But apart from that suspicion, the fearful scandal which so sensational an affair must make would mar his career, his life, his young daughter's life! Larry's suicide with this girl would make sensation enough as it was; but nothing to that other. Such a death had its romance; involved him in no way save as a mourner, could perhaps even be hushed up! The other—nothing could hush that up, nothing prevent its ringing to the house-tops. He got up from his chair, and for many minutes roamed the room unable to get his mind to bear on the issue. Images kept starting up before him. The face of the man who handed him wig and gown each morning, puffy and curious, with a leer on it he had never noticed before; his young daughter's lifted eyebrows, mouth drooping, eyes troubled; the tiny gilt crucifix glinting in the hollow of the dead girl's arm; the sightless look in Larry's unclosed eyes; even his own thumb and finger pulling the lids down. And then he saw a street and endless people passing, turning to stare at him. And, stopping in his tramp, he said aloud: "Let them go to hell! Seven days' wonder!" Was he not trustee to that confession! Trustee! After all he had done nothing to be ashamed of, even if he had kept knowledge dark. A brother! Who could blame him? And he picked up those sheets of paper. But, like a great murky hand, the scandal spread itself about him; its coarse malignant voice seemed shouting: "Paiper! … Paiper! … Glove Lane Murder! … Suicide and confession of brother of well-known K.C. … Well-known K.C.'s brother. … Murder and suicide. … Paiper!" Was he to let loose that flood of foulness? Was he, who had done nothing, to smirch his own little daughter's life; to smirch his dead brother, their dead mother—himself, his own valuable, important future? And all for a sewer rat! Let him hang, let the fellow hang if he must! And that was not certain. Appeal! Petition! He might—he should be saved! To have got thus far and then, by his own action, topple himself down!

With a sudden darting movement he thrust the confession in among the burning coals. And a smile licked at the folds in his dark face, like those flames licking the sheets of paper, till they writhed and blackened. With the toe of his boot he dispersed their scorched and crumbling wafer. Stamp them in! Stamp in that man's life! Burnt! No more doubts, no more of this gnawing fear! Burnt? A man—an innocent—sewer rat! Recoiling from the fire he grasped his forehead. Burning hot.

Well, it was done! Only fools without will or purpose regretted. And suddenly he laughed. So Larry had died for nothing! He had no will, no purpose, and was dead! He and that girl might now have been living, loving each other in the warm night, away at the other end of the world, instead of lying dead in the cold night here! Fools and weaklings regretted, suffered from conscience and remorse. A man trod firmly, held to his purpose, no matter what came of it!

He went to the window and drew back the curtain. What was that? A gibbet in the air, a body hanging? Ah! Only the trees—the dark trees—the winter skeleton trees! Recoiling, he returned to his armchair and sat down before the fire. It had been shining like that, the lamp turned low, his chair drawn up, when Larry came in that afternoon two months ago. Bah! He had never come at all! It was a nightmare. He had been asleep. How his head burned! And leaping up, he looked at the calendar on his bureau. "January the 28th!" No dream! His face hardened and darkened. On! Not like Larry! On! On!

[*1914*]

HAD A HORSE

I

SOME quarter of a century ago, there abode in Oxford a small bookmaker called James Shrewin—or more usually "Jimmy," a run-about and damped-down little man, who made a precarious living out of the effect of horses on undergraduates. He had a so-called office just off the "Corn," where he was always open to the patronage of the young bloods of Bullingdon, and other horse-loving coteries, who bestowed on him sufficient money to enable him to live. It was through the conspicuous smash of one of them—young Gardon Colquhoun—that he became the owner of a horse. He had been far from wanting what was in the nature of a white elephant to one of his underground habits, but had taken it in discharge of betting debts, to which, of course, in the event of bankruptcy, he would have no legal claim. She was a three-year-old, chestnut filly, by Lopez out of Calendar, bore the name Calliope, and was trained out on the Downs near Wantage. On a Sunday afternoon, then, in late July "Jimmy" got his friend, George Pulcher, the publican, to drive him out there in his sort of dog-cart.

"Must 'ave a look at the bilkin' mare," he had said: "that young 'Cocoon' told me she was a corker; but what's third to Referee at Sandown, and never ran as a two-year-old? All I know is, she's eatin' 'er 'ead off!"

Beside the plethoric bulk of Pulcher, clad in a light-coloured box cloth coat with enormous whitish buttons and a full-blown rose in the lapel, "Jimmy's" little, thin, dark-clothed form, withered by anxiety and gin, was, as it were, invisible; and compared with Pulcher's setting sun, his face, with shaven cheeks sucked-in, and smudged-in eyes, was like a ghost's under a grey bowler. He spoke off-handedly about his animal, but he was impressed, in a sense abashed, by his ownership. 'What the 'ell?' was his constant thought. Was he going to race her, sell her—what? How, indeed, to get back out of her the sum he had been fool enough to let "young Cocoon" owe him, to say nothing of her trainer's bill? The notion, too of having to confront that trainer with his ownership was oppressive to one whose whole life was passed in keeping out of the foreground of the picture. Owner! He had never owned even a white mouse, let alone a white elephant. And an 'orse would ruin him in no time if he didn't look alive about it!

The son of a small London baker, devoted to errandry at the age of fourteen, "Jimmy" Shrewin owed his profession to a certain smartness at sums, a dislike of baking, and an early habit of hanging about street corners with other boys, who had their daily pennies on an 'orse. He had a narrow calculating head, which pushed him towards street corner books before he was eighteen. From that time on he had been a surreptitious nomad, till he had silted up at Oxford, where, owing to Vice-Chancellors, an expert in underground life had greater scope than elsewhere. When he sat solitary at his narrow table in the back room near the "Corn"—for he had no clerk or associate—eyeing the door, with his lists in a drawer before him, and his black shiny betting book ready for young "bloods," he had a sharp, cold, furtive air, and but for a certain imitated tightness of trousers, and a collar standing up all round, gave no impression of ever having heard of the quadruped called horse. Indeed, for "Jimmy" "horse" was a newspaper quantity with figures against its various names. Even when, for a short spell, hanger on to a firm of cheap-ring bookmakers, he had seen almost nothing of horse; his racecourse hours were spent ferreting among a bawling, perspiring crowd, or hanging round within earshot of tight-lipped nobs, trainers, jockeys, anyone who looked like having "information." Nowadays he never went near a race-meeting—his business, of betting on races, giving him no chance—yet his conversation seldom deviated for more than a minute at a time from that physically unknown animal the horse. The ways of making money out of it, infinite, intricate, variegated, occupied the mind in all his haunts, to the accompaniment of liquid and tobacco. Gin and bitters was "Jimmy's" drink; for choice he smoked cheroots; and he would cherish in his mouth the cold stump of one long after it had gone out, for the homely feeling it gave him, while he talked, or listened to talk on horses. He was of that vast number, town bred, who, like crows round a carcase, feed on that which to them is not alive. And now he had a horse!

The dog-cart travelled at a clinking pace behind Pulcher's bob-tail. "Jimmy's" cheroot burned well in the warm July air; the dust powdered his dark clothes and pinched, sallow face. He thought with malicious pleasure of that young spark "Cocoon's" collapse—high-'anded lot of young fools, thinking themselves so knowing; many were the grins, and not few the grittings of his blackened teeth he had to smother at their swagger. "Jimmy, you robber!" "Jimmy, you little blackguard!" Young sparks—gay and languid—well, one of 'em had gone out!

He looked round with his screwed-up eyes at his friend George Pulcher, who, man and licensed victualler, had his bally independence; lived remote from "the Quality" in his Paradise, "The Green Dragon"; had not to kow-tow to anyone; went to Newbury, Gatwick, Stockbridge, here and there, at will. Ah! George Pulcher had the ideal life—and looked it: crimson, square, full-bodied. Judge of a horse, too, in his own estimation; a leery bird—for whose judgment "Jimmy" had respect—who got "the office" of any clever work as quick as most men! And he said:

"What am I going to do with this blinkin' 'orse, George?"

Without moving its head the oracle spoke, in a voice rich and raw: "Let's 'ave a look at her first, Jimmy! Don't like her name—Calliope; but you can't change what's in the Stud-book. This Jenning that trains 'er is a crusty chap."

"Jimmy" nervously sucked-in his lips. The cart was mounting through the hedgeless fields which fringed the Downs; larks were singing, the wheat was very green, and patches of charlock brightened everything; it was lonely, few trees, few houses, no people, extreme peace, just a few rooks crossing under a blue sky.

"Wonder if he'll offer us a drink?" said "Jimmy."

"Not he; but help yourself, my son."

"Jimmy" helped himself from a large wicker-covered flask.

"Good for you, George—here's how!"

The large man shifted the reins and drank, in turn, tilting up a face whose jaw still struggled to assert itself against chins and neck.

"Well, here's your bloomin' horse," he said. "She can't win the Derby now, but she may do us a bit of good yet."

II

The trainer, Jenning, coming from his Sunday afternoon round of the boxes, heard the sound of wheels. He was a thin man, neat in clothes and hoots, medium in height, with a slight limp, narrow grey whiskers, thin shaven lips, eyes sharp and grey.

A dog-cart stopping at his yard-gate and a rum-looking couple of customers!

"Well, gentlemen?"

"Mr. Jenning? My name's Pulcher—George Pulcher. Brought a client of yours over to see his new mare. Mr. James Shrewin, Oxford city."

"Jimmy" got down and stood before his trainer's uncompromising stare.

"What mare's that?" said Jenning.

"Calliope."

"Calliope—Mr. Colquhoun's?"

"Jimmy" held out a letter.

> "Dear Jennings,
> "I have sold Calliope to Jimmy Shrewin, the Oxford bookie. He takes her with all engagements and liabilities, including your training bill. I'm frightfully sick at having to part with her, but needs must when the devil drives.
> "Gardon Colquhoun."

The trainer folded the letter.

"Got proof of registration?"

"Jimmy" drew out another paper.

The trainer inspected it, and called out: "Ben, bring out Calliope. Excuse me a minute," and he walked into his house.

"Jimmy" stood, shifting from leg to leg. Mortification had set in; the dry abruptness of the trainer had injured even a self-esteem starved from youth.

The voice of Pulcher boomed. "Told you he was a crusty devil. 'And 'im a bit of his own."

The trainer was coming back.

"My bill," he said. "When you've paid it you can have the mare. I train for gentlemen."

"The hell you do!" said Pulcher.

"Jimmy" said nothing, staring at the bill—seventy-eight pounds three shillings! A buzzing fly settled in the hollow of his cheek, and he did not even brush it off. Seventy-eight pounds!

The sound of hoofs roused him. Here came his horse, throwing up her head as if enquiring why she was being disturbed a second time on Sunday! In the movement of that small head and satin neck was something free and beyond present company.

"There she is," said the trainer. "That'll do, Ben. Stand, girl!"

Answering to a jerk or two of the halter, the mare stood kicking slightly with a white hind foot and whisking her tail. Her bright coat shone in the sunlight, and little shivers and wrinklings passed up and down its satin because of the flies. Then, for a moment, she stood still, ears pricked, eyes on the distance.

"Jimmy" approached her. She had resumed her twitchings, swishings, and slight kicking, and at a respectful distance he circled, bending as if looking at crucial points. He knew what her sire and dam had done, and all the horses that had beaten, or been beaten by them; could have retailed by the half-hour the peculiar hearsay of their careers; and here was their offspring in flesh and blood, and he was dumb! He didn't know a thing about what she ought to look like, and he knew it; but he felt obscurely moved. She seemed to him "a picture."

Completing his circle, he approached her head, white-blazed, thrown up again in listening, or scenting and gingerly he laid his hand on her neck, warm and smooth as a woman's shoulder. She paid no attention to his touch, and he took his hand away. Ought he to look at her teeth or feel her legs? No, he was not buying her, she was his already; but he must say something. He looked round. The trainer was watching him with a little smile. For almost the first time in his life the worm turned in "Jimmy" Shrewin; he spoke no word and walked back to the cart.

"Take her in," said Jenning.

From his seat beside Pulcher, "Jimmy" watched the mare returning to her box.

"When I've cashed your cheque," said the trainer, "you can send for her"; and, turning on his heel, he went towards his house. The voice of Pulcher followed him.

"Blast your impudence! Git on, bob-tail, we'll shake the dust off 'ere."

Among the fringing fields the dog-cart hurried away. The sun slanted, the heat grew less, the colour of young wheat and of the charlock brightened.

"The tyke! By Gawd, 'Jimmy,' I'd 'ave hit him on the mug! But you've got one there. She's a bit o' blood, my boy; and I know the trainer for her, Polman—no blasted airs about 'im."

"Jimmy" sucked at his cheroot.

"I ain't had your advantages, George, and that's a fact. I got into it too young, and I'm a little chap. But I'll send the —— my cheque to-morrow. I got my pride, I 'ope." It was the first time that thought had ever come to him.

III

Though not quite the centre of the Turf, the Green Dragon had nursed a coup in its day, nor was it without a sense of veneration. The ownership of Calliope invested "Jimmy" Shrewin with the

importance of those out of whom something can be had. It took time
for one so long accustomed to beck and call, to mole-like procedure,
and the demeanour of young bloods to realise that he had it. But
slowly, with the marked increase of his unpaid-for cheroots, with the
way in which glasses hung suspended when he came in, with the
edgings up to him, and a certain tendency to accompany him along
the street, it dawned on him that he was not only an out-of-bounds
bookie, but a man. So long as he had remained unconscious of his
double nature he had been content with laying the odds, as best he
might, and getting what he could out of every situation, straight or
crooked. Now that he was also a man, his complacency was ruffled.
He suffered from a growing headiness connected with his horse.
She was trained, now, by Polman, further along the Downs, too far
for Pulcher's bob-tail; and though her public life was carried on at
the Green Dragon, her private life required a train journey over
night. "Jimmy" took it twice a week—touting his own horse in the
August mornings up on the Downs, without drink or talk, or even
cheroots. Early morning, larks singing, and the sound of galloping
hoofs! In a moment of expansion he confided to Pulcher that it was
"bally 'olesome."

There had been the slight difficulty of being mistaken for a tout by
his new trainer Polman, a stoutish man with the look of one of those
large sandy Cornish cats, not precisely furtive because reticence and
craft are their nature. But, that once over, his personality swelled
slowly. This month of August was one of those interludes, in fact,
when nothing happens, but which shape the future by secret
ripening.

An error to suppose that men conduct finance, high or low, from
greed, or love of gambling; they do it out of self-esteem, out of
an itch to prove their judgment superior to their neighbours', out
of a longing for importance. George Pulcher did not despise the
turning of a penny, but he valued much more the consciousness that
men were saying: "Old George, what 'e says goes—knows a thing or
two—George Pulcher!"

To pull the strings of "Jimmy" Shrewin's horse was a rich and
subtle opportunity absorbingly improvable. But first one had to study

the animal's engagements, and, secondly, to gauge that unknown quantity, her "form." To make anything of her this year they must "get about it." That young "toff," her previous owner, had of course flown high, entering her for classic races, high-class handicaps, neglecting the rich chances of lesser occasions.

Third to Referee in the three-year-old race at Sandown Spring—two heads—was all that was known of her, and now they had given her seven two in the Cambridgeshire. She might have a chance, and again she might not. He sat two long evenings with "Jimmy" in the little private room off the bar, deliberating this grave question.

"Jimmy" inclined to the bold course. He kept saying: "The mare's a flyer, George—she's the 'ell of a flyer!"

"Wait till she's been tried," said the oracle.

Had Polman anything that would give them a line?

Yes, he had The Shirker (named with that irony which appeals to the English), one of the most honest four-year-olds that ever looked through bridle, who had run up against almost every animal of mark—the one horse that Polman never interfered with, for if interrupted in his training, he ran all the better; who seldom won, but was almost always placed—the sort of horse that handicappers pivot on.

"But," said Pulcher, "try her with The Shirker, and the first stable money will send her up to tens. That 'orse is so darned regular. We've got to throw a bit of dust first, 'Jimmy.' I'll go over and see Polman."

In "Jimmy's" withered chest a faint resentment rose—it wasn't George's horse; but it sank again beneath his friend's bulk and reputation.

The "bit of dust" was thrown at the ordinary hour of exercise over the Long Mile on the last day of August—the five-year-old Hangman carrying eight stone seven, the three-year-old Parrot seven stone five; what Calliope was carrying nobody but Polman knew. The forethought of George Pulcher had secured the unofficial presence of the Press. The instructions to the boy on Calliope were to be there at the finish if he could, but on no account to win. "Jimmy" and George Pulcher had come out over night. They sat together in the dog-cart by the clump of bushes which marked the winning-post, with Polman on his cob on the far side.

By a fine, warm light the three horses were visible to the naked eye in the slight dip down by the start. And, through the glasses, invested in now that he had a horse, "Jimmy" could see every movement of his mare with her blazed face—rather on her toes, like the bright chestnut and "bit o' blood" she was. He had a pit-patting in his heart, and his lips were tight pressed. Suppose she was no good after all, and that young "Cocoon" had palmed him off a pup! But mixed in with his financial fear was an anxiety more intimate, as if his own value were at stake.

From George Pulcher came an almost excited gurgle.

"See the tout! See 'im behind that bush. Thinks we don't know 'e's there, wot oh!"

Rather wide, the black Hangman on the far side, Calliope in the middle, they came sweeping up the long mile. "Jimmy" held his tobaccoed breath. The mare was going freely—a length or two behind—making up her ground! Now for it!—

Ah! she 'ad the 'Angman beat, and ding-dong with this Parrot! It was all he could do to keep from calling out. With a rush and a cludding of hoofs they passed—the blazed nose just behind the Parrot's bay nose— dead heat all but, with the Hangman beat a good length!

"There 'e goes, 'Jimmy'! See the blank scuttlin' down the 'ill like a blinkin' rabbit. That'll be in to-morrow's paper, that trial will. Ah! but 'ow to read it—that's the point."

The horses had been wheeled and were sidling back; Polman was going forward on his cob.

"Jimmy" jumped down. Whatever that fellow had to say, he meant to hear. It was his horse! Narrowly avoiding the hoofs of his hot, fidgeting mare, he said sharply:

"What about it?"

Polman never looked you in the face; his speech came as if not intended to be heard by anyone:

"Tell Mr. Shrewin how she went."

"Had a bit up my sleeve. If I'd hit her a smart one, I could ha' landed by a length or more."

"That so? " said "Jimmy" with a hiss. "Well, *don't* you hit her; she don't want hittin'. You remember that."

The boy said sulkily: "All right!"

"Take her home," said Polman. Then, with that reflective averted air of his, he added: "She was carrying eight stone, Mr. Shrewin; you've got a good one there. She's the Hangman at level weights."

Something wild leaped up in "Jimmy"—the Hangman's form unrolled itself before him in the air—he had a horse—he dam' well had a horse!

IV

But how delicate is the process of backing your fancy! The planting of a commission—what tender and efficient work before it will flower! That sixth sense of the racing man, which, like the senses of savages in great forests, seizes telepathically on what is not there, must be dulled, duped, deluded.

George Pulcher had the thing in hand. One might have thought the gross man incapable of such a fairy touch, such power of sowing with one hand and reaping with the other. He intimated rather than asserted that Calliope and the Parrot were one and the same thing. "The Parrot," he said, "couldn't win with seven stone—no use thinkin' of this Calliope."

Local opinion was the rock on which, like a great tactician, he built. So long as local opinion was adverse, he could dribble money on in London; the natural jump-up from every long shot taken was dragged back by the careful radiation of disparagement from the seat of knowledge.

"Jimmy" was the fly in his ointment of those balmy early weeks while snapping up every penny of long odds, before suspicion could begin to work from the persistence of enquiry. Half-a-dozen times he found the "little cuss within an ace of blowing the gaff on his own blinkin' mare"; seemed unable to run his horse down; the little beggar's head was swellin'! Once "Jimmy" had even got up and gone

out, leaving a gin and bitters untasted on the bar. Pulcher improved
on his absence in the presence of a London tout.

"Saw the trial meself! 'Jimmy' don't like to think he's got a stiff
'un."

And next morning his London agent snapped up some thirty-
threes again.

According to the trial the mare was the Hangman at seven stone
two, and really hot stuff—a seven-to-one chance. It was none the
less with a sense of outrage that, opening the *Sporting Life* on the
last day of September, he found her quoted at 100-8. Whose work
was this?

He reviewed the altered situation in disgust. He had invested about
half the stable commission of three hundred pounds at an average of
thirty-to-one, but, now that she had "come" in the betting, he would
hardly average tens with the rest. What fool had put his oar in?

He learned the explanation two days later. The rash, the unknown
backer, was "Jimmy"! He had acted, it appeared, from jealousy; a
bookmaker—it took one's breath away!

"Backed her on your own just because that young 'Cocoon' told
you he fancied her!"

"Jimmy" looked up from the table in his "office," where he was
sitting in wait for the scanty custom of the Long Vacation.

"She's not his horse," he said sullenly. "I wasn't going to have him
get the cream."

"What did you put on?" growled Pulcher.

"Took five hundred to thirty, and fifteen twenties."

"An' see what it's done—knocked the bottom out of the
commission. Am I to take that fifty as part of it?"

"Jimmy" nodded.

"That leaves an 'undred to invest," said Pulcher, somewhat
mollified. He stood, with his mind twisting in his thick still body.
"It's no good waitin' now," he said; "I'll work the rest of the money
on to-day. If I can average tens on the balance, we'll 'ave six thousand
three hundred to play with and the stakes. They tell me Jenning
fancies this Diamond Stud of his. *He* ought to know the form with
Calliope, blast him! We got to watch that."

They had! Diamond Stud, a four-year-old with eight stone two, was being backed as if the Cambridgeshire were over. From fifteens he advanced to sevens, thence to favouritism at fives. Pulcher bit on it. Jenning *must* know where he stood with Calliope! It meant—it meant she couldn't win! The tactician wasted no time in vain regret. Establish Calliope in the betting and lay off. The time had come to utilise The Shirker.

It was misty on the Downs—fine-weather mist of a bright October. The three horses became spectral on their way to the starting-point. Polman had thrown the Parrot in again, but this time he made no secret of the weights. The Shirker was carrying eight seven, Calliope eight, the Parrot seven stone.

Once more, in the cart, with his glasses sweeping the bright mist, "Jimmy" had that pit-patting in his heart. Here they came! His mare leading—all riding hard—a genuine finish! They passed—The Shirker beaten, a clear length, with the Parrot at his girth. Beside him in the cart, George Pulcher mumbled:

"She's The Shirker at eight stone four, 'Jimmy'!"

A silent drive, big with thought, back to a river inn; a silent breakfast. Over a tankard at the close the Oracle spoke.

"The Shirker, at eight stone four, is a good 'ot chance, but no cert, 'Jimmy.' We'll let 'em know this trial quite open, weights and all. That'll bring her in the betting. And we'll watch Diamond Stud. If he drops back we'll know Jenning thinks he can't beat us now. If Diamond Stud stands up, we'll know Jenning thinks he's still got our mare safe. Then our line'll be clear: we lay off the lot, pick up a thousand or so, and 'ave the mare in at a nice weight at Liverpool."

"Jimmy's" smudged-in eyes stared hungrily.

"How's that?" he said. "Suppose she wins!"

"Wins! If we lay off the lot, she *won't* win."

"Pull her! "

George Pulcher's voice sank half an octave with disgust.

"Pull her! Who talked of pullin'? She'll run a bye, that's all. We shan't ever know whether she could 'a won or not."

"Jimmy" sat silent; the situation was such as his life during sixteen years had waited for. They stood to win both ways with a bit of handling.

"Who's to ride?" he said.

"Polman's got a call on Docker. He can just ride the weight. Either way he's good for us—strong finisher, and a rare judge of distance; knows how to time things to a T. Win or not, he's our man."

"Jimmy" was deep in figures. Laying-off at sevens, they would still win four thousand and the stakes.

"I'd like a win," he said.

"Ah!" said Pulcher. "But there'll be twenty in the field, my son; no more uncertain race than that bally Cambridgeshire. We could pick up a thou——as easy as I pick up this pot. Bird in the 'and, 'Jimmy,' and a good 'andicap in the bush. If she wins, she's finished. Well, we'll put this trial about and see 'ow Jenning pops."

Jenning popped amazingly. Diamond Stud receded a point, then re-established himself at nine to two. Jenning was clearly not dismayed.

George Pulcher shook his head, and waited, uncertain still which way to jump. Ironical circumstance decided him.

Term had begun; "Jimmy" was busy at his seat of custom. By some miracle of guardianly intervention, young Colquhoun had not gone broke. He was "up" again, eager to retrieve his reputation, and that little brute "Jimmy" would not lay against his horse! He merely sucked in his cheeks, and answered: "I'm not layin' my own 'orse." It was felt that he was not the man he had been; assertion had come into his manner, he was better dressed. Someone had seen him at the station looking quite a "toff" in a blue box-cloth coat standing well out from his wisp of a figure, and with a pair of brown race-glasses slung over the shoulder. Altogether the "little brute was getting too big for his boots."

And this strange improvement hardened the feeling that his horse was a real good thing. Patriotism began to burn in Oxford. Here was a "snip" that belonged to them, as it were, and the money in support of it, finding no outlet, began to ball.

A week before the race—with Calliope at nine to one, and very little doing—young Colquhoun went up to town, taking with him the accumulated support of betting Oxford. That evening she stood at sixes. Next day the public followed on.

George Pulcher took advantage. In this crisis of the proceedings he acted on his own initiative. The mare went back to eights, but the deed was done. He had laid off the whole bally lot, including the stake money. He put it to "Jimmy" that evening in a nutshell.

"We pick up a thousand, and the Liverpool as good as in our pocket. I've done worse."

"Jimmy" grunted out: "She could 'a won."

"Not she. Jenning knows—and there's others in the race. This Wasp is goin' to take a lot of catchin', and Deerstalker's not out of it. He's a hell of a horse, even with that weight."

Again "Jimmy" grunted, slowly sucking down his gin and bitters. Sullenly he said:

"Well, I don't want to put money in the pocket of young 'Cocoon' and his crowd. Like his impudence, backin' my horse as if it was his own."

"We'll 'ave to go and see her run, 'Jimmy.'"

"Not me," said "Jimmy."

"What! First time she runs! It won't look natural."

"No," repeated "Jimmy." "I don't want to see 'er beat."

George Pulcher laid his hand on a skinny shoulder.

"Nonsense, 'Jimmy.' You've got to, for the sake of your reputation. You'll enjoy seein' your mare saddled. We'll go up over night. I shall 'ave a few pound on Deerstalker. I believe he can beat this Diamond Stud. And you leave Docker to me; I'll 'ave a word with him at Gatwick to-morrow. I've known 'im since he was that 'igh; an' 'e ain't much more now."

"All right!" growled "Jimmy."

V

The longer you can bet on a race the greater its fascination. Handicappers can properly enjoy the beauty of their work; clubmen and oracles of the course have due scope for reminiscence and prophecy; bookmakers in lovely leisure can indulge a little their own calculated preferences, instead of being hurried to soulless conclusions by a half-hour's market on the course; the professional backer has the longer in which to dream of his fortune made at last by some hell of a horse—spotted somewhere as interfered with, left at the post, running green, too fat, not fancied, backward—now bound to win this hell of a race. And the general public has the chance to read the horses' names in the betting news for days and days; and what a comfort that is!

"Jimmy" Shrew-in was not one of those philosophers who justify the great and growing game of betting on the ground that it improves the breed of an animal less and less in use. He justified it much more simply—he lived by it. And in the whole of his career of nearly twenty years since he made hole-and-corner books among the boys of London, he had never stood so utterly on velvet as that morning when his horse must win him five hundred pounds by merely losing. He had spent the night in London anticipating a fraction of his gains with George Pulcher at a music-hall. And, in a first-class carriage, as became an owner, he travelled down to Newmarket by an early special. An early special key turned in the lock of the carriage door, preserved their numbers at six, all professionals, with blank, rather rolling eyes, mouths shut or slightly fishy, ears to the ground; and the only natural talker a red-faced man, who had "been at it thirty years." Intoning the pasts and futures of this hell of a horse or that, even he was silent on the race in hand; and the journey was half over before the beauty of their own judgments loosened tongues thereon. George Pulcher started it.

"I fancy Deerstalker," he said: "he's a hell of a horse."

"Too much weight," said the red-faced man. "What about this Calliope?"

"Ah!" said Pulcher. "D'you fancy your mare, 'Jimmy'?"

With all eyes turned on him, lost in his blue box-cloth coat, brown bowler, and cheroot smoke, "Jimmy" experienced a subtle thrill. Addressing the space between the red-faced man and Pulcher, he said:

"If she runs up to 'er looks."

"Ah!" said Pulcher, "she's dark—nice mare, but a bit light and shelly."

"Lopez out o' Calendar," muttered the red-faced man. "Lopez didn't stay, but he was the hell of a horse over seven furlongs. The Shirker ought to 'ave told you a bit."

"Jimmy" did not answer. It gave him pleasure to see the red-faced man's eye trying to get past, and failing.

"Nice race to pick up. Don't fancy the favourite meself; he'd nothin' to beat at Ascot."

"Jenning knows what he's about," said Pulcher.

Jenning! Before "Jimmy's" mind passed again that first sight of his horse, and the trainer's smile, as if he—Jimmy Shrewin, who owned her—had been dirt. Tyke! To have the mare beaten by one of his! A deep, subtle vexation had oppressed him at times all these last days since George Pulcher had decided in favour of the mare's running a bye. D—n George Pulcher! He took too much on himself! Thought he had "Jimmy" Shrewin in his pocket! He looked at the block of crimson opposite. Aunt Sally! If George Pulcher could tell what was passing in his mind!

But driving up to the Course he was not above sharing a sandwich and a flask. In fact, his feelings were unstable and gusty—sometimes resentment, sometimes the old respect for his friend's independent bulk. The dignity of ownership takes long to establish itself in those who have been kicked about.

"All right with Docker," murmured Pulcher, sucking at the wicker flask. "I gave him the office at Gatwick."

"She could 'a won," muttered "Jimmy."

"Not she, my boy; there's two at least can beat 'er."

Like all oracles, George Pulcher could believe what he wanted to.

Arriving, they entered the grand-stand enclosure, and over the dividing railings "Jimmy" gazed at the Cheap Ring, already filling up with its usual customers. Faces and umbrellas—the same old crowd. How often had he been in that Cheap Ring, with hardly room to move, seeing nothing, hearing nothing but "Two to one on the field!" "Two to one on the field!" "Threes Swordfish!" "Fives Alabaster!" "Two to one on the field!" Nothing but a sea of men like himself, and a sky overhead. He was not exactly conscious of criticism, only of a dull "Glad I'm shut of that lot" feeling.

Leaving George Pulcher deep in conversation with a crony, he lighted a cheroot and slipped out on to the Course. He passed the Jockey Club enclosure. Some early "tolls" were there in twos and threes, exchanging wisdom. He looked at them without envy or malice. He was an owner himself now, almost one of them in a manner of thinking. With a sort of relish he thought of how his past life had circled round those "toffs," slippery, shadowlike, kicked about; and now he could get up on the Downs away from "tolls," George Pulcher, all that crowd, and smell the grass, and hear the bally larks, and watch his own mare gallop!

They were putting the numbers up for the first race. Queer not to be betting, not to be touting round; queer to be giving it a rest! Utterly familiar with those names on the board, he was utterly unfamiliar with the shapes they stood for.

'I'll go and see 'em come out of the paddock,' he thought, and moved on, skimpy in his bell-shaped coat and billycock with flattened brim. The clamour of the Rings rose behind him while he was entering the paddock.

Very green, very peaceful, there; not many people, yet! Three horses in the second race were being led slowly in a sort of winding ring; and men were clustering round the further gate where the horses would come out. "Jimmy" joined them, sucking at his cheroot. They were a picture! Damn it! he didn't know, but that 'orses laid over men! Pretty creatures!

One by one they passed out of the gate, a round dozen. Selling platers, but pictures for all that!

He turned back towards the horses being led about; and the old instinct to listen took him close to little groups. Talk was all of the big race. From a tall "toff" he caught the word Calliope.

"Belongs to a bookie, they say."

Bookie! Why not? Wasn't a bookie as good as any other? Ah! and sometimes better than these young snobs with everything to their hand! A bookie—well, what chance had he ever had?

A big brown horse came by.

"That's Deerstalker," he heard the "toff" say.

"Jimmy" gazed at George Pulcher's fancy with a sort of hostility. Here came another—Wasp, six stone ten, and Deerstalker nine stone—top and bottom of the race!

'My 'orse'd beat either o' them,' he thought stubbornly. 'Don't like that Wasp.'

The distant roar was hushed. They were running in the first race! He moved back to the gate. The quick clamour rose and dropped, and here they came—back into the paddock, darkened with sweat, flanks heaving a little!

"Jimmy" followed the winner, saw the jockey weigh in.

"What jockey's that?" he asked.

"That? Why, Docker!"

"Jimmy" stared. A short, square, bow-legged figure, with a hardwood face! Waiting his chance, he went up to him and said:

"Docker, you ride my 'orse in the big race."

"Mr. Shrewin?"

"The same," said "Jimmy." The jockey's left eyelid dropped a little. Nothing responded in "Jimmy's" face. "I'll see you before the race," he said.

Again the jockey's eyelid wavered, he nodded and passed on.

"Jimmy" stared at his own boots; they struck him suddenly as too yellow and not at the right angle. But why, he couldn't say.

More horses now—those of the first race being unsaddled, clothed, and led away. More men—three familiar figures: young "Cocoon" and two others of his Oxford customers.

"Jimmy" turned sharply from them. Stand their airs?—not he! He had a sudden sickish feeling. With a win, he'd have been a made man—on his own! Blast George Pulcher and his caution! To think of being back in Oxford with those young bloods jeering at his beaten horse! He bit deep into the stump of his cheroot, and suddenly came on Jenning standing by a horse with a star on its bay forehead. The trainer gave him no sign of recognition, but signed to the boy to lead the horse into a stall, and followed, shutting the door. It was exactly as if he had said: "Vermin about!"

An evil little smile curled "Jimmy's" lips. The tyke!

The horses for the second race passed out of the paddock gate, and he turned to find his own. His ferreting eyes soon sighted Polman. What the cat-faced fellow knew, or was thinking, "Jimmy" could not tell. Nobody could tell.

"Where's the mare?" he said.

"Just coming round."

No mistaking her; fine as a star; shiny-coated, sinuous, her blazed face held rather high! Who said she was "shelly"? She was a picture! He walked a few paces close to the boy.

"That's Calliope. … H'm! … Nice filly! … Looks fit. … Who's this James Shrewin? … What's she at? … I like her looks."

His horse! Not a prettier filly in the world!

He followed Polman into her stall to see her saddled. In the twilight there he watched her toilet; the rub-over; the exact adjustments; the bottle of water to the mouth; the buckling of the bridle—watched her head high above the boy keeping her steady with gentle pulls of a rein in each hand held out a little wide, and now and then stroking her blazed nose; watched her pretence of nipping at his hand: he watched the beauty of her exaggerated in this half-lit isolation away from the others, the life and litheness in her satin body, the wilful expectancy in her bright soft eyes.

Run a bye! This bit o' blood—this bit o' fire! This horse of his! Deep within that shell of blue box-cloth against the stall partition a thought declared itself: 'I'm —— if she shall! She can beat the lot! And she's—well going to!'

The door was thrown open, and she led out. He moved alongside. They were staring at her, following her. No wonder! She was a picture, his horse—his! She had gone to "Jimmy's" head.

They passed Jenning with Diamond Stud waiting to be mounted. "Jimmy" shot him a look. Let the —— wait!

His mare reached the palings and was halted. "Jimmy" saw the short square figure of her jockey, in the new magenta cap and jacket—*his* cap, *his* jacket! Beautiful they looked, and no mistake!

"A word with you," he said.

The jockey halted, looked quickly round.

"All right, Mr. Shrewin. I know."

"Jimmy's" eyes smouldered at him; hardly moving his lips, he said, intently: "You —— well don't! You'll —— well ride her to win. Never mind *him*! If you don't, I'll have you off the turf. Understand me! You'll —— well ride 'er to win."

The jockey's jaw dropped.

"All right, Mr. Shrewin."

See it is," said " Jimmy" with a hiss.

"Mount jockeys!"

He saw magenta swing into the saddle. And suddenly, as if smitten with the plague, he scuttled away.

VI

He scuttled to where he could see them going down—seventeen. No need to search for his colours; they blazed, like George Pulcher's countenance, or a rhododendron bush in sunlight, above that bright chestnut with the white nose, curveting a little as she was led past.

Now they came cantering—Deerstalker in the lead.

"He's a hell of a horse, Deerstalker," said someone behind.

"Jimmy" cast a nervous glance around. No sign of George Pulcher!

One by one they cantered past, and he watched them with a cold feeling in his stomach. Still unused to sight of the creatures out of which he made his living, they *all* seemed to him hells of horses.

The same voice said:

"New colours! Well, you can see 'em, and the mare too. She's a showy one. Calliope? She's goin' back in the bettin', though."

"Jimmy" moved up through the Ring.

"Four to one on the field!""Six Deerstalker!""Sevens Magistrate!" "Ten to one Wasp!""Ten to one Calliope!""Four to one Diamond Stud!""Four to one on the field!"

Steady as a rock, that horse of Jenning, and his own going back!

"Twelves Calliope!" he heard, just as he reached the stand. The telepathic genius of the Ring missed nothing—almost!

A cold shiver went through him. What had he done by his words to Docker? Spoiled the golden egg laid so carefully? But perhaps she couldn't win even if they let her! He began to mount the stand, his mind in the most acute confusion.

A voice said: "Hullo, 'Jimmy'! Is she going to win?"

One of his young Oxford sparks was jammed against him on the stairway!

He raised his lip in a sort of snarl, and, huddling himself, slipped through and up ahead. He came out and edged in close to the stairs where he could get play for his glasses. Behind him one of those who improve the shining hour among backers cut off from opportunity, was intoning the odds a point shorter than below. "Three to one on the field." "Fives Deerstalker." "Eight to one Wasp."

"What price Calliope?" said "Jimmy," sharply.

"Hundred to eight."

"Done!" Handing him the eight, he took the ticket. Behind him the man's eyes moved fishily, and he resumed his incantation.

"Three to one on the field … three to one on the field. Six to one Magistrate."

On the wheeling bunch of colours at the start "Jimmy" trained his glasses. Something had broken clean away and come half the course—something in yellow.

"Eights Magistrate. Eight to one Magistrate," drifted up. So they had spotted that! Precious little they didn't spot! Magistrate was round again, and being ridden back. "Jimmy" rested his glasses a moment, and looked down. Swarms in the Cheap Ring, Tattersalls, the stands—a crowd so great you could lose George Pulcher in it. Just below a little man was making silent, frantic signals with his arms across to someone in the Cheap Ring. "Jimmy" raised his glasses. In line now—magenta third from the rails!

"They're off!" The hush, you could cut it with a knife! Something in green away on the right—Wasp! What a bat they were going! And a sort of numbness in "Jimmy's" mind cracked suddenly; his glasses shook; his thin, weasley face became suffused and quivered. Magenta—magenta—two from the rails! He could make no story of the race such as he would read in to-morrow's paper—he could see nothing but magenta.

Out of the dip now, and coming fast—green still leading—something in violet, something in tartan, closing.

"Wasp's beat!" "The favourite—the favourite wins!" "Deerstalker—Deerstalker wins!" "What's that in pink on the rails?"

It was *his* in pink on the rails! Behind him a man went suddenly mad.

"Deerstalker—Come on with 'im, Stee! Deerstalker 'll win— Deerstalker 'll win!"

"Jimmy" sputtered venomously: "Will 'e? Will 'e?"

Deerstalker and his own out from the rest—opposite the Cheap Ring—neck and neck—Docker riding like a demon.

"Deerstalker! Deerstalker!"

"Calliope wins! She wins!"

Gawd! His horse! They flashed past—fifty yards to go, and not a head between 'em!

"Deerstalker! Deerstalker!" "Calliope!"

He saw his mare shoot out—she'd won!

With a little queer sound he squirmed and wriggled on to the stairs. No thoughts while he squeezed, and slid, and hurried—only emotion—out of the Ring, away to the paddock. His horse!

Docker had weighed in when he reached the mare. All right! He passed with a grin. "Jimmy" turned almost into the body of Polman standing like an image.

"Well, Mr. Shrewin," he said to nobody, "she's won."

'Damn you!' thought "Jimmy." 'Damn the lot of you!' And he went up to his mare. Quivering, streaked with sweat, impatient of the gathering crowd, she showed the whites of her eyes when he put his hand up to her nose.

"Good girl!" he said, and watched her led away.

'Gawd! I want a drink!' he thought.

Gingerly, keeping a sharp lookout for Pulcher, he returned to the Stand to get it, and to draw his hundred. But up there by the stairs the discreet fellow was no more. On the ticket was the name O.H. Jones, and nothing else. "Jimmy" Shrewin had been welshed! He went down at last in a bad temper. At the bottom of the staircase stood George Pulcher. The big man's face was crimson, his eyes ominous. He blocked "Jimmy" into a corner.

"Ah!" .he said; "you little crow! What the 'ell made you speak to Docker?"

"Jimmy" grinned. Some new body within him stood there defiant. "She's my 'orse," he said.

"You—Gawd-forsaken rat! If I 'ad you in a quiet spot I'd shake the life out of you!

"Jimmy "stared up, his little spindle legs apart, like a cock-sparrow confronting an offended pigeon.

"Go 'ome," he said, "George Pulcher; and get your mother to mend your socks. You don't know 'ow! Thought I wasn't a man, did you? Well, now you—well know I am. Keep off my 'orse in future."

Crimson rushed up on crimson in Pulcher's face; he raised his heavy fists. "Jimmy" stood, unmoving, his little hands in his bell-coat pockets, his withered face upraised. The big man gulped as if swallowing back the tide of blood; his fists edged forward and then—dropped.

"That's better," said "Jimmy," "hit one of your own size."

Emitting a deep growl, George Pulcher walked away.

"Two to one on the field—I'll back the field—Two to one on the field." "Threes Snowdrift—Fours Iron Dook."

"Jimmy" stood a moment mechanically listening to the music of his life, then edging out, he took a fly and was driven to the station.

All the way up to town he sat chewing his cheroot with the glow of drink inside him, thinking of that finish, and of how he had stood up to George Pulcher. For a whole day he was lost in London, but Friday saw him once more at his seat of custom in the "Corn." Not having laid against his horse, he had had a good race in spite of everything; yet, the following week, uncertain into what further quagmires of quixotry she might lead him, he sold Calliope.

But for years betting upon horses that he never saw, underground like a rat, yet never again so accessible to the kicks of fortune, or so prone before the shafts of superiority, he would think of the Downs with the blinkin' larks singin', and talk of how once he —— had a horse.

[*1923*]